THE BAR SINISTER

THE BAR SINISTER

Sheila Simonson

Walker and Company
New York

First published in the United States of America in 1986 by the Walker Publishing Company, Inc.

Published simultaneously in Canada by John Wiley & Sons Canada, Limited, Rexdale, Ontario

Book designed by Irwin Wolf

Library of Congress Cataloging-in-Publication Data

Simonson, Sheila, 1941-
   The bar sinister.

   I. Title.
PS3569.I48766B3   1986   813'.54   86-1321
ISBN 0-8027-0880-3

Printed in the United States of America

10 9 8 7 6 5 4 3 2 1

This one is for Anne McCaffrey,
quid pro quo.

THE BAR SINISTER

Part I
Emily
1812-1813

= 1 =

EMILY FOSTER, RELICT of the late Edward Foster, Esq., of Wellfield House, seethed in her cramped corner of the publick coach as it jolted up the long flat Hampshire hill to the market town of Mellings Magna. From the other seat three male passengers eyed her black bonnet with varying degrees of indifference. Beside her a farmer's wife with a basketful of household sundries overflowed into Emily's lap.

Emily clenched her hands into fists on the strings of her reticule. Her jaw ached—for the past three hours she had been clenching her teeth. Under the best of circumstances she hated to be late. And today of all days! She should never have consented to go to Winchester. *How very like a lawyer*, she fumed to herself, *to keep a mere widow waiting whilst he secures some landowner's interest.*

She had missed the noon coach. Now her employer, who had been bringing his children to live with her, would take them elsewhere. "Fiddle," she said softly. "Fudge." And, greatly daring, "Damnation."

Fortunately Emily's lapse from gentility was lost in the clamour as the coach pulled into Mellings Magna. Mellings Parva, her destination, was one stop further on and there would be a wait.

Everyone, including the farmer's wife, got out. "Stretch your limbs, ma'am," she advised Emily kindly. "Mortal stuffy, they coaches," and she stepped down with a series of grunts and wobbles that shook the vehicle.

1

Why not? Emily thought gloomily. *My sitting here won't make the coachman swill his ale faster.* She climbed down into the noisy yard and straightened her bonnet. It was pouring rain and already quite dark. Four o'clock of a November evening.

She scuttled for the inn's publick room. There was no time to retire to a private chamber like a proper lady, and if there had been Emily was not sure she had money to pay the charge. The publick room was dark, noisy, and crowded, and smoky from an imperfectly drawing chimney. Ignoring the stares of the curious and the impertinent, Emily made for the fire. Stuffy the coach might be. It was also quite cold.

When she had thawed her hands and her eyes had begun to sting from the smoke, she retreated to a quiet corner to view the scene. A muttered curse persuaded her the corner was occupied.

"I beg your pardon," Emily said politely.

The woman whose foot she had stepped on gave her a tired, gap-toothed smile. "Jaysus, think nothin of it, missus. Ye didn't wake the babby." She was suckling a dark-haired child who snorted, gave a pull at the discouraged-looking teat, and relapsed into somnolence. The woman covered herself casually.

Emily returned a constrained smile and retreated. Presently she found a vacant space on the other side of the hearth and sat down on a three-legged stool. It wobbled, but held.

Beyond the oak dining table the farmer's wife stood drinking a mug of ale and exchanging good-natured badinage with an old gaffer who waved a clay pipe whenever he wished to emphasise a point. He said something in a cackling, reedy tenor, and the woman laughed heartily. Passengers from the London mail, mostly men, crammed the benches at the laden table. A plainly dressed young woman Emily took to be a servant ignored the occasional leers of her travelling companions and ate stolidly. Beside her a thin girl in a grey bonnet picked at a plate of boiled chicken.

Squeezed between grey-bonnet and a sour-looking clerk sat—or rather, knelt—a tiny girl, whose tangled brown curls and round rosy face cleared the table by a scant inch. The child was drinking a dish of soup with careful concentration. Each time she guided the spoon to her mouth without dripping its contents she gave a small triumphant nod. Twice as Emily watched, the little girl spilled a bit, once on the cloth and once on the square of linen tucked into the neckband of her serge travelling dress. Both times she scowled, set her small jaw firmly, and bent to her task with renewed deliberation.

She did not seem to be very hungry. A mug of milk by her plate remained untouched. It was rather as if she were practising a difficult art she meant to master. She ignored the other diners, even when one of the red-faced farmers addressed her as his honey and asked if she wanted a sweetie.

Perhaps she is deaf, Emily thought, dismayed. *She cannot be alone.* Grey-bonnet ignored the child, however, being caught up in worries of her own, and when the little girl spilled her soup on the tablecloth the sour clerk twitched his elbow away with the air of one who will not be inconvenienced by someone else's brat. *She is* alone, Emily thought, indignant. The child finished the soup and wiped her mouth efficiently on the square of linen.

"*Emilia. La leche.*" A male voice, low but imperative.

The child turned her head. "*No.*"

"*Sí. Ahora mismo.*"

An expression of extreme martyrdom and self-sacrifice overspread the rosy features. The child said something dignified in the same language, grasped the mug firmly in both hands, and took three swallows, grimacing. She set the mug down without spilling. "*Bastante?*"

Apparently she received confirmation that she had drunk enough, for she grasped the startled clerk's sleeve without

3

selfconsciousness, steadied herself, and clambered down. The clerk grumbled a protest but the little girl paid no heed. She pranced from the table into the shadows on the far side of the room, where several men stood talking in low voices. The man who had addressed her took her hand and drew her off to the stairs. He lifted her to the third step and began to button her into a pelisse.

My employer, Emily deduced. As there were not a great many Spanish-speaking children to be found in Hampshire coaching inns, her conclusion did not require the exercise of superior logic. And the misplaced Irishwoman suckling the black-haired baby would be the wet nurse. Emily felt some relief. They were late, too.

Ought I to put myself forward? she wondered, and decided on the whole she would prefer to wait and watch. There would be few passengers for Mellings Parva. Time enough for introductions. Emily slid the stool gently back and blended into the shadows.

Captain Richard Falk, Fifty-second Light Infantry, lately a widower, father of Thomas and Emilia Falk and Emily's employer. He was not above the middle height, she noted with some disappointment. She preferred tall men. Falk was thin but well proportioned and did not move clumsily. She watched as he guided his daughter to a vacant place against the wall. He hoisted the child up so that she sat on his left arm, wriggling slightly but apparently content.

Father and daughter had the same colouring—dark brown hair with a touch of auburn and thick-lashed, well-spaced dark eyes. Captain Falk's features, like his daughter's, were regular, even handsome, or would have been but for two circumstances. His complexion was deeply weathered, as if he had been broiling under a sun considerably warmer than that of Hampshire. Lines radiated from the corners of his eyes. That might have indicated profound good humour, but Emily doubted it. He looked cross. Probably he had been squinting at the Spanish sun. The

4

other circumstance was his expression, a slight but fixed scowl. But perhaps he did not frown all the time.

Emily wondered how long he and the children had been in England and what Captain Falk had been doing. Not visiting his tailor, clearly. British army officers rarely wore uniform except on duty and Captain Falk was no exception. He wore boots, breeches, and a brown coat which looked to have seen better days. His cravat was rumpled, his hair wanted trimming, and he ought to have shaved. In short, he seemed neither amiable nor prosperous, and Emily's gloom deepened. At least his daughter was not visibly afraid of him, but her well-behaviour argued strict discipline. Strict discipline was not one of Emily's strong points.

When the coach was called up at last Emily took her gloom out into the drizzle. Presently the farmer's jolly wife emerged, followed by Captain Falk, the little girl, and the Irish wet nurse, protesting in fluent argot with her charge on her arm. There were no other passengers, not even the cackling gaffer.

"Jaysus, sor," the wet nurse moaned, "if I jounce five more miles in yon bluidy contraption I'll cast up me accounts for sure and then where'll ye be?"

Captain Falk growled something.

"Whisht, now, what's a bit of a mist?"

"Very well. Climb up with the guard if you must."

"Thankee, sor. 'Tis a kind heart ye have. Here." She thrust the blanket-wrapped baby, apparently still sleeping, at its father. To Emily's surprise he did not drop it, but balanced his bundle on one arm and fumbled with the ties at his throat. "Take my cloak, then, Pegeen. You'll be drenched."

"Right, your honour, and mind ye don't wake the bhoy." She scrambled with fair grace up to the guard's perch and sat beaming down, gap-toothed, through the rain.

"After you, ma'am."

Emily started. Falk's voice, sharp and exasperated.

5

The farmer's wife had resumed her place in the coach and Emily was blocking the man's way. She tumbled in, higgledy-piggledy, and settled herself by her earlier seat-mate.

The little girl climbed in, followed by her damp father with his squidgy bundle. He removed his hat, and his daughter shook the wet from it, some of the drops spattering Emily. The child's air of deliberation deserted her when her father had taken his seat, and she began to chatter in excited Spanish, bouncing and peering out the window, though it was now too dark to see anything.

The vehicle gave a lurch and they swayed and clopped out of the innyard. The Mellings coach was not famous for speed, which was probably fortunate, considering the condition of the road.

"Pretty child." The farmer's wife smiled at Captain Falk and nodded. "Foreign, eh?"

The captain scowled at her and did not reply.

"Well!" She settled her plump thighs more firmly on the seat and began to favour Emily with a thorough condemnation of foreigners, the government's war policy, and the price of sugar.

Emily squirmed and her spirits sunk even lower. Captain Falk did not seem amiable, and her neighbour's parochial grumblings were scarcely designed to sweeten his temper.

What of it? Emily thought crossly. *He may take his children elsewhere with my goodwill.* But she knew very well she had fallen in love with the little girl at sight. *Emilia—she even shares my name.* Her grosser self retorted, *Very confusing that will prove, madam, the baby is not even a year old, and the wet nurse the veriest camp follower.* Resolutely Emily repressed the voice of reason. The little girl was rosy and curly and amazingly well conducted.

I should make myself known, Emily reflected. The farmer's wife talked on. Emily waited for a pause in the bucolic monologue. The price of wool was down, it seemed. Corn up.

6

Across from her the little girl gave up the window view and squirmed over to her father's side, palpably asking for something. He did not smile, but his low reply apparently satisfied her, for she insinuated herself under his arm and listened to his quiet Spanish with an occasional chirp and wriggle.

Through her seatmate's garrulity Emily could hear him speaking. It sounded as if he were telling a story. The child's neatly shod feet jabbed the air from time to time. Gradually she slid lower in the seat. After a while her eyelids drooped and she fell asleep abruptly, as very young children do. Her father asked her a low-voiced question. When she did not reply, he stopped talking, rearranged her more securely, closed his eyes, and seemed to sleep, too. The coach swayed. The dim light from the unshrouded window brushed the child's sleeping face and her father's right hand, which was capable-looking with long blunt-tipped fingers.

With a slight start Emily realised that the farmer's wife had ceased grumbling some time before and was staring at the sleeping trio with unabashed curiosity. Well, it had been an impressive performance. Emily shuddered to think how her son Matt would behave in such circumstances.

Matt was four. This little señorita could not be more than three. "Two under three," the solicitor's letter had read. "The son and daughter of an officer serving in the Peninsula. Their mother is deceased and he must find an English home for them."

Emily's tender heart had been wrung even as her rational self pointed out how odd it was that the officer in question did not send his children to his family or his wife's family. However, the fee offered was ample, the solicitor sounded respectable, and Emily wanted young children, younger than Matt. She meant to give Matt rivals in the nursery. The other applicants had not met her simple requirements. *Really, the twelve-year-old idiot son of a marquess would not do.* When she placed her advertisement Emily had expected a wider choice of children. Captain Falk's had been the only acceptable offer.

Even so her father had objected vehemently. He disapproved the war, the army, Emily's profiteering, and other people's brats. Her mother-in-law had also made it plain she thought Emily deranged, but opposition only stiffened Emily's backbone, and when she found in her father's unwed sister Frances an unexpected ally, she burnt her bridges and writ the solicitor that she would welcome Captain Falk's children.

Bad luck to their scowling sire, I shall welcome his children. Emily closed her eyes, smiling a little as she recalled Aunt Fan's unforeseen intrusion into the domestic brangle.

"Do be still, Henry. Good for Emma. Needs something to take her mind off her troubles, and the money won't hurt."

Dear Aunt Fan. Frances Mayne had come to Mayne Hall at Lady Mayne's death when Emily was twelve, and grumbling the while, had taken over the housekeeping. Emily had always supposed her aunt would escape Mayne Hall at the first opportunity, but when Sir Henry Mayne invited his newly widowed daughter to make her home with him and act his hostess, Aunt Fan had been surprisingly firm with him.

"Nonsense. Emma has her own house and she will be wanting to oversee young Matt's estate. Be practical, Henry. Can't keep your children under your eye forever."

And Emily's father, rumbling his displeasure, had given the idea up. He had ridden over to Wellfield House every day in the month after Edward's death, all the same.

At first, in the shock of her double loss—for the fever that had killed her husband had also taken the life of their two-year-old daughter—Emily had been grateful, but Sir Henry was no passive observer. When he began to take the reins from her grasp Emily had had to deal with him. She must learn to manage the estate herself. Edward had made her Matt's guardian. It was her duty, and besides, she needed to be busy. She would accept Papa's advice but he must not be running things. So went her arguments.

It had taken more than a year to convey the full impact of her message to her father and there had been some injured feelings. That he had opposed her scheme of baby-farming without being able to prevent it showed she was finally emerging from the permanent nursery of the mind to which he had mentally consigned all of his children.

Emily swayed with the coach and regarded her dozing employer through half closed eyes. *You do not know it, my dear sir*, she thought, *but your children are my passport to an independent life.*

2

THE CARRIAGE LURCHED again, and this time the baby gave a muffled yowl. Captain Falk opened his eyes (Emily wondered if he had really been asleep) and gave the bundle a competent jiggle and pat. The baby sobbed a few times and lapsed again into silence.

"I'll take him, if you like," Emily offered.

Her employer stared. His eyes looked wary, dark as midnight.

"I am Mrs. Foster."

"Indeed."

"I should have made myself known to you sooner, sir."

He grunted. Very gracious.

"The baby," Emily prompted.

"He's asleep. And rather wet."

"Oh, dear."

He did not dignify that with a response. After a moment he said acidly, "If you are indeed Mrs. Foster then perhaps there's some hope we'll be met."

"My father's coachman has been waiting for you at the Rose and Crown in Mellings since one o'clock," Emily retorted. "He's probably drunk as a wheelbarrow."

"We arrived in Mellings at half past twelve."

Dismay smote Emily. "Mellings Magna! Oh dear, weren't my directions clear?" Manifestly they were not. A further thought struck her. "Noon? You cannot have come from London."

"Portsmouth," Captain Falk said tersely.

"But you writ from London."

"I'll edify you with an account of my travels later, ma'am. We certainly set out in the small hours from Portsmouth."

"The small hours! No wonder the children are tired!"

"You think it would have been preferable to start at noon and arrive at three in the morning?" His daughter had flung up a starfish hand. He tucked it neatly back and straightened the skirt of her pelisse.

"Could you not have journeyed by easy stages?"

"No."

Emily blinked. She was unused to such bluntness—rudeness, really. He ought to have hired a chaise. "Well, we're nearly at Mellings. Parva," she added hastily at his unvoiced snarl. He had white, slightly crooked teeth. "I shall see them both snugly in bed as soon as we reach home."

When he made no comment she said in careful, neutral tones, "The, er, person in the guard's box is the baby's wet nurse, I take it."

"It would certainly seem so."

Emily flushed. "I was not expecting to accommodate strange servants."

"I presume you were also not expecting me to bring a suckling child without its nurse. Be reasonable, madam. Mrs. McGrath has her wages of me, and she is clean and a hard worker."

"I shall be feeding her."

"It would look odd indeed if you didn't."

Unwillingly Emily grinned. "I starve my servants, of course. And beat them. Come, sir, let's not bicker."

He shifted the sodden baby on his left arm. "I'm peaceful by nature."

" 'As any sucking dove.' "

His mouth twisted in an answering grin. "Your hit, Mrs. Foster."

The farmer's wife had been listening to their exchange

with interest. Now she snorted and the captain gave her a wry glance.

"The little girl has excellent manners," Emily interposed, tactful. *Unlike her father.* "Does she speak no English at all?"

"A few phrases."

"What can you have been thinking of?"

"Spanish is her mother tongue," Captain Falk said coolly.

Emily bit her lip. "Yes, I see. I'm sorry." She meant she was sorry his wife had died, but he misunderstood her.

"She'll learn English quickly. She is forward for her age."

"So I observed."

"Mellings Parva," the coachman bawled, and the vehicle lurched to a stop.

The farmer's wife bestowed a smile on Emily, a scowl on Captain Falk, and descended. Emily followed suit, handed down by the guard. When she stood on solid ground she turned back.

"Has your daughter wakened? Yes, I see she has." Emily smiled into the sleepy hazel eyes. *"Buenas días, Emilia."*

The child's mouth formed an *O* and she turned to her father. A spate of treble Spanish followed. He translated drily, "She says it is *buenos tardes*, is it not, and the lady speaks strangely."

Emily laughed. "Oh, dear, and I tried so hard. Ask her, please, if she will come down to me. You may tell her that my name is also Emilia."

"Is it?"

"It is Emily."

Emily heard herself introduced as Doña Emily. The child slid from her seat, bobbed a creditable curtsey, and without further ado launched herself from the top step.

Fortunately Emily caught her in midair. She gave her small namesake a hug and set her down, murmuring, "You're quite a handful, I see. Rather like Matt. Shall you come for a ride in my papa's carriage?"

Emilia blinked up at her and gave a tentative smile.

"Pegeen, where in the devil . . ." Captain Falk had

extricated himself from the coach with a single lithe movement. "Lord, woman, you're blue as megrim."

"It was that cold I like to fell off," the wet nurse agreed from behind Emily. The woman's teeth were chattering. "Is the great man not awake then?"

"Asleep. Wet." Captain Falk's style was decidedly terse. "Change him, Peg, if you please. In the inn. This lady is Mrs. Foster. She assures me a carriage awaits us, but I daresay she's cutting a wheedle."

Emily gave him an indignant look and led the parade into the inn. As she entered with her charges, the proprietor of the Rose and Crown bustled up, all attention.

"No, thank you, Willis. I shan't require a private parlour today, but do show Mrs. McGrath where she may change young Thomas." That, according to the solicitor's letter, was the baby's name. "And roust Papa's coachman from the table beneath which he is no doubt sleeping. I shall require him to pole up the carriage at once."

Willis, eyes bright with curiosity, complied. Emily did not enlighten him. Everyone would hear of her eccentric undertaking soon enough.

The inn was uncrowded. The few old men by the hearth ignored the intrusion. Emily led her small companion to a vacant armchair. She sat, lifting the child to her lap. Although Emilia stiffened she did not resist. "What a pretty bonnet," Emily murmured. "And a pretty girl, too. I hope you like rabbits, because there are five already and Matt says there are kittens in the barn."

The child regarded her with large, unblinking eyes, hazel, flecked with colour, and thickfringed.

"She doesn't understand you."

"I know," Emily said calmly. "Children listen to the tone of one's voice as much as to the words."

"Interesting if true." Captain Falk sat rather heavily on a nearby bench.

"You played the trick yourself in the coach."

He looked up, eyes narrowed.

"I don't speak Spanish at all well so I couldn't follow the story you were telling young Emilia, but it very nearly put *me* to sleep."

That startled a smile from him. "Very dull tale. It always seems to work."

Emily smiled, too, and gave her charge a jiggle. The little girl bounced enthusiastically. "Aha, do you know that one? Here comes the lady—pace, pace, pace. Here comes the gentleman—trot, trot, trot. Here comes the trooper—gallop, gallop, gallop."

Emilia leapt up and down to the verse with an energy that showed her to be unaffected by long travel in coaches. Her delighted laugh rippled like clear water.

Emily laughed, too, rather breathless. "Whoa! *Basta!*"

The child quietened after one more small bounce.

"I have the feeling I may learn Spanish rather more rapidly than your daughter English."

Captain Falk was watching with an unfathomable expression in his eyes, which were, Emily noted, not black after all, but hazel like his daughter's and also flecked with colour. In his case, green.

He inclined his head in response to her remark but said nothing. Not a forthcoming man. *No small talk*, Emily thought critically. Her other critical thoughts she pushed to the back of her mind. *After all*, she told herself with conscious charity, *he has been travelling all day and half the night and is probably tired. No doubt he is ordinarily civil and clean-shaven.*

She jounced the willing Emilia several more times and talked to her of Matt and rabbits and chickens. Presently she had the satisfaction of finding the little girl, quiet and boneless as a puppy, curled against her side and playing with the strings of her reticule.

When Mrs. McGrath returned at last Captain Falk rose and gave her his seat on the bench. The baby was awake and fractious.

Watching the nurse comfort him, Emily reflected rue-fully that young Thomas was going to give her father a shock. He was a pretty child, but quite the most un-English-looking baby Emily had clapped eyes on. His hair was black and straight, his complexion olive, and his enormous eyes black as midnight. Every inch the foreigner and not yet in leading strings. He seemed to want to creep on the mucky floor. The wet nurse contained his wriggling as long as she could, then let him stand at her knee. He clutched one of her fingers and glared balefully about.

"There's a wee gentleman," Mrs. McGrath said brightly in the tones of one who has reached the limit of endurance. "Will ye walk, Tommy? Show the lady your paces, there's a good babby."

Tommy glowered and sat with a resounding thump on his draggled petticoats. He let out a screech of pure rage. Before he turned quite purple his father scooped him up and strode with him to the yard.

Emily and Mrs. McGrath exchanged glances.

"I hope he may not dump his son in the horse trough," Emily ventured.

The wet nurse looked shocked. "No, now, missus, him-self has a way with the bhoy. Ye've no need to fret. He'll show Tommy the horses and bring him back when he's stopped his screeching."

"I daresay. You've had a tiring journey, Mrs. McGrath."

"Me name's Peggy, missus. A long journey, aye. The coach wasn't a patch on the bluidy ship. Five days was all she took from Lisbon, like a bluidy yacht race it was, and the gale howling in the rigging all the way like the souls of the damned. Amy, there, was sick as a cat. Her da kept her on deck, thanks be to God, and didn't she bounce back when we made port like one of them India rubber balls, but we was that worried about her."

As if in response Emilia gave a small bounce.

"Do you call her Amy?"

"I do, and the captain does most of the time. 'Twas her ma called her Emilia."

"I see." That, at least, would simplify matters. "Er, is your husband also with the army, Peggy?"

"His honour's batman." A shadow passed over the woman's face. "Left him in Belém, we did. He's a hot-tempered ould devil, is McGrath, but I'm homesick for him already, would ye credit it? He's me third."

"Your third husband?"

"Aye, since Vimeiro. Buried two of 'em, God rest their souls, and when Jerry—that's McGrath—popped the question I said yes like a shot, for don't it stand to reason a nofficer's servant'll last longer than a sojer?"

"Er, I daresay."

"I've no wish to be widowed again. Whisht, I'd no wish to be shipped off to England, missus, if it comes to that. It's a strange, hard place, to be sure, and what me da would be after saying if he found me plumped down in the midst of a lot of Sassenachs . . . well!" She heaved a sigh.

Emily began to be amused. "What can't be cured must be endured," she intoned.

Peggy gave her a doubtful look.

"I believe that's my father's coachman. Will you fetch Captain Falk for me?"

Peggy went without argument.

Emily looked at the apparition before her and sighed, too. "At least you're still here, Dassett. Can you drive?"

Dassett looked as virtuous as he could. His eyes and nose were red. "Certainly, Miss Emily. Stuck me head under th' pump. Carriage's poled up."

When the carriage reached Wellfield House at last, the bells had rung eight in the village and it was quite black outside. Peggy McGrath was frankly snoring, Amy-Emilia was sound asleep, and Emily held the baby, upon whom the visit to the horse trough had apparently acted as a draught of opium. Captain Falk kept his own counsel. Emily did not think he slept, but he said nothing.

"Ahem. We're here," she announced feebly. It was not at all the way she had meant to welcome the children to her home. Dassett threw open the carriage door and pulled down the steps with a flourish. At least he had not run them into a ditch.

=3=

EMILY CARRIED THOMAS in, directing Dassett to bear the sea chest and portmanteau that constituted the Falk chattels to the nursery.

"The portmanteau's mine," Captain Falk said shortly. "Where shall I put Amy?"

By this time Emily's cook-housekeeper had bustled into the foyer with candles, curtseys, and tongue-cluckings. From behind Mrs. Harry peered the flushed face of Phillida, maid-of-all-work.

"The nursery," Emily said with equal brevity. "Follow me. Mrs. Harry will lead the way. Is Matt asleep?"

"I've just tucked him in, ma'am." Phillida, eager to oblige. "Shall I wake him?"

"Lord, no! That is—no, certainly not. Miss Amy and Master Tommy must be put to bed at once. Warm the sheets, Phillida, if you please."

Phillida darted Captain Falk a sidelong glance and scuttled to obey.

"Has the old cradle been set out?" Emily called after her.

"Yes, ma'am." Phillida vanished.

They had reached the first-floor hallway and Emily was breathless from the swift climb. "The nursery is on this floor," she contrived to say between gasps. "I've given Matt one nook opening on the schoolroom and your daughter the other. Mrs. McGrath can have a bed in the nursery proper."

Captain Falk made no comment. She glanced at his face but it was unrevealing.

18

"I had not yet engaged a nursemaid," she continued, leading the way, "so perhaps it's fortunate that Mrs. Mc-Grath will be staying. Ah, here we are." She lowered her voice. "Matt sleeps through that door, and you may lay Amy here, unless you think she should sleep with Mrs. McGrath tonight."

"That might be wise."

"I daresay. Well, let's go into the nursery, then." To her relief a fire of sea coal burnt in the nursery, and when Mrs. Harry had lit a pair of candles on the wide dressing table the room looked cheerful enough. Emily laid the sleeping Thomas on the low trundle and turned to face the others. Mrs. McGrath was staring about, jaw slightly agape. Captain Falk held his daughter.

"The cradle is here, Mrs.—er, Peggy." Emily pointed. "If you'll make Tommy ready, perhaps I can undress Miss Amy. Captain Falk, I daresay you'll be wanting a glass of wine. Pray follow Mrs. Harry. I'll join you in the drawing room directly."

Captain Falk laid his daughter on the trundle as directed. He stood looking down at both children for a moment. Then he turned on his heel and followed Mrs. Harry from the room.

No sentimental outbursts there. Emily sighed and issued a spate of orders. Presently both children were snug abed without having been wakened. Matt hadn't stirred either. Emily tidied her hair in her own room and trudged back downstairs to the small withdrawing room.

Captain Falk, his back to the door, leaned on the mantel. He was contemplating the fire, head bent, one foot on the fender. He looked as if he wanted to kick the coals.

"They'll both do now," Emily said.

He turned in one movement, like a cat. Emily was glad she was not a French outpost. He was certainly a wary man.

"They're asleep, and Mrs. McGrath is settling in with a cup of tea. Will you not sit, sir?"

"No, thank you," he said, curt. "I must return to the inn at once. If you'll direct your servant to find my gear."

"The inn!"

He said, in tones of repressed exasperation, "I can't remain here. It's nearly nine o'clock."

Emily stared. "I daresay you're confusing me with some green maiden of your acquaintance. Of course you'll remain here. I've ordered a room prepared for you."

Captain Falk scowled. "Upon my word, ma'am, are English villages so transmogrified that a single woman may entertain a man for the night without occasioning gossip? A new day is upon us."

"I think my credit sufficient to pull through one evening in your company," Emily said sweetly. "Besides, I've sent Dassett for my Aunt Fan."

Captain Falk's brows, really his most expressive feature, shot up.

"My father's sister," Emily explained. "She'll be here very soon. Grumbling. I assure you she's a famous gooseberry."

That seemed to throw him off balance. After a moment he said wryly, "Then I look forward to making her acquaintance." .

"Now will you sit?"

"I'm standing, ma'am, because if I sit I shall fall asleep."

"Oh."

"I daresay I'd be in the same case," he said with rough kindness, as if such a sentiment were alien to his character, "even if I'd found the right Mellings to begin with. My children are not restful travelling companions."

Emily, who always responded to the least sign of humanity in otherwise unredeemed villains, smiled. "Then I'll order up a supper for us, sir, whilst my housemaid makes your room ready. I'm sharp-set, I confess."

He did not immediately reply.

"Did you dine at Mellings Magna?"

"No. I wasn't hungry."

"Oh, dear, you must be starved."

"I'm more in need of lint and hot water than food, Mrs. Foster. Do you run to such items?"

"Lint," Emily repeated blankly.

"I've bunged up my arm and I should change the dressing."

"You've been wounded! How dreadful. Is it a grave injury?"

He looked embarrassed. "No. In fact it's just—"

"Just a scratch," Emily snapped, annoyed.

He smiled, this time in genuine amusement, and the effort certainly improved his looks. "As a matter of fact, it was rather nasty. I was going to say it's just about healed. Not quite, however."

"Then by all means let us change the dressing."

"Us?"

"Your right arm?" He had held the children on his left arm.

"Well, yes."

"Then you must find it awkward to tie the bandage. I shall do so with ease."

"I might be left-handed."

Emily frowned. "Are you?"

He laughed. A rusty sound. "No. And it *is* awkward."

"Come along, then."

Emily and Captain Falk, the latter in shirt-sleeves, were belowstairs in the Wellfield kitchen when Aunt Fan finally drove up in the carriage.

The kitchen was warm and cheerful, and Mrs. Harry bustled in and out doing appetising things upon Emily's new patent range, which Captain Falk regarded with more interest than he exhibited in Emily's performance as Ministering Angel. He had used the scullery pump to good purpose and now looked less travel-stained and wider awake.

"Remarkable piece of ironmongery."

"I like it." Emily decided to cut the grimy bandage from his forearm and applied the scissors with precision. "It's convenient for heating water." Most of the linen strip came off easily enough, revealing what looked like a weal from the inner wrist toward the elbow. The chief injury, however, lay in the bunched muscle below the joint. The crusted cloth would require soaking. Emily set herself to the task. "Have you never seen a cookstove?"

"Not of that size." He drew a sharp breath.

"Did I hurt you?"

"No. The water's rather hot, however. You'd better let me rip the remainder off."

"Rip! I presume you mean it to heal at some point in the not too distant future. Have a little patience, if you please."

He was silent but not, she perceived, in a mood of meek acquiescence. He watched her critically. Self-consciousness made her clumsy and in the end she ripped a bit of lint. That opened the injury and it bled. Not a great deal, but the wound was ugly—inflamed on the edges and not properly closed.

"How was it caused?"

"Half spent ball."

"*Half* spent!"

"If it hadn't been half spent you'd be admiring a very nice stump."

Emily cast him a look of dislike and cleaned the area carefully, dusting it with basilicum powder. When she had tied a neat and considerably cleaner and less bulky bandage, she glanced at him, triumphant. "There! That should do until tomorrow."

"I trust so." He rolled the sleeve down, adding with grudging generosity, "For an amateur you show up well."

" 'Praise from Lord Henry is praise indeed'."

"My Christian name is Richard."

"But not Lord Richard."

She thought he looked at her queerly but he said nothing. He rose and shrugged into his seedy coat with his usual economy of movement.

"Beg pardon, Mrs. Foster, I'm sure. Will you be wanting supper in here?"

Emily was scandalised. "In the dining room, Mrs. Harry. Good heavens!"

Mrs. Harry eyed Captain Falk uncertainly.

"She thinks I'll feel more at home here belowstairs," Captain Falk explained in a voice of sweet reason.

"The dining room," Emily snapped. "And have Phillida show Miss Mayne in directly she comes."

Mrs. Harry sniffed. "Very good, ma'am."

"Unnecessary," said a familiar gruff voice from the stair. "I'm here." Aunt Fan in militant black descended with firm tread. "What's the meaning of this, Emma?"

Captain Falk awaited her scrutiny without visible signs of alarm.

Emily tidied away the scraps of lint and the basin. "Merely a little rough surgery, Aunt. Captain Falk has injured his arm."

Aunt Fan fixed her victim with her direct blue gaze. "You're late, sir."

Captain Falk inclined his head.

Emily intervened. "I misdirected him. The children are in bed."

"Small blessings," Aunt uttered. "Dassett is foxed, Emma."

"I am sorry, Aunt Fan. He waited all afternoon at the Rose and Crown for Captain Falk, and temptation overcame him."

Aunt snorted. "Ramshackle business. You oughtn't to have gone to Winchester. Well, that's water over the weir. How d'ye do, sir. I'm Frances Mayne." She extended her hand.

Captain Falk shook it. "Richard Falk."

"Falk, eh? Odd sort of name. Not English."

"I made it up," said Emily's impossible employer.

"Indeed. No family."

As Aunt Fan's remark was a statement it required no answer, and he gave none.

"Baseborn?" she barked, suddenly.

23

"Yes."

"Thought so."

Emily gaped. She had not entertained any such thought. Aunt Fan might've hinted. However, neither her aunt nor Captain Falk seemed disturbed by the harrowing revelation, and Aunt forged on.

"Children legitimate, I trust."

"They have been ratified by the *Inquisición* and my colonel, ma'am. In advance."

"Ha. What you wanted, young man, was a Protestant clergyman."

"English clergymen are in short supply in Spain and Portugal."

"I daresay. No chaplains?"

"I have never seen a Church of England chaplain in the field," Captain Falk said thoughtfully. "No doubt such creatures exist. They're reputed to enjoy the rank of major. Certainly they draw upon regimental funds."

Aunt clucked her tongue. "Dereliction of duty. The Church is in a shocking state, in my opinion. Fuel for the Methodists' fire."

"Fuel for someone's fire," Captain Falk agreed, a gleam of devilment in his eyes.

Aunt Fan regarded him with suspicion. She was a devout churchwoman.

Emily judged it time to intervene again. "If you'll go up to the dining room, Aunt, Mrs. Harry can bring the supper. Captain Falk?"

He stood aside to let her pass.

Presently Mrs. Harry regaled them with hot soup, cold meat, fresh bread, a bowl of crisp new apples, and a good ripe Stilton.

Rather to Emily's surprise, Captain Falk ate little and slowly. At least his bad manners did not extend to the table. Aunt Fan kept urging more sherry on him. Emily wondered why her redoubtable aunt had taken a fancy to the man. Probably because they were both blunt-spoken to a fault.

A bastard. Emily could not quite like that. The by-blow of some City merchant or wayward gentleman, no doubt. At least he didn't claim high connexions. In one respect the news were welcome. There would be no grandparents or aunts and uncles to descend upon Wellfield House and rob Emily of the children.

She was already their partisan, she realised ruefully, young Amy's in particular. Poor child, she was in need of a defender, what with a dead mother and ramshackle father. As for the little boy, Emily began to look forward with malicious pleasure to the sensation his appearance was going to make among her neighbours and kin. Papa, for instance. Sir Henry did not like foreigners.

Captain Falk and Aunt Fan—primarily Aunt Fan—were engaged in a discussion of Viscount Wellington's strategy. Emily listened to the interchange with some surprise. She had always supposed that her aunt's enthusiasm for the military adventures of the Nation sprang from a desire to set Sir Henry's back up.

Captain Falk was not informative. He toyed with a barely tasted glass of Sir Henry's best sherry and made appropriate noises when the older lady paused for breath. Emily wondered when her aunt would notice that she was conducting a monologue.

"Very cautious game his lordship is playing," Aunt pronounced. "When will he take the bit in his teeth again, eh? Show us his mettle."

"I've no idea, ma'am. I'm not on the Staff."

"*Hrrmph*. Like a bit of dash myself. Sir John Moore, now, had style."

"And look where it brought him," Captain Falk muttered.

"What's that? Not partial to Moore?"

"I served under him in Egypt and here at Shornecliff. He was a very fine trainer of light infantry."

Sir John Moore was Aunt's particular Hero. She had actually worn mourning for him. Now she bristled. "He did what he could in Spain, sir."

"I daresay. What I chiefly recall of his dash through Spain is that it was dashed uncomfortable."

That was blighting. Unnecessarily, Emily thought. However, Aunt Fan had been asking for a set-down so Emily did not spring to her defence.

Aunt glared. "What regiment are you with, sir?"

"The Fifty-second."

"Brought off at Vigo?"

"No."

"Well, the rear guard behaved very well," Aunt conceded magnanimously.

"Yes, we did."

For reasons unknown to Emily this lack of becoming modesty caused her aunt's belligerance to moderate and she spoke with surprising mildness of Lord Paget and the evacuation of Corunna. Emily began to find the replaying of bygone battles tedious.

"We'll have to speak of your arrangements for the children, sir," she said in the first lull.

Captain Falk cocked an eyebrow.

"In case you should meet with an accident." For Emily that was blunt.

Captain Falk's lip curled in response to her euphemism. "I've made a will. It's at my solicitor's." Emily opened her mouth to voice a protest but he forestalled her indignation by reaching into his breast pocket and drawing out a neat sheaf of papers. "Everything writ down, ma'am. Read it at your leisure."

"Is there a guardian?"

"My solicitor and Captain Conway."

"Captain Conway," Emily mused. "Where shall I find him?"

"In Portugal. He's with the Rifles."

"Wonderful! What if both of you meet with a mischance?"

"Emma!" Aunt Fan snapped.

"I beg your pardon, Aunt, but I must be practical."

"You certainly do think ahead," Captain Falk murmured. "I'll come up with something, I daresay, in case my demise and Tom's are simultaneous."

Emily refused to be baited. "I'd appreciate it, sir. Direct your man of business to write me the particulars."

He gave an ironical half bow.

"And the, er, pecuniary arrangements?" Mention of money always embarrassed Emily. She felt her neck go hot.

"Dear me, no delicacy at all." Clearly Falk had taken in her discomfiture. His voice was bland. "You'll continue to be paid. I shouldn't wish you to be put to any inconvenience, Mrs. Foster."

"It's not my convenience you should be consulting, sir, but your children's comfort and well-being."

He regarded her without expression over the wineglass which he turned slowly with long, brown fingers. Candlelight winked on the rim. "I have lately come into a windfall." He set the glass on the table. "A small legacy from an, er, godmother. I've put the sum in trust for my children. There should be no legal complications. I presume there would also be a pension. Tom would see to that."

"Very well." Emily would have been happier with more detail. Perhaps her dissatisfaction showed.

Captain Falk said with a flash of temper, "I'm a poor man, ma'am, and like to remain so, for I have no private means and no connexions. If you don't wish to take on the care of my children under the terms you agreed to, I'll release you. I wish you will tell me now, for I've little time to make other arrangements."

Emily kept her voice cool. "I can't be expected to buy a pig in a poke."

"Two, surely."

Emily raised her brows.

"Piglets."

Emily was forced to smile. "I do intend to take on your children and I concede that I can't object to your terms.

Now, if you wish to retire, sir, Aunt Fan and I shall excuse you. You've had a long day." She rang for Phillida.

He rose to go but could not resist one parting shot. "I trust you won't require too much leisure to read my letter of instruction, Mrs. Foster. I mean to leave on the morning coach."

Emily stared.

"There is one from Mellings Parva at eleven, or so the innkeeper said."

Emily took a long breath. "You act with despatch, Captain Falk. Phillida, is the captain's room ready?"

"Oh, yes, ma'am," said that damsel, blushing and bobbing a curtsey. "Hot water's laid on and fire poked up."

"Then perhaps you'll show him up."

Captain Falk executed a bow. "Miss Mayne, Mrs. Foster."

Emily nodded a gracious dismissal. Rather like Queen Charlotte.

"Good night, sir," Aunt Fan said, gruff. "Moore did his best, you know."

He was startled into a rare, unironic smile. "And that was very good, all things considered."

4

THE PARCEL FROM Lisbon arrived in good time for Boxing Day. As Emily had expected nothing of the sort it threw her off stride. It contained neither message nor letter, only the three neat packages—a largish one for Amy, a much smaller one for Tommy, and one that was labelled, crisply, "Matthew." Emily stared for a long time at the wrappings before setting the gifts aside with the children's other Christmas boxes.

Amy was not speaking. Once or twice in the first week Emily caught her whispering a question to Peggy McGrath, but these lapses into speech grew less frequent as the days passed, and finally ceased altogether. Emily felt helpless. She supposed anyone else would be grateful that the child was docile, but she couldn't help remembering the little chatterer of the coach, and the confident, self-contained miss who had drunk soup so skillfully in the inn. Matt was scornful of his new sister, too inclined to dismiss her as "stupid," a word Emily began to wish he had never heard. He found the baby endlessly fascinating. Amy he ignored.

Emily's father had inspected her charges. Predictably, he found Tommy's looks uncongenial. Sir Henry cross-examined Mrs. McGrath until the woman hid when she heard him coming, and he kept grumbling objections that Aunt Fan's report to him had clearly fueled, although Emily thought Aunt Fan could not have said anything very dreadful. Aunt had liked Captain Falk.

As the word *bastard* did not surface in Sir Henry's mutterings, Emily deduced her aunt was being unnaturally discreet and charged her with deception.

"What Henry don't know won't hurt him."

"Aunt!"

Aunt Fan gave her stare for stare. "Are you regretting your undertaking, Emma?"

"No," Emily muttered, and in a stronger voice added, "No, though I wish I spoke Spanish. Poor Amy."

Aunt hewed to the point. "If you mean to keep the brats you'll have to deal firmly with your father."

"Firmness is one thing, deception another."

"Is it important?"

Emily gaped. "Can you ask?"

"Is it?"

"Not to my feelings for the children," Emily said slowly.

"I should have said it gave you pause."

Emily bridled. "Oughtn't it? God knows what the man's breeding is."

Aunt took a reflective sip of tea—they were in the withdrawing room. "I think you may take it he ain't the child of a dockwhore and a costermonger."

"Aunt Fan!"

"Army commissions don't grow on bushes like blackberries."

"I know that," Emily muttered.

"He married the brats' mother."

"So he said," Emily rejoined, darkly.

Aunt Fan set her cup down and examined a digestive biscuit. "Not in your style to be mistrustful, Emma. Easy enough to check whether Captain Falk was wed. Write his colonel. As for the rest, his speech was educated, he was open as day about his name and status, and his manners were unexceptionable."

That stung Emily. "He was extremely rude."

Aunt Fan rejected the biscuit. "He didn't spit on the

floor, wear spotted neckcloths, or eat with his fingers. What more do you ask? *You* were rude, my dear, prying into his pockets like a bailiff. I could have sunk."

Emily eyed her aunt resentfully. "I had to know."

"You did not have to rake over Captain Falk's finances in my presence."

"He was leaving next morning," Emily said, sullen.

Aunt Fan was not moved. "And had everything spelled out for you in that letter, clear as day. There was no need to ask."

"Well, I didn't know that."

"Never mind," Aunt Fan said briskly. "What's done is done. As for your father, if you feel compelled to tell him your employer is someone's by-blow, be prepared to stand by your guns. Henry," she added dispassionately, "is a trifle conventional."

At that Emily could not forebear laughing.

Aunt Fan did not join in her mirth. "And you take after him, my dear."

That gave Emily pause. She brooded over her possible resemblance to her father for several days. She loved him dearly, but one does not wish to encompass a parent's faults as well as his virtues. Sir Henry was a trifle stuffy, a trifle complaisant, a trifle high in the instep. It was mortifying to consider one's own stuffiness.

After all, Emily conceded finally, in the middle of the night, *that Captain Falk is a bastard is not his fault. It's probable that he has even suffered some inconvenience from the fact. Do not wax Gothick, Emily. It's not your business to be visiting the sins of the parents on their children.*

The children, in fact, occupied Emily sufficiently so that she soon tucked their father in the back of her memory and, apart from the parcel from Lisbon, thought of him rarely. Tommy was delightful. Emily had forgot how interesting an infant could be, every day changing, every day learning. He was a sweet-tempered child, his ills straightforward. A tooth peeking through was the worst Emily knew of him, and he regarded her from the first with the same trust he gave his nurse. Amy, alas, was another story.

At first Emily had thought it would be easy, for she had established a rapport with Amy even before Captain Falk left. He had taken a swift, unemotional farewell of his children—a pat for Tommy, a hug and a brief, calm exchange in Spanish with Amy—and marched out of the door apparently without any second thoughts. Emily had directed her groom to drive him to the inn in the old gig. That was that.

When Amy spent the first few days of her father's absence clinging to Peggy McGrath's skirts, Emily had thought the little girl's behaviour unremarkable. Though she made further friendly overtures to the child, Emily did not force the issue.

As the days turned into weeks, however, it became clear that something was seriously amiss. Amy did not talk. Not only did she make no attempt to speak to Emily and Matt, Phillida and Mrs. Harry, she also stopped speaking to Peggy, who could understand her Spanish. At first Emily was inclined to blame the Irishwoman.

"Are you sure you didn't say something to frighten her?"

Peggy looked shocked. "No, then. His honour wouldn't like it, for all he's a great one for telling her tall tales himself. Eee, will ye look at Tommy?" She leapt up.

Tommy had crept to the nursery scuttle and was tasting a nice lump of coal with the air of a connoisseur. That was the end of that conversation. After all, Tommy was Peggy's work. Though she was perfectly good-natured with Amy, the Irishwoman's mind was on the baby and on her own homesickness for her husband.

Emily tried various tacks with Amy. She brought out her old dolls. She read little stories and rewarded Amy with sweetmeats for listening. She brought a kitten into the house. More to the point, Emily studied the tattered

Spanish grammar one of her brothers had found for her in a Winchester bookshop.

With the help of her own French, her papa's Latin, and diligent guesswork, she contrived to construct certain basic messages. She wasn't sure of her pronunciation, however, and the grammar's vocabulary was better suited to ordering hogsheads of wine than to asking a three-year-old if she wanted to play in the stables with the kittens. *Los gatos— gatinos?* That sounded heavy-footed. Amy stared at Emily and said nothing.

Amy said nothing all the way through Advent. She said nothing when Emily bathed her, brushed her brown curls, cut her meat for her, took her for a carriage ride.

"Is the brat mute?" Sir Henry thundered when Amy shrank from the advances he made to her over high tea at Mayne Hall. He turned back in disgust to Matt, who was talkative enough for two children, and began the ritual of losing to his grandson at draughts.

Emily held Amy close and glared at her father's broad back. *"Pobrecita,"* she whispered. *"Dolce niña."*

Amy shivered but said nothing. It had been a mistake to bring her to Mayne Hall. Sir Henry's idea of coping with foreigners was to add *o* to selected nouns and repeat everything three times, more slowly and loudly each time. For an instant Emily saw him as Amy must have, all bristling brows and wind-reddened features, shouting incomprehensible gibberish.

As soon as she could pry Matt from the draughtsboard and his tea cakes, Emily fled home to Wellfield House, and thereafter Amy stayed with Peggy when Emily and her son made their weekly visits to Sir Henry.

Emily began to dread the coming ordeal of Christmas. She had three brothers, two of them older than she, and married, with large families of children. Her younger brother, James, was still unwed at seven and twenty, and something of a rake. Like other rakes before him he was prudish in the extreme where the repute of his kinswomen was concerned. When he heard of Captain Falk's overnight sojourn at Wellfield House, James flew into the boughs. He was ready to call Falk out and heartily disappointed to find the man had already fled the country. Although Emily was equal to depressing the pretentions of her brothers and withered James with a few well-chosen phrases, his rodomontade promised ill with regard to the family's probable feelings about Captain Falk's children.

As James and the other Mayne males converged on their ancestral home, Emily toyed with the idea of refusing to bring the children for the traditional goose and plum pudding dinner. But Matt would have been crushed by such a decision and so would Emily's father. At least Papa did not demand Emily's presence on Boxing Day.

The huge dinner party on Christmas evening was every bit as appalling as Emily foresaw. Christmas was the one day of the year at which all the grandchildren except infants in arms dined with their elders. As a rule Emily found the sight of so many scrubbed nieces and nephews diverting. This year she kept seeing the event through the eyes of a frightened three-year-old abandoned in the midst of gabbling strangers.

All the while Emily exchanged chitchat with her sisters-in-law, admired their offspring, explained for the hundredth time why she had taken in someone else's brats, nodded and smiled and sampled the overrich viands, she knew the child who shrank beside her was utterly desolate. Emily kept Amy's cold little hand in her own and wished time would fly.

The child ate nothing and said nothing. On Emily's right Matt wriggled and giggled. The noise level rose and fell as course followed course. At last, as abruptly and inexplicably as an eclipse, the candles were snuffed. Into the appalling darkness a liveried footman, his face lit from beneath and distorted with his efforts, bore in the flaming pudding.

It was too much for Amy. She began to sob, softly at

first, then wildly, hysterically. There was nothing for it but to beat a quick retreat.

"Stay by your Aunt Jane," Emily hissed at Matt as she rose with the rigid, wailing child in her arms. Matt nodded, wide-eyed. Everyone was staring, Sir Henry balefully. Emily fled.

That night, alone in her darkened bedchamber, Emily almost made up her mind to write Captain Falk that she could not keep his daughter. It had taken nearly an hour to calm the little girl, and she instantly withdrew once more into her shell of silence. But what would become of Amy if Emily did not keep her?

From Peggy McGrath's casual remarks Emily had begun to draw a picture of the perils attendant on following the army. She envisaged Amy captured with the baggage, as might have happened that very year had Captain Falk not providentially been wounded in the siege of Burgos and compelled to leave his duties before the army made its disastrous retreat into Portugal. No. Even in settled, comfortable circumstances, life was a fragile thing—as Emily's own daughter showed, dead at two of the same fever that had killed Edward Foster.

Resolutely Emily beat back the tide of melancholy that recollection always brought. No. She would not abandon Amy. But what she would do to reach the child Emily could not think. It was well past midnight before she climbed, shivering, into her now cold bed. She cried a little, but that did no good. Finally she fell into a restless sleep.

5

As a rule the children took their breakfast in the nursery, but Emily had always made Boxing Day breakfast a feast, and Matt expected to find his gifts by his special place in the breakfast room. She did not like to disappoint him. Indeed she meant to reassure him of his importance to her now that the other children claimed so much of her attention. Amy had certainly claimed her attention on Christmas Day. Accordingly Emily rose early. Feeling somewhat the worse for wear, she donned her prettiest grey morning gown and tiptoed in to wake Matt.

She had a very good private chat with him. He had found a sixpence in his portion of pudding and he told her of that and of trouncing his cousins at spillikins, and he didn't dawdle overmuch at his dressing either. When he was scrubbed and looking fair and fresh in his best nankeens and the new navy jacket with gilt buttons, Emily peeked in on Peggy and her charges.

The wet nurse was suckling Tommy. Amy lay on her trundle, thumb in mouth. She wouldn't look at Emily.

"What's wrong with her?" Matt demanded, scornful.

"Hush, Matt. Will you dress her and bring the two of them down directly, Peggy?"

"I will that." Peggy glanced at Amy. "Her ladyship woke twice in the night, missus. Bad dreams."

"Did you make her a glass of hot milk?"

"Yes, but she wouldn't take it. She don't like milk, missus."

"Oh dear, I forgot. I'm sorry, Peggy." Emily went to the trundle and touched Amy's hair. Amy held her breath. *"Pobrecita,"* Emily murmured. *"Dolce niña."*

"Er, it's *dulce*, missus."

"Dulce," Emily repeated wearily. "Bring them down when they're ready, please, Peggy. Matt and I have something to do first."

Ordinarily Emily delighted in her son's pleasure as he played the lord of the manor. Now she watched almost absentmindedly as he gave the grinning groom, Phillida, and Mrs. Harry their customary vails. He made a small neat speech thanking them for their faithful service. When they applauded his efforts he beamed and looked up at Emily for approval. Abruptly, she knelt and gave him a bear hug. He was a quick, confident little chap. She really did not deserve such a paragon.

"You were splendiferous," she whispered and he giggled at the wonderful new word, and Mrs. Harry and Phillida made much of him. The groom, eager to be off home for the day, shuffled his feet. Presently Phillida and Mrs. Harry, who had taken Christmas with their families, began to bustle about, anxious to serve the breakfast, so Emily and Matt took leave of them.

"Will there be presents?" Matt asked, jumping along at her side.

"Just a lump of coal," Emily teased.

"Oh, Mama."

Emily relented. "Yes. I think so. One or two."

Matt gave a joyous leap. "Dozens!"

"Well, not quite so many. Will you help me, Matt? Amy's papa sent gifts from Portugal."

Matt made a face.

"There's one for you, too," Emily said gently.

"Oh."

"Here." She unlocked the china cabinet in the dining room. "This little one is for Tommy. Carry it in to the breakfast room for me, please."

Matt bore the small box in very carefully and set it by the place Emily indicated. He looked at the four set places, covertly comparing the small piles of gifts by each plate to see which was biggest. "Where do I sit?"

"Where you always sit. Tommy is beside you. Here."

"What does that say? Mat-thew," he spelt out, screwing up his face at the unfamiliar black letters. "Ha!"

Emily set the larger parcel marked *Amy* by the other place. "Did you look by the curtains?"

Matt turned, eyes wide as saucers. A rocking horse as tall as he was and handsomely accoutred stood by the window. He emitted a shrill whistle. "For me?"

"For the nursery," Emily said firmly, but Matt was already beside the horse, inspecting its equipage with satisfied grunts. He would have to be brought to share. At the moment, with Amy passive and silent, that was not a problem. Emily watched her son mount his charger, and sighed.

Phillida served the meal, for once dropping nothing. Matt kept pinching his packages. Occasionally he had to be reminded to swallow. Peggy McGrath held the bright-eyed Thomas on her lap and ate heartily. She was totally unembarrassed to be eating with the family, Emily saw with relief. From time to time the nurse popped a choice morsel into Tommy's rosebud mouth, all the while commenting with hyperbolic Hibernian approval on the table, the setting, the food, and the beauty of the children.

Amy sat beside Emily, who induced the girl to down a bit of toast and several spoonsful of porridge. Amy looked pretty in her best wool gown. Brown became her, but Emily vowed to make the child some less utilitarian garments. Although, she thought, that would be beside the point if Amy were to spend the rest of her early years in a brown study.

"Can't we open them now, Mama?" Matt had reached the limit of his patience.

Emily said, resigned, " 'May we not.' Yes, Matt. But one at a time, and starting with Peggy."

"Me!" Peggy looked delighted and scandalised. "Faith, missus, there's no need for it."

"It's the custom," Emily said gently. "Go ahead, Peggy. The first is from Matt."

Peggy's presents were perhaps a trifle predictable. There were a small net purse with a gold guinea—the lord of the manor's gift—a length of soft wool from Emily for a new gown, and a lace cap with a blue ribbon through it, which was also from Emily in lieu of something from the Falk children. Tommy chewed on the purse, Peggy exclaimed, Matt looked pleased with himself and not too impatient. Amy stared.

At least she was staring *at* something, and not just into thin air. Emily opened her own trinkets. Matt had constructed a handsome penwiper, Phillida a reticule covered with any number of glued periwinkle shells, and Mrs. Harry had sewed a set of fine lawn handkerchiefs, which, as she was a notable needlewoman, were a handsome gift. Emily rather thought she liked the penwiper best.

"My turn?" Matt, dancing with impatience.

"Yes, very well. You're next oldest."

He ripped through his gifts like a gale, silver paper flying, and did not seem at all discommoded to find among them a box of lead soldiers (from Emily) and a box of wooden soldiers (Captain Falk). Indeed, when he had approved his other gifts, Matt set the soldiers up all around his place. It seemed likely that the wooden ones would be overborne by the leaden ones.

"Thank your papa," Matt said politely to Amy.

Papa. Amy did not speak but Emily could have sworn her lips moved.

Emily picked up the largish, oblong parcel from Lisbon. She took a deep breath and plunged. "This is for you." She set the packet beside Amy's left hand. "From your papa, Amy. *De su papa.* Tell her, Peggy, please."

Peggy obliged with a short burst of Spanish.

Amy's eyes widened and she touched the package gingerly.

"Shall I help you open it, darling?" Emily tore open the paper without any delicacy at all. The parcel was stoutly wrapped. Emily fumbled the last tie loose and lifted the lid. A handsome bisque doll dressed in the Spanish style reposed in the box, a note pinned to the gown. Emily puzzled the message out. *Á Amy. Feliz Navidad. La señora se llama 'Doña Inez.' Papa.* And in English, *Someone for Amy to talk to.* Carefully, her fingers trembling, Emily removed the doll and put it in the little girl's lap.

"*De papa,*" Amy whispered.

"Yes, darling. I mean, *sí. De papa. Para tí.* Peggy, tell her that the doll is called Doña Inez and that it is to keep Amy company." Emily gave up the paraphrase and quoted, "Someone to talk to."

Peggy looked game but baffled, and tried a few sentences.

"*De papa,*" Amy said aloud. She asked a question, hands clutched on the doll, eyes bright.

Peggy burst into laughter.

"What is it?"

"She wants to know if it's a saint, missus."

"No. My word!" Emily was too intent on the small secular miracle occurring to be diverted into theology. "Tell her a friend, *una amiga.* Tell her Doña Inez can understand her."

"*Doña Inez?*" Amy finally caught at the name through Emily's clumsy pronunciation. "*Oh, claro! Claro!*" And she began to jabber away to the doll as if she had never heard of silence.

Peggy beamed. "Will ye listen to that?"

"Very happily." Emily leaned back in her chair, limp as an old dishclout with relief. "Whew. What is she saying?"

"I can't follow her when she goes along at that clip, missus. Something about his honour and a carriage and a big ball of fire."

The plum pudding. The blasted plum pudding. "I wish I knew why she stopped talking."

Peggy jiggled Tommy and removed a napkin ring from his mouth. "Have ye thought that mebbe she didn't understand why the captain went off?"

Emily said, "Yes, of course I thought of that, but he did explain."

"He told her he had to go away. I've turned it over in me mind, missus. When Doña Isabel died Amy didn't understand, and they all kept telling her her mama had gone away to God. She didn't know *muerte*. Could it be that, d'ye think?"

Emily stared at Peggy's good-natured face with consternation. "I ought to have thought of it. She was afraid to let her father out of her sight. How clever of you, Peggy."

Peggy flushed. "Whisht, missus, haven't I known Amy since she was born? She's a deep one."

"Doña Inez," Amy said happily and stuffed a half eaten piece of toast into her mouth. Crumbs fell on the doll's gown. She brushed them off fastidiously, then looked from Emily to Peggy. A long question, uttered through the remains of the toast, rattled out.

Peggy answered her, smiling.

"What now? Who is Doña Inez?"

"Nobody, then. It's only a story his honour was always spinning for her. They was making it up together as they went along, see."

Emily did see. "I wonder if he would write a bit of it down for her from time to time?"

"I dunno, missus," Peggy said doubtfully. "They always talked Spanish and he'd have to put it in English for you, wouldn't he? I ain't a scholar."

"Well, I'll write him at once in any case. And Peggy, in future I shall rely on you to tell me what's on Amy's mind."

"I ought to told you yesterday straight off when it come to me. The thing is I wasn't sure of meself," Peggy said frankly. "Ye're a kind lady, missus, but 'twas such a mad notion ye might've laughed at me."

"Oh, Peggy."

Peggy flushed but stuck by her guns. "Sure and I know I ain't a proper nursemaid for a house like this. I do me best and I'm willing to learn, but it's hard sometimes when I'm homesick for the ould divil in Portugal."

"Do you want to go back?" Emily asked gently. "You may stay here as long as you choose, but I don't like to be keeping a wife from her husband."

Peggy's face cleared. "Whisht, missus, if I went back McGrath'd kill me for sure." It transpired that her husband was ambitious to open a publick house in Cork on their joint savings. Peggy would have elaborated on this scheme, which seemed to have her allegiance, but at that point Tommy was found to be chewing through his gift from his papa. When he had been given the coral the packet contained for proper, approved chewing, Amy was discovered halfway to the rocking horse, determined to give Doña Inez a little outing. Matt protested, Amy gave him glare for glare, and everyone waxed very merry.

=== 6 ===

When Sir Henry arrived that afternoon Emily felt almost equal to dealing with him. He huffed a bit. Emily explained. As he was a sentimental man at heart and thoroughly approved daughters who were attached to their fathers, he was soon thinking of Amy as a prodigy of sensibility, a miniature heroine tragically abandoned by her callous parent. As this fiction was clearly preferable to his looking upon Amy as a damnable nuisance, Emily did not correct it.

Sir Henry insisted upon being shown up to the nursery, where he regaled Matt by finding sugarplums in the boy's hair, performed the same enchantment for the wide-eyed Amy, and concluded his visit with Captain Falk's daughter on his knee. He even bestowed a pat on Tommy's petticoats, though it was clear to Emily that the baby's foreign looks still rankled. Tommy, unmoved by Sir Henry's opinions, chewed on his coral and drooled.

That evening Emily wrote Captain Falk a full account of Amy's ordeal. Within the month she received the first installment of the phantastical adventures of Doña Inez. The story was penned in a neat, almost clerklike hand, together with a civil greeting for Miss Mayne, which delighted Aunt Fan, and an equally civil thank you to Emily for writing, which from its very restraint caused Emily to feel shame that she had not sent him a report of his children sooner. She vowed to write once a month.

It was baffling to step into the saga of Doña Inez *in medias res*, and, of course, the problem of telling the tale through Peggy McGrath complicated the narration. Emily took to reading the stories through at least once in English after the labourious translation process and it proved a good way to teach Amy English sentences. The child picked up English vocabulary as a magnet does pins. By the end of the next year Peggy's offices were more ceremonial than necessary. Amy received the stories with uncomplicated delight, and indeed, they were delightful, if a trifle odd.

Doña Inez was a very young Spanish lady who lived in the Sierra Morena with a group of bandit cousins. She rode astride in a black habit with cherry-coloured ribbons and she fell into all kinds of perils from which she always escaped, triumphant, through the courage of her spirited pony, Eustachio, and her own boundless ingenuity.

Everywhere Doña Inez went, however, she was accompanied by a dogged, bewildered, middle-aged duenna, Doña Barbara by name. Doña Barbara rode an anonymous mule, wrung her hands a great deal, and always, no matter how dire the straits to which she and the heroine were reduced, found upon her person the means of making a nice cup of chocolate.

It was not long before Emily caught Matt eavesdropping on these phantasies. Each episode, of course, had to be repeated several times a week with embellishments until the new installment arrived. Emily invited her son to listen.

"It's girls' stuff." He looked down his snub nose. "Silly."

Emily did not wish to encourage him in toploftiness. "Very well, Matt. Go away."

He went.

She soon caught him at it again, however. "Captain Falk writ the story," she ventured, cautious. "He is a soldier. I shall tell him you said his story was silly."

"Mama!"

"Well, perhaps I won't if you'll listen politely instead of sulking."

So Matt sat at the big nursery table with Amy and Peggy

and Emily whenever Captain Falk's letters arrived, and he and Amy were soon playing at Doña Inez and the Bandits for hours in the nursery, and later, as the weather improved, in the stables. Matt played all the bandits at once.

In an early letter to Portugal Emily ventured to hint that the inclusion of at least one male character by name would be wholly acceptable to her son. That was how Doña Inez acquired a cousin, Don Julio, who appeared from time to time in an heroick light. It was Doña Inez's story, however. Even Matt accepted that.

As for herself, Emily grew very fond of the duenna, Doña Barbara. Fellow feeling, no doubt. She finally expressed her preference to Captain Falk. He obliged with a crisp little episode featuring Doña Barbara as a baffled heroine which had Emily in stitches. Amy and Matt regarded this departure from the plot line with amazed scorn. Middle-aged duennas were not supposed to be heroines, it seemed, so Emily wrote her employer that he had best return to old ways. She thanked him, however.

By October, when Captain Falk sent Amy a plumpish black-clad doll named Doña Barbara for her fourth birthday, Emily had begun to entertain much friendlier feelings for her employer. Although their letters had come, insensibly, to contain more than quixotic fictions and accounts of Tommy's teething, an invisible boundary of reserve remained and Captain Falk never crossed it. Perhaps that was just as well. It is comparatively easy to be witty, even friendly, on paper. In the flesh Emily had not found the man agreeable, nor did she moon over him now. Not moon, exactly. Merely, she allowed herself to wish him well.

That she took to reading the war news in her father's London newspaper with greater interest than she had heretofore felt was perfectly reasonable. She asked to borrow the papers with some self-consciousness, but no one commented on her sudden patriotism, not even Aunt Fan, who had always read the war news.

It had been necessary, for example, after Emily had carefully perused the casualty lists, to require Captain Falk to send an account of the Battle of Vitoria for Aunt's edification. His reply came quicker than its predecessors. The advance of the army into northern Spain had opened the northern ports to English shipping and one could now almost count on three weeks, or with luck a fortnight, between letters.

The account Captain Falk sent of King Joseph's captured baggage was very funny, though Peggy McGrath was dismayed to have missed the prime chance for plunder of the entire war. She spent several days lamenting the cruelty of her fate to Emily's unexpressed shock. Though she had grown fond of Peggy, Emily knew she would never wholly understand the woman.

Emily did not understand Captain Falk, either. It took her several days to realise that she knew little more of the battle after reading the Vitoria letter than she had known before. Other officers wrote letters, some of which were published in the newspapers, with excellent accounts of the fighting. Captain Falk's was vague and prosaic. Emily did not, she wrote him, expect the real-life equivalent of Doña Inez but rather more detail would be welcome to Aunt Fan and to his obliged servant, Emily Foster. This time the reply was slow in coming.

She had received the account of Vitoria in early July and fired off an immediate reply, which she calculated ought to have been in his hands well before the first of August. With luck she could expect something by the fifteenth. She sat back happily to await a fuller account.

On the third, however, the first word came of Soult's counterattack through the epic Pass of Roncesvalles. The Army of the Pyrenees were hotly engaged over a wide front. Aunt Fan read the daily dispatches eagerly, Emily with dread.

She had made a very stupid mistake. If Captain Falk were killed now she must not only deal with Amy's baffled grief but also with Matt's. As for her own feelings, her mind shied away from examining them. It would be quite dreadful to have no more of Doña Inez and Doña Barbara.

At the end of the week she was relieved to find an amiable answer to her request for more detail of Vitoria. Captain Falk pointed out that he had spent the first part of the battle pinned down behind a hedge with his company and the latter part in dogged pursuit of the retreating French, so his field of vision had been limited, and oughtn't Emily to consult the newspapers? They were never accurate, but journalists quite often saw more than ten yards on either side. That was prosaic. Unfortunately it also made good sense.

Smiling at her own disappointment Emily started to turn the page to peruse Doña Inez's latest adventure when the date on the first page caught her eye—23 July 1813. The day *before* the French attacked. What good was that!

Ten days elapsed with no word from Spain. It was true that the newspaper accounts did not list Captain Falk among the casualties. It was also true, as Aunt Fan pointed out with unconscious cruelty, that the returns were scattered and incomplete. The fighting had dragged on for a week, and it had been fierce.

Matt and Amy drank in the latest episode of Doña Inez with oblivious glee. Indeed they demanded its retelling so often Emily grew downright snappish. That baffled them. Guiltstruck, Emily forced herself to read the tale again *con brio*.

When the letter came at last it contained no apology for the delay—indeed, Emily realised ruefully, it showed no consciousness that there had been delay. It was briefer than usual, and rather hard to decipher, being composed, as the author pointed out, in a tent during a downpour. Doña Inez's adventure was a lackluster affair. The children heard it with their usual hopeful enthusiasm. No taste.

Emily did not ask for any details of the Battle of the Pyrenees. A week before Amy's October birthday the newspapers reported that the Duke of Wellington had crossed the Bidassoa into France.

Amy received Doña Barbara the doll with complaisance. There were other gifts. Sir Henry gave her a handsome English doll, a milkmaid blonde with a fetching straw bonnet who entered into a complex three-way relationship with the black-clad Spanish ladies. Emily allowed the little girl to use one of the window seats in the nursery as a doll parlour. When Matt came the superior male, as he still sometimes did, Amy would turn her back on him and retreat to the company of her ladies, with whom she carried on long discussions in Spinglish.

For the most part Amy and Matt squabbled amiably. They even worked out a system for sharing the rocking horse. It began to look jaded from too much galloping over the plains of La Mancha.

Emily felt some satisfaction that her reasons for taking up baby-farming were proving out so well. She ought to have been pleased that Sir Henry now accepted her curious household—he even boasted about it to his friends—but her feelings were not so simple. She had grown thoroughly entwined in the lives of the Falk children. She triumphed at Tommy's first step (March), rejoiced when Amy finally learned to count in English (April), and flinched when Tommy's first word was *Mama* (May).

The trouble was, she foresaw only unhappiness for herself and the children whether Captain Falk lived or were killed. If he lived, and, as now seemed possible, the war ended, he would take the children away to some garrison town—or even, God forbid, India. If he were killed . . .

Unfortunately for Emily's sanity, the Duke of Wellington seemed determined to give her no respite. The army had not gone into winter quarters as usual. In stately succession followed the battles of the Nive and Orthez. Glorious, said Aunt Fan. Emily had never been so out of sympathy with her aunt's sentiments.

To complicate matters, the winds in the Bay of Biscay

waxed surly. The army had invested Toulouse before Emily received word that Captain Falk had got his majority by brevet (the Nive) and been slightly injured in a fall from his horse (Orthez). "Just a scratch," he wrote, with what she considered unnecessary malice.

As the bells of Mellings Parva announced Bonaparte's abdication and the subsequent costly victory of Toulouse, Emily received a curt note, *sans* Spanish romance, to the effect that Captain Falk, now Major Falk, was coming home.

That was her first interpretation of his letter. Rereading after her initial flurry of relief subsided, she was forced to another version. Owing to his rise in rank he was compelled to exchange into a new regiment, and that regiment were bound for North America where the former colonists were still in arms. He meant first to escort a wounded friend to England. Time pressed. If she had questions that required his response perhaps she had best write his solicitor. In short he was not "coming home" to Wellfield House.

That infuriated Emily. Surely he owed his children as much consideration as he owed a mere friend. She wrote a scathing letter and posted it, fuming, to Toulouse. She placed no reliance on his sense of parental duty, however, so she did not tell the children that their father would soon be in England. Thus, when Peggy's black-avised husband rode up one fine May evening leading a fat, intelligent-looking pony, Matt and Amy were galvanised with joy.

"Eustachio!" they cried with one voice.

Part II
Tom Conway
1813

= 7 =

Tom Conway felt slack and dull with too much sleep. If he lay still the pain was a mere nagging below his left shoulder blade. Except for the crackle of the fire and the dripping of rain off the eaves the room was still. He could hear the sound of Richard Falk's pen scratching across foolscap. Tom turned his head.

Richard, in shirt-sleeves, his deplorable French coat thrown carelessly across the back of his chair, bent to his task.

" 'Scribble, scribble, scribble, Mr. Gibbon.' "

Richard's hand stilled before he went on with his writing. After a few minutes of steady application he stopped, sanded the page, and stood. He held the sheet to the light of the flickering candle, scowling at it. Then he set it down and picked up the candle. "I take it you've decided to rejoin the living."

Tom drew a sharp breath as unwelcome recollection came flooding back. "Temporarily. You're a damned provocative sort, Richard. From anyone else I'd take that as a slip of the tongue."

"From me it had to be deliberate." Richard's face, momentarily illumined by the unsteady light of the candle, was drawn and tired. A smear of ink decorated one cheekbone. He set the candle on the small table by the couch upon which Tom lay, and went to the scullery. There was a clanking noise and presently Richard returned minus the smear and bearing two half filled glasses.

"If I drink another brandy," Tom said dreamily, "I shall puke on your boots."

"Not for the first time."

"I was devilish seasick, wasn't I?"

Richard's rare smile lit his face. He put the glasses down and sat on the rickety chair by the bedside. "Epically." He stretched, arching like a cat, and pressed the heels of his hands to his eyes.

"Epically. Is that what you're working at?"

Richard cocked a quizzical eyebrow. "My latest epic? It's finished. I was just copying the last chapter for the printer."

"When did you find time to write it?"

"Not aboard ship, to be sure." Richard took up his brandy, warming it in his hard, capable hands. He took a swallow, and leaning his head against the high back of the chair, gazed at nothing.

What a clump of contradictions he was. Tom closed his eyes, drifting. *A cross-grained, sour-tongued, inconsistent . . . bastard.* He opened his eyes, staring at the freshly limed ceiling. The timbers were heavy black bars across the white. *Black and white. Life and death. Death. Bastard*, he thought, and realised with a clutch of dismay that he had spoken the word aloud.

Richard said quietly, "Now who's provoking?"

"How long have we been here in Rye?" Tom turned his head to look at his friend, then looked away. There was no use apologising. With Richard there never was. *Son of a whore.*

"Nearly a fortnight. Tomorrow you are going to walk with me along the strand."

"Delightful. What if it's still pouring rain?"

"In the teeth of a gale, if necessary."

"Why?"

"Because you're beginning to resemble one of the lower vegetables. I find that disturbing."

Tom took another careful breath and was surprised to find that the pain stayed at the same level. It could almost be called an ache. "Very well." Realisation struck him. "A fortnight! My God, Richard, how much time do you have left to you?"

"Eight days. I can stretch it to nine. Time to walk to Deal. Or we could make a sentimental pilgrimage to Shornecliff. Do you recall the delights of Shornecliff? Running up sheer bluffs in full gear. Prancing about in a December surf—"

"What about your children?"

"Flourishing, I trust."

Tom twisted and regretted the movement. "You will board the mail coach tomorrow and set out for Hampshire. For Christ's sweet sake," he gasped, "you've not seen them in two years!"

"Twenty months." Richard's voice was calm. "Lie back, you lout. You'll rip something open."

Tom obeyed, gritting his teeth against the sickening contraction of his ruined back muscles. For a time he thought he would indeed puke on his friend's boots. Presently the room stopped heaving. Something cool touched his sweating face. A wet cloth.

"My God, how shall I stand it?"

The cloth touched his brow again.

"How?" he repeated, angry.

"I don't know how," Richard said quietly, "but you will."

"Easy for you to say."

Richard did not respond.

Presently Tom's breathing steadied.

" 'Thou knowest, 'tis common, All that lives must die, Passing through Nature to Eternity.' " Richard's voice was wry and sad.

Tom said bitterly, "Aye, it is common. But not easy."

He felt the cloth touch his face again. Richard did not speak, for which Tom was grateful. He knew he was behaving badly. When he could command his patience, he said, "Where's Sims?"

"I sent him to see about food. You'll have to eat something solid for a change."

Tom swallowed. "You can stop soothing my fevered brow."

Richard rose and carried the cloth and a basin which had apparently been sitting on the uneven floor into the scullery. Tom followed him with his eyes. Richard was a long time about his chore. The back door opened. Was he leaving? *Do I care?* Tom stared at the ceiling. A spider dangled coyly from the middle beam, almost motionless in the still air. "Did you give up?" Tom whispered. The spider continued to dangle.

He heard the back door close. Richard entered, his hair damp. "Raining," he said unnecessarily. "Spring squall. It'll blow over by morning." He walked over to the spindly secretary, shoving his hair from his eyes with an impatient hand. "Damn."

"What is it?"

"I've blotted my blasted copybook." He leaned one hand on the desk and moved the sheet of foolscap carefully out of range.

"Why do you write that tripe?"

"Money."

"Is there money in it?"

Richard straightened, wriggling his shoulders as if they ached. "Enough. I screwed twenty more pounds out of Hitchins this time." He turned, a fugitive smile in his eyes. "I thought I could intimidate him better in person than by post. I was right."

Tom felt his mouth quirk in unwilling response.

"Easier?"

"Yes."

"Good. What do you say to the brandy now?"

"I say no. Finish your own, however."

Obediently, Richard sat once again by the daybed and toyed with the brandy glass.

"Fool."

Richard raised his glass in ironic salute and tossed off the contents.

"I want you to leave tomorrow," Tom said and knew he lied. The realisation surprised him.

"When you're on your feet."

"No. Tomorrow. Your children . . . "

"I don't intend to go to Hampshire."

"Then why the devil did you come home with me? I thought that was the excuse you gave Daddy Hill." General Hill was notoriously softhearted.

Richard set the empty glass carefully on the small table. "Why?"

"To see Hitchens and deliver the manuscript."

"If you think I need a nursemaid—"

"If I hadn't come Bevis would have. Your affinity for the sea is well known."

"Sims—"

"Rather hard on Sims, don't you think? It took two of us. Three," he amended thoughtfully. "McGrath lent a hand, too."

"Where's McGrath?" McGrath was Richard's servant, a black Irishman with a villainous squint and the disposition of a camel.

"Dallying with his wife."

"In Hampshire?"

Richard inclined his head.

Tom drew a breath. "Then I think you should join him."

"I never meant to go down to Mellings. Why should I?"

"Why! My God."

Richard rose, walked to the leaded window and stood staring out at the distant mass of the sea. He did not speak.

"I don't understand you."

"You're not required to."

"God damn your eyes," Tom said softly. "I may not be required to, but I will." Very slowly and with exquisite care he rolled to his left side and swung his long, breeches-clad legs over the edge of the couch. It was sudden sharp motion that hurt.

He levered himself to a sitting position by careful inches, his arm shaking with the strain of bearing his weight. He straightened. When he thought he would not faint, he said, "Tell me."

Richard whirled. In half a second he was across the room, eyes dark with anxiety. "Tom, don't . . . you can't . . . "

Tom fended his friend off with a shove of his undamaged right arm. "I can do whatever I put my mind to," he said through clenched teeth. "Tell me."

"Yes. Very well, but let me help you lie down first. You're not ready for heroicks quite yet."

"What about . . . walk . . . on the strand . . . tomorrow?"

"Hush." Frowning, Richard slipped his right arm around Tom's shoulders, bracing one knee on the bed frame and one booted foot on the floor. "Easy, now. There. No more of that tonight." His touch was hard, and cold from the damp air, but he seemed to know what to do and he was deft and surprisingly gentle. Lying back down was less hurtful than sitting.

Restored to his former state, Tom glared at the ceiling. The eaves dripped musically. The spider had swung up, pulling her lifeline with her. The filament quivered. "Tell me," he said gratingly.

Richard resumed his seat. "I came with you because I knew what the sawbones would tell you. Lord Bevis was oversanguine."

"You *knew*?" The surgeons had told Tom he would be lucky to live five years. Loose metal and bone fragments were wandering about his insides, and one piece, a nasty chunk of brass, lodged dangerously near his spine. Though the surgeons' verdict had not been unexpected it had been a hard blow.

"Another lapse of the tongue. I didn't know what they'd say. I surmised. In any case I thought they'd hack you about again. I didn't think you should should be alone. Besides, you'd be needing to find lodgings, and I meant to see to that and to be assured you were well served before I left. And on your feet, if possible."

Tom digested that. "But I had Sims by me."

"Sims will do. I know that now, but I had to be sure."

"Why?"

"Oh, the devil—"

"Don't avoid me. Why?"

There was a long pause. "I may be a bastard," Richard said drily, "but I'm capable of ordinary friendship."

Tom closed his eyes.

Richard's voice was rough. "I've known you a long time, Tom. You're my son's godfather and you stood by me when Isabel died. What more reason do you need?"

Tom unclenched his hands slowly, finger by finger. "You've placed me under a very heavy obligation."

"There is no obligation. I did what I had to do."

"And devil take the hindmost?"

"Something like that."

Tom lay very still.

"I was afraid they'd make you take laudanum."

"How did you know about it? My God, Egypt." Tom had been wounded some years before in Egypt. Owing to the stupidity of the surgeons and his own nineteen-year-old ignorance, he was given addictive quantities of opium. Withdrawal had not been pleasant. He had not used it in a decade. He still recalled the nightmares.

"Then I am grateful," he said, "and very much obliged."

Richard shifted in the chair.

"It was good of you to put up with my whining."

"No whining. A lot of swearing."

Tom heard his friend rise and looked up at him. Richard stood, rubbing his arms, the habitual scowl between his brows.

"Is it so very different?" he asked abruptly.

Tom stiffened. "What?"

"Knowing. We've all been under a death sentence in a way." He rubbed his arms again, shivering. "I don't express myself well. I'm sorry. It's want of sleep."

Tom stared.

"The longer we were over there the shorter the odds. I always thought the axe would fall sooner or later. I still do. It's a matter of time. You've five years left to you."

"With luck," Tom said bitterly.

"With good luck. I think you should rest for a few months. Then find something to do."

"Tatting?"

"You said yourself you can do anything you put your mind to. Take up Greek or architecture or . . . or accounts. You've a head for figures. Do something demanding."

"Perhaps I'll write a novel."

Richard's shoulders slumped. He turned away and walked back to the window. Tom saw that it had gone pitch dark out. Unlikely that Richard could see far beyond the gate.

Presently Richard jerked the curtains together. "Try to sleep if you can. I've letters to write. Sims will be along soon."

"You'll need your candle."

"Yes. In a moment." He riffled through the stack of freshly copied sheets, squared the pile, and stuffed it in a stiff paper folder of the sort that ties with ribbons. He mended his pen and bent close to scribble the direction.

"Richard . . . "

"What is it?" He finished and straightened, turning. His hair flopped over his forehead in a dark wing.

Tom's voice was harsh. "You'll have to talk about your children. There is the small matter of their guardianship. If you should meet with an accident—"

"If I'm killed you're stuck with them. I'm sorry to burden you with such a charge, but it's too late to change things. They can be left with Mrs. Foster. My will is with my solicitor."

"You have great faith in the estimable Mrs. Foster."

"I have no choice."

"*I* am not so sanguine," Tom said with deliberate brutality. "You've only her word for it that they're well and happy, Richard. How if she's lying to you? She could be. Even if she's honest she may take it into her head to marry, or sell the manor and emigrate, and then where would they be, poor brats?"

"You have the authority to make other arrangements." Richard did not move. His face was a blur in the dim light.

"What if other arrangements are needed now? What if I stick my spoon in the wall in the next sixmonth? You'll have to think about them, Richard, at the very least."

"Do you imagine I ever think of anything else?"

8

RICHARD'S VOICE WAS so quiet that for a moment his words did not register.

Tom had been watching the spider methodically spinning strand after tiny strand. He jerked his head sharply and was rewarded with another spasm that left him gasping. "If you feel that way, then I wonder you won't go to them." He squinted, but it was impossible to make out his friend's expression. Richard stood beyond the pool of candlelight.

Richard took his jacket from the chair back and put it on with deliberation. Tom bit back an automatic sarcasm. He didn't have to see the coat, he remembered it very well—the fabric visibily sleazy, the cut foreign. It had annoyed Tom, who was as fastidious in such matters as he could afford to be, for six weeks.

Richard said calmly, "I could give them only a few days. And don't cover yourself with guilt. Two weeks or two days—the effect would be precisely the same. I'd come galloping on the scene, probably frightening them. They're not used to strangers. I'd disturb their routine, confuse them, and to what purpose? I'd just have to leave and I daresay that would confuse them, too."

"And what if you're killed?"

Richard shrugged. "I think it unlikely they remember me. Amy was two when I saw her last. Perhaps she does have a few dim recollections, but Tommy wouldn't know me at all. I hear of them regularly, and I daresay they hear of me. Thanks to Mrs. Foster, they probably think of me as Father Christmas."

"Surely not."

"As a shadowy figure who writes letters," Richard amended, not smiling, "and sends gewgaws on their birthdays. That's tolerable. Do you fancy I'd want them to go into paroxyms of grief over me if I were killed? I find the idea revolting."

He went to the fire, added a careful ration of sea coal, and stood looking down at it. Apparently his handiwork didn't satisfy him, for he reached for the poker and began jabbing at the coals. The flaring orange light showed his set profile. The bunched muscle of his jaw jumped.

Tom chose his words with caution. "If they were mine, I'd want to see them, say good-bye to them."

"My Christ," Richard said softly, "I couldn't bear it." He gave the fire one further tired poke and set the iron in its place with exaggerated care, which was necessary, Tom saw with astonishment, because his hand was unsteady.

Surprise was succeeded by bewildered pity. Tom closed his eyes. He could think of nothing to say. He was not a parent himself and could only guess at the feelings attached to that state. He had always vaguely supposed them pleasant. It now occurred to him that fatherhood, in Richard's circumstances, was something akin to tragedy. *For a man of feeling* . . .

Was the idea so absurd? *One need not wear one's feelings on one's sleeve.* Richard had a reputation for aloofness and withering sarcasm, but sarcasm is a fair defence against feeling.

They had known each other since boyhood. Richard had been a high-strung lad whose bad dreams annoyed his fellows by night and whose belligerence by day made friendship a constant hazard. They had been thrown together because they were both left at Parson Freeman's rectory, where they were being schooled, during the holidays. Later they had lost track of each other for long stretches of time and neither troubled to write. Even in the Peninsula they had not sat in one another's pockets.

Tom had always accounted Richard a friend, but not a close one, and he had accepted guardianship of Richard's children in the patronising conviction that Richard could very likely find no one else. Now he was in Richard's debt.

If Richard were in my shoes, would I take such pains for him? Tom turned the thought over in his head. *No. What a self-satisfied prig I am. Full of conscious virtue and blind as a sow. Saint Thomas Conway, patron of orphans and universal good fellow.* Self-disgust kept him silent.

Richard leaned on the mantel, head bent, still staring into the fire.

"Will you tell me how things are left?" Tom said at last.

Richard straightened. "I've writ everything down. I meant to go over it with you later."

"Tell me."

Richard took a long breath. "They won't be a charge on you. You needn't think that. There's enough to see them educated and a small dower for Amy."

"How the devil did you contrive that?" Tom was astonished.

"Cheeseparing, and four very bad novels."

"In two years?"

"I'd finished the first before Isabel died." He walked over to the bedside table and took up the other brandy glass. "If the government decide to honour their debts there'll be three months' arrears and whatever prize money they award. I told the colonel to direct it to my solicitor when I exchanged." He swirled the liquour in the glass. "That might see Tommy into a clerkship."

"Not into the army."

"No." He gave a short laugh. "Over my dead body."

Tom said quietly, "Sell out. Before you run out of luck."

"And do what?"

"Write."

Richard stared at him. "I haven't another book in me."

"Send Don Alfonso to King's Town and stay home yourself." Don Alfonso was the hero of Richard's later works, a highborn Spaniard of extravagant pride and stupidity. A good satire, Tom thought, but one the general reader was unlikely to recognise. The books sold because the plots, improbable though they might be, moved like lightning. "Did you model Don Alfonso on old Cuesta?"

That startled a smile. "As Don Gregorio might have been at twenty-five, with touches of Joachim Blake."

"A clever invention."

"Nonsense," Richard said flatly. "I write the purest tripe. The great British publick prefer it to art."

Tom chuckled. "I only read the one. It was damned amusing."

Richard said nothing. The brandy sloshed in slow circles.

There was an uninhibited crash at the front door and Sims entered, laden with viands from the nearest inn.

Despite the humiliation of having Sims feed him in the manner of a robin stuffing its nestling's craw, Tom surprised himself by eating with a fair appetite. Sims's imperturbable cockney cheer was equal to that, or as Tom well knew, any other occasion. Nevertheless Tom determined to take no more meals lying down.

Sims swept up the crumbs deftly. "Try a bit o' cheese, major. Nice crumbly cheddar. Nothing like it. There's a bit o' berry tart if you've a fancy for it. Sip o' ale first? Right you are." He trundled over to the table where Richard was picking at a slice of boiled chicken, and poured a swig into a pewter tankard.

"Try not to spill it all over him," Richard said shortly.

Sims was offended and returned to Tom's side muttering, but he didn't spill much.

Richard rose. "I'm going for a walk."

"No 'urry, Major Falk, sir."

The door closed.

Sims clucked like a hen. "Not 'alf civil tonight, is 'e?"

"He's tired," Tom said pacifically. "Er, how long have I been lying here, Sims, and why? Not another metal fragment."

"No, now. Pulled a couple of stitches when we come down from London in Lord Bevis's flash carriage. Road like a cart track the last five mile. That didn't 'elp. You was doing well enough 'til the ague set in." He met his master's gaze blandly. "Been more'n a week. 'E said," Sims jerked his head in the direction of the door, " 'E said wot you wanted was Peruvian bark, but the 'pothecary balked. Wanted to dose you with laudanum. Rare set-to that was. I told the quack you didn't use it, but 'e thought 'e knew best. Major Falk threw 'is drops out the door and they 'ad words."

"I can imagine." Tom suppressed a laugh. It hurt to laugh. He was relieved to know that the surgeons hadn't been at him again. "The ague, you say. You're sure?"

"Sure as death," Sims said with characteristic want of tact. "Dosed you with bark, Major Falk did. 'Ad to pour it down you, four, five different times. Nasty stuff. 'E said I should keep a supply of the bark to 'and. That right, Major?"

"Yes. Thank you, Sims. If you've been spelling Richard off and on for a week you'll be tired, too. Turn in early."

"Oh, I took forty winks on me couch of ease this morning. Major Falk said 'e'd cope. 'Ad 'is scribbling to keep 'im 'appy. 'E's writ a book, ain't 'e?" Sims looked impressed.

"Four. No, more than that. The first few were too dreadful to count."

"Cor. Is 'e famous then?"

"No." Tom stared at his man and decided not to try to explain pseudonyms. Richard's was Peter Picaro. Alliterative and appropriate. Peter Piper picked a peck of pickled peppers.

" 'Ere, wot's so bleeding funny?"

"Sorry, Sims," Tom choked back a laugh. "A stray thought."

"It's a fair treat to see you pulling out of the dismals," Sims said generously. "More like yerself, if I may say so, Major."

"You may. Thank you, Sims. Did I have the wit to cash a bank draught before I left Town?"

"Aye. We're in clover."

"Then take a crown, or whatever you need, and be off to the inn. What's it called?"

"The Dolphin, sir."

"To the Dolphin. You can return the crockery and settle the account. Have a pint or two before you come back."

Sims looked pleased at that and vanished in a trice, having built up the fire and lit a fresh candle before his exit. It was some time before Richard returned.

=9=

Tom drowsed, but he wasn't tired. *Slept out*, he thought. The spider on the center beam seemed to have retired for the night. It was raining and beginning to blow.

At last the front door opened quietly. Sims was incapable of such delicacy.

"Where's Sims?" Richard snapped.

"At the Dolphin. Probably under the table by now."

"I told him not to leave you."

"I daresay he thought my orders took precedence of yours." Tom felt a stab of annoyance. *Officious bastard*. "Do you fancy I'll fall on my sword if I'm left alone?"

"You might turn feverish again. I can do without another night of wrestling with you." Richard latched the door.

"I daresay." Tom squinted. "Richard, you lunatic, you're soaked to the skin. Take that appalling coat off and change your shirt or *you'll* be needing the Peruvian bark."

Richard crossed obediently to the fire and, removing the offensive garment, dragged out a dilapidated firescreen. He hung the coat on it, where it dripped a melancholy puddle onto the flags. "You don't like my Bordeaux jacket?"

"Is that what it is? No. I do not."

"Pity."

"Change your shirt."

"In a moment." Richard knelt and held his hand to the fire.

"You might've had your tailor choose a less obnoxious shade of blue."

"What tailor? It was ready made for an *avocat* who unfortunately succumbed to the typhus. M'sieur assured me it suited milor' to a perfection. Besides it was dagger cheap and you'll allow I needed a new one."

Tom closed his eyes. He tried to recall if he had given Richard money for the remove from London. He felt a cool hand on his forehead and looked up into Richard's composed features. A drop of icy water hit Tom's nose. "What the devil?"

"Sorry. Wet hair. I wanted to see if you need another dose."

"No!—that is, I'm perfectly well."

"All the same, one more glass . . . "

Tom groaned theatrically.

A spark of laughter lit his friend's eyes. "I perceive you are greatly improved. It will do you good, however."

"That's what all quacks say of their revolting potions. Where are you going?"

"To change my shirt." He disappeared beyond Tom's range of vision and returned, pulling a fresh shirt over his lean torso. His hair had been towelled and stood up in tufts.

"You look a guy."

Richard entered to the scullery. He came back with a glass of murky liquid. "Don't try to sit up. I'll prop you."

"Good God."

"Stop imagining horrors," Richard said rather sharply. "You're almost healed. When you've healed completely you'll have to work at it a bit. In a month or so it won't play the devil with you all the time. Standing and walking would be well enough now. Bending and sitting will take longer, that's all."

"I do not love thee, Dr. Falk."

"No reason you should. No, don't try it. Just lean on my arm. I'll pull you up."

Tom leaned. He drank the stewed bark off and made a face. Richard removed the glass. When he lay flat once more and the worst twinges had subsided, Tom took a careful breath. "I'll need a replacement in the wings—as the children's guardian. Have you thought of that?" He was proud of his own matter-of-fact tone.

"No. Not really." Richard sat on the chair and stretched his booted legs out, staring at them.

"Bevis."

"No."

"Do you dislike Bevis?"

"I don't dislike him. He's an affable man. I don't know him well enough." Richard chewed his lip. "Forgive me. I realise he is your close friend, but I judged him somewhat volatile."

"In his tastes perhaps. Not in his sense of duty."

"That is high praise."

Tom sighed. "Whom do you suggest?"

"Travers. No, he's bound for America, too. I forgot."

"Who else?"

Richard said bleakly, "There aren't legions to draw from. I haven't your gift for friendship."

"They're dead, aren't they? I'm sorry, Richard. I have been somewhat more fortunate, but apart from Bevis I haven't a great many friends I could entrust children to, either."

"Then it will have to be Bevis." Richard rose, levering himself up on the chair back. The chair protested. "I'll draw up instructions for my solicitor."

"Have you thought to ask your family for help?"

His hand clenched on the curved wood. "Christ!"

"I wish you will hear me out."

"I'd sooner see them on the parish," Richard said fiercely. "Are you mad?"

"There is such a thing as an excess of stubborn pride. The Duke of Newsham is a great landowner. I think the Ffouke estate could bear the charge of two small children."

"I can see," said Richard with false calm, "that I am going to have to tell you a story."

Tom frowned. "That's not necessary. I appreciate your reluctance. God knows, I'd have to be stricken blind, legless, and penniless before I'd apply to the Earl of Clanross. It is far better not to be a relation at all than a poor one."

Richard went to the secretary. Paced like a cat.

"It is not a question of your comfort, however, but your children's. There's a difference. Stop prowling, Richard."

"I think I should tell you a story. I have a knack for that, haven't I? You once called me a blackguardly liar."

"That was some few years ago." Almost twenty in fact. They had both been twelve when they first met.

"You were right," Richard snapped. "I am a liar, a fairly gifted one. Like panders and whores and hangmen, I have learnt to turn a moral defect into coin of the realm."

"I hardly think—"

"Nevertheless, the story I am going to tell you now is the truth. When I've done, perhaps you'll see why I prefer not to put my children in the power of Newsham or the dowager duchess."

Tom stared. The man was speaking of his own mother.

"I am going to tell you how I discovered I was the Duchess of Newsham's bastard."

"Richard, for God's sake—"

" 'Stop dramatising yourself,' " Richard mocked, his voice thick, " 'Be sensible.' Do you see this candle?"

"I can scarcely avoid it. You're shaking hot wax on me."

"Then mark me. What I shall say is the plain truth." He placed his left hand square in the flame and held it there.

Tom didn't trouble with words. He swung both arms up hard against Richard's right elbow and the candle fell to the flags.

THE ROOM PLUNGED into darkness and Tom plunged into a black pit of pain. It was beyond his power to keep from crying out, but he did not faint, which was rather surprising. He stuffed his right sleeve in his mouth and waited. After a nauseating time he opened his eyes on a room lit only by the dying fire.

"What other tricks do you intend to divert me with?" he said with all the sarcasm he could muster. He was exceedingly angry. *Bastard, indeed. Charlatan.* "Snake charming? Sword swallowing?" Except for the rain, there was absolute silence. The smell of burnt flesh offended the air. "Richard!"

"What?"

Tom turned his head. Richard was backed against the dark bulk of the table, halfway across the room. He was motionless, head bent, cradling his left hand. How had he got there? *Leapt sidewise like a cat*, Tom thought sourly. "Of all the fool tricks. That was not necessary."

"Perhaps not."

"Perhaps!" Tom's wrath broke through.

Richard said dully, "I am quite stupid from want of sleep. You caught me off guard. I thought . . . "

"What did you think? Well?"

"I thought you were the last man to make such a suggestion. I thought I could trust you."

The silence extended. Tom chose his words. He was still angry, but confusion began to edge out his wrath. "I made my suggestion reluctantly." His voice grew sharp again. "You will allow the circumstances are awkward, the choices limited."

"Yes."

Another thought struck him. "When did you finish the book?"

"What?"

"The latest episode in the riotous career of Don Alfonso."

"A quarter past ten."

"This morning. I see." He did. Want of sleep did explain a great deal. "And spent half the night wrestling me, and how many nights before that? I rather think you should go to bed."

"I am now wide awake." Richard raised his head. His face was a white blur, white as his shirt. "Unfortunately."

"Oh, go mend your hand. It stinks."

That took some time. The wind, with a wonderful sense of melodrama, had decided to howl, and rain battered the windows. Richard had not lit the candle. *Groping about in a dark scullery*, Tom thought, exasperated.

"Sit down," he snapped, when his lunatic friend returned. "I refuse to crane at you."

The chair scraped.

"Light the candle."

"I don't know where it's rolled to."

"Never mind. Does the roof of this little chateau leak? I can't say I approve your taste in architecture."

Richard did not play. His voice was listless with exhaustion and defeat. "Bevis's agent said it was sound. It's private. The rent is fair. You should be in the town, however."

"So that my opportunities will be greater for, what was it, Greek and bookkeeping?" Richard said nothing. In friendlier tones Tom went on, "It's a reasonable idea. I just wasn't ready to be making plans."

"I know."

"I think you should tell me your story."

73

Richard moved across the dark room to the window. His voice, when it came, was composed, lifeless. "I was raised with the duke's children in the Abbeymont nursery. I don't know why. Perhaps some bargain the duchess struck when she consented to return to her connubial vows. I learnt I was baseborn fairly young. It was not . . . a devastating realisation. The duke had bastards. I thought I was one of them. Very young children accept things as they are."

"I daresay you're right," Tom murmured, recalling several fairly bizarre features of his own childhood which had not seemed strange to him at the time. "Go on."

"It was not until I was eight or nine that I began to wonder. Do you know how such establishments are conducted? There are wet nurses, nursemaids, tutors, a presiding governess for the girls—that sort of thing. Rather formal. Lady This and Lord That. At first I thought my name was Lordrichard. One word."

"But . . . "

"I still don't understand it. From time to time the duchess would make visitations and we would be paraded for her inspection. She powdered her hair. I don't know what its true colour was." He drew a breath. "The duke's visits were rarer and more abrupt. I was invariably hustled out of sight. I began to wonder why."

"Didn't you ask?"

"Oh, yes. And got no answer. 'Now, Lord Richard, you know you must not speak of such things. And mind your tongue.' As a rule I did. When I turned twelve I thought I should put it to the test. Sarah goaded me, rather. Lady Sarah. My half sister. She was two years older."

Tom waited.

Richard paced restlessly, stumbling a little on the uneven flags. "We decided I should confront the duke."

"My God."

"It was a dare. Like walking the ridgepole or jumping a three-barred gate, no hands. I thought I'd try it."

"What happened?"

"The next time the duke descended on us and I was sent

off, I sneaked back into the Presence. He saw me at once, of course, and asked who I was."

"And you found out your origins?"

"Yes. He beat me to a bloody pulp."

"What!"

"There were preliminaries, I daresay." Richard had returned to his post by the dark window. "I don't recall. He—the duke—had a loud voice and he made the situation quite clear to everyone, but I chiefly recall being thrown against a large mahogany table."

Tom held his breath.

"He cracked my head and several ribs and bust my left arm," Richard said dispassionately. "By the time he'd finished there was quite a commotion. I dimly recall Sarah screeching."

"Didn't your mother intervene?" Tom burst out.

"The duchess wasn't there. I came to my senses in Parson Freeman's rectory some weeks later."

Tom frowned. "But what . . . why were you taken to the rectory?"

"I don't know," Richard snapped. "I wasn't given an explanation and I'm no longer curious. They got rid of me."

"Christ, Richard. Freeman wasn't there."

"Lord Clanross had already sent him off across the Atlantic to rescue you from your imaginary pirates. His wife nursed me and told me how dreadful you were. I conceived an extravagant admiration for you, Tom."

Tom shut his eyes. He had contrived by luck and a glib tongue to run off to Nova Scotia after his mother's death. He still looked upon the feat as something of a triumph. The Earl of Clanross had sent Parson Freeman to fetch him back.

"I imitated you four times, with no success at all. I didn't even reach the next market town. No ingenuity." Richard laughed. It was not a very jolly sound but there was honest amusement in it. "However, I put your exploits in my first book so there was some profit in the example."

Tom felt his cheeks flush. "Cawker."

"You spun some fairly tall tales yourself. I collect you fetched up in Boston blacking boots."

"In Halifax," Tom muttered. "Mucking out stables."

"No pirates?"

Tom shook his head. "Did you hear from them afterwards?" By 'them' he meant the duchess, but Richard took him literally.

"Lady Sarah writ me after Vimeiro that the duke had died."

Tom digested that. "After fifteen years' silence you must have been startled to see her hand."

"I was appalled," Richard said wearily. "I thought I'd put them off the scent."

"What do you mean?"

Richard walked back to the chair and sat, head down like a spent runner. "I think I must have been jumping at shadows those first few years, but I'd had a fright, you know." He lifted his head. "Have I been chasing phantoms, Tom? The duke was a vindictive man. I think he made other attempts on my life."

"Tell me."

=== 11 ===

OUTSIDE THE WIND gave a melodramatic blast that rattled the windowpanes. Tom waited.

Richard was groping. "Shipping a fifteen-year-old off to the Indian Army doesn't strike me as a receipt for longevity."

"No, but it's done. Or was then."

"I didn't question it at the time. I was glad to go. You took up your commission somewhat later, I think."

"I was seventeen. Better prepared."

Richard shrugged. "Two years would not have prepared me for India. The thing is, I kept getting into scrapes."

"That, at least, is not startling."

Richard pinched the skin between his brows and drew his hand down across his face. "They were not all of my making."

"Your scrapes? I see."

He rubbed his jaw with his right hand. The left dangled. "There were incidents. It's all very shadowy. I stopped eating anywhere but the mess, after a time, and I was careful to avoid being alone. When we were called out on campaign—Tipoo Sultan's war—the tricks stopped."

"Seringapatam."

"Yes. Away from garrison I was safe enough, I think. Except for the usual inconveniences of campaigning." His voice was wry. India had been his first taste of war. "I volunteered for the expedition to Batavia and you know the confusion that followed when that was cancelled. I was ill on the troopship, but so was damned near everyone. Bad water."

"That was the army that came to Egypt, wasn't it?"

"Yes. Overland from the Red Sea."

Tom winced. He had had a very bad time in Egypt himself, but he had heard tales of the Indian relief column that curled his hair. Scant food, bad water, scorpions, sunstroke—and an outbreak of plague once the troops reached Cairo.

But Richard's mind was not on scorpions and sunstroke. He sat straighter, conforming to the chair. "After that it changed."

"Their tactics?"

"I'm not sure there was a 'they,' or a he." He eased his shoulders against the chair back. The wind gusted again and the panes rattled on cue. He cocked his head. "Is that Sims?"

"No. He's not been gone long enough. 'Spring squall?' " Tom quoted in gentle mockery.

Richard shrugged. "It will blow itself out by morning. Where was I?"

"Egypt."

"Cairo and Alexandria. I called on you."

"I remember. You were burnt black. I didn't recognise you."

"Then we're even." Richard's teeth gleamed in the darkness. "You had enormous moustachios and your arm in a sling."

"And a sleepy droop in the eyes from all that opium."

"It was the devil of a thing to happen to you, Tom. I was sorry to hear of it."

"Inconvenient," Tom agreed. "Tell me about the duel."

"You knew of it?"

"Everyone did."

Richard was silent.

"I thought you'd lost your temper," Tom prompted.

"In the end, I did. We were all short-tempered by that

time, and at first I just put it down to the heat and the waiting. Then things began to change in the mess. Snickers, sidewise looks, *sotto voce* comments. My friends started to look worried, but there was nothing to pin down. I never did know what went on, but I was slowly being sent to Coventry and damned uncomfortable it was."

He paused, ordering his thoughts. "There was an older man, a lieutenant with a reputation as a brawler. He kept pushing me. I said something. I don't even recall what it was, but it was trivial. He picked up on it. There were witnesses and when he challenged me, I had to fight. You know how it used to be."

"Yes, I see." Duelling had been epidemic in the army.

Richard had been silent, reflecting. Now he said more brusquely, as if he meant to be done, "Hertford, that was my opponent's name, was a dead shot, which has never been the case with me. I had the choice of weapons. I made him fight with swords."

Tom choked on a laugh. No one fought with swords anymore.

"You taught me the foils." The smile gleamed again. "Swords are different, of course. I was rusty, but Hertford had never used a sword and he was slow. I thought I could take him."

"And did."

Richard's voice was uncertain. "I daresay you'll think me a fool, but that was a damned ugly sensation. When I tried to pull my weapon out, it rasped on bone. He screamed. I dream of it sometimes, though I've done worse things since."

Tom shuddered. After a moment, he said, "He didn't die, as I recall."

"He recovered quickly once we put out to sea. He said nothing to indicate that anyone had put him up to it. We were both brought before the court martial. The witnesses, thank God, told the truth—that he'd forced it on me. He was cashiered."

"And you were acquitted."

Richard inclined his head. "With an undeserved reputation for swashbuckling and the strong feeling that my superiors did not look upon me with favour. I was correct."

"Half pay."

"Yes. We reached Colchester Garrison just in time for the Peace of Amiens. I was the first to go."

Tom grimaced. As he recalled with vivid clarity, living on an ensign's pay was not an easy trick, though rather easier abroad than at home. An ensign's half pay was derisory. "I was lucky to avoid that. They sent me to Ireland. How did you live?"

"Very obscurely. In the circumstances I thought it prudent."

"On half pay you could hardly have done otherwise."

"I could live on it now." Richard's tone was dry. "At the time I had grandiose notions of what was owing to my consequence."

"Fresh linen, hot shaving water, the occasional newspaper, a private room."

"Yes. I decided that genteel starvation didn't suit me."

"So you writ a book."

"I popped my watch, my greatcoat, and a spare pair of boots and bought some paper." He sounded almost cheerful. "I was pleased when it sold. It fetched twenty guineas, which was more than it was worth. I marched off with my booty and bought a bowl of hot stew. It was my first hot meal in a fortnight and I couldn't finish it."

"My God."

"It took more than one campaign to wean me of my taste for luxury."

Tom had to smile at that. "Did you do your scribbling in London or Colchester?"

"London. It's easier to lose oneself in London." He stood up. "I lost my phantom pursuers."

"They picked up the scent again when you rejoined the regiment?"

"I didn't rejoin the regiment."

Tom whistled. " 'Strewth. You didn't sell out!"

Richard walked over to the hearth and knelt by the fire. "I was still on the muster, but I worked at writing till I turned twenty-one." He began methodically rebuilding the fire. His motions were clumsy. Hand hurting.

Tom did some rapid calculations. He and Richard had been born within a fortnight of each other. "January eighteen five, some months into the war. I recall I was surprised to find you with the Fifty-second."

"Surprised to find me using a different name." Richard poked the fire and was rewarded with a satisfactory pulse of light.

"I thought that was your affair."

"For which I thank you." As if blinded by the flames, Richard groped his way to the dining table. "Shall I light the candle?"

"If you wish," Tom said quietly. It occurred to him that Richard had found it easier to speak his piece in the dark. "You made the exchange on the proceeds of your other book, I collect."

"There were two more books, three altogether. I only claim one of 'em. I saved what they brought in and lived by copying letters and legal documents." He returned to the hearth and lit the candle with a spill. "I changed my name by deed poll." He took the candlestick in his left hand, cupping his right about the flame, and carried the candle to the table. "Better?"

"Thanks. Why Falk?"

"You mean, why not Fitz-something? I meant to stay in the army, so I tried to make it look like a simplified spelling rather than a name change. Old Craufurd's name was always being spelled different ways. Why not mine? I thought Folk would occasion less comment than something completely different."

I nearly made a joke of it, Tom thought, aghast.

Richard was saying, "The law clerk misread my scrawl

as 'Falk.' I didn't correct him. The clerk at the Horse Guards was suffering from eye trouble and actually asked me how to spell it."

"Luck."

"It gave me three years free of the Ffouke family," Richard said simply. "How Sarah traced me I don't know."

"With the duke dead surely you'd no more cause to fear."

"Do you think I had cause?"

Tom met his friend's troubled eyes. "I don't know," he said honestly. "It's hard to believe a peer of the realm would . . . " His voice trailed off. *Not a tactful thing to say.*

Richard's mouth set. He pulled his left sleeve up to the elbow. "The bone the duke broke cut the skin. You can see the scar, rather faint, next to that sabre slash I took at Fuentes."

"You don't have to prove anything, Richard, and I would have believed you without the candle trick." Tom put conviction in every syllable, but he wasn't sure he would have credited the story if Richard had just blurted it out.

Richard's eyes dropped. He smoothed the sleeve.

"The duke is dead," Tom ventured. "Surely your eldest brother is not of the same stamp."

"I don't remember Keighley. He's fifteen years my senior. Lord John's a rakehell. Lord George was five when I left. They've no cause to love me or mine and some reason to wish me dead."

"Why?" Tom asked, bewildered.

"Because the duke left me out of his will."

"Did you expect a legacy?"

A wry smile twisted Richard's mouth. "It's a legal question. For all his rodomontade in the Abbeymont schoolroom, the duke neglected to blot me out legally. A tirade in front of nursemaids doesn't constitute repudiation of paternity. I'd lived twelve years as Lord Richard Ffouke. He should have branded me a bastard or cut me off without a shilling. That would have been final."

Tom blinked. "Upon my word, you should sue."

"For my 'share'? Don't be simple. I'm not his son. Besides, I'd no money then for lawyers, and I haven't now. Keighley—Newsham, I should say—could command the best in the realm. Or hire footpads. He writ me to that effect. I still have the letter."

"Lady Sarah informed you of the legal question. You've an ally."

"Sarah? She brought hell on me when I was twelve. I'm too old to play her games now." He spoke without rancour but with absolute finality. "I prefer a decent obscurity—for myself, and for Amy and Tommy, too. Believe me, Tom."

"It'll have to be Bevis, then."

"If there's no other choice." He shoved his hair out of his eyes. "I'll go to Mellings. I decided you were right, but I won't leave until Wednesday."

"That'll give you two days."

"Two days too many," Richard said with sudden bitterness.

"Go to sleep."

"Very well." He got clumsily to his feet. "Tell Sims it's his turn for the floor."

"A pallet?"

"Yes, by the fire. Very snug."

"Richard."

Richard turned back. He was cradling his left hand. "Shall I fetch something for you first?"

"No. If you were my father, Richard, I'd want to be able to say I'd met you."

He thought Richard flushed.

"Good night."

"Good night," Tom said to the ceiling. Sims was going to be late and rather drunk. Ample time for thinking. For the first time since the Chelsea surgeons had passed their death sentence on him, Thomas Conway found he wanted to think.

Part III
Emily, Sir Robert Wilson
1814-1815

= 12 =

EMILY HAD FALLEN in love with the Author of Doña Inez. She brought herself to admit her feelings the day Eustachio arrived. Emily fell in love frequently. It was her secret vice, cultivated since girlhood, when she had tumbled head over ears in love with her father's new bailiff because he had guinea-gold hair.

Emily had never done anything about her little passions. Virtue? Rather prudence, perhaps, or cowardice. She did not suppose she would do anything about this passion, either, but she had now been a widow for four and a half years. Sometimes she felt as if her widow's weeds were a nun's habit, or as if, at five and twenty, she had taken on the mantle of middle age. Sometimes she wanted to do something quite mad—run off with a band of gypsies or take up opera dancing. It was in this spirit of secret recklessness that she had indulged her epistolary passion for Richard Falk. It was not quite a safe thing to do, and that was why she did it.

As the "doing" so far consisted only in writing him cheerful details of his children's lives and rereading the brief notes that prefaced each installment of Doña Inez for signs of the man behind the pen, her risk had not seemed very great. But there was risk. The uncertain, up-and-down state of mind that had driven her to write the furious letter to him when she thought he would not come to see the children had taught her that much. Her anger had been disproportionate. The children did not miss him. How could they? Amy would surely have missed his letters—Matt as well. But none of the three children remembered Richard Falk as a real presence. Emily was the one who wanted to see him in the flesh.

She also had to admit to herself that part of her anticipation stemmed from plain vulgar excitement. She was exceedingly curious to see him again. She wanted to compare the man with the writer of absurd adventures. She reminded herself that she had not been enchanted with him at their first meeting. Indeed, he had struck her as remarkably cross-grained. In all likelihood she would find him repellent, and probably that would be for the best.

Peggy McGrath's welcome of her spouse was nearly as vociferous as the children's enthusiasm for Eustachio. Emily did not take to McGrath. A sour-faced, short-tempered, ugly man, his glowers intimidated Matt, though Amy chattered away to him happily enough. Out of delicacy Emily gave the connubial pair a private room in the untenanted second floor and took Tommy into her own bedchamber. He cried for his Peg a bit the first evening, but he was a sunny child, and Emily distracted him easily enough with his new territory. When he found next morning that his nurse had not entirely deserted him, he decided to accept her husband with only an occasional reproachful glance from his sloe-black eyes.

Amy coerced McGrath into saddling Eustachio with one of Emily's discarded sidesaddles, an insult that Matt bore so ill he forgot to be afraid of McGrath. Thereafter everyone rubbed along tolerably well—for the next week. Amy, like Doña Inez, decided she preferred to ride astride.

It was not possible to pump McGrath about his master. Emily had thought the Irish loquacious. Peggy certainly bore out that impression, but McGrath's idea of civil speech was confined to grunting and scowling. When Emily ventured a cautious question about his master's well-being, McGrath scowled. When she allowed that Major Falk must be pleased with his promotion, McGrath grunted. Given her husband's unprepossessing qualities, it was curious that Peggy took on a rosy glow in his presence. The horse McGrath had ridden belonged to Major Falk. McGrath declined to stable the creature on Emily. "Orders." Grunt. Scowl.

Major Falk himself finally appeared on the late coach as McGrath was about to settle with the innkeeper for the horse's board, so he did not come to Wellfield House until morning. Warned by Peggy's welcoming screech—she had spotted her master from the window on the second-floor landing—Emily put off the apron she had donned for her daily descent to the kitchen, tidied her cap and her emotions, and went down to greet her employer. If the pulse pounded in her throat it did not pound so hard that she was incapable of reason.

Phillida had stuck the major in the chilly withdrawing room where he stood looking not greatly different from what Emily remembered, except he was clean-shaven and somewhat tidier. His hair was cropped short. He had a new coat. Emily did not approve the coat. It looked vaguely foreign.

"Good morning, Major Falk."

"Mrs. Foster."

"I am glad to see you well. You will wish to go up to your children directly, I daresay. I have not prepared them for your coming, so I beg you will go slowly with Tommy." Emily was proud of this civil, businesslike, uneffusive greeting.

Major Falk followed her obediently up the stairs and said nothing. At least he didn't grunt, Emily reflected, philosophic. It was not in her to maintain a dignified silence. She kept up a polite chatter. The children loved the pony, Tommy now spoke seven separate words and two sentences, Amy was learning to write her name, the weather was agreeably mild, was it not, she hoped he had had a pleasant voyage. She did not await his reply and ushered him into the schoolroom *sans* ceremony.

His daughter indulged no adult tergiversations. She launched herself at him with a delighted shriek.

"Papa," Tommy echoed, experimental.

It was not as affecting a reunion as it might have been, but it was satisfactory. Major Falk accepted Tommy's wariness without comment. He listened to his daughter's mostly English chatter with grave attention, and when Matt showed signs of sulk, drew Emily's son into a discussion of the pony's points which developed into a riding lesson. That took up most of the afternoon.

Emily had decided it was time her father met her employer. That evening, Major Falk bore with Sir Henry's Corn Law monologue without satire. No sparks flew. When Major Falk had gone off to the inn at Mellings Parva, Sir Henry made mild approving noises. Aunt Fan said nothing disparaging. Emily did not voice her own exasperation. It was all too tame. Major Falk left the next afternoon with McGrath. The children continued to speak of their father afterwards, casually, as one might speak of an uncle one saw on occasion. Amy did not repeat her silent mourning.

Emily told herself she was a fool to have wished for more. Presented with a full account of his friend's sufferings, she had had to accept her employer's decision to stay so long with Major Conway. Indeed she was glad Major Falk had never received the scorching letter she posted to Toulouse, and she admitted to herself that loyalty to one's friends was always commendable. Commendable. *Convenable*. Conventional.

Before he took his leave, Major Falk said, flat and emotionless, "Write Tom Conway if I'm killed. He'll know what to do."

That seemed to give Emily an opening. "I trust it will not prove necessary, sir. Er, what arrangements—"

"Tom knows what to do," he repeated. "No complications to trouble your head over, unless you mean to give the children up."

"No. Oh, no, of course I don't." Exasperation sharpened Emily's voice.

Falk went on, oblivious, "That's settled then. Write Tom."

At that point Peggy brought his freshly scrubbed children down to the foyer, where the major and Emily awaited them. Peggy was inclined to be distraught and dramatic. Major Falk sent her out to lament over her departing husband and took Tommy, who gave his father a wet kiss of the sort he bestowed on all comers.

"Bye, Papa." He wriggled to be put down, and his father obliged with a small pat on the little boy's petticoats. "Bye," Tommy repeated, cheerful. "Bye-bye."

The major had knelt by his solemn-eyed daughter and took her in a cautious embrace.

"Don't go."

"I have to."

Amy's face screwed up.

He said something soft and rapid to her in Spanish, adding in English, "Shall you write to me, *querida?*"

"I can write my name."

"Yes, and very clearly, too."

"I'll write," Amy said with dignity, "if you will, *tambien*. Bring me *un paroquet*, *Papa*, and write me of Doña Inez in America."

Tommy whirled in a gleeful circle. "Bye, Papa."

"Oh, sir, I'll keep my heels in." Matt clattered down the stairs. His shirttail hung out. "I promise."

"Hush, Matt." Emily intercepted her son at the foot of the stair. Tommy was still whirling and chanting. *He is going to knock over that table*, Emily thought, distracted. She lunged after Tommy just in time to prevent a vase of late daffodils from crashing to the polished tiles of the entry. "Bye," said Tommy impudently. "Bye, Mama Em."

"Oh, Tommy." Half laughing, Emily turned, and stopped with her smile frozen on her lips. Major Falk still knelt holding Amy, his hands cramped desperately on her small shoulders and his eyes clenched shut.

"You're squeezing me, Papa."

91

"Like a lemon," he said in an almost ordinary voice.

Amy giggled.

He released her and rose slowly, his face composed and colourless.

"Shall I write you every month as usual?" Emily wanted to say something splendid and healing, but her voice rattled out dry and precise as peas on a shuttle.

"Yes, if you will. The winds from America are somewhat erratic. Don't be alarmed if my replies are delayed as much as three months. Good-bye, Matthew." He shook hands with Emily's son.

Three months! Emily did not voice her despair. It was rather too late for that. "Shall we come out with you?"

"No!" He added more quietly, "I shall have to detach Peggy from McGrath."

"Poor Peggy."

"Poor McGrath," he said drily. "Good-bye, Mrs. Foster."

"Bye!" Tommy shrieked. "Bye! Bye! Bye! Bye!"

13

THE FIRST LETTER came within the month by a packet Major Falk's ship met off the Lizard. It contained a spirited account of Doña Inez and Eustachio on the high seas, and Doña Barbara seasick in the scuppers. Emily responded immediately and warmly. Amy and Matt added careful sentences about the pony. The second letter followed the first within a week. Doña Barbara was back to brewing chocolate and Eustachio had had a narrow escape from sharks. After that the letters stopped.

By September Emily was reading the American news with grim attention. The army had burnt the city of Washington. There was no mention of Major Falk. She told herself not to play the hysterical female. Contrary winds.

Finally, when Amy's birthday passed without a parcel, Emily wrote Major Conway. Because she was unsure of how she ought to address a dying man she kept her language stiff and formal. The reply was delayed. When it came it was marked from a village in Lancashire, not Rye, whence she had directed her letter.

Major Conway, it appeared, had taken on the position of estate agent on one of Lord Dunarvon's manors which was just now being opened to coal mining. "Fascinating new engines," the major wrote with obvious enthusiasm. "Dunarvon talked of installing one of Stephenson's circular rail roads—steam-powered, of course—if the vein proved rich, and by the way don't worry. Richard always lands on his feet." Major Conway's clear unconcern set Emily's mind temporarily at rest but another silent, letterless fortnight unnerved her and she wrote again.

"I'm sure there is no cause for alarm yet," the major replied by return post, "but as you may have questions for me in my role as guardian-of-record, perhaps you might consider meeting me in London in ten days' time. I must travel there on a matter of business in any case." He added further soothing comments, which meant he knew no more of his friend's whereabouts than Emily did.

It took Emily five minutes to decide to go.

For several days after their early arrival in Town, Emily and Aunt Fan amused themselves with raids upon cloth warehouses, arcades, and book emporia. Emily bought toys. She had a sinking feeling there would be no toys from America for Christmas, so she was perhaps overlavish. *They are all three such good children*, she reflected from the safe distance of sixty-odd miles.

She found a handsome cloisonné snuffbox for her father. She also indulged herself in a sinfully expensive bonnet. It was blue with a deep poke and an enormous feather dyed to match that curled over her left eye. She liked it so well she wore it back to the hotel and told the garrulous modiste to burn the old mourning-grey. She was glad she had done so over Aunt Fan's protests, for when she and her aunt entered the solemn foyer in a flurry of bandboxes and parcels she bumped into Major Conway.

"My dear Mrs. Foster." The proprietor, a man of wonderful dignity, allowed her a tight smile. "This gentleman has just been enquiring for you. Shall you receive him?" He retreated five discreet paces.

"Oh, dear. Major Conway, you're early!" Distracted, Emily pulled off her glove and held out her hand. "How do you, sir?"

"Very well, ma'am."

Emily peered around the feather into a pair of tired grey eyes.

"I like your bonnet," the major said in a pleasant baritone. He was a tall man. "Matches your eyes."

Emily smiled. "I knew how it would be when I read your letters, sir. You know precisely what to say. I shall probably fall in love."

The grey eyes lit and he smiled delightfully. "I can't see any objection to that, ma'am, but I think we should conduct our courtship in a less publick arena."

Emily and Aunt Fan had had time to dispose themselves on the small sopha before their caller arrived at their first-floor suite. When Phillida, with a coy giggle and a flounce, announced the major, Emily rose. Welcoming pleasantries died on her lips. "My dear sir, you look quite white. Shall you take a glass of . . . oh dear, we have nothing stronger than ratafia."

He gave a faint, twisted grin. "I am afraid—under circumstances—I can accept nothing less than cognac."

"Brandy." Emily nodded. "The very thing. Unfortunately we haven't any."

"Yes, we have." Aunt Fan whisked from the room.

Emily stared after her. "Dear Aunt Fan, always prepared for emergencies."

"It is scarcely that," Major Conway rejoined in a rather steadier voice. "Why I should be suddenly afflicted with . . . this nuisance, when I trotted up three flights yesterday, I don't know."

"Well, that's probably the cause," Emily said reasonably. "If you'll sit in that chair by the fire, sir, you'll feel more comfortable directly."

The major sat by careful degrees. By the time he was settled and looking less green, Aunt had returned with a stoppered bottle plainly labelled *Tonic* in raised letters. Aunt Fan poured a healthy dollop into what Emily took to be her tooth glass. Aunt did not precisely say now be a good boy and drink it all down but that was the gist. Major Conway obeyed. Presently he regarded them both from half closed grey eyes.

"And to think I asked them to send up a mere tea," he murmured.

"Did you, sir?"

"Yes. I thought you might require soothing."

Emily laughed, relieved. "I should like tea of all things. Can it be had in one's rooms? Aunt and I have been taking ours downstairs with the common herd."

"Common? In Crillon's?"

Emily pulled out a gilt armchair and sat. "It is rather an exalted place."

"I could have installed you in Dunarvon's town house, but you'd find it oppressive. It's in holland covers." His returning smile faded. "My conduct just now relieves me of the tedium of explanation. When Richard left we had agreed that I would be needing a replacement. I asked you to come because I wished to make you known to my successor. Don't look so distressed, Mrs. Foster," he added, wry. "Crillon's staircase won't kill me. Bevis had leave. I thought you might as well meet him."

Emily frowned. "Mr. Bevis? That sounds unlikely."

"Lord Dunarvon's heir," Major Conway said. "Viscount Bevis. We are friends. He is just now on leave from Brussels, where he is on the Prince of Orange's staff, but I daresay he will be selling out. In any case I think he'll do. Richard is acquainted with him."

"Acquainted," Emily echoed, rather faintly.

He grimaced. "You are too acute, ma'am. Richard objected to Bevis on the grounds that he does not know him well, but neither Richard nor I could fix on anyone nearer. And I do know Bevis. He is the best of good fellows. I think you'll find him agreeable."

"Will he kiss my hand in the French style?"

The major's grey eyes lit. "I think it extremely likely. Bevis has excellent taste."

Caught in her own mild joke, Emily blushed. "You flatter."

"I never offer Spanish coin," he said gently. "I thought it time to commence our courtship."

That drew a smile. "I shall be glad to meet Lord Bevis, Major, though I trust there will be no occasion to prolong the acquaintance. Have you had word of Major Falk?"

He frowned. "He was used to write you regularly?"

"I writ him an account of the children at least once a month. He responded as soon as he received my letters. There have been delays before, but six weeks was the longest I ever had to wait. I know the American winds are even less cooperative than those in the Bay of Biscay. A sixmonth, however . . . " She fell silent.

He did not comment at once. When he spoke, he seemed to choose his words with care. "I sent an enquiry through Richard's regimental adjutant. You must understand that Richard is rather inclined to stumble into adventures."

Emily waited. *Adventures.*

"Other people lead orderly, regular lives. Richard is constantly falling into scrapes." He grimaced, as if the word were not to his taste. "He does not seek disasters. They find him out. However, I daresay he'll turn up like a bad penny as soon as the peace is signed."

"Scowling and flinging off sarcasms like squibs." Emily sighed. "No doubt you're right."

Major Conway said drily, "I perceive you have seen Richard at his best. What a fool he is."

Emily raised troubled eyes. "I have only met your friend twice. He was worried, I collect. And quite desperately tired."

"You're a perceptive woman."

"It did not take a great deal of perception to see that," Emily rejoined. "Will you tell me how things are left?"

Major Conway frowned. "Richard did not?"

"He told me not to trouble my tiny head, and that you would know what to do."

Major Conway raised his brows.

"Oh, not in so many words." Emily's pent-up exasperation burst through, surprising her. "I wonder why it is that men suppose women incapable of rational judgement. I am not a widgeon, sir. I have run my son's estate since my husband's death." She raised her chin. "And improved the receipts. I should be far more at ease if I could make plans for Amy and Tommy. As it is I am wondering whether to prepare Amy to earn her bread or to marry a duke. I had inclined to the former," she added darkly, "but if her affairs are to be dealt with by belted earls I perceive I erred in my assumption."

Major Conway went off into the whoops.

Presently his mirth tickled a grin from Emily. "It is not funny."

"No. Merely absurd." Major Conway shifted his long legs and gave way to a final suppressed chuckle. "There would be a small pension, of course. I—or Bevis—would see to that, and I daresay we could find young Thomas a place in a school for officers' sons."

"As I thought," Emily said, resigned.

"There's rather more than five hundred pounds."

Emily whistled and caught herself up guiltily. "I beg your pardon, sir."

The major regarded her with a bemused air. "Pray don't apologise, Mrs. Foster. I've never met a lady who could whistle. I beg you will marry me at once."

"I had to teach my son, Matt," Emily said absently. "To whistle, that is. Five hundred pounds." She tapped her forefinger on the chair arm. "The legacy, I daresay. What a blessing Major Falk's godmother chose to die at such an opportune moment." She looked up to find the major staring at her in blank incomprehension.

"The legacy. He made it over to the children when he brought them to me."

"There was no legacy."

It was Emily's turn to stare.

"I do not know why Richard should spin such a tale," Major Conway said slowly. "No doubt he had reasons. If his children have anything at all it is because he sweat for it."

Emily regarded him for a long moment without blinking, then shook her head. "I do not understand."

"I do." The major closed his eyes and rubbed his brow as if his head ached. "Richard has never had anything but his pay, Mrs. Foster. And a certain gift for improbable prose fictions."

"Explain."

He lowered his hand. "Richard is an author. In the past three years, since Doña Isabel's death, he has sold four novels."

"Novels?"

"Yes."

"He produced the money by scribbling books!" Emily digested the idea. "Are they good novels?"

"You are a remarkable woman."

She met his admiring grey gaze. "Don't rush your courtship. I collect the literary merit of Major Falk's works is immaterial. What is material is that he lied to me, from first to last. What other deceits has he practised on me, I wonder?"

There was a pause. Major Conway frowned. "Is it so important? You cannot have been under any illusion that Richard is prosperous. He seemed to think there would be enough to educate the children and provide Amy's dowry."

"Ample." Emily's mouth set.

"What do you mean to do?"

Emily exploded. "Do? I shall give him a piece of my mind. That arrogant, satirical, deceitful—why do you smile?"

"Relief, ma'am, believe me. I thought I should find myself with two children on my hands."

Emily was shocked. She contrived to assure him that, far from abandoning the children, she meant to keep them by her as long as she might. She grew emotional on the subject. It was a good thing that the tea cart arrived in the midst of her high flight or she might have betrayed her feelings. All her feelings.

— 14 —

THE TEA CART was a miracle of gleaming china, starched linen, and exquisite cakes and sandwiches. Aunt Fan dealt with the footman in short order. As Emily and, she suspected, the major had quite forgot her aunt's presence, they exchanged guilty glances.

"Better adopt the brats." Aunt dispensed the steaming Bohea with the competence of thirty years' practice. "Sugar, Major?"

"Er, no. Thank you."

"Ought to. Perk up your spirits. Very invigorating, sweet tea."

"I am wholly restored," Major Conway said. "Adopt, Miss Mayne?"

Aunt, having wrested a table, another chair, and the tea apparatus into place before the fire without discommoding herself in the least, had taken up her position as behind a redoubt. "Eat a sandwich, sir. Put some flesh on your bones. Not the cucumber."

Major Conway meekly consumed a slice of bread and butter. "Adopt?" he repeated, rather thickly.

Emily had heard this exchange in stunned silence. *Adopt.* She did not at all like the implications of the word. Perhaps Aunt Fan sensed her revulsion.

She addressed Emily directly, eyes sharp. "Your father won't balk. Attached to young Amy. Taking little thing. Only sensible course, Emma. Mother dead, father in foreign parts, no relations. Bring 'em up as your own. Doing it already."

Emily tried to order her thoughts. In the early days of her acquaintance with the children, adoption had occurred to her, though she had supposed her widowed state might cause legal complications. Now it was the last thing she wanted, for it would sever her only link with their father. She took a gulp of tea. Richard Falk's single revealing moment with his daughter presented itself before her mind's eye.

"It won't do," she blurted, relieved to have found the right argument. "Major Falk would never consent."

"I wonder how you know that," Major Conway said quietly. "Richard's attachment to his children is more than a matter of duty. He needs them." He set his cup on the table. "More than they need him, I fancy."

"Often the case with parents," Aunt Fan offered.

Emily stared at her.

"Don't be a fool, gel. Look at your father. Like a broody hen. Always has been. Should have let young James go up to London. Couldn't bear it."

Major Conway drew a sharp breath.

Emily turned. "Are you well, sir?"

"Yes, quite. A thought merely."

"What if Major Falk is indeed dead?" Aunt asked in practical tones. "Likely to be kin to kick up a dust? What about the mother's family? Foreigners."

Emily's stomach knotted. She set her cup down.

"If Richard were dead then Mrs. Foster would be free to act as she wished." Major Conway accepted the fresh cup Aunt Fan thrust into his hands. "Doña Isabel's family— excepting *el Jefe*—are all dead. I don't believe he would raise objections. He gave his sister to Richard freely, and in Spain the father provides for his children."

How could he speak so coolly of the unspeakable? Emily pushed the thought of Major Falk's death aside. "Will you tell me something of the children's mother, sir? They will be asking questions."

Major Conway discovered the teacup and set it down three quarters full. "Doña Isabel . . . Lord, I daresay I should give you the whole story, or as much of it as I know. Then perhaps you'll comprehend what I mean by Richard's propensity for scrapes."

"Scrapes?" Emily echoed, mechanical.

The major smiled at her. "And no, the marriage was not a scrape. I chose my words clumsily. It was, so far as an observer can judge, a very good thing for both parties—though not, of course, in a worldly sense." He turned to Aunt Fan. "I daresay you recall the retreat we made on Corunna."

"Eighteen eight and nine," Aunt Fan said tersely. "Sir John Moore killed. Should never have happened." Whether she meant the retreat or Moore's death at the battle that was fought to cover the embarkation was unclear. Matt had been teething, Emily recalled, and Edward was still alive.

"I was with the Light Bobs," the major said. "Rifles. Richard, of course, stayed with the Fifty-second through the war, so we saw rather more of each other then than later."

"Rear guard," Aunt interposed.

He smiled. "Paget would wish you to mention the cavalry."

"Uxbridge."

"His lordship's conduct of the rear guard was held to be brilliant, though we didn't feel brilliant. We had made our way past Astorga and we'd kept the French at bay, though the other regiments left a damned shambles in our path. Sorry."

"Justified," said Aunt Fan. "No supplies."

Major Conway grinned. "I should leave you to tell it, ma'am. My memory is befogged at some points."

Aunt Fan nodded graciously. "Bound to be. Go on."

"There we were, stretched out blocking the *correo* in a storm of sleet. We'd fought off and on all day, none of us had eaten—in fact there was nothing to eat, and we'd been on short commons for some days before that. It was cold and miserable."

Emily shivered.

"We'd holed up in the shell of a half destroyed barn," the major was saying. "At least it was shelter. Someone had unearthed a little wine. We contrived a fire and settled in for the night. Into this charming scene rode Richard. He said we were to pull back another half mile. You may imagine the huzzas with which he was greeted. We weren't in a reasonable frame of mind. Neither was he. We gave him a swallow of the wine and sent him on his way. He'd four more outposts to reach."

He looked up at the ladies and smiled. "On the edge of your seats, I see. Perhaps I should take up writing narrative."

"Do go on," Emily snapped.

"Very well. You may wonder why an officer of the line was doing staff duty, but the truth is no one else was to hand with a living, breathing horse on which to trundle through the sleet. It goes without saying Richard was in no better case than the rest of us, all grime and beard and sarcasm. I didn't think he could make it. He didn't."

"Captured?" Aunt Fan asked.

"No. He gained the last outpost and came back with the platoon part of the way. Then they lost him. He was supposed to be guiding them, so they went back a few yards. His horse had fallen dead. Richard had cracked his skull on a rock in the fall and didn't seem to want to wake up."

Emily made a noise.

He looked at her briefly. "To their credit they carried Richard as far as they could, which was to our ruined barn, I fancy. We'd left it by then. He was still unconscious, and doesn't recall any of it to this day. They laid him in shelter, but his chances of surviving and not being taken by the French were remote. He was posted missing. Everyone assumed he was dead."

Aunt Fan sniffed.

The major drew a long breath. "When I heard, I kept

imagining him lying in a snowbank with the wolves at him." He shook his head frowning. "We were no longer very close, Richard and I. There were men I was closer to who were lost in the retreat, but I kept thinking about Richard. I daresay it was because we were schooled together. We've known each other a long time."

Aunt sniffed again, loudly, and poured him another cup of tea.

He didn't touch it. "You may imagine my relief when Richard joined us after Talavera, looking fit as a fiddle with his Spanish wife riding pillion behind him on a captured French horse." He smiled at their reaction. "Richard's colonel was taken aback—to see him again, and to find he was wed. Spanish marriages were not yet allowed, but Richard presented him with a *fait accompli*. Doña Isabel's brother was a *guerrillero* chief of some stature and ferocity. It was not thought prudent to cross *el Jefe*. And young Amy was, er, on the way."

"My word," Emily said faintly. "What was Mrs. Falk like?"

"Small. Richard is not above the middle height and she came to his shoulder. Black hair, olive complexion, snapping black eyes with lashes about a yard long. I daresay she was more striking than pretty. She was capable of being haughty when she chose to, and she had a temper like a rocket, soaring off in every direction at once. She was ferociously jealous."

Emily tried to repress a surge of jealousy. She cleared her throat. "Did you like Mrs. Falk?"

"Oh, we all tumbled in love with her at once." Major Conway smiled reminiscently, oblivious to Emily's feelings. "She could have trod on red jackets all the way to Lisbon, but she never had eyes for anyone but Richard. They had wonderful arguments."

That sounded familiar. "Go on," Emily said, glum. Clearly the marriage was made in Heaven.

"Such arguments. Crescendoes of insults in the most

lisping Castillian." Major Conway laughed. "Doña Isabel was from the region of Old Castile near Aranda del Duero. It was a treat to hear them go at it. Richard speaks fluent Spanish. He'd have had to, after a sixmonth with *el Jefe*'s little band of cutthroats."

"Heavens."

"They had found Richard wandering in a daze, half frozen. Doña Isabel nursed him back to health. That sounds romantical and perhaps it was, but it cannot have been an easy time. The *guerrilleros* were pressed by the French, and the region was devastated from two armies having fought over it. The band came south when Wellington moved on Oporto. Richard reported in but he stayed with the irregulars as liaison until the Fifty-second rejoined the army."

"Doña Isabel was with the *guerrilleros* the whole time?"

"Her family and village had been destroyed by the French. She had no one to turn to but *el Jefe*, and indeed she was lucky to enjoy a brother's protection."

"I see." Emily wondered whether she would have had Doña Isabel's courage.

Major Conway misread her hesitation. "If you're asking yourself whether she was a lady, ma'am, I think the answer is yes. Her father was *alcalde*—a sort of J.P. *Hidalgos*, I fancy, but not wealthy. She could read and write in Spanish."

"But not in English, I take it."

He looked surprised. "She couldn't even speak English, Mrs. Foster. No need to. Richard spoke Spanish with her. We all admired Doña Isabel," he added, rather stiffly, as if disapproval were written on Emily's face. "She had great courage and she was devoted to Richard and her children."

"I'm sure she was. A heroine." The model for Doña Inez? Gloom swept over Emily. How could she hope to rival such a splendid ghost?

"Follow the camp?" Aunt asked.

"Not until after Amy was born. After Busaco. When

Masséna finally withdrew things were easier, and that became possible. Before that Richard found quarters for her near Lisbon. I think she preferred the camp." Major Conway looked at his hands. "They did not have a great deal of time. Tommy was born early in eighteen twelve and Isabel died in April."

"But Major Falk didn't bring the children to me until the autumn of that year," Emily protested. "Tommy was nearly nine months old. Creeping."

"Richard would not have left his company in other hands during a campaign, and I collect he hadn't heard from Hitchins either. Hitchins is his publisher."

That brought Emily crashing back into the present. She cast her eyes heavenward. "Publisher!"

"Fairy godmother?" Major Conway offered tentatively.

Emily fell into the whoops. "Oh dear, I ought not to laugh. Your friend, sir, is a blackguard."

"A lunatic," the major agreed. "And a Grub Street hack. But not, I think, a bad father."

"Letters most particular," Aunt said. "Good grasp of detail. Bought Amy a pony."

"The pony belongs to Amy and Matt," Emily corrected. "In that respect, sir, your friend has been most considerate. He always includes Matt in his gifts, and that has averted considerable strife. Matt is not used to playing second fiddle."

Major Conway's mind was elsewhere. "I wonder if you have considered the difficulties attendant upon keeping Richard's children. Surely mine is not the only offer of marriage you have received, ma'am. Are not three children, two of them a stranger's, an encumbrance?"

"To my many suitors? I've found Amy and Tommy exceedingly convenient, sir. They saved me from two solicitors and the Master of Hounds. The master was most importunate."

He laughed at that. "How if you form an attachment, ma'am?"

Emily's blood froze. *Does he know? Ah, he means an attachment to someone other than Richard Falk.* "I daresay it's possible."

"You speak as if the likelihood were remote. Are you averse to marriage?"

Emily forced a smile. "My taste is overnice. The solicitors had damp hands and the master is inclined to roar." She added, for he looked troubled, "Do not be anxious in my behalf, Major Conway. I should not give my affections to a man who disliked children. It is one of my criteria for suitability."

To her relief, he did not pursue the matter further. "Shall the two of you take dinner with me tomorrow in the hotel? I'll engage Bevis to come."

"Of course. Aunt?"

Aunt Fan nodded decisively.

"And the theatre afterwards?" The offer was cautious.

"I'd like it of all things!" Emily beamed. "How very kind in you, sir. It has been ages since I have seen the inside of a theatre. Pray, Aunt, approve."

"Very well, Emma. Do you good," Aunt Fan said gruffly. "Do us both good. Now, Major, off with you. Recruit your strength."

"Against the rigours of dinner and the theatre?" Major Conway grinned. Emily decided she was in love with his eyes. "Very well. Thank you, ladies. It has been a most agreeable afternoon."

"And enlightening," Emily said in her driest tones. That provoked a chuckle. "Shall I help you up, sir?" But Major Conway declined her offer and rose under his own power with only a grimace or two.

When he had gone Aunt Fan said gruffly, "Good man. Waste."

Emily understood her. After a moment she said, "I wonder how we shall occupy ourselves until dinnertime tomorrow."

"Buy the books."

Emily stared.

"Major Falk's novels," Aunt Fan snapped. "You've no head, Emma. All sentiment."

Emily choked on a laugh. "How if they are improper?"

"Bound to be." Aunt's eyes gleamed.

With some searching of secondhand bookstalls they found three of the novels. The most recent was not yet in print.

Dinner and the theatre were splendid and Lord Bevis the pattern card of viscounts. He was so charming as to defy belief. *Dazzling the country cousins*, Emily thought as they rode home from the theatre in a wonderfully appointed town carriage with the arms of a belted earl emblazoned on the doors.

She stifled the thought. After all, Lord Bevis was an amiable man and it was no punishment to look at him. Not only was he classically handsome by nature, but art, in the person of a superb and obviously English tailor, had enhanced his healthy masculine beauty. He wore conventional evening clothes. It was a pity to have missed seeing him in dress regimentals. *Ah well*, Emily mused, *one cannot have everything*. When it came to dealing with guardians, though, she hoped Major Conway would confound his physicians and live forever, and she wished Major Falk would write.

= 15 =

It was March before Emily finally received letters from Major Falk—five at once. For some reason her relief expressed itself in an orgy of housecleaning. The impulse was almost exhausted, and she was dusting the top of an *armoire* in one of the vacant guest chambers and considering bundling the children into the gig for a visit to her papa, when Phillida interrupted her.

"Lady Who?" Emily asked, arrested in a mid swipe of the feather duster.

Phillida fairly writhed with impatience and curiosity. "Please, ma'am, she says she's Miss Amy's aunt."

The chair Emily stood on wobbled dangerously. She dropped the duster. "Er, show her ladyship into the withdrawing room," she contrived to say through her astonishment. "Inform her that I'll be down directly I've made myself presentable." Lady Sarah Fumble Mumble. Phillida occasionally had difficulty conveying the simplest messages. Whom could she mean? Emily had no intention of dealing with any ladyship when she herself wore a gown covered with cobwebs. She dashed to her own room, splashed the grime from her hands and face, and scrambled into her best tea gown. Ladyship? Aunt? Surely not.

A woman—lady, at least in the vulgar sense—rose as Emily entered the drawing room. The caller was in her thirties, pretty in an equine way, with dark brown hair and direct hazel eyes.

"Mrs. Foster?"

Emily kept a wary distance. "I am Emily Foster. I don't believe I've had the pleasure."

"I'm Sarah Ffouke-Wilson. I was Sarah Ffouke."

"Indeed." Emily had no need to counterfeit blankness. *Foke? Folk? Ffouke.*

"The late duke of Newsham's daughter," Lady Sarah supplied as Emily finally made the connexion.

Emily said slowly, "If that is so, ma'am, I do not at all understand your condescension in calling upon me. There can be no . . . There must be some mistake. My servant told me you claim kinship with the children in my care."

"They are my brother Richard's children. Half brother."

Emily was dumbfounded. When she could command her voice she ventured, "Major Falk a natural son of the Duke of Newsham? You will pardon me, Lady, er, Sarah, if I find that hard to believe."

Lady Sarah looked surprised in her turn. "You knew Richard was baseborn?"

"He made no secret of the fact. He also led me to believe he had no family living. Now I come to think of it," she added, wrath kindling, "he never said so directly."

"I daresay he felt it." A faint flush touched Lady Sarah's cheekbones. She ran her tongue across her lips. "There was a—a break. I have not seen Richard in twenty years. None of us has."

"Why?"

"It is all very complicated." Lady Sarah twisted the tan gloves in her hand. "My brother is not the duke's son, Mrs. Foster, but the duchess's. By Lord Powys."

"Good God." Emily gestured Lady Sarah to a chair and sat down herself.

Lady Sarah made a business of arranging her skirts with nice precision on the stiffest chair in the chamber. She smoothed her green velvet travelling dress. "I see that you have heard the story. Quite a famous scandal in its day."

Emily said faintly, "Yes. Lord Powys was killed, was he not?"

110

Lady Sarah nodded. "In a duel. Very Gothick. My father challenged him. My father was rather Gothick, if it comes to that." She did not look at Emily.

Emily made a push to collect her wits. "There was a break, you say, twenty years ago?"

Lady Sarah inclined her head.

"Major Falk cannot have been more than twenty at that time, and you, I should judge, somewhat younger—twelve or thirteen."

At that Lady Sarah looked up. A spark of wry amusement in her eyes abruptly convinced Emily that the woman was indeed kin to Major Falk. "You flatter me, ma'am, and malign Richard. He was twelve. I am two years his senior."

Emily assimilated that.

Lady Sarah's brief amusement faded. "Until that time Richard lived at Abbeymont in the duke's household. It was . . . My mother had made it a condition of her return, that Richard should be raised with her other children, and my father had apparently agreed. When Richard was twelve, however, there was an incident which made it clear to my mother that Richard would be safer elsewhere."

"Safer?"

"Safer," Lady Sarah repeated. "*Maman* had Richard removed from Abbeymont. She told no one where she had sent him. As far as I knew he had just disappeared. We were not encouraged to ask where. When he turned fifteen *Maman* used her influence with the Duke of York to procure a commission for Richard in a regiment that were to be sent abroad. It was all very difficult to contrive, for she had to plan her strategems with the utmost secrecy."

"Why?" Emily was more bewildered than ever.

"She feared for Richard's life. My father, you see, was intermittently mad. Violently mad."

Emily digested that. After a long moment she rose and yanked the bellpull.

Lady Sarah looked puzzled.

"I am going to send for a nice, dull pot of tea," Emily explained.

Lady Sarah flushed. "Believe me, Mrs. Foster, *I* am not mad. I am trying to tell you why—"

"Yes, yes," Emily soothed, faintly hysterical. "I can see that. I should explain that my family are ordinary country people who live ordinary dull lives. Ever since Richard Falk swam into my ken I have been subject to unexpected jolts of melodrama. I find that tea is the only composer. Ah, Phillida, tea, if you please. Are the children having theirs?"

"Yes, ma'am. Mrs. Harry thought you would wish it."

"Thank you."

Phillida remained, gawking.

"Thank you, Phillida. Tea." The maid left, casting curious glances over her shoulder as she fled out the door.

"No wonder he concocts phantastical plots," Emily murmured to herself. "They must come naturally."

"I beg your pardon?"

"Your brother," Emily said kindly. "He is a novelist. Did you not know of his *sub-rosa* career as Peter Picaro?"

Lady Sarah shook her head, hazel eyes wide.

Emily rose and went to the secretary. She picked up the rather battered cloth-bound book that was lying on the blotter and handed it to her visitor without comment.

The tea arrived directly. Phillida contrived not to spill great quantities. When she had been induced to leave, Emily poured. Neither of the women spoke. Emily's mind was racing to no very clear purpose. She had rarely been so confused in her life.

Lady Sarah turned the pages of the book with apparent fascination. "Richard writ it?"

"Yes. That is volume one of the first Don Alfonso novel. Major Falk writ several other novels, I believe, when he was very young, and he has done three since that one. The last is not yet in print. They are not at all suitable reading for ladies."

That startled a smile from Lady Sarah. "Oh dear, forgive me. It is so . . . so unexpected."

Emily said with a certain grim fervour, "Everything about your brother is unexpected."

"Do you dislike Richard?" Lady Sarah's voice was hesitant.

With an heroick effort Emily kept her own voice colourless. "He is my employer."

Lady Sarah sighed. "I don't know Richard at all."

"If it has been twenty years since you saw him that is not to be wondered at." Emily took a calming breath. "Forgive me, but I still do not understand your purpose in coming to me. Major Falk is in America. His children are too young to be of interest to anyone not deeply concerned for their well-being. I know nothing of their father's private affairs." She uttered the last with irony, mild, she thought, in the circumstances.

"You know more than I," Lady Sarah shot back. "I wish to see my niece and nephew, Mrs. Foster. I was attached to Richard when we were children. I meant to assure myself that his children were well cared for." She gave Emily a swift glance. "I've done that, but I'd like to see them all the same."

Emily thought the request over, taking her time. "I am not at all sure Major Falk would wish it."

Lady Sarah bristled. "Upon my word, Mrs. Foster, you can't believe I would corrupt them."

"No. I shan't give you the opportunity."

Lady Sarah stared. She gave an uncertain laugh.

"I have met Major Falk twice only." Strange but true. "We've corresponded, but it would be impertinent in me to claim to know his feelings. I do know that he is protective of Amy and Tommy."

Lady Sarah stiffened.

"Do you not think," Emily continued, grave, "that he would have told me of the connexion if he wished to acknowledge it?"

"If *he* wished . . . " Lady Sarah's voice trailed off in purest astonishment.

Her surprise clarified Emily's feelings. "Yes, if he wished to acknowledge it. If I follow you correctly, he has lived his adult life without reference to your family. It is probable that, as far as he is concerned, there *is* no family. He has provided for his children. They are healthy and happy with a good home and the assurance of their father's concern. They do not need to be patronised by a duke's daughter. They are Major Falk's children, and that is no bad thing."

Lady Sarah turned pale. "You speak plain, Mrs. Foster."

"I could speak plainer," Emily rejoined. "You say you were attached to your brother, but twenty years of silence argue at least indifference."

"I did not know the children existed until a fortnight ago. Bevis told me—"

"I thought Lord Bevis an agreeable man," Emily interrupted. "I did not think him a common gossip."

The fire went out of Lady Sarah. "We are old friends," she muttered. "I had not met Bevis since he went out to the Peninsula. I asked him if he had seen anything of Richard and he told me he had the guardianship of Richard's children."

"That is not true, strictly speaking."

"Oh, he explained the complications." Lady Sarah set her teacup on the table. "He said that Richard had gone off to America and that nothing had been heard of him in a sixmonth."

"I received letters last week."

"He's alive then?" Lady Sarah sat up very straight.

Emily nodded.

Lady Sarah looked so relieved Emily could not but be moved. "Major Falk fell ill shortly after he arrived in America," she volunteered. "Hence the lack of letters from King's Town. He says he has resumed his duties. With the war over I daresay he will be returning in the next month or so."

"Was he . . . did he take part in that terrible affair in New Orleans?"

"I do not know, Lady Sarah."

Lady Sarah bit her lip. "Then you can't say that he is well."

"No. He was not listed among the casualties, however." Emily set her own cup down. "I read the casualty lists very carefully. Indeed it sometimes seems to me that I have done little but read casualty lists in these past months."

"You have had an anxious time, Mrs. Foster."

"One becomes hardened to uncertainty. I did not realise quite how anxious I had been until the letters came last day week."

"Will it console you to know that I have been reading those same lists for five years?" Lady Sarah's voice was so low as to be almost inaudible.

Emily must have betrayed surprise, for her visitor went on, defensive, "When my father died, my mother told me what had become of Richard. I writ him directly. That was just after Sir Arthur—the Duke of Wellington—first landed in Portugal. I did not know what to write in my letter and I daresay I put my foot wrong. Richard's reply made it clear that he wanted nothing to do with any of us." She rose and her tan gloves slipped to the carpet. She knelt to retrieve them, voice muffled. "It was so shaming. I greatly fear your instinct is correct, Mrs. Foster. Richard would not wish me to know his children." Emily saw that her guest's eyes were bright with unshed tears. "I had best take my leave of you."

Emily weakened. "Perhaps he would not wish the children to know of the connexion, but he couldn't reasonably object to your meeting them. Tommy will be napping by now, but Amy and Matt are in the schoolroom awaiting their writing lesson. Matt is my son. They will be delighted to have their lesson postponed."

"Oh, if I could see them!" Lady Sarah closed her hands on the errant gloves. "You are very kind."

Emily, knowing she did not merit the praise, flushed. "In the ordinary course of things I am not quite so rude."

"I ought to have writ you first, but I couldn't think what to say," Lady Sarah said humbly. "You could call me Lady Wilson. It is my style now after all. Robert, my husband, is a baronet. You—you could tell them I am merely a new neighbour."

Emily smiled at that. "They won't require an explanation, ma'am. My callers are frequently dragged up to inspect the schoolroom."

=== 16 ===

WHEN THEY REACHED the schoolroom door, however, Emily had second thoughts. For some reason she always supposed the big shabby chamber would seem as delightful a place to visitors as it was to her. Looking with aristocratic eyes at the faded chintzes, the serviceable but ancient carpet, strewn now with Matt's soldiers, and the dishes still uncleared from the children's nuncheon, her heart sank.

Amy let out a whoop. She was deep in the persona of Doña Inez. The rocking horse crashed forward and back. Matt, asprawl on the carpet, deigned to look up at the visitor.

"Must we do our lesson now?" He was a child who always came straight to the point.

"In a few minutes." Emily did not betray her chagrin aloud. "Amy, dismount, if you please. We have a guest."

Amy shot a mischievous grin over her shoulder and crashed back and forth several more times, curls flying.

"Emilia!"

The crashing stopped and the little girl slid down from her mount. She put on her best penitent expression and bobbed a creditable curtsey. *Minx*.

Matt stood up with an air of resignation and brushed the knees of his nankeens. His soldiers had clearly sustained heavy losses. They lay on their backs staring at the ceiling in scarlet and green ranks. There were probably cobwebs on the ceiling.

Emily cleared her throat. "Children, this is Lady Sarah

Ffouke-Wilson. Lady Sarah, my son, Matthew Foster, and Amy Falk." Matt ducked a bow. Amy, hazel eyes bright with curiosity, curtseyed again. Emily's courage failed her. "Lady Sarah is a new neighbour," she mumbled.

Lady Sarah was made of sterner stuff. She extended her hand. "How do you do, Matthew."

Matt gave the hand a pump. His tow-coloured hair flopped.

"Do you mean to be a soldier."

Matt regarded her with scorn. "I'm the squire. Squires tend to their land. That's just a game I play when it's too wet to ride Eustachio."

"Er, very logical," Lady Sarah responded. "I take it Eustachio is a pony."

Matt's eyes brightened and he launched into a poetic appreciation of Eustachio's points. "Of course, Amy and I have to share him," he added, aggrieved.

"My papa gave Eustachio to *me*." Amy glowered at him.

"You're just a girl."

"Ha!"

Emily considered sinking into the carpet. "That will do. If you can't deal comfortably neither of you shall ride."

"Oh well, it's raining anyway," Matt said philosophically. "Amy has rotten manners."

"Both of you are complete savages. Pick up your soldiers, Matt. Amy, I wish you will show Lady Sarah your dolls."

Amy led the way to her window seat dollhouse. The seat overflowed with her booty. Amy pulled Doña Inez and Doña Barbara from their repose among the pillows, the coverlets and doll dresses, and the lesser doll personages she had been given by Sir Henry. "Are you a real lady?" she asked. "A *lady* lady? I shall be a lady if I mend my manners and don't shout at Matt. Nobody calls Mama Em 'Lady Emily.' *She's* a lady."

Lady Sarah looked ruffled, but she said a swift recover. "I'm a duke's daughter. It's the custom. However, I had to learn not to shout at people, too. What beautiful dolls."

Amy straightened their mantillas and viewed her ladies dispassionately. "They're Spanish like my mother. I had them forever. Doña Barbara is a grown-up."

"Yes, I can see that. Do they speak to each other?"

"Sometimes." Amy regarded her enigmatically. "They were used to speak Spanish but I taught them the English. Doña Barbara is the duenna. Papa sent them to me."

Lady Sarah cleared her throat. "Do you miss your papa?"

Amy stared. "You know Papa? *Ai*, I mean, *do* you know Papa?"

Emily gave Lady Sarah a warning glance.

Lady Sarah said cautiously, "I used to. A long time ago."

Amy's face fell. "I thought you saw him sooner. He doesn't write for a long time. Then, ha, five letters at once, with proper stories. He's over the ocean." She made a wide gesture in the general direction of the Atlantic. "You wish—*do* you wish to see Tommy? He's only two and a half."

"Yes."

"He's stupid. He won't ride Eustachio."

Emily wished Amy had not soaked up Matt's vocabulary with such spongelike thoroughness.

"Even so, I'd like to see Tommy," Lady Sarah said.

Amy gave a wonderful Spanish shrug. "Through here," she hissed in a whisper loud enough to wake the dead. "Don't wake him."

"I'll be quiet."

Emily followed them to Tommy's room. Peering over Lady Sarah's shoulder she saw with relief that Tommy had indeed fallen asleep. He sprawled on his cot with the abandon of infant slumber, one plump hand flung over the edge of the covers and his petticoats about his neck. His straight black hair clung damply to his forehead. One cheek showed the imprint of a button. Emily tiptoed to his side and straightened his garments. He sighed and turned over.

Out, Emily pantomimed. They returned to the schoolroom. "He's an amiable child," she murmured, "but a small bear if he misses his *siesta*. What is it, Lady Sarah?"

"He looks . . . he doesn't look like my—like Major Falk."

"*I* look like Papa," Amy said complaisantly. "Tommy looks like our mama. *Verdad*. Peggy says so. Doña Isabel was Spanish, you know."

"Yes," said Lady Sarah in a less suffocated voice, "so I was told. Well, Amy, I am very glad to meet you, but I must say good-bye, now. Thank you for showing me your brother and your dolls. Should you like another doll?"

"No, thank you. I need a riding crop. Good-bye." Amy curtseyed again. "*Lady* Sarah." That was impudent and an impudent grin crossed Amy's features. Emily frowned at her, not very severely.

"Good-bye, Matthew." Lady Sarah was being thorough.

"Bye." Matt had taken up his favourite picture book and looked up impatiently. At Emily's maternal glower he rose and executed a reluctant bow. "Good-bye, ma'am. When you come again you may see Eustachio. If it's not raining."

"Thank you," Lady Sarah said gravely. "You're very kind."

Downstairs Emily saw that the encounter had shaken Lady Sarah. Her eyes were very bright and her colour high.

"Shall I send for more tea?"

"No, oh no, thank you. And thank you for letting me meet them. They are quite beautiful."

"And occasionally rag-mannered," Emily said drily.

"I like children with spirit. Your son is also a charming boy, Mrs. Foster. I have three sons. I had a daughter, too, but she died." Lady Sarah's hands fluttered.

Emily swallowed. "I'm sorry. I lost a daughter, too. That's why I was so glad to have the charge of Amy. Does it disturb you to find Tommy foreign-looking? I assure you he is wholly English in his ways, if a baby may be said to have nationality. Of the three he is the easiest and most amiable of temper."

"You speak as if all three were your children."

"Do I? I ought not to, but I feel as if they are."

"Please. It seems to me most admirable."

"They see their father very seldom."

Lady Sarah twisted her gloves again. "Is he . . . is Richard a good father? I beg your pardon, Mrs. Foster. You are bound to tell me he is, I know, but young Amy spoke of him with such detachment that I had to ask."

"Perhaps I have encouraged Amy's detachment. Major Falk's profession is so very chancy. Indeed, I think he wishes it, for he does not create emotional scenes when he does see them." For reasons obscure to herself Emily did not tell her guest anything more of Major Falk's relationship with his children. It seemed an unwarranted invasion of his privacy. "Pray come into the withdrawing room and sit down, Lady Sarah."

"Oh no, I must go." She pulled on the maltreated gloves. "Shall you allow me to see them again, Mrs. Foster?"

"No."

Lady Sarah's eyes flew to Emily's.

"Not immediately." Emily frowned, thinking. "I shall write Major Conway and ask his advice."

"That is Bevis's friend, is it not?"

"Your brother's friend. They have known one another for a long time, I believe. Major Conway will be able to guide me. I shall write Major Falk, too, of course."

Lady Sarah departed soon thereafter, polite but unsettled. She borrowed Don Alfonso and gave Emily her direction. Knowlton. Wilson of Knowlton.

Emily had heard of Knowlton. Everyone in Hampshire knew of Knowlton. She shook hands and showed her unexpected guest out in a thoughtful mood. Although she felt some exasperation that she had been exposed to this surprise attack, she acknowledged that it could be no very pleasant thing to confess oneself the product of a notorious scandal. There was something odd about the twenty-year silence. Had the Duke of Newsham really been mad? His daughter had announced the fact baldly, as if she did not expect contradiction. It was all baffling and worrying.

That evening Emily sat down at her desk and writ Major Conway a full account of Lady Sarah's visit. His answer, which came by return post, did not contribute to her peace of mind.

"My dear Emily," he began (in the months since the theatre party they had reached first-name friendship):

"I am sorry to say I cannot advise you to permit Lady Sarah's visits under any circumstances. I daresay she is an amiable woman and that her motives are pure as the driven snow, but Richard would not wish the Ffouke connexion to be encouraged. He will probably call Bevis out for betraying the children's whereabouts to his sister.

Lady Sarah will have explained to you Richard's unhappy parentage. She has probably not told you what he suffered at the late duke's hands, nor do I mean to, but the duke behaved with great cruelty. Legal complications arising from the will now make it a matter of some concern that none of the Ffouke family have any dealing with Amy and Tommy. I do not wish to frighten you, but I must ask you to keep a close watch on the children when strangers are about. I wish you will hire an extra groom so that someone may keep an eye on them at all times. I am enclosing a draught on my bank.

This precaution is chiefly a means of averting Richard's wrath from Bevis's and my own head. I shall write Richard directly and ask for his instructions. In the meantime I prefer excessive caution to overconfidence. Pray humour me and believe that you need not expect the situation to continue very long.

If I had not just undergone another tiresome bit of surgery, I should come to you myself. As it is I can only fire off letters in all directions. I have writ Lady Sarah. She will be shocked to receive a bear garden jaw from a complete stranger, I daresay. However, my letter should relieve you of the embarrassing task of showing her the door. I have also rung a peal over Bevis. Richard was not eager to name Bevis as guardian. It seems his mistrust was well-founded, though it goes without saying that Bevis blundered from the best of motives. Richard's connexion with the Duchess of Newsham was not widely known in the army. I had forgot Bevis is her grace's cousin. I should have warned him to keep mum.

Forgive me for alarming you. I can only act as Richard's friend. He has borne enough grief at the hands of the Ffouke family to make association unthinkable, even if Lady Sarah and her brothers are filled with benevolence.

> *Yours, in haste and some*
> *perturbation of spirit,*
> *Tom Conway.*

To say that these news caused Emily agitation would be an understatement. She hired a man at once and would have carried the problem to her father and Aunt Fan but that it seemed so private a matter she could not feel easy taking her father into Major Falk's confidence. For days she jumped at shadows. She even found an excuse to avoid going to church on Sunday. Fortunately the rains continued, so the children did not think their confinement to the house odd. Nothing happened and Emily began to feel easier.

A week later, just as the news of Bonaparte's escape from Elba reached Mellings, Major Conway writ her another note:

Dear Emily,

You may pull back your outposts. I have had a reassuring, and very stiff, letter from Lady Wilson. As Richard has never questioned her motives I think you may take it that there is nothing to fear. To be on the safe side, however, pray keep the groom until Richard's return. I have Lady Sarah's promise that she will trouble you no further.

Your relieved and obedient servant,
Tom C.

P.S. Bevis is penitent but puzzled. I have had no word from Richard. That is to be expected.
P.P.S. Damn *Boney.*

On the heels of Major Conway's letter came a brief note of apology from Lady Sarah by a curious young footman who also bore the three volumes of Don Alfonso.

Emily took the note and the novel and tipped the footman, whom she directed the new groom to see off the premises. She sent no reply. If Lady Sarah were honest, as Emily was inclined to think, the whole affair could only have been profoundly humiliating. If she were not, Emily did not mean to reassure her.

— 17 —

MARCH WORE INTO April. The emperor of the French was reestablished in the Tuileries making constitutions, and, one presumed, armies. The Duke of Wellington continued in Vienna. In Brussels the Prince of Orange emitted nervous military noises in his temporary role as allied commander. Richard Falk was still on the high seas.

The clash of nations interested Emily not at all. She was too absorbed in Falk melodrama. For some reason the easing of her immediate vigilance made her jumpier than the original state of siege. She slept badly. More than once she woke in the middle of the night sure that Amy and Tommy had been smothered in their beds.

Feeling the fool, she nevertheless rose and assured herself that they were alive and safe in the nursery. The third time it happened she had to explain something of her apprehension to Peggy McGrath, who promised with almost all the holy vows of heaven to say nothing to the children. Peggy's eyes gleamed with excitement, however, and she looked like a war-horse that has heard the bugle. It crossed Emily's mind that the nurse relished a bit of action.

Presently Emily became hardened to apprehension herself and learned to sleep again. Indeed, she slept so soundly that when Phillida woke her one wet spring night, the maid had to shake her several times before her eyes blinked open.

"Oh madam, please wake up. He's here."

"What? Who?" Emily focussed her mind. "He?"

"Captain Falk."

"Major," Emily corrected, cross and half awake. Then the news sank in. She sat up and tore off her nightcap. "Hand me my robe." She gazed blearily at the hands of the clock, which showed half past twelve. "Where have you put him?"

"In the foyer. There's no fire in the withdrawing room. Oh madam, such a turn he give me, knocking like that. I thought we was invaded for sure."

Emily struggled into her slippers and robe and ran a brush over her tumbled hair. "Mmm . . . Very well. Make up the fire in the kitchen and put a kettle on. Leave me a light, witling."

Phillida lit a candle with her own taper and scuttled out, muttering under her breath.

Shielding her flame from the draughts, Emily walked as quickly as she dared down the stairway. It had never seemed so vertical. She had time to rehearse one or two soothing, explanatory, and reproachful speeches. Her heart thumped in her throat. Below in the unlit foyer she could just make out Major Falk's dark presence. He seemed to be leaning on the hall table. When he saw her light he straightened with a jerk. In the dim glow of the candle Emily could see that his cloak was mud-splattered and his jaw unshaven.

When she reached the lowest steps and saw his eyes she abandoned her rehearsed speeches. "They're all right. Truly. Sound asleep upstairs in their beds. Come, I'll show you."

He followed her in silence. The subdued clank of his spurs assured her that he was just behind her.

At Tommy's chamber he stood, stiff as a board, hands clenched, while she tucked the little boy's covers about him. Tommy flung off the tickling edge of the quilt with an irritable grunt and settled into his form like a hare. At Amy's door Major Falk did not wait for Emily. He knelt in one swift motion by the edge of his daughter's cot, and very carefully, because his hand shook, touched her brown curls.

That was too much for Emily. She set the candle by Amy's bed, went out into the dark schoolroom, and had a good, albeit silent, cry. She had reached the stage of wiping her streaming eyes on the sleeve of her robe, having somewhere misplaced her handkerchief, when Peggy stirred in her nook by the fire and made an interrogatory noise.

"Hush," Emily whispered, sniffing. "Go back to sleep."

That only spurred the nurse awake. She climbed from her truckle and stumped over to Emily, plaits flopping. "What is it, missus?"

"Major Falk."

"Himself!" Peggy did not shriek aloud, but she had no delicate scruples about intruding on her employer's reunion with his child. She swarmed over him. It was a wonder Amy didn't waken.

Presently he came out of Amy's room with the candle in one hand and his other arm about Peggy's shoulders. "Yes. Be still, Pegeen." At least he kept his voice low. "McGrath is very well, but I left him aboard the troopship. I came ashore at Falmouth."

Emily stared at the two of them illuminated in the puddle of light from the single candle. Major Falk looked composed if exhausted, Peggy bright-eyed. Emily herself might have vanished. Her employer was wholly absorbed in reassuring the servant, a kindness Emily must have approved had she been less distraught herself. As it was she sniffed again, rather loudly.

Apparently he took in her indignation, for he gave Peggy a last tired hug and handed Emily the candle. "Thank you." It was said with such simplicity that Emily's self-pity died in her throat.

Major Falk had returned his attention to the nurse. "Go back to bed, Peg. I'll tell you everything in the morning." To Emily's surprise, Peggy obeyed without protest.

When Emily and Major Falk reached the kitchen, he said abruptly, "I must see to my horse. I left him tethered in front of the house. Is there a way out?"

Emily pointed. "Turn left. I'll cut some meat and bread for you. Wake the groom if you need help." He disappeared and Emily sent the fascinated and protesting Phillida to bed.

Waiting for him, Emily had plenty of time to regret her tumbled hair, to wish that someday they could meet in ordinary, civilised circumstances. Her thoughts were turbulent and her acts domestic. She had cut and arranged quite a creditable midnight supper and brewed a very strong pot of tea by the time he stumbled back into the kitchen with his saddlebags over one arm.

He looked at the food and then at his hands. "Scullery?"

Emily pointed again. "I'll take your cloak and the bags." He handed them to her and disappeared into the scullery.

Emily set the bags on a chair and hung the cloak by the fire. Phillida could brush the mud off in the morning. It was the same cloak he had worn the year before. It had been threadbare then. It now boasted what looked like a scorch mark and a three-cornered tear. McGrath could not be a very efficient servant. The cloak was damp, but not soaked. Major Falk must have escaped the rainstorm of the afternoon. Or, more likely, ridden through it and been dried off by the wind in its wake.

He had removed most of the mud from his person. Emily watched him cross the flags. His hair was wet and he was wearing faded regimentals. It was the first time she had seen him in uniform. She did not like it.

"Falmouth," she murmured. "Three days' hard riding."

"Two and a night." He added, defensive, "There was a moon."

"Splendid. I daresay you remembered to eat now and then."

He took a long breath. "I got your letter and Tom's ten days ago. The ship came up to us off Ushant with orders and mail."

"For heaven's sake, sir, sit and eat. I can wait for explanations."

"Then you are a rare woman."

"A pearl beyond price," Emily snapped. "Sit. Eat."

He obeyed. He ate two slices of beef and a piece of bread with a restrained ferocity that told Emily all she wanted to know about his journey. However, he stopped at that and shoved the plate away. "Has Lady Sarah come back?"

"No, and I don't think she will. Major Conway writ her a very strong letter."

"Where's Knowlton?"

"About seven miles beyond Mellings Magna on the London road."

"Very well," he said heavily. "I'll have it out with her tomorrow. God, today. What time is it?"

"Past one o'clock, I rather think."

"Today then. I hope I've not left it too late." He looked at the fire, shivering a little. "I'm posted to Brussels."

Emily repressed an automatic protest and poured two cups of tea.

His hands curved on the cup and he stared into the amber liquid. "I wish you will keep the groom."

"I mean to." Questions hovered on her tongue but she bit them back. Not the hour for lengthy explanations. She sipped at her tea. He did not, but sat warming his hands, head bent.

Presently he looked up at her. "I'm sorry to bring this down on you. If I hadn't been fool enough to trust Bevis's discretion they would never have heard of Amy and Tommy."

"They?" Emily said gently.

"The Ffoukes." He explained the legal problem tersely.

"Good God." For the first time Emily perceived his apprehension as having a basis in fact, and the hair stood up on the back of her neck. "But that's—"

"Gothick," he finished, grim. "I know. I have to find out if Sarah has blabbed to the duke."

"She assured Tom Conway she would tell no one."

He was silent.

"Will you know if that's true when you've spoken with her?"

He shrugged.

"I thought her candid," Emily ventured.

"Perhaps she is." He sounded so blue-devilled and withal so tired Emily rose and stalked to the hearth.

"What are you doing?"

"Placing coals in a warming pan. Phillida has turned down your bed but the sheets want warming."

He began to laugh, head in hands.

"I collect," Emily said with severity, "that you spent last night under a hedge."

"Only after the moon set," he said meekly.

— 18 —

SIR ROBERT WILSON was a plump middle-aged gentleman some years older and some inches shorter than his noble wife. He had wed for love. She had not. In the seven years of their marriage, he thought she had learnt to love him. Certainly she trusted him, and knowing her history, he felt that to be a considerable achievement.

Twenty-eight when they wed, handsome, wealthy, and sophisticated, Lady Sarah Ffouke had seemed an unlikely wife for a country gentleman. However, she had taken so contentedly to the management of his household, to the small neighbourhood, and to the mixed pleasures of maternity, that their annual London seasons grew shorter and shorter. She liked to keep in touch with her old friends. Once or twice a year she invited parties to Knowlton, but she seemed happily settled in the role of squire's wife. She had given him three sons. Sir Robert did not like to see her troubled.

When the butler entered the breakfast room where they sat over a light nuncheon and announced that one Major Falk wished speech with Lady Sarah, Sir Robert watched his wife turn pale.

"Falk? Is that—"

"Richard." Sarah's hands fluttered to her throat.

"Shall I go to him first?"

"Oh, Robin, if you will . . . "

"You needn't see him at all, you know."

She stared at him, half shocked, half hopeful. "He's my brother."

"My dear, he is your mother's by-blow. No one would think it odd if you were to refuse to see him."

She closed her eyes for a moment, still very pale, but said nothing.

"Well, Sarah, I'll go in to him and see what the fellow wants. If you don't come in a quarter hour I'll send him on his way."

Her gaze seemed to follow him out of the room. Leaving the hall he encountered his butler. "Where have you put Major Falk?"

"The red salon, sir. A stranger, is he not?"

"Yes. Thank you, Bowles. Tell her ladyship where we are, however. She will make for the withdrawing room, I daresay."

The butler looked puzzled for an instant before his features reassembled into a perfect blankness. He was a very correct servant. Wilson hesitated at the door to the red salon, which was ajar. Then he pushed it open and entered.

Falk had not made himself at home. He was standing on the Turkey carpet and he looked up from contemplation of its pattern when Wilson spoke.

"Major Falk? I am Robert Wilson. How d'ye do?" Wilson deliberately did not extend his hand. No need to be effusive.

Apparently Lady Sarah's half brother agreed. "Servant, sir. Your man mistook me. I wished to speak with Lady Sarah."

"But you will concede that a husband has the right to meet his wife's, er, acquaintances?" Wilson spoke with an effort at coolness which sounded supercilious in his own ears. He was startled and unsure why he should be so.

He had expected—what? The fawning vulgarity of a shirttail relation? Perhaps a slightly shopworn copy of Lord George, or a blustering swaggerer like Lord John. What Wilson had not envisaged was a thin, weather-beaten

132

man of middle height who frowned at him from eyes the exact shape and colour of his wife's.

Lady Sarah took after the Ffoukes, but her eyes were her mother's. Falk's features, with allowance for a tropic tan and harsh lines of experience, hardship, and, Wilson thought, an uncertain temper, were a masculine version of the dowager duchess of Newsham's. At sixty-five, the dowager was still a handsome woman.

Wilson's question, as it was meant to, threw his unwanted guest off balance, and Falk's frown deepened. However, the man said, noncommittal, "No doubt. I trust Lady Sarah is in good health."

He does not know that I am privy to the relationship, and is willing to keep me in the dark in case Sarah has not told me of it, Wilson thought, again surprised. That argued a kind of loyalty—and experience of the reception bastards were apt to receive of the respectable. Wilson felt slightly ashamed of himself.

He cleared his throat. "Let us not hide our teeth. You are Sarah's half brother, are you not, come to ring a peal over her? She received an impertinent letter from a gentleman who said he writ at your behest. It cut up her peace."

"I cannot think my friend was impertinent." Major Falk brushed his hair from his forehead. It wanted trimming. "That's not Tom's style. I hope he was plain."

"He was plainspoken. I find the situation obscure."

Falk's eyes narrowed. "I daresay you do. Lady Sarah should have no difficulty understanding it, however. She assured my friend that she would not inform Keighley—the present duke, that is—of my children's whereabouts. I came to hear her repeat that promise. And to find out what further damage she has done."

"Upon my word—"

"I daresay Lady Sarah's action was not malicious."

"Malicious!" Sarah stood in the doorway. "Richard, how can you?" Her eyes flashed. She looked, her indulgent husband thought, quite magnificent.

133

Her brother regarded her without expression. "Eavesdropping? You weren't used to play the coward, Lady Sarah."

"And you weren't used to wax slanderous, Lord Richard."

He drew in a sharp breath. "Don't be insulting."

"Why not, when you are?"

They glowered at each other. Presently a flicker of wry humour touched Major Falk's eyes. "I had not meant this to be a social call, ma'am."

The fire went out of Sarah. "And here we are quarrelling like cat and dog, or brother and sister." Her hazel eyes brimmed. "Oh, Richard, it is good to see you. How . . . how have you been?"

Her brother was made of sterner stuff. "Very well," he said flatly. "How many of your obnoxious family have you told of my children?"

Sarah flushed, but kept her dignity. "None, except *Maman*."

"That was exceedingly stupid," Falk said through his teeth. "And she has no doubt spread the news broadcast to the duke, your other brothers and sisters, and half the Ton."

"I did not tell her where I found your children. Merely that I had seen them and that they are healthy and happy."

"So far," he said bitterly.

"You cannot imagine *Maman* means them harm."

"I have no idea what obscure motives move through her grace's brain, and pray do not enlighten me. It's the duke and your amiable brothers whose intentions I question."

"Keighley wouldn't—"

"Oh, wouldn't he? You writ me a letter some years ago, Lady Sarah. I wonder if you remember the tenor of it."

"I writ you three letters."

His brows drew together. "I received one."

"I writ you that my father was dead. That was the first."

He nodded. "That one reached me. Well?"

"Well what?"

"You told me," he said slowly, "that owing to the duke's carelessness I had some legal claim on the estate. I paid you the courtesy of assuming that you were warning me not to try the claim before the courts, and of course I replied that I would not. I also sent a statement to that effect to your eldest brother."

Sarah sank into the nearest chair. "I wasn't warning you. I was *inciting* you. I thought you ought to have something."

He stared at her. "My God, madam, nothing would induce me to claim kinship with the Duke of Newsham. If I thought I were his son on whatever side of the blanket I'd slit my throat."

Wilson, who remembered the late duke with revulsion, fought an impulse to applaud and said in his pleasantest voice, "I really think you should sit, Major. And that I should ring for sherry. Airing the family linen is such dry business, is it not?"

"I prefer to stand, sir. I have very little time and I'm not in the mood for small talk. The late duke tried once to kill me."

Wilson cocked an ear. He had heard Sarah's version of the incident and he was curious.

Falk went on, however, without elaboration. "When he failed of his object, he had me pursued to India. He very nearly destroyed me. When you writ me of his death, Lady Sarah, I had several minutes of profound relief, until I realised that he had provided his sons with a motive for continuing the hunt. So I signed an oath before two unimpeachable witnesses that I'd not try to pass myself off as a Ffouke heir. It wasn't a pleasant task, as you may imagine, but I hoped it would satisfy them. I sent the statement to the present duke. Should you care to see his response?"

Sarah nodded, mute.

He drew a paper from the breast of his tunic and handed it to her without further comment.

135

Wilson was possessed of a keen desire to read over his wife's shoulder. He rang for the butler instead. "Sherry, Bowles," he murmured when the man appeared. Bowles nodded and vanished.

Neither Sarah nor her brother noticed the byplay. Sarah had gone pale as she read. Now two spots of colour burnt on her cheekbones. "How utterly sickening of Keighley. Richard, I swear to you, I didn't know." She began to crumple the dog-eared letter.

In a single swift movement he was at her side and had taken her wrist.

"You're hurting me."

Wilson started forward.

Falk took the letter and released his grip. "I beg your pardon, but that is the only legal evidence I have of Keighley's intentions. If something should happen . . . "

"I see," she whispered. "Oh, I see. And your children—"

"Represent precisely the same threat to the estate that I do," he interrupted, completing her thought. "Not a very large threat, considering Newsham's power, but I have no faith in his moderation. It would be easy for him to cause them harm, particularly if I were not alive to see to their protection. I am posted to Belgium," he added wearily. "I have just returned from an unpleasant year in America. Do you see why I have the wind up?" He smoothed the letter as if it were a sonnet from a lover.

Sarah nodded without looking up. Her hands clenched in her lap. Wilson was deeply sorry for her, but unable to think of anything constructive to say.

At that point, happily, Bowles entered with the sherry tray. He set it at Sarah's elbow and withdrew. Sarah was in no state to be playing the hostess, so Wilson poured the three glasses himself. Sarah took hers, still silent.

Wilson met his brother-in-law's frown and said placidly, "I am of a persevering nature. If you'll take a glass, Major, we'll call it restorative rather than social." He had the satisfaction of seeing the grim lines about the other man's mouth ease. At least Falk had a sense of humour. Falk sat, docile enough, and took the proffered sherry.

"Excellent." Wilson seated himself on a rather uncomfortable gilt chair between brother and sister, a not quite neutral body between contending armies. "Now, Sarah, you've told the dowager that the children exist, but not where. She is apt to surmise they live within a reasonable distance of Knowlton. Is your mother likely to have passed the information to his grace?"

Sarah looked at him uncertainly. He gave her a reassuring smile and sipped his sherry.

"*Maman* hasn't spoken to Keighley or Caroline in a sixmonth. Caroline is Newsham's duchess," she added, looking at her brother for the first time in some minutes. "They have three daughters. *Maman* is fond of the girls, but she and Keighley do not agree."

Falk took a swallow of sherry. He did not comment.

"I've said nothing to anyone else, Richard. Truly. Except Robin, of course."

"Of course."

Wilson ignored the sarcasm. He gave Sarah a brief smile and turned back to her brother. "Then I think our path is clear. In the morning I shall put the chaise to and leave for the dowager's residence in Yorkshire. Do you ride with me far as London, Major, as your time is limited. Lodge that incriminating letter with your solicitor." He finished his sherry in two judicious sips, reflecting.

"Thank you, Wilson, but I can't impose on you so far."

"I think you ought," Wilson said mildly. "If you will give me your trust."

Falk finished his sherry and rose. "It won't wash. There are Lord John and Lord George. Not to mention your sisters, ma'am. I shall have to remove the children to a place of safety. If I can find one in the time left to me," he added, savage.

"No!" Sarah jumped up and went to him, touching his arm. He jerked away as if he had been stung. Wilson, angered, made to interpose himself and thought better of it. His wife stood very still rubbing her rejected hand on the skirt of her gown.

Sarah was not the sort to give up easily, however. She raised her chin. "What kind of parent can you be to speak so casually of taking Amy and Tommy from Mrs. Foster's care? She has given them her home. And her heart."

"I did not speak casually." He turned from her and stared out the window, the set of his shoulders eloquent of stubbornness.

"The dowager lives retired," Wilson observed. "Lord John never visits her and Lord George would not leave London in the Season for the wilds of Yorkshire. Nor would your sisters, my dear. There's a chance the dowager may have writ them, but it's only a chance. If I act with despatch I may be able to forestall her. Pray reconsider, Major. I'm at your service."

Major Falk turned slowly. "Why?"

"Not because of your conciliating manners, to be sure."

Falk did not smile at this sally.

Wilson sighed. "I have never dealt easily with the duke. He opposed Sarah's marriage to me on specious grounds, and we keep our distance when we are forced into company. Unlike you, sir, I do not believe him capable of sustaining a vendetta. He is far too indolent. However I, too, have children, and I have sufficient imagination not to dismiss your fears. He is a proud man and mean in money matters."

Falk was rubbing his brow as if he had the headache.

"I always pull Sarah's chestnuts out of the fire," Wilson murmured.

The hand stilled.

"The one you ought to look out for is Lord George."

Falk dropped his hand and regarded Wilson, frowning.

"Think it through. Newsham's duchess has so far produced daughters. True, she's a youngish woman and perfectly healthy, but, who knows? She might be thrown from a carriage or choke on a bone. Or the duke might, more to the point. Lord John will never marry. His tastes do not lie in that direction." Wilson watched the other two to see the effects of his little phantasy. "That leaves Lord George to succeed—and he is your junior, sir."

Sarah's jaw dropped. She closed her mouth with a snap.

Falk's thin face went blank. After a moment he said, drily, "And pigs may fly. If you've no objections I'll deal with one disaster at a time. Besides there is one irrefutable witness that I am not the duke's son. The dowager."

"I wondered when you would arrive at that. It presents a simple solution to all your difficulties."

To his surprise Falk looked neither indignant nor relieved, merely uncertain. He turned to his sister. "You know the dowager. Will she make a witnessed statement for Newsham's lawyers?"

Sarah stared at him and then at Wilson. She was flushed. "You have both taken leave of your senses. Expose her folly to the world? Every feeling revolts! How could you think of asking *Maman* to humiliate herself, to—to rake up a dead scandal."

"It is not as if she would be asked to perjure herself," Wilson murmured. "She has merely to confirm what the world already believes. Her 'folly' is notorious and has been for some thirty years."

"Thirty-two years and four months at least." Incredibly Falk appeared to be suppressing laughter. "It is a little odd, to be sure, to be asking one's parent to swear to such a thing."

Wilson snorted.

Sarah was powerfully unamused. "You're both despicable. It is not a joke. *Maman* is five and sixty years old, and frail. You know how ill she was this winter, Robin. She has suffered enough." At that she broke off, looking confused.

Falk said delicately, "Do you believe my children should be made to suffer, too? Very scriptural of you, Sarah."

Sarah's eyes filled with tears. "I . . . Of course not, Richard. Oh, if I knew what was right . . . "

Her brother, with some tact, turned back to Wilson. "It

seems to me unlikely that the dowager would make the effort."

"I am a persuasive and insinuating fellow."

"You are, by God, but you'd be trying to overcome some thirty years of inertia. Rather like moving the world without a lever."

"That is not true!" Sarah burst out.

"What isn't?"

"Inertia. *Maman* rescued you."

Falk scowled. "From the duke's clutches? Come, Sarah, she wasn't even there. That much I do remember."

"No, but when Papa stormed off she arranged for you to be taken to the parson, what was his name?"

"Freeman."

"And she paid for your education. She sold her diamonds and had paste copies made. For three years she schemed and contrived to get you safely out of the country, and what is more she succeeded. If the duke knew of your whereabouts in India it was not her doing. She will be very surprised to hear that he found you. Indeed, I shan't tell her so. She is proud of her efforts."

Falk regarded his sister in silence. Wilson thought he was skeptical. After a moment he said rather heavily, "That's water under the bridge. Will she consent to make a statement now?"

"I—I don't know," Sarah faltered. On a firmer note she added, "I know she will wish to help in some way, if she can be brought to believe in the danger."

Falk withdrew the letter from the breast of his tunic and handed it to Wilson without a word.

"Then you will entrust me with the matter?"

"I have no choice." Perhaps that seemed as ungracious to Falk as it sounded to Sir Robert, for Falk flushed. "I beg your pardon. I shall be in your debt, sir."

Wilson rather thought he would. "A copy should suffice for the dowager, Major. I am persuaded you ought to place the original with your solicitor. Let us meet tomorrow at the coaching inn in Mellings Magna. Ten o'clock."

The next half hour was spent in practical arrangements. Gradually Sarah began to look less agitated. Wilson was as conscious of his wife's feelings as if she had shouted them aloud. It was grossly unfair that Sarah should be rebuffed because of her father and the present duke. She had feared her father. That fear had left marks on her character which no amount of husbandly kindness and approval could wholly erase. It angered Wilson that it should be so, and he felt some resentment against Falk for calling up the bad old times, but there was no help for it, and the poor devil was not to be blamed for trying to protect his children.

When he left, Sarah would have made some sisterly gesture but Falk's manner precluded it. Wilson saw him off and returned to find his wife crying in a tired way on the sopha.

He drew her to him, patting her hair. "What a prickly lot your brother is."

"He kept calling me Lady Sarah, as if we had not been in leading strings together."

"Well, you *are* Lady Sarah. Tell me, Sal, have I done the right thing?"

"Oh, Robin, I am thinking of poor *Maman*. I hate to cut up her peace. Richard is not in the least grateful to her."

"It is not to be wondered at. She sent him off to the Indian army." Wilson smoothed her hair. "If I contrive to draw the duke's fangs, Falk will have reason to be grateful."

"Is it such a terrible place?"

"India? The climate is appalling, our troops are perpetually devastated by disease, and if my calculations are correct, your brother arrived in time for the Mahratta War. The dowager cannot have predicted that, but I daresay it may have coloured your brother's feelings a trifle."

Sarah gave a sad, assenting sniff.

"In any case it is nothing to do with you."

"I feel so guilty."

"You meant everything for the best. Where is your brother's novel? I am now agog to read it."

"I sent it back to Mrs. Foster." Sarah straightened and

gave him a tentative smile. "It is quite shocking and very funny. I have writ to Hatchard's for copies of all his books."

"Lord, you'll bankrupt me." Wilson smiled back. "Shall you come up and help me pack for the journey? I mean to pick your brains, Sal. Your *Maman* and I go on very comfortably in the general way, but I confess to some trepidation in this case."

"Take her a box of *marrons glacés*. The kind with silvery paper. And be sure to compliment her on her hair. She is wearing it in a new style."

Wilson watched his wife's air of concentration with affectionate amusement. Having made up her mind to cooperate, she would do so in a large way. There was nothing mean about Sarah.

=== 19 ===

EMILY DID NOT expect Major Falk to return. He had taken his gear, such as it was, with him to Knowlton, so she was understandably startled when Phillida showed him in to her small library. Emily had been doing accounts.

"My word, I thought you must be halfway to London by this time." She forced herself to sound detached.

"And here I am on your doorstep again." He looked glum.

"Well, what happened?"

"We talked."

"That is certainly an achievement," Emily snapped, maddened, but he was tone-deaf to sarcasm for once.

"Sarah had writ the dowager duchess."

"Is that bad?"

"Discretion is not the dowager's middle name."

Emily shivered. "What is to be done?"

Major Falk did not meet her eye. "Wilson seems to think he can reach her in time to prevent her from spreading the good news. I am less sanguine, but it's worth a try."

"Wilson?" Emily frowned. "Ah, Lady Sarah's husband. I haven't met him. Is he inclined to be helpful? You must have exercised a great deal of tact and diplomacy."

A brief smile lit his eyes, faded. "Not in my line of country. Wilson is a clever man, or perhaps not being a blood relation is an aid to clear thinking. He is also very protective of his wife. I think he means to ease Sarah's mind, which is fortunate because I wouldn't relish bearding the dowager in her den. Nor do I have the time. She lives in Yorkshire."

Emily thought about that, and thought in general. "What do you wish me to do?"

He was silent for a long time. Finally he asked, diffident, "Would you prefer that I remove the children? I'll take them to Belgium with me. Peggy can come."

"No!"

"It's an obvious precaution."

Emily began to panick. "And have them follow in the baggage train of the army? I won't allow it."

"They were born in the baggage train of the army."

Emily did not mince words. "And their mother died in it."

Falk stiffened. "I could find someone in Brussels to keep them."

"And what if Bonaparte sacks Brussels?"

"Have you no faith in the British army?"

"I have no faith in any army." Emily stuck out her jaw. "You will leave them here. The groom will watch them. I shall watch them. I'd slay anyone who touched either of them. In any case, nobody has molested them so far."

"And what if I am killed when Boney sacks Brussels? Tom cannot come to help you," he said quietly. "Bevis will be with the staff. Can you protect the children for the rest of their lives? That was not in the terms of our agreement."

"If necessary I will. You forget, sir, that I am not a helpless, solitary creature. I have a father and brothers to call on." She took a hasty turn of the small room. " 'The terms of our agreement.' I wonder you can speak in that cold-blooded, legalistic way. Amy and Tommy are not a parcel of land or a team of horses you have given me the lease of. I love them. Matt thinks they are his sister and brother. My father treats Amy like a favoured granddaughter. They are family, sir. Family is not merely a matter of blood. If it comes to that I have more right to them than you. They scarcely know you."

Major Falk did not reply.

Emily stared at him, appalled at what she had said. If she had hated him she could not have said anything more wounding. What was wrong with her? "I beg your pardon, sir. I spoke in haste."

He met her stare and gave a short unamused laugh. "You do fight fire with fire. Perhaps Wilson may cajole the dowager into swearing to my illegitimacy. If he succeeds there will be no more danger to them and you may lower your guard."

Emily was silent. She hoped her confused feelings were not writ large on her face.

Falk went on in a dry, businesslike voice, "Wilson will call on you when he returns from Yorkshire to tell you how he fared. Even if he reports success I wish you will keep the groom. I'll write you from Belgium if I think it's safe to dismiss him."

Emily swallowed. "May I explain the situation to my father?"

"Need you?"

She sighed. "No."

"Then I wish you will not." He looked at the carpet. "I am past being embarrassed by Lady Sarah's family, but it seems to me safer to keep the story close. In any case, I still haven't decided what the children should be told of their connexions." He said the word with palpable distaste.

"You ought to make up your mind."

He looked up, rueful. "I thought I had. I didn't bargain on Sarah's excursion into aunthood."

It was indeed all Lady Sarah's doing. Emily reflected with nostalgia on the long period when she had been happy in the illusion that the children had no kin to trouble her. It had been a comfortable fiction. With all her heart she wished Lady Sarah had not punctured it. "Why did she come in the first place?"

"Sarah? I have no idea. I neglected to ask."

Emily sighed again. "There's no use crying over spilt

milk. I have a question for you, which I have hesitated to put."

"What is it?"

"What do you mean to do when there is a real peace?"

"That seems problematic. Boney is set for another ten years."

Emily forged on, stubborn, "You might be posted to a garrison in England. Would you take Amy and Tommy to Manchester?"

"I shouldn't dare," he said drily.

Emily flushed to the roots of her hair. "In spite of what I said in the heat of the moment, I am always aware that they are your children, sir."

"It's a mistake to plan too far ahead. Don't give yourself the megrims, ma'am. With any luck I'll be killed directly and neither of us will have to think about Manchester."

"You're a horrible man."

"So I've been told."

Emily bit her lip. "And I am a curst shrew. I ought to have learnt to mind my tongue by now."

Falk raised his brows. "We all have our limitations."

That reduced Emily to silence once more. Fuming silence.

"Are the children in the paddock? I ought to review the troops."

"Again?"

"Not if you dislike it," he said politely.

"Oh, it is of all things what I wish." Emily stalked to the open door. "Matt will probably try to leap a ditch for your edification and break his neck."

"Nonsense. I have a sobering influence on your son. He calls me sir and obeys me implicitly."

"Perhaps you should take *Matt* to Belgium," she rejoined, and, at that, he smiled.

What a strange, contrary man he was. She supposed other satirists might also be incapable of sustaining the high tragic note, but Major Falk, with enough Gothick meat in his dish to create a perfect stew of emotion, seemed to prefer to back off from it into irony. It was, on the whole, an endearing peculiarity, but she hoped he had no more surprises in store for her, and she wished with all her heart that he did not have to go so soon.

Lady Sarah and Wilson called within the week, Sir Robert travel weary. Emily eyed him with curiosity. Introductory and polite murmurs about the weather, Bonaparte, and everyone's health eventually dried up.

Emily took the plunge. "You are to report to me, I believe, Sir Robert. I feel like a brigadier."

Sir Robert returned her smile but looked as if he would prefer to be elsewhere. "I found my brother-in-law an exacting commander."

"He can be wearing." That was true but perhaps disloyal. Emily wondered at herself. She kept saying things that contradicted her real feelings. Or perhaps her feeling for Richard Falk was as much a fiction as the story of his godmother's legacy. She was not in love with him, she reminded herself. She was in love with his letters.

Wilson sighed. "The dowager balks at the humiliation of swearing that Richard Falk is not her husband's son."

"You are unfair, Robert."

He shot his wife a quick glance. "That is the effect of the dowager's resistance. We spent two days and a long evening sidestepping the issue. I learnt a great deal of her marriage to the duke which I ought not to know. She is frail, and I could not bring myself to press the matter as I ought to have done."

Wilson fiddled with his handsome watch fob. After a moment he caught himself at the nervous practice and looked up at Emily with a rueful smile. "She charmed me, Mrs. Foster, as she always does, and I came away convinced that she had made enormous concessions. When I turned what she had actually said over in my mind I found that I had got her firm promise to tell no one of the children."

"And that's all?"

"Yes." Wilson was not pleased with himself.

"And she has told no one of the children?"

"Fortunately she has not. She has told no one except for her maid, who is seventy, French, and so high in the instep she doesn't speak to the butler, who couldn't understand her anyway."

Emily said slowly, "Then it seems the immediate crisis is over."

"Richard should be satisfied," Lady Sarah interjected.

"No doubt I'll have his opinion in the next few days." Emily had received no word from Major Falk since his abrupt and unceremonious departure and she was beginning to worry.

Wilson made an effort to sound soothing, but he was clearly dissatisfied with the fruits of his efforts. "I writ from Town on my way home. It will take rather more than a spoken promise to satisfy him, I fear, but I think *you* may be easy, Mrs. Foster."

Emily remained uneasy, but she did not say so. There was no point in compounding the misery. She rang for Phillida. "Shall you take a glass of sherry? My father assures me it is tolerable."

From the alacrity with which Phillida responded to the summons it seemed likely she had been eavesdropping again. Emily shooed her away and poured. "Lady Sarah?"

"I thought you relied on tea in these situations, Mrs. Foster."

"Your brother has driven me to drink."

Lady Sarah smiled absently. "Has the furor disturbed the children?"

"No. They were curious about the groom at first, but he helps with their pony, so they accept him. My other servants have been baffled. Amy, of course, was delighted to see her father, if only briefly. He brought her a doll. In his saddlebags."

Lady Sarah sighed. "If only I had not rushed to see them without consulting Richard first."

"The man was incommunicado," Sir Robert snapped,

"You *couldn't* consult him. Indeed, if the dowager had consented to make a statement, you might have congratulated yourself, my dear."

"She will never agree. It's the witnesses who trouble her, Mrs. Foster." Lady Sarah set her glass down and leaned forward. "*Maman* fears they'd talk. She fancies the old scandal is dead and does not wish to revive gossip."

Emily could think of nothing to say to that. It seemed a trivial consideration.

"Can you understand?"

"Oh, I can understand." In spite of herself, Emily's anger broke through. "Major Falk may feel otherwise. After all he has had to live with the scandal all his life. I daresay he thinks the burden unfairly distributed."

Lady Sarah's eyes lowered. "We have all lived with it. But *Maman* is an elderly lady, Richard a young man. He has made his own life in spite of it."

"And now he is trying to save his life," Emily said, quietly. "Do you understand that?"

Lady Sarah and Sir Robert frowned at her with almost identical expressions. It was odd how two faces so dissimilar in bone structure could look so alike. Emily wondered briefly if she had come to resemble Edward Foster in the course of her own marriage.

Sir Robert shifted his heavy thighs on the gilt chair. "Ah, the present duke may have writ a few threatening remarks in the heat of the moment. I would not put it past him to block Major Falk's promotion or have him sent to a post of danger, but direct action is not in Newsham's style."

"You don't appear thick-witted, sir, I meant that Major Falk's children *are* his new life. When I first learned of his parentage from Lady Sarah I was inclined to think the course he adopted dishonest, but now—leaving aside our flurry of melodrama—I think he made the right judgement." She turned on Lady Sarah. "You must admit that the children are better off with no connexions at all than with kin who despise them and wish them ill."

Lady Sarah paled. "No one could despise them."

Emily raised her brows. "Consider them a nuisance and an embarrassment, if you prefer. That is the same thing."

Lady Sarah bit her lip. Her husband was watching her. He looked as tired and anxious as his round features would allow. Another bystander, Emily thought, with a surge of fellow feeling.

Wilson said, "If they do not know they are despised, they cannot be made to feel despicable. Do you imply, Mrs. Foster, that further visits from Sarah to the children would be unwise?"

"Their father did not forbid her to visit them."

"Nevertheless—"

"*I* shall be glad to receive Lady Sarah at any time."

"Oh, stop talking around me as if I were a post," Sarah muttered. "I shan't meddle farther, Mrs. Foster. I promise."

Emily was content with that and presently showed her guests out. They did not ask to see the nursery.

Part IV
Sir Robert
Wilson, Emily
Summer, 1815

— 20 —

LADY SARAH LAID the dog-eared newspaper down and took a sip of her breakfast coffee. "If it is a great victory why does the duke write so dismal?"

"Wellington is not a man given to enthusiasm." Sir Robert had been repressing uneasiness for the entire twenty-four hours since news had come of the victory at Water-loo, all through the bell ringing, the *feu de joie* of the local militia, the obligatory ale with his tenants and port with his neighbours.

So had Sarah. "Richard," she said, tentative.

"There was no word of your brother in the despatch. I'm inclined to be optimistic. However, outside his staff and certain noblemen, the duke mentioned no one by name under the rank of brigadier. My optimism may be founded on sand."

"Shall I write Mrs. Foster?"

"We know no more than she. Wait, Sal."

So they waited.

Richard Falk's name did not appear on the first incomplete casualty lists. That raised their hopes, but then, except for the Guards, few names appeared for that entire wing of the army.

It struck Wilson as odd that he should be feeling hope at all. Sarah's feeling for her brother, compounded of guilt and nostalgia, he was beginning to comprehend. His own was decidedly odd.

There were the novels, of course, or rather the novel.

Wilson had so far only read one, but he was susceptible to literary merit. At first he was incredulous. The man he had met so briefly could not have writ so lighthearted and withal so charming and bizarre a romp through the pomposities of Spanish society.

There are two kinds of satirist. One writes from loathing and indignation. The other writes from a strong sense of absurdity and usually gives the impression of being secretly grateful to the objects of his criticism for providing him with cause for laughter. Falk, like Henry Fielding, was of the second sort. Although Wilson admired them less than the stricter satirists, he had often found himself wishing he could give such authors a glass of his best-run brandy. Indeed he had once had the pleasure of doing just that for Mr. Sheridan. Wilson felt the same sense of instinctive fellowship for the author of Don Alfonso, although his brother-in-law in the flesh inspired no such warmth.

Now, poring over the latest close-printed casualty list, Wilson realised his anxiety was for the writer, not the man. As he came to that perception he saw in the column of print, *Falk, R.*

He blinked. *Falk, R. lt. col., 28th Foot, missing, presumed killed.* He felt a moment of dismay so strong he dropped the paper. Should he tell Sarah? No, he would have to be sure. He rose and rang for his valet, who came as usual on noiseless feet.

"Pack a portmanteau for me, Kennet. I am going up to London for two days. Formal rig won't be necessary . . ." His voice trailed off and he stared vaguely at the Stubbs painting of an early Derby winner that hung above the mantel. "Full rig, Kennet. I shall go to White's. Perhaps someone will know something."

"Very good, sir."

"Why are you hanging about?"

"Shall I accompany you, sir?"

"No. Dash it, yes, I daresay you ought to come. Can't go about in crumpled linen."

Kennet looked scandalised that such a plan had crossed his master's mind even for a moment.

Wilson burnt the newspaper on the study grate and told his wife only that he meant to enquire for her brother at the Horse Guards. He wished to spare her the grisly rumours he was sure were rife in the capital. An appeal to her maternal instincts generally succeeded where reason did not. In the end he persuaded her to stay home with the boys.

Three days later he returned to her and there was now no point in hiding newspapers. She met him at the front entry.

"Mrs. Foster sent to tell me Richard has been wounded. Did you know that when you left?"

He kissed her. Her cheek was stiff to his touch. "I read 'missing, presumed killed.' I wanted to be sure."

"You might have told me. He's my brother."

"My dear, I wanted to spare you the uncertainty."

She gave him a disbelieving stare, but wifeliness overcame her and she caused the servants to take his driving coat. She even sent for refreshment.

When he had settled into his favourite chair and taken his first sip of sherry, however, she leapt to the attack. "I must go to Richard at once."

"You cannot, Sarah. At such a time, Brussels is no place for a lady."

"Then you must go. Find Richard and bring him here."

He took a swallow of sherry, rinsing the dust from his throat. Over the rim of the glass he searched his wife's face. She looked her full age. For a moment pity made him helpless to speak.

"You must, Robin." This time she was pleading.

"I shall go to him, of course, Sarah, as soon as may be. I have already directed my man of business to make enquiries. These financial types have connexions in Antwerp."

"If you delay he may die before you reach him."

"He may be dead already, my dear," Wilson said gently "The word was, 'gravely wounded.' "

"Then go at once."

"Very well, in the morning. But bringing your brother here is out of the question. He will be far too ill to move."

"Then you shall stay with him until the doctors say he may be moved. For God's *sake*, Robert."

Wilson rose. Sarah rarely used his full Christian name preferring Robin. He preferred Robin, too. He paced to the long window and stood looking out. The sun was setting in a pastel glow. "We cannot bring him here, Sally."

"We can and we will."

Wilson did not turn. "Shall you tell your sons that he is their uncle?"

"Yes," Sarah said, fierce.

Wilson turned, brows raised. "Have you changed your loyalties? What of your mother?"

"I don't believe *Maman* would wish me to leave Richard in the care of strangers."

That was too much like fustian for Wilson. "It's late in the day for the dowager to succumb to maternal concern she does not feel. You forget I've spoken with her of her by blow. Your brother has served in the army more than half his life. I daresay he has been hit before and must certainly have been in the care of strangers."

"You are hateful, Robert."

"I hope not." He went to her and stood looking down at her. "I find your baseborn brother rather more interesting than your legitimate brothers, Sarah, and I am certainly ready to serve him. It is the dowager who would not inconvenience herself for him. If you cause Richard Falk to be brought here openly, as your brother, there will inevitably be gossip and the gossip will light on her grace's head She is fond of our sons. Will she be happy when they look at her askance? Will *you* be happy?"

Sarah's jaw set.

Wilson sighed. "Very well. It may take me a month."

Sarah began to cry. "Oh, Robin, you are so good to me."

"I know it, madam." He smoothed her hair. "I can't think why. You'd best prepare your mother. No. We can't bring him here."

Sarah peered at him from behind the flimsy lace handkerchief with which she had been touching her eyes. "Newsham?"

"Yes." Wilson sat with disgusted energy on the chair nearest her. "What a stupid tangle. Well, I'll go to Brussels and see what may be done. I wish the dowager may be brought to acknowledge her guilt unequivocally. Do you try to persuade her this time, Sarah. Then we may whistle at Newsham and have the colonel—he is now a lieutenant colonel. Did you know that?"

Sarah nodded and blew her nose.

"Then we may have the colonel to visit whenever we and he wish it." Absurd to be thinking of the social amenities. The man was, in all probability, already dead.

Perhaps Sarah read his thought, for her gloom did not lift. "I'll try, but I don't think it will do any good. She is adamant."

Wilson sighed. He, too, thought it improbable that the dowager would soften. She could be very stubborn indeed.

Emily had taken her new gig out early because of the heat. Even so, a billow of dust followed her from farm to cottage to farm like a tame ghost. The weather had been relentlessly beautiful since the week before Water-loo. Nature ought to weep.

Emily was beginning to deal with the probability of Richard Falk's death. The numbness had not yet worn off, but she knew from past experience what would happen when it did wear off. In sequence, fury, a burst of grief, and long months of misery afterwards. Prickles of anger shot through the dull fog of her disbelief. It was doubly unkind of fate to deal her such a blow when she had finally come to terms with her muddled feelings. She did indeed love the author of Doña Inez. He was probably dead. A dead letter. Emily's mouth twisted at the sourness of the irony.

"Halloo!"

Emily reined back for a haywain that lumbered into the lane from an adjacent field.

"Good day t'ye, Miz Foster. Champion haying weather."

Her lips formed a smile for Mr. Proudy, one of her major tenants. He had his third son with him. The boy had grown half a foot in the past year and gangled at her from the slippery top of the piled hay. The wagon lurched. Willie Proudy grinned down at her and grabbed at his pitchfork to keep from sliding off.

Her team switched restlessly as the revenant dust settled upon them, but she held them back until the Proudy wain turned off. She tasted grit. A fine buff powder sifted down on the shoulders of her habit. Still she waited until she had the lane to herself again. She did not need to be gaped and grinned at.

The hay was early. Her father thought they might make an extra crop. Perhaps she ought to feed another milch cow through the winter this year. Eustachio was not a big eater. There ought to be enough hay to feed another cow. Mrs. Harry would be glad of the milk for cheeses. Emily clucked and eased the ribbons and the patient bays stepped along the lane.

Wild roses flared in bloom in the hedgerows. The air was thick with dust and the scent of roses. On her left hand her father's cornfields, each stalk of wheat heavy with promising grain, swelled up as far as the old apple orchard. Off to her right she could see a generous wealth of her own demesne, rye and blue wheat, lucerne on the rich bottom. The tidy fields were tidily squared by hedges and ditches under the gunmetal sky.

Everything in good order, she told herself, as the gig passed into a small stand of oak. The shade was welcome after the blinding sunlight. She should sell some timber this year. Of course the price would fall with the war over. Abruptly she pulled over on the verge and yanked a square of linen from the pocket of her skirt. She had been crying again without knowing it. Leaking tears like an old cistern. She scrubbed at her eyes.

The battle had taken her by surprise. She hadn't been thinking of battles, her mind on the Duke of Newsham and Lady Sarah and Byzantine plots. *Fiction*, she thought, furious, mopping her face. *Phantasy*. All the while the familiar bugaboo, Bonaparte, had been moving his flesh and blood legions in for the kill. She ought to have expected it. For three years now she had expected it. She'd been used to the idea. Damnation to Lady Sarah Wilson for distracting her from reality. It wasn't fair.

The horses were gorging themselves on a toothsome clump of cow parsley. A horsefly, discouraged by the *flickflick* of their undocked tails, decided to sample Emily's damp face. She swatted at it violently. One of the bays looked back at her.

"Oh, the devil. *Giddap*." She flapped the reins and the obedient team left off munching.

This will not do, Emily, her sensible self told her in accents reminiscent of Aunt Fan. The horses plodded slowly up the long hill home. *You are a mature woman with responsibilities. Life—children, horses, cows, vegetable marrows, roses—must go on, and you are in charge of this particular slice of life.* "Duty calleth, stern daughter of the voice of God." *That was Mr. Wordsworth, wasn't it? He was always right, Wordsworth.*

By the time she turned into the approach to Wellfield House, Emily was in tolerable command of her emotions once more. The sight of Lady Sarah's barouche drawn up before the front door jolted her heart, but her pulse steadied. At the stables, she gave the groom her reins, stepped down calmly, and walked back to the house to face the verdict.

She took the side door that led through the kitchen, stopping to bathe her hot face under the scullery pump.

Mrs. Harry greeted her cheerily, rattled pots on the range, went on with her work. In the hall Emily laid her gloves and bonnet on the narrow table and smoothed her hair. Her face stared somberly back at her. She looked flushed and tired, but her eyes weren't noticeably swollen. She brushed the dust from her habit with great care.

Phillida came into the hall, mobcap askew, eyes curious. "Oh, Mrs. Foster, that Lady Sarah's in drawing room—"

Emily cut her off. "Yes, I know. Bring the sherry tray."

"Sherry?" Phillida gaped. It was not yet eleven o'clock.

"You heard what I said," Emily snapped. "Bring it at once." She made herself go into the withdrawing room.

Lady Sarah was pacing the carpet. She stopped dead when Emily entered. "He's still alive."

Emily sat with a thud on the nearest chair.

"Oh Lord, I oughtn't to have blurted it out. I beg your pardon, Mrs. Foster—Emily . . ."

Emily took a gulp of air and the room stopped spinning. Lady Sarah was leaning over her, eyes anxious. Emily forced a smile. "These are good news indeed. Has Sir Robert—"

"Robin found Richard five days ago and writ me that evening. The letter . . . just a note, really . . ."

Emily took from her the single crossed sheet and focussed on Sir Robert's finicking hand. Sarah had the kindness to keep still. She sat on the edge of a straight-backed chair.

Emily read the letter through twice. Finally she gave up, shaking her head. "I don't seem to be taking this in. What . . . Is he—is your brother very bad?"

"Yes." Sarah ran the tip of her tongue over her lips as if they were dry. "Yes, very bad, but Robin thinks there's some hope of his eventual recovery."

Emily closed her eyes, opened them, unclenched her hand on the crumpled letter. "I beg your pardon, Lady Sarah. You will be thinking I've lost my wits as well as my manners." She smoothed the sheet with trembling fingers and handed it back. "When I saw your barouche at the door I foolishly assumed the worst." She gave a shaky but creditable laugh. "I'm obliged to you for coming."

"I had Robin's letter last evening." Lady Sarah smiled a tremulous smile. "By special messenger. I put the barouche to at half past nine this morning. I could have sent one of the grooms with a note last night, but I thought I ought to tell you myself."

Emily looked at her guest, seeing her for the first time. Sarah's eyes were shadowed with sleeplessness and she looked as if she had thrown her clothes on at random. Her hair escaped the summer straw bonnet in wisps.

"You're very kind, Lady Sarah. I'm grateful."

"Shall you tell the children?"

"Yes."

The two women exchanged stark glances. Sarah looked down at the shell-pink gloves she was twisting in her hands. They did not match her buttercup yellow gown.

"Sherry, ma'am." Phillida crashed through the door. The tray tilted dangerously.

"Thank you. Leave us, if you please."

Phillida did not please. She trailed out, gawking over her shoulder.

"Shall I pour?" Sarah's abused gloves slid to the floor.

"If you will be so kind," Emily said carefully. "My hands seem to be shaking."

"Here."

"Thank you." Emily swallowed a mouthful of the sweet wine and sat very still. As it began to warm her, she took another, slower sip and groped for something to say. "I—the letter . . . Sir Robert writes in very general terms. A head injury?"

"Yes, and a bad wound in the shoulder joint."

"Which arm?"

"He doesn't say."

Emily swallowed the remains of her sherry and rose to pour herself another glass. "More?"

"Please. I shall be disguised. I couldn't eat breakfast."

Emily, her energy sweeping back with a rush, rose and stalked to the bellpull. "That at least we can remedy. You'll take an early nuncheon with me, I hope. I couldn't eat either. I find myself suddenly ravenous."

Sarah rummaged in her reticule. "Oh, dear . . . I oughtn't . . . it was such a relief to hear. . . ." She took out a wispy lace handkerchief and wiped her eyes. "Yes! By all means, Emily. What a sensible woman you are. I could eat my horses. Without mustard."

Both ladies laughed immoderately at this unremarkable joke. Emily did not feel at all sensible.

When Lady Sarah had gone at last Emily made straight for her bookroom, which was dark owing to an overgrowth of ivy, and had a thorough cry. Then she marched upstairs, washed her face, changed into a cool muslin gown, and made herself break the news to Amy.

Amy and Matt were frightened, but not terrified, and Matt was unnaturally kind to Amy for several hours afterwards. He promised to let her ride Eustachio as much as she wanted for a week. Peggy McGrath, though visibly shaken, had the good sense not to screech. Tommy dumped a bowl of bread and milk on the floor.

Apprised of the news by a note which the new groom carried to Mayne Hall, Sir Henry and Aunt Fan rallied to Emily's side. It was nearly midnight before she again had time to think.

She lay in her darkened bedchamber staring dry-eyed at the flounced canopy of the bed. It was foolish to feel so light, so hopeful. That Richard Falk had been alive five days ago was no guarantee that he still lived. If only she could drop everything and go to Belgium to see for herself. What special merit had Sir Robert Wilson that he should be so privileged? And what did he know about caring for invalids? She thought of plump, good-natured Sir Robert with something approaching dislike.

Kind of Lady Sarah to bring the news herself, directly. It

almost compensated for the fact that, thanks to her meddling, Richard Falk had gone into battle with an unquiet mind. Almost.

I must write him at once. Emily sat up, galvanised. He will need to know his children are safe and well. At last, something to do. That was the worst of it, to be sitting about waiting with nothing to do. What had Sir Robert's letter said? *Still unconscious from a severe head wound.* Sighing, Emily lay back once more against the pillows. *Wait for morning. Wait.* After a long time staring at the canopy she finally drowsed off on that thought. It was going to be a long wait.

= 21 =

A FORTNIGHT AFTER he found his brother-in-law, Sir Robert Wilson sat in his ornate room in the Hôtel Bretagne in Brussels and wished himself home in Hampshire. He was writing Sarah, and his facility with the pen had deserted him. Crumpled paper littered the floor.

What was he, a sedentary man, amateur of letters, doing in Brussels that others could not have done better? The previous day Richard Falk had recognised him for the first time—and flinched.

Well, he must write. Sarah would be imagining horrors if he didn't. He drew the sheet of paper to him, dipped his newfangled steel pen in the inkwell and began again:

> *My dearest Sal,*
>
> *You will be wishing me in Hades—or home—for not writing sooner, but I have been waiting on events. I can now supply you with a fuller account of your brother's condition than I gave you in my first letter. Pray share the information with Mrs. Foster. I fear her anxiety must be nearly as great as yours.*
>
> *Richard will probably live. I have now got him a comfortable room with friends of Brotherton. [Brotherton was Wilson's man of business.] The family— they are well-regarded merchants—are most attentive. The worst of it is the head wound.*
>
> *At first I thought Richard had been blinded, for they bandaged his eyes. I am assured there is no danger of*

*that, however. Merely he had complained of the light.
He still has wretched headaches. The scar on his forehead
will be covered by his hair, and the surgeons no longer
believe his skull cracked. His memory is partially af-
fected, however, with regard to the battle. Fragments of
a musket ball and silver lace from his epaulette are still
lodged near the point of his right shoulder. Those are the
worst injuries, the rest resolving into cuts, bruises, and
slashes, ugly but not serious. He is still exceedingly ill,
my dear Sarah, which, now I have reread my catalogue
of grue, I think you will credit. He cannot be moved.
Indeed they mean to try another surgery on the shoulder
when he has gained a little strength.*

*You were quite right to make me come. The Bruxel-
lois are everything that is kind—to our wounded and to
those of the French so fortunate as to have survived three
days and nights on the field. As you may imagine,
however, the city overflows with the injured and the
medical capabilities of both military and civilian doctors
are stretched to the limits. Your brother was lucky to
have been left only one night and half a day without
attention. His servant, McGrath, accompanied the cart
which brought Richard and ten others to Brussels, and
McGrath found an artisan with an empty room to
which Richard could be taken. Otherwise he must have
lain overnight in the wretched vehicle. All this on top of
his injuries left your brother very near death.*

*He has suffered intermittently from fevers associated
with his wounds, and because of the head injury he was,
in any case, quite unconscious for six days. He has been
bled rather more often than I should myself recommend,
but then I am no physician. For long stretches of time,
he sleeps or lapses into delirium. It was only yesterday
that I could be certain he recognised me. That, indeed,
was not entirely a happy chance.*

*When I assured him repeatedly that his children were
safe he seemed easier, but I could tell that the sight of my*

inoffensive phiz gave him a jolt. My dear, I do not at all enjoy being looked upon as a Bird of Ill Omen. Nor do I like being absent from my home, my sons, and my Sally. You must consider me fixed here for at least a month, however. I have seen Richmond and Lady Frances Webster. The Duke (of Wellington, I mean) is said to be near Paris. What exciting times we live in, to be sure. I find I prefer dullness. My best love to the Boys and my dearest love to my Sarah.

Your devoted and peripatetic husband,
R. Wilson.

Wilson sanded the missive, sealed it, and set it aside for the hotel servants to post. He had not told his wife the whole truth. The second surgery was being executed as he writ. Wilson hoped he was not squeamish, but he had no intention of stopping within five streets of the sickroom until the operation should be safely done with. His man, Kennet, felt even more strongly, and indeed threatened to quit when Wilson tentatively suggested he spell the weary McGrath at night. Fortunately Madame Duvalier was less pinthearted, and she commanded her servants' unqualified obedience. At least Richard would be well-attended.

Wilson dined in solitary gloom in the now half deserted dining room of the hotel. When he had first come it had echoed with excited conversation in four or five languages, but most of the civilian employees of the various armies had gone on now toward Paris, and many of the curious had drunk their fill of sensation as well. Ordinarily a gregarious man, Wilson was glad to be alone. He needed to think. If his brother-in-law survived the second surgery, which was by no means a foregone conclusion, there was going to be a problem of another order altogether.

In his first week in Brussels, Wilson had discovered that Richard Falk was being transformed into a mythic hero. He had distinguished himself. That much the formal reports made clear. Already certain names and certain deeds had caught the imagination of the body of English—mostly curiosity-seekers, wounded soldiers, and officers' families—still in the Belgian capital. The process of telling and retelling heightened the drama of what had happened on the eighteenth of June. Sometimes, indeed, fancy replaced fact. Wilson suspected that was the case with the charge of the Union Brigade. It might also be the case with his brother-in-law, although, as with the cavalry, some fact seemed to lie behind the fiction.

Richard had been serving on General Barnes's staff as a liaison with the Dutch-Belgians, apparently because his French was fluent, the Dutch-Belgian troops were restive, and the general was desperate for experienced officers. That explained the otherwise mysterious brevet promotion to lieutenant colonel.

At Quatre Bras Richard had stayed beside the Belgian regiment's colonel, a young count, and between them they had brought the untried recruits off without dishonour. That, Wilson was given to understand, was something of an achievement. It was at Quatre Bras that Richard had taken the shoulder wound.

At Water-loo the count and a good number of his officers were killed in the cannonade that preceded Ney's first assault on the centre. The survivors of the regiment looked as if they must panick, as a young regiment of their compatriots had already done. Wilson was not sure what had transpired, but it appeared that his brother-in-law had rallied the frightened men, taken direct command of the regiment, and stayed with them, holding them firmly to their duty, until they—and he—lay in a blood-stained heap.

The story grew daily in detail and interest. Everyone, it seemed, had a stake in it—the old Peninsulars because Richard was one of them, the rest of the English because he was English, and the Belgians because, on a day in which their countrymen had been uncertain, Falk had shown that Belgians fought very well when they were led with spirit.

Considering that many of the Bruxellois had strong Bonapartist leanings—so, for that matter, had the troops—

Wilson thought it odd that they should take such obvious satisfaction in what seemed to him simple self-slaughter. *La gloire*, in his strong if unspoken opinion, was an overrated commodity. It looked as if his brother-in-law had come by rather a lot of it. Falk's name was on everyone's lips. Wilson thought the Duke of Newsham was going to like that even less than his grace liked Wilson's own officious interference with the course of nature. Wilson had received a very stiff letter from Abbeymont.

With Richard's name a byword, Wilson reflected, it was only a matter of time before some well-meaning soul pointed out that he was half brother to the Duke of Newsham and some other contributor tossed in a sentimental allusion to his motherless children, at which point God knew what mischief would be set afoot.

There was only one solution. The dowager must be brought to a sense of her obligations.

At the merchant's house next morning Wilson took in the straw spread on the cobbles and the general air of tiptoe in the foyer and his heart sank. Madame appeared almost immediately.

"How is he?" Wilson stepped resolutely inside.

"Asleep, Monsieur Huilsong, thank the good God. Such a terrible night. Jeannot is watching now."

"May I see him?"

"He will not waken for some hours, God willing."

"I'll not disturb his rest, madame. I wish merely to see for myself."

"Very well, but no noise, if you please." Her stiff black silk rustling like leaves, madame led the way upstairs.

The sickroom was shuttered and still as a tomb, except for Richard's slow breathing. Jeannot, a pert young woman in neat cap and bands, curtseyed to them silently. She had been knitting.

Wilson stood for a long time looking down at his brother-in-law. Richard lay too still. The tropic tan which had made him black as a gypsy had begun to fade to an unpleasant grey-brown, and no natural healthy colour showed even in his lips, which were bitten. By now Wilson was used to the angry scar that slashed up from the right brow. The hair was beginning to cover the shaven area. He was used to his brother-in-law's near skeletal thinness, too, but the new stillness appalled him.

Always before, even in sleep or delirium, a lively tension had informed Richard's rest. Now his hands lay as open and slack on the linen sheet as a dead beggar's. It was as if he had nothing more to ask.

Abruptly Wilson turned and strode from the room. He took polite leave of madame, but his determination must have shown, for she eyed him curiously. When he reached his small sitting room at the hotel he sat at the secretary and commenced a very long, very blunt letter to the dowager duchess of Newsham.

A week later he made a formal call on his brother-in-law. He thought of it that way. In the interim he had called every day but Falk was seldom awake. Twice Wilson found him in the grip of a low fever. There had been no grand crisis, merely days of drift. When Richard was awake he seemed disinclined to talk. Madame and the surgeon considered their patient stronger now. He could talk if he would. Wilson felt apprehensive, however. He dressed with particular care to give himself courage.

Richard lay still and unresponsive under Wilson's first gentle essay at small talk. After the third vacant pause Wilson decided to move to the point. "The sawbones consider you may be moved in a fortnight."

"Oh? Where?" Richard's tone was dull, indifferent.

"You may wish to go to Monsieur le comte, of course." The comte was elder brother to the late Belgian colonel. "I believe you know the chateau, and he is anxious to extend his hospitality."

Richard's brows drew together in a slight but definite frown.

Emboldened, Wilson went on, "He considers you saved his brother's honour, and the regiment's."

Richard did not reply.

"I wonder if you realise you have become something of a celebrity, Richard." No response. "Your authorship of Don Alfonso is an open secret, thanks to a brother officer of the Fifty-second, who is *hors de combat* and has nothing better to talk of. One Captain Browne."

Richard licked his lips. "Harry.."

Wilson drew a breath. "Monsieur le comte's wife's cousin is even now embarked on a translation, and a bookseller in the Rue Bois had fifty copies of the last novel shipped to him from London as soon as your friend spread the news. They were snapped up directly."

"Hitchins had better stump up with the royalties."

Wilson felt a vast relief. Not only conscious but recognisably Richard. He pushed on, gentle but inexorable. "Fame and fortune. Delightful, of course. Was this Captain Browne of the Fifty-second acquainted with your late wife?"

"Harry? No." There was a long frowning silence. "Oh, God, he knew of her. Everyone did."

"And of her children." Wilson rose and poured a glass of water from the carafe on the bedside table. "Please don't agitate yourself, Richard. I have some news for you and a request, but madame will throw me out if I drive you into a fever."

"The devil . . ." Richard's head turned on the pillows. "I wish I could think."

Wilson raised his head and helped him sip some of the water. Very little spilt. When Richard lay back again, staring at him, Wilson said sharply, "You are not to worry. Lie still. I wanted to be sure you would understand me."

Richard blinked. "Have I been wandering? My head . . ."

"A nasty knock. You have seemed somewhat disconnected."

The hazel eyes closed. He did not at all like the idea. "I see. How long?"

"Close on a month now. We have all been most concerned."

After a pause Richard said with some of his wonted energy, "My wits are more or less gathered. Tell me your news." From the set of his mouth it was clear he expected nothing good.

"I writ the dowager the afternoon of your second surgery. You were weak and I had begun to get the wind up. Your friend, Browne, was regaling everyone with Don Alfonso, there was already some talk of a knighthood, and my presence had been noted."

"Go on."

"I was very plain with the duchess. I don't think she'll forgive me easily. However, she has signed a witnessed statement. I have it here."

Richard's brows drew together as if he were trying to puzzle out the meaning of this.

Wilson drew the letter from his breast pocket. "I need your instructions. I can send this to your solicitor, or to Newsham's, with a covering letter. Either course seems reasonable."

"Yes." Richard's voice came out in a croak.

"There is another possibility. If you will entrust me with the statement, I shall go over to England immediately and take it to the duke myself. He is in residence at Abbeymont."

Richard closed his eyes. A very slight flush tinged his cheekbones. "I should be very much obliged to you."

Wilson sighed. "I'll do my possible, Richard. I failed you in May because I hadn't the backbone to be plain with the dowager. I don't blame you for hesitating to trust my goodwill."

"I can't very well deny your goodwill."

"Madame has had to depute a squadron of her daughters to deal with your crowd of well-wishers. If you mean to thank me for your present surroundings, you need not suffocate in gratitude."

Richard frowned.

Wilson said gently, "Shall I leave tomorrow for Abbeymont? I have no gallant reservations about being plain with Newsham. I should consider myself your deputy."

There was a long silence. Wilson thought his brother-in-law was groping for words. At last Richard said merely, "Thank you. I am obliged to you."

"Good-bye, then." Wilson executed a bow. "I'll return as soon as may be."

22

WILSON ENJOYED THE prospect of bearding Newsham. Sarah's eldest brother always made him feel an encroaching mushroom. As Wilson's family had played a prominent role in Hampshire affairs since the reign of Henry VI, that was a trifle unfair.

If Newsham had displayed some overweening talent to justify toploftiness—for tying a cravat, say, or backing Derby winners—Wilson thought he might have felt less resentment, but Newsham was chiefly gifted in pride of lineage. The duke was sarcastic but not witty. Educated at Eton and Oxford, he now read almost nothing. He was just another wealthy man who collected gold snuffboxes. Wilson considered him a dead bore.

It gave Wilson some pleasure when he reached Abbeymont to find Lord George also in residence. Accordingly, when the ladies had retired for the evening and Lord George began to gather his cronies for a night of deep basset, Wilson interrupted him.

"I wonder if you will join the duke and me, George. I've something private to say to both of you."

George, impatient, excused himself to his friends and the duke led the way to the study. When all three had been provided with sufficient snuff and brandy to sustain dialogue, the duke turned to Wilson, one brow raised.

"We understand you have been busy in Brussels, Wilson."

"Yes."

"Sarah's doing."

"Certainly Sarah's doing. My wife has excellent judgement."

Lord George was heard to utter something about the cat's paw.

Wilson said, bland, "You'll eventually have cause to learn the power of a woman, George."

"No need for lessons." George took a pinch of snuff and sneezed. "Ladybird I took in tow last spring cost me a pretty penny. Damme if Jack don't have the right idea. Leave 'em all alone. Harpies."

The duke looked bored, as well he might. "Very amusing, George, and, er, enlightening, but you intrude on Wilson's patience. Can't you see that he's pregnant with news?"

This heavy-footed reference to his girth gave Wilson sufficient starch to proceed without scruple. "What a master of metaphor you are, Duke. I can't call what I have in my budget news, precisely. It's more like last week's mutton."

Lord George guffawed. He was apt to do so without much cause.

Wilson went on, "I have here a message from the dowager designed to gladden your existence. Perhaps you'll just read it, Newsham, and I can explicate later."

"By all means." The duke reached out a hand. "Her grace has decided to kiss and make friends, eh? About time. Eight months . . ." His voice trailed off. "Upon my word." The statement was brief. It announced unequivocally that Lord Richard Ffouke, *alias* Richard Falk, was not a son of the fourth duke of Newsham.

Newsham read the note almost at a glance, reread it, and handed it to Lord George without comment.

George whistled through his teeth. "Oh, by Jove, that's something like!"

"It will stand up in a court of law, I believe." Wilson took a luxurious sip of the duke's brandy.

Lord George handed him the paper. "I say, good of you, Wilson. The old lady saw reason, eh?"

The duke was less sanguine. "Odd timing, Wilson. Why now?"

Wilson made his eyes wide. "What was the timing to do with anything? It saves you from a potentially embarrassing situation. Your half brother is no longer an obscure lieutenant buried in Portugal. Sooner or later the connexion will be generally known."

"I collect you will see to that." The duke's lip curled.

"Oh no, Duke, you mistake my motives."

"I know Sarah's sentiments well enough."

Wilson set the paper on the occasional table at his side. "Sarah's feelings are her affair. They are unchanged, of course." He picked up his drink and eyed the duke over the rim of the snifter. "What you may not yet know is that Falk has a son. Quite legitimate. A sturdy three-year-old named Thomas. There is a daughter, too, but that is less to the point. The children reside in Hampshire not twelve miles from Knowlton."

Lord George goggled. For a long moment the duke, too, was mute with surprise. "These are news indeed." He rose and stood looking at Wilson without expression.

The hair on Wilson's neck prickled, but he gave stare for stare.

The duke shrugged, finally, and went to the decanter. "Who is the fortunate mother? Some camp follower, I collect."

Wilson took a breath. "Mrs. Falk is deceased. She was the daughter of a Spanish *hidalgo*."

"A foreigner? Pah." There was a silence and the clank of glass on glass. Lord George joined his brother and poured a stiff tot. Wilson began to enjoy himself.

The duke resumed his seat. "Have you been busy in our interests, Wilson? Somehow I doubt it."

"I wonder at you, Duke." Wilson took a reflective sip. "What more can you desire? You now have assurance that neither your half brother nor anyone acting in his children's behalf can make a claim on the estate. Nor will there be any doubts concerning the succession in the case of your demise without heirs male."

"It's early days to be counting on that," the duke snapped.

"*I* have no interest in the matter."

Lord George was studying the amber depths of the brandy decanter as if his life depended on it.

The duke cast his brother a sharp glance. "No. You're altogether too disinterested, Wilson."

Sir Robert maintained his silence.

The duke slammed his glass down with controlled violence, rose again, and began pacing. "I wish I knew your reasons. You dash off to Brussels without a word to anyone and I next hear of you succouring the dowager's by-blow. That's plain enough. You—or Sarah—mean to embarrass me. And now you bring me this." He flicked immaculately kept fingers at the paper Wilson had laid on the table. "On the face of it you've done me a service."

Wilson inclined his head. "It's the dowager who has served you. I'm merely the bearer of glad tidings."

"Does your friend, the prodigal, know of this document?"

"If you mean your half brother, yes. I wonder why you can't refer to him by name."

"Major Falk, then."

"Colonel," Lord George interposed, startling both men.

"Eh?" The duke glowered at his brother.

George screwed up his face in an effort to remember. "Lieutenant colonel, Twenty-eighth Foot. Read it in the *Gazette*."

"Colonel Falk, then," the duke snapped. "Falk. Pshaw."

"It's his legal name," Wilson offered. "By deed poll."

The duke stared at him, mouth tight.

"Colonel Falk thought it would be best to bring the dowager's statement to you rather than place it with his solicitor."

Lord George's face was clouded with the unaccustomed effort of thought. "I don't see it. Chap must be mad. He could sue."

"I think not," Wilson interrupted. "Perhaps he could, but he won't. He wants nothing to do with any of you. Because of the gravity of his recent injuries, it seemed urgent that he take this step to protect his children's safety." Wilson watched both men closely as he spoke.

The duke's eyes narrowed. Lord George gaped. Wilson thought George's surprise genuine.

"That's an abominable suggestion," the duke said coldly.

"Oh, I agree. Not without some foundation in fact, however." Wilson held the duke's gaze steady.

The duke's eyes lowered. He began to pace, running a hand over his balding forehead. "If you mean my father's actions, that India business, the duel—for God's sake, that was the work of a madman."

Wilson exhaled carefully. He had had some doubts about the campaign of persecution. *A duel?* He controlled his surprise with an effort. "So you knew of that business? I wondered."

The duke was still off balance. "Not at the time, of course. M'father's man of business laid the scheme before me when the late duke died. There were expenses."

Wilson felt an icy stab of anger. "I daresay. And you decided to call off the hounds from motives of economy. Good of you."

"I don't like your tone."

Lord George said irritably, "If you're going to speak in riddles, gentlemen, I've a better use for my time."

"The duke has just made an indiscreet admission, George." Wilson took a breath, feeling his path. "Well, tit for tat. Sarah has read the letter you writ Colonel Falk when you succeeded to your father's honours, Newsham. So have I. So has the dowager."

The duke went still. "What letter? I may have spelled out a few home truths—"

"You spelled out a few threats, Duke. Very effective."

"Be plain."

"You, sir, are not a madman, but you took advantage of the probable effects of a madman's malice. For gain."

"Falk had no claim on the estate."

"The lawyers had their doubts, hadn't they? So had you."

"What the devil are you suggesting?" Lord George exploded.

Wilson turned his head. His neck was beginning to ache from craning at the two of them. "Menaces, Lord George. Menaces. That letter is with Colonel Falk's solicitor." He rose. "I wish to hear no more talk of *my* motives, my lord Duke. Look to your own."

"Do you threaten me?" A muscle by the duke's mouth jumped.

Wilson walked to the long study table and twirled the globe. "There would be no point in exposing your conduct to censure, so long as you leave your brother—I beg your pardon, your half brother—and his children, strictly alone."

"That I can promise." The duke's lip curled again.

Wilson matched his tone. "Can you? No opprobrious comments when your friends ask you about the relationship? No raised eyebrows and meaningful snickers? No nasty *bon mots* at the club?"

"My conduct among my friends is not subject to your criticism, Wilson."

"Not yet," Wilson said softly. He stabbed his finger at the globe at random, hitting Spitzbergen.

"Damme, Wilson," Lord George exploded. "It don't matter what Keighley says among his friends."

"It didn't matter."

The duke was incredulous. "Are you suggesting that my mother's bastard means to cut a figure in Society?"

"I think nothing more unlikely, if you mean the London clubs," Wilson retorted. "Colonel Falk is just now an object of considerable interest, however. He may cut a figure, as you put it, without making any effort to do so."

"Pho."

"He is to be invested with the Order of St. Lewis. There's talk of a new order of the Bath for which he would certainly be eligible. Political pressure might be exercised in his behalf."

The duke gave a short, contemptuous laugh. "By you?"

"By the Prince of Orange. Among others."

Both men stared at him.

"I think he would refuse." Wilson wished he had had greater opportunity to talk with Richard. "Unless he decides to remain with the army. As a lieutenant colonel he'll be given the choice of staying on in spite of his injuries, and he may still see that as the best means of providing for his children. I hope not."

The duke was apparently still turning Wilson's revelations over in his mind. His expression was not pleasant.

"Well, by Jove, a collateral field marshall." Lord George guffawed. "Dashed amusing thought."

"He has other choices." Wilson drifted to the glassed-in bookcase and stared at the expanse of calf-bound volumes, chaste and uncut, which decorated the wall. "Colonel Falk is a novelist of some merit. Did you know that?"

"A scribbler of romances? Good God."

"He would be better described as a satirist."

The duke stiffened.

George's transparent features reflected dawning horror. "Good God, Wilson, the scoundrel ain't going to put us in a book!"

The duke's voice grated like filed steel. "I should be obliged to stop publication of any such libel."

"Libel? Of course. Who could doubt it?" Wilson sat again in the comfortable chair, settled back, smoothed the black silk of his evening breeches.

"I can see to it that Falk never publishes another line," the duke snarled. "You may tell him so with my compliments."

"More menaces, Duke?"

The duke bit his lip.

"You must see how ill-advised you would be to follow any such course."

"It's blackmail. I'll not stand for it."

Wilson lost his temper. "I wonder who is victimising whom? There was a time when you might have come to terms with Falk at no very great cost, of money or pride. Instead you persuaded him that you meant to carry on your father's vendetta. Richard is not a fool, Duke. To the contrary. He has given you the most solemn assurance that he will make no claim on you. And you now have the duchess's statement as well. To continue your game of persecution one step farther would be a pointless exercise of malice. Richard is not now without friends."

Unexpectedly Lord George seconded Wilson. "Stands to reason, Keighley. Water-loo. Circulating libraries. Fight one, not both. Better give it up."

The duke wheeled on him. "When I require your opinion, George, I'll ask for it."

"Needn't fly into the boughs. No legal question now, thanks to m'mother's statement. Ignore the chap, there's the ticket."

"Your brother shows uncommon good sense, Newsham." Wilson was surprised. Perhaps there was more to Lord George than met the eye.

The duke took up his pacing again. "What do you want of me, Wilson?" He stopped, glaring. "I warn you I won't tolerate your damned interference in matters that don't concern you."

That was fustian and Wilson treated it with the contempt it deserved. "I want your word—in George's presence, if you please—that you'll make no further move of any kind against Richard Falk or his children. Neither directly nor indirectly."

There was a pregnant pause. "Or what?"

"Sarah will dissociate herself from you publicly." Wilson picked up his snifter, discovered it was empty, and set it down.

Lord George took the hint and poured him another.

"Sarah is not without influence in Society," her fond husband murmured. "I think you'd find ostracism uncomfortable, Duke. Your duchess and your daughters would dislike being turned away from Almack's. Your other sisters and John and George would very properly resent being dragged through a new scandal."

"By God, sir, you'll live to regret this," the duke snarled.

Wilson had been bullied at his school. The duke's manner recalled the experience. "Pray do not make threats against me, sir! Neither I nor my wife is in any way dependent upon you. We live very well without your favour," Wilson heard himself shouting.

Lord George watched, mouth agape.

Wilson tempered his tone. "I wish you will think, Duke. I should like a scandal no more than you. You're under the illusion that the word of a peer runs unquestioned. That is not so. It has never been so. Whilst your brother was an unconsidered subaltern in an unfashionable regiment posted abroad, you had the whip hand. No doubt of it. Now times have changed."

Wilson met the duke's eyes. The man was sweating. "As for Richard's illegitimacy, you have only to look at men like Beresford—Marshall of Portugal, a baron in his own right, and a Knight of the Bath. Or young Burgoyne of the Engineers, more to the point. They say he is a coming man. Indeed, duke, there is a fashion for bastards. Especially blue-blooded ones."

The duke made a contemptuous noise.

Wilson's voice hardened. "No one will question your brother's merits. Merely they will wonder why a man of such obvious gifts should have been kept so long in poverty and obscurity. You must learn to expect impertinent questions. The matter has already gone that far without Sarah's interference, or mine." He set the glass down. "If the truth should come out with the full weight of Sarah's indignation behind it . . ." He allowed his voice to trail off.

The duke and Lord George were both staring at him as at a fakir, Lord George flushed and the duke very pale. The duke's eyes glittered unpleasantly, but Wilson saw with relief that he was thinking, turning what had been said over in his mind.

The Duke of Newsham was no genius, but if his understanding was ordinary it was extraordinarily tenacious of self-preservation. He had grown up in the shadow of his mother's impropriety and his father's madness. His aversion to scandal was deep and honest. Wilson relied upon it.

Watching Newsham struggle with his pride, Wilson felt a sudden incongruous stab of pity. Almost gently he said, "George pointed out your wisest course. Ignore Colonel Falk. I'm sure he'll return the courtesy. Give me your word, Duke, and be done with it."

Rather to Wilson's surprise the duke's eyes dropped. "Very well," he muttered. "You have it."

"Sir?"

"You have my word. No action of any kind—so long as that damned scoundrel keeps his satires to himself."

Wilson shook his head. "That won't do. I trust Richard will live to write any number of novels and I hope he sticks to satire. He does it extremely well. I will engage to see that he avoids direct reflexions upon your family."

"Is that your word?"

"Yes." Wilson gave a half smile. "And I'll bridle Sarah's wrath. At least in publick."

The duke's hands clenched. "Then you have my word, Wilson. I'd esteem it a favour if you'd remove yourself from my sight."

Wilson rose and picked up the duchess's statement.

"I'll keep that." Newsham took a step toward him.

"No, I think not. I'll send a copy of it to your man of business. Whatley, is it, in the City? Good evening, George."

"Wilson," Lord George murmured.

The duke was rigid with offended dignity. He did not bow as Wilson walked out.

= 23 =

It seemed to Emily that everything was touched in gold that summer. By August there was even a golden haze in the air. The children flourished. The new groom showed himself amiable as well as observant and spent hours coaching Matt and Amy, so that they both showed creditably on Eustachio. Amy was riding astride. Emily could not like that but it was tedious for the groom to be changing saddles all the time, and besides, the example of Doña Inez weighed with her. Doña Inez always rode astride.

The children still demanded that Emily read them the old stories, most of which they knew by heart. She found it harder to do so with each repetition. It was going to be some time before Doña Inez set out on a new adventure. That much was clear from Wilson's letters to Lady Sarah.

Emily herself received a brief, formal note from Colonel Falk toward the end of July. He acknowledged her letters and instructed her to keep the groom. The handwriting was foreign, the signature nearly illegible. Nevertheless Emily felt enormous, irrational relief when she saw it. He was alive.

Wilson writ glumly. The only favourable development of the month was the dowager duchess's witnessed statement, which probably made Emily's amiable groom unnecessary. Lady Sarah showed Emily that letter with visible reluctance, nor did Emily press for detail. She had formed a low opinion of Lady Sarah's mother, compounded partly of moral aversion and mostly of exasperation. She wondered how any woman could be so careless of her children's welfare.

When Lady Sarah brought the dowager to call, joy did not gush and stars twinkle. Emily had been bottling fruit. By the time she had made herself presentable to a duchess both ladies were ensconced in the withdrawing room.

Lady Sarah rose as Emily entered. "Emily—Mrs. Foster, I wish to make you known to my mother."

"Your grace." Emily directed a grim curtsey at the seated figure.

The duchess did not rise. She was an incredibly fragile lady, at least in appearance. The hand she extended, blue-veined and marked with the freckles of age, felt like a collection of bird bones. Her hair was pure white, white as a wig, but soft-looking, and she dressed with exquisite attention to detail. Her silver-grey gown, her soft cashmere shawl, which seemed redundant for a warm day, her neat slippered feet, the lace mitts, the tiny lace cap, all said palpably, "I am an old lady now, but in my day I made the mode."

The duchess was small and small-boned and she settled back into the comfortable chair she sat in with the air of one who has always commanded homage. When she regarded Emily from bright hazel eyes and smiled gently, just wide enough to show she had kept her own teeth, white and slightly crooked, Emily found herself uttering conciliatory and welcoming phrases. The resemblance of the dowager to her son was unsettling, and Emily resented her own response.

The duchess apologised gracefully for not rising.

Lady Sarah said, nervous, "*Maman* wished to make your acquaintance, my dear Emily, and since the weather was so very fine we ordered up the barouche."

The duchess added, with a trace of malice, "Sally is trying to indicate without being quite blunt that she disapproves my impulsive behaviour." She gave Emily a straight ook from the uncanny hazel eyes. "I meant to catch you unprepared, Mrs. Foster."

With an effort, Emily infused coldness into her voice. "May one ask why, ma'am?"

The duchess flashed a mischievous smile, very much like Amy's. "I thought you might show me the door if you was warned."

Aware she had been read like a book, Emily said nothing.

Lady Sarah bit her lip. "*Maman*—"

"Hush, my dear. It is one of the few prerogatives of age to speak bluntly. I wish to meet my grandchildren, Mrs. Foster."

Emily regarded the duchess steadily. "I daresay I cannot refuse you, ma'am."

"But you would if you could," the duchess finished on a wry note reminiscent of her son.

Emily said quietly, "I would ask their father's permission. If I could."

"And you don't think it would be forthcoming."

Emily's initial anger renewed itself. "I don't know, your grace. I'm not Colonel Falk's *confidante*. We deal comfortably enough, but he is a reserved man."

"And protective of his children." The duchess made a rueful *moue*. "As I have reason to know."

Recalling the humiliation the dowager had undergone, the admission of her folly before witnesses, Emily blushed.

"Do I offend your sensibilities, Mrs. Foster?" The duchess was amused.

"My sensibilities are less to the point than your son's, ma'am. He does not trust you, or any member of your family."

"Emily!" Lady Sarah was shocked.

The duchess's amusement faded. "That is blunt indeed."

Emily kept her voice cool. "Forgive me. You've placed me in an awkward position."

The duchess gave a decisive nod. "Yes, I see that. You are a young woman of character."

"You flatter, ma'am. In the circumstances, you surely don't expect me to toad-eat you, nor do I understand why you are suddenly overcome with a yearning to see two children whose existence you didn't trouble to find out for yourself."

"That is precisely the reason." The duchess was still gentle-voiced but bright spots of colour burnt on her high cheekbones. "I was curious. Vulgarly curious."

Emily gritted her teeth.

"You disapprove me, I think."

"It's not my place to censure your conduct, your grace, but I'd dislike it very much if you were to confuse Amy and Tommy."

"Confuse?" The duchess's brows shot up.

Emily groped for the right words. "You cannot mean to acknowledge them, and they're bound to wonder why a duchess should find them interesting."

"Why should I not acknowledge them?"

Lady Sarah stared at her mother.

After a pause Emily said, "Because the duke cannot like it."

"I'm not subject to Keighley. He is a fool and a bore." For the first time she sounded like an old lady, a testy old lady.

Emily compressed her lips. "It may be that Colonel Falk would not like it."

"My son is a prude?"

"No. He may eventually tell the children of their paternal descent, ma'am. Very likely he will, but I don't think his hand should be forced." It was too much for Emily's patience, and she went on recklessly, "*They* are not bastards, your grace. Why should they be made to trouble their heads over such matters?"

A long silence ensued. The duchess watched Emily, hazel eyes unwinking. "Are they happy children?"

"I hope so," Emily snapped. "Happier than *your* children."

The duchess paled. Lady Sarah jumped up and went to her mother. "That was uncalled for."

The duchess patted her arm almost absently. "Hush, Sarah. The truth will occasionally out. Perhaps you're right, Mrs. Foster." She sighed. "I had no talent for motherhood, but rather to my surprise I find myself a tolerable grandmother. Oh, don't bother to protest, Sarah. We have never discussed my conduct as a mother, but you must know I speak the truth."

Lady Sarah subsided, but she looked troubled.

"I did not love the late duke nor, after the first years of my marriage, could I respect him," the duchess pronounced, dispassionate. "I also resented bearing his children. I've since learned to value Sally as I ought, and George, who is silly but amiable. I have some respect for John—he won't speak to me. The other girls and Keighley seem to me rather dull personages, and Keighley is capable of both malice and greed. In spite of that, I'm fond of Keighley's girls. They visit me at the Dower House. Perhaps there is something in watching a child grow and change."

Emily cleared her throat. "I believe it is so, your grace."

The duchess gave a wry smile. "I daresay you're more maternal than I by nature. If so, perhaps you'll understand why I did not allow myself to watch Richard grow up."

Emily swallowed her astonishment.

"I could have indulged such feelings toward Richard. I was fond of his father. Powys was a romanticist, but a kind man at heart and amazingly handsome. He was fair. Sally tells me neither of Richard's children is fair. A pity."

"But they are both handsome." Emily felt her resolution giving way. "Amy resembles you. Tommy will be a dark-eyed Latin type, a devil with the ladies if he troubles to exert himself."

"Lazy, is he? Powys was inclined to be lazy unless something"—she gave a wry smile—"or someone caught his interest."

Emily was in over her head and knew it. "I'd say Tommy was placid rather than lazy. Amiable."

The duchess gave a decisive nod of her head. "Like George."

Emily hesitated, embarrassed. Tommy resembled himself. "They're at play in the garden, ma'am."

The duchess frowned. "Don't weaken, Mrs. Foster. You are quite right. I ought not to confuse them."

Oppressed by a sense of *déjà vu*, Emily went on, "Perhaps not. But if you stood by the French doors in the dining room you could watch them and . . . and satisfy yourself as to their appearance and perhaps their state of mind."

"My dear, I am too shortsighted."

"Opera glasses," Lady Sarah interjected, inspired.

Emily pulled the bell for Phillida. "The very thing."

"You persuade me." The duchess had a charming laugh, like crystal bells.

Thus the duchess, leaning on her silver-headed cane, walked into the dining room and sat by the windows for a time, perhaps half an hour, watching Amy and Matt squabble under the ancient apple tree. Tommy was plucking overblown dandelions and chasing the fuzz. From time to time all three children teased the latest batch of kittens. Peggy minded them whilst she pared potatoes.

Emily could not help thinking how casual the scene must appear to ladies accustomed to ranks of nursemaids and governesses. The duchess said nothing, nor did Lady Sarah.

Her grace and Sarah took their leave quietly and Emily spent the balance of the afternoon feeling horrible guilt, but in what cause she was not certain.

She worried the strange visit over in her mind until exasperation drove her to write a letter. She was not comfortable writing Colonel Falk—by Wilson's account he was still very ill—so she writ Wilson. She also writ the duchess a long epistle describing the children's regimen and their small foibles and talents. It seemed the least she could do, but she knew it was no substitute for receiving the children's homage. Finally she wrote Tom Conway, too, but that was merely a sop to her sanity. She and Tom were innocent bystanders, after all. He would understand her feelings.

Perhaps homage was the chief satisfaction the duchess took in being a grandmother. Emily did not doubt her grace's grandchildren would pay her homage. The duchess had enough charm for ten grandmothers. A pity she had not been able to charm her own children.

Richard Falk resembled his mother, but he did not have her charm. Emily thought that was a good thing. She liked him better without it. With charm he would have been a dangerous man.

It was Sir Henry Mayne who provided the household with its first real distraction from worry. For Matt's seventh birthday Emily's father gave her son a pony, and Emily a shock.

"Well, my dear?" Sir Henry beamed at Emily and smacked his breeches-clad leg with his crop. "Well?"

They were standing in the stableyard. Sir Henry pointed the butt of his crop at Matt's gift. The spotted pony was somewhat leaner than Eustachio. Matt and Amy were already talking to it. Eustachio, brought out for comparison, watched them tolerantly.

Emily kissed her father. "Papa, how splendid."

"He's a good boy, is Matthew." Sir Henry harrumphed deep in his throat. "Made up my mind to buy him a mount when I saw how he took to Falk's gift horse."

Emily suppressed a grin. Sir Henry had thought Eustachio a "demned imposition." "Now perhaps Matt and Amy will not quarrel so much. And Amy can use the sidesaddle."

Sir Henry gave an indulgent snort. "Rides like a trooper, little minx."

"Yes, indeed, which is all very well now, but it will not be at all the thing when she is Miss Falk."

"Or Miss Ffouke."

Stunned, Emily could not immediately speak.

Sir Henry sighed. "I daresay it ain't my business, but I can put two and two together. Lady Sarah Ffouke-Wilson. The Duchess of Newsham. Young Falk is the duchess's by-blow, ain't he?"

Emily's tongue thawed. "How did you know that?"

Sir Henry's brows twitched. "Her grace's *affaire du coeur* with Powys was a great scandal the year I first sat for Mellings. Year William was born. Young whippersnapper's the right age."

Emily swallowed. "I didn't like concealing anything from you, Papa."

"Thought I'd kick up a dust." *Slap* went the crop against his dusty buckskins. "Might have, when the brats first came. Whole business smelled of fish."

"I'd have told you, dust or no dust, Papa, but I could not betray a confidence." Emily took a breath and explained as briefly as she could the events of that spring and the peril in which the children had lain. Her father grasped the legal problem directly but all the comings and goings required considerable elucidation. In the end he shook his head.

"Never could see sense in that sort of intrigue. People making life complicated for themselves. Newsham was a bully boy. Mad as a hatter. Pity Powys didn't kill him in the duel. Better all round. Well, Emma you've taken on quite a tangle. You're sure you don't want to . . . disengage?"

Emily stared. "What do you mean?"

"Give the children up," Sir Henry said without roundaboutation. "Not at once, but as soon as Falk recovers. I daresay this sister of his would see them comfortably established. Sir Robert Wilson is a man of means."

"No! I couldn't." Panick rose in Emily's throat.

"You may have to. If Falk is reconciled to his family—"

"He wants nothing to do with them."

"The more fool he," Sir Henry snapped. "Newsham is a magnate, always a power in the land, though the present duke's a lightweight. There's blood and wealth there, my dear. Even a left-handed connexion—"

"I can't believe that would weigh with Richard Falk."

"Come, come. You've seen the man thrice."

Emily shook her head. She *knew*.

"If you're fixed in your mind then there's no more to be said." Sir Henry heaved a sigh. "He writ me."

"Who?"

"Falk. Colonel now, eh?"

Emily nodded.

"Very proper. Wants to see more of his children. Asked me to find a house for him on a short lease."

"Does he mean to set up his own nursery?"

"No, no, calm yourself. Wanted a cottage in walking distance of Wellfield House. Didn't wish to compromise you. Don't like the inn at Mellings Parva."

"Oh." Emily was baffled, but pleased and relieved. "I thought Lady Sarah and Wilson meant him to come to Knowlton."

"They may. Ain't in *his* mind."

"But a cottage."

"I know. I don't like the idea either. Writ him to come to me at Mayne Hall."

Emily blinked hard. "Oh, Papa, how kind of you."

"*Hrrmph*. Not at all. Honour to have a Water-loo man under my roof. At least, that's what Fanny says."

Emily choked on a laugh. "Dear Aunt Fan. So *military*."

Sir Henry grinned. "Something in what she says."

"When doese he come?"

"Toward the end of August."

"This month?" Emily beamed. "How splendid. He must be very much improved in health. Shall I tell the children?"

"Unaccountable young man. Better wait till you know for sure. Daresay he'll write you."

That was a grievance. "I wonder he did not write me in the first place. *I* could have helped him find a house."

Sir Henry looked shocked. "Most improper. I must warn you, Emma—getting altogether too independent. Watch yourself, m'gel."

Emily let that pass. She wrote Lady Sarah the news at once, not stopping to consider the consequences.

=== 24 ===

SARAH, DISMAYED BY Emily's news, writ her husband, and Wilson, in his turn, was hurt and confused, for he had assumed his brother-in-law would come to Knowlton.

Richard's recovery was slow, but he had got past the point of danger. He could not read because of the head wound, nor write because of the shoulder injury. After three operations he was weak as a kitten, but no longer in much pain, except when one of the blinding headaches came on, and they were now infrequent. He was on the mend. Indeed he had reached that stage of itch and ennui in which his temper, never very biddable, was on a short fuse. Wilson had been tiptoeing about his brother-in-law's sensibilities for days, but Sarah's letter dispersed his caution.

"Sarah informs me you've leased a house of Sir Henry Mayne," he said without preamble as he entered the sickroom.

"Then she knows more than I," Richard said shortly. "I asked him to find me a cottage." He was lying, propped, on a chaise longue with the window open to a view of Bruxellois chimney pots, and he regarded Wilson without enthusiasm. The room was hot.

"A cottage. Upon my word, Richard, what game are you playing at? You will come to Knowlton as soon as may be, and let us hear no more of cottages."

Richard shut his eyes and did not reply.

Wilson moderated his tone from wrath to exasperated patience. "I don't understand you. There's no danger in your coming to us. I assure you, Newsham has been muzzled. The duke is still sulking at Abbeymont and don't mean to show his face in Society before Michaelmas. If it's the dowager you don't want to meet, she is taking the waters at Bath."

Richard frowned. When he spoke his voice was stiff. "I'm very much obliged to you, Wilson, and oppressively grateful, but I'm not going to sit in your pocket."

"I don't *require* gratitude," Wilson roared. "And I don't see what that has to do with your letting a cottage in Mellings Parva."

"I want to see my son and daughter."

"It's no great distance from Knowlton to Wellfield House. Or you could bring them to Sarah. They'd enliven the nursery, I daresay."

Richard gave a brief grin. "I daresay." The smile faded. "No. They're comfortable as they are."

"They wouldn't be discomfortable at Knowlton."

"Would they not?"

Wilson stopped short in his nervous pacing of the chamber and glared at his brother-in-law. "You may be justified in pursuing an intransigent attitude toward the Ffouke family, Richard, but I'm damned if I see why you won't accept *my* hospitality."

Richard gazed at the chimney pots. "Since I entered the army I've been poked, slashed, punctured, grazed, and on one occasion, blown arse over teakettle into a ditch lined with *chevaux de frise*. Nobody considered that cause for celebration. Not to mention cholera, dysentery, Guadiana fever, and yellow jack. All of a sudden I have offers of hospitality from you; from Henry Mayne, who considered his daughter had come down in the world to associate with my children; from Monsieur le comte; from madame; from Lord Dunarvon, for God's sake; and from half a dozen persons I'm not acquainted with. Am I transmogrified, I ask myself, by a mere whack on the noggin? Thank you all the same, Wilson. I prefer not to be exhibited like a two-headed calf."

"Knowlton is not Bartholomew Fair," Wilson snapped, but he felt a twinge of guilt. There would be a certain social cachet in having a Hero of Water-loo under his rooftree.

"I'm not a freak of nature."

"You're a damned perverse care-for-nobody with the manners of a—a . . ."

"A bastard," Richard supplied helpfully.

For the first time Wilson felt some sympathy for his late father-in-law.

"Oh, go away, Wilson," Richard muttered. "I'm in a foul temper."

"Evidently."

Richard took a breath. "I want to see my children. I need a place to work. Hence the cottage. I didn't think much beyond that."

Wilson was not placated, but his ears pricked at the word 'work.' "Do you mean to write another novel?"

"I have the feeling I'm about to be put on half pay by a Grateful Nation," Richard said, wry. "I daresay I'll have to write another novel. That is, if I can still lift a pen."

"I have an excellent bookroom. You're welcome to write in it."

"I doubt that I could."

That was a facer. Wilson's deepest, most cherished motive was to show Richard his book collection and enjoy a few intelligent words on the art of literature. He had even thought he might show Richard the reviews he contributed regularly to the *South Briton*. Sir Robert was diffident about his own literary talents, however. Rebuffed, he retreated into description. "I assure you my bookroom is pleasant and quiet." He cleared his throat. "I have an early edition of *The Pilgrim's Progress* I'd like to show you."

Richard flushed. "My God, I'm a hack, Wilson, not an Author. I wouldn't know how to write without interruption. Be reasonable, man. The bust of Molière would intimidate me."

"That's arrant nonsense. There is no bust of Molière."

"You're quibbling."

195

"I'll hide the engraving of Milton dictating to his daughters."

Richard gave a crack of laughter, and clutched at his head with his good hand.

That forced a reluctant smile from Wilson. "I don't see—"

"No, you don't." Richard's tone was no longer hostile. "I'm damned if I can explain. It has something to do with the circumstances under which I writ the other books. I'll have to have McGrath parade the village children through the dooryard from time to time, firing off squibs and beating on pans, to set up the proper atmosphere. Habit is a wonderful thing." He cocked a friendlier eye at his brother-in-law. "You ought to go home to Sarah, Wilson. I'm in rude health."

Wilson made an indignant noise of protest.

"Well, at least you'll allow I'm rude. Go home. I mean to be in Hampshire by the end of the month and I promise faithfully to call on you and my sister. There's no need for you to cool your heels in Brussels any longer."

"The arrangements—"

"There's nothing to arrange. When I can travel McGrath will pack my traps and we'll be off. I must go up to London, in any case."

"They can't expect you to report so soon."

"They don't. *I* mean to settle things, however. The Horse Guards will be cutting down the establishment as quick as may be. They'll be delighted to rid themselves of another line officer on any pretext."

"Then you won't make a push to stay in?"

Richard said drily, "I think I've had enough."

"I thought you might find it in your interest to remain with the army."

"I've no wish to be shipped off to India."

Wilson shuddered. "There's the Army of Occupation."

"I believe my regiment are bound for the Indies. Even if they aren't, I shouldn't like France now."

That shocked Wilson. "But Paris!"

"What pleasure could anyone take in being loathed in Paris? You can't be imagining the French will welcome us."

"They seem docile enough."

"They're relieved and exhausted. In a sixmonth they'll spit on us. When we entered the south, you know, it was different. Many of those people were Royalists. Paris is another story. I hear Bonaparte has been captured."

"Yes."

"Will he be tried?"

"Exiled, I think."

Richard was silent for a long moment. "Let's hope they find a snugger prison this time."

"Do you remember the battle, Richard?" Wilson ventured, hesitant to raise the subject.

"Bits of it, early on." Richard's mouth twisted. "I shan't strain after the missing parts. I recall Quatre Bras very well."

"They will be investing you with the French order soon."

Richard closed his eyes. It was hot in the chamber and he was sweating—had been for some time.

Wilson went to the window to seek out a breeze. "I'll stay for that. You shouldn't have refused the Bath."

"If I meant to stay on in the army I wouldn't have refused. As it is, there's no point."

"It is an honour."

" 'That I dream not of,' " Richard quoted inappropriately. "A political game, Wilson. You know that as well as I. The government mean to placate the Belgians."

There was some truth in the observation, but only some. Wilson was troubled. Because he had never understood the military frame of mind, he had listened to the harbingers of Richard's glory with baffled attention. Sir Walter Scott, it was said, wished to write a History of Water-loo. Wilson had supposed his brother-in-law to be something of a fire-eater, and it surprised him that Richard would spurn a place in Sir Walter's history. That kind of glory Wilson did understand. Very strange. Wilson turned back from the window.

"I can't convince you to convalesce at Knowlton?"

"No. But I thank you."

Wilson sighed. "Very well. I'm sorry for it. I daresay you'll do as you wish, however. I'll stay for your bout with the French court Wednesday."

"Thank you. You may prop me up."

"With pleasure. I'll write Sally to expect me in a fortnight."

Owing to a favourable wind, Sir Robert was home within ten days, and glad of it. That evening, when they were alone in Lady Sarah's withdrawing room, he sat on a satin-covered chair and faced her at last. "Well, Sal, your brother is now a *chevalier* of France. I must say he speaks the language very well."

"French governesses," Sarah said tersely. She had been disappointed not to see Richard. "We all speak good French."

Wilson hadn't thought of that. He was inclined to overlook the fact that Richard had spent his first twelve years in the late duke's household.

"Why did he not come home with you?" Sarah, intent, worried.

"He won't be fit to travel for another fortnight." Wilson evaded her eyes.

Sarah waited, tapping her foot, for his explanation.

"There was nothing to be gained from my staying on."

"You might have persuaded him to come here."

"That's out of the question."

"Why?"

Wilson sighed. "I'm not sure why, Sarah. I just know it is. I was angry with him when he first refused me."

"After all your trouble in his behalf . . ."

Wilson said, rueful, "You think he should be more grateful, is that it? I'd like to deal with Richard on an equal

198

footing some day, but I'm afraid that won't be possible whilst he feels himself obliged to me. Let be, Sally. God knows he has reason to be prickly. And now I wish to hear no more of Richard. How are you, and how are my boys?" The right questions in the right order.

— 25 —

Sir Henry Mayne was nearly as baffled by Colonel Falk's conduct as Lady Sarah when Richard wrote him a polite but firm refusal of hospitality and repeated the request for a cottage. But Sir Henry was not as military-minded as his sister Frances, and contained his disappointment with only a few grumbles, which he directed at Emily. "Ungrateful whelp" was the strongest term he uttered. Emily understood him to be reconciled to finding Colonel Falk a house.

"There's the Lodge."

Emily shook her head. "It's a five mile walk from the Lodge to Wellfield. Besides, it's too large."

"He don't want a dashed hovel."

"No, of course not, Papa. There's Aunt Maud's little house."

Sir Henry guffawed and Emily was forced to a reluctant answering smile. Her great-aunt had lived out her twilight years in a tiny ornate bandbox that still reeked of femininity.

"There is Watkins's cottage at Mellings Parva." Watkins had been Sir Henry's first bailiff and his father's before him, a venerable old man who treated the infant Emily to bull's-eyes as she walked with her nurse to the village.

"Dash it, not a gentleman's residence."

"If we were near a town I daresay Colonel Falk would let rooms. Watkins's cottage is more spacious than that, and it is in fair condition, isn't it?"

"Well . . ."

"You've not let it!" Sir Henry had been looking for a tenant for the cottage since Watkins's death the previous winter.

Sir Henry shook his head, "No, but I don't like the idea."

"Oh, Papa, times change. I daresay Colonel Falk would be perfectly content with Watkins's house. There are four rooms, the windows are large, the kitchen has a pump, and there's a proper writing desk—unless you've hauled off the furnishings."

"It's as it was in Watkins's time. Place wants a coat of lime. Tiles loose. Dash it, it's cluttered with the old man's gewgaws."

"Do you mend the tiles. I'll give it a good cleaning," Emily said firmly. "And you may take out the lumber. Watkins's cottage will do very well."

Still grumbling, Sir Henry acceded.

As August dragged on, Emily, having seen the cottage refurbished, changed the water in the vases she had confidently placed on every flat surface. Then she changed the flowers. Sir Henry received a bank draught for three months' rent, which inspired him to stump up with a load of wood and an extra bookcase. Emily aired the linen and dusted. It rained—proof positive the roof no longer leaked—and cleared off again for what would probably be the last wine of summer.

On her third flower changing expedition Emily took polishing cloths and a duster and made a thorough, critical inspection.

The kitchen-scullery–dining room of Watkins's cottage was a large low-ceilinged room made surprisingly light by two small windows and a fresh coat of lime. The gay chintz curtains Emily had hung made it cheerful. The hearth shone with scrubbing and so did the round oak table. Watkins had left an oak dresser, too, against the interior wall. In it Emily had placed such dishes and cutlery as she judged Colonel Falk might need, including three sturdy pewter mugs for the children.

Emily swept the already spotless flags briskly and took the blue bowl of marigolds from the table to the pump for fresh water. A few drops of priming and a hearty push on the handle produced a stream of artesian water. The interior pump was the one great luxury the cottage boasted— the well water was reputed to be the sweetest for several miles around.

She had emptied the vase of stale water and laid the unfaded flowers on the slate drainboard. She stood dreamily letting the water pulse over her hands. It was a warm day and the cool rush felt pleasant. Slowly the stream waned to a trickle and Emily filled her bowl. She replaced the marigolds, critically nipping off a brownish bloom with her fingers, dried the bowl and her hands on her apron, and turned.

Richard Falk was standing in the door from the passage, watching her silently. Emily clutched the bowl to her bosom and stared. It was improbable that she was seeing visions in broad daylight.

"Hullo, Mrs. Foster." His voice at least sounded familiar. "Playing the housemaid?" The remark, while not flattering, was reassuring.

Emily flushed, laughing a little, and set the bowl on the table. "Caught in the act. How do you, sir? I'm very glad to see you." She yanked the apron off and advanced to him, her hand outstretched in welcome.

He took it left-handed, which made her flush again. His right arm was still in a sling and his right coat sleeve hung empty. She ought to have thought. However, his clasp on her still damp paw was warm and quite real, and Emily's happiness overpowered her confusion. "We'd nearly given you up for this week," she confided, smiling at him. "The children have been wonderfully impatient. Did you drive from Dover? Have you come in Sir Robert's carriage? Where's McGrath?"

At her tumbling questions he smiled, too, leaving Emily breathless. "To answer you in reverse order, McGrath is at the inn with our gear. We came on the mail coach. From London."

"Good heavens."

He looked a little pale but otherwise remarkably well, Emily thought, and well turned out in a new brown coat and buckskins. And remarkably handsome, too. She was apt to forget what a handsome man he was. He wore his thick brown hair longer than usual, to hide the scar, she supposed. It served the purpose and she liked the effect much better than a proper Stanhope crop.

He noticed that they were still holding hands and disengaged gently. "Shall you show me the house? I wasn't sure I'd picked the right cottage, but there was an ominous-looking woman with a broom across the lane, so I chose this one."

"How fortunate you didn't go up to her. Mrs. Hibbert feuded with Watkins for years. She's our local witch."

He was startled into laughter, a pleasant and thoroughly distracting sound.

Emily contrived not to throw her arms around him. *Propriety, Emily, propriety.* "You've had a tiresome journey. Ought you to have walked from the inn?"

"Nothing wrong with my legs." He was still amused. "Lead on, ma'am."

She showed him Watkins's parlour, with the rosewood secretary for his writing and the settle and the chairs for the children. It was a less attractive room than the kitchen, smaller because the bedroom behind it cut off a third of the space, but the red Turkey carpet had cheered it up. She was glad she'd brought that and the bowl of daisies on the mantel.

"I daresay you'll be wanting more room for books. Papa will bring the estate carpenter down to you when you've settled in. The bedroom is rather poky. There's room above for McGrath and Peggy to have a little privacy. Do you think it will do? It's not at all far to Wellfield House. Half a mile along the lane."

"Mrs. Foster—"

"And I think you should be calling me Emily," she went on, greatly daring. Her cheeks felt hot but she made herself finish. "We've been acquainted for a long time now, Richard, and I abhor ceremony. Besides, I'll never remember to call you Colonel. I've only just got used to Major." She crashed to a stop and ventured a look at him.

His eyes were grave. "You're very kind. Emily." He let out a long breath and looked about the room. "I like the house. It's far better than anything I could have found for myself."

"I thought perhaps you'd find it too small."

"Small!" His brows shot up and he grinned, with the predictable effect on Emily's pulse. "You have an extravagant idea of my expectations. I've just spent two months in a back bedchamber with a panorama of chimney pots. This looks like Versailles."

Emily laughed. "I've saved the best for last." She led him down the narrow passageway to the back door. "You see, I knew you'd be wanting to have the children to yourself some of the time, and no cottage, however spacious, can contain such spirited children without bursting. When you writ Papa to find you a house I remembered Watkins's garden."

A bit of weeding and pruning had improved the overgrown plot out of all compass. Emily gazed about her with satisfaction. The afternoon sun showed the garden at its best. The apple trees were heavy with green fruit, the grass a trifle brown, perhaps, but tidy, just right for romping children. Sir Henry had caused his carpenter to put up a swing in the far tree, and the bench beneath the nearer one shone with new paint. Along the grey stone wall the autumn flowers, freed from choking weeds, flared in cheerful riot, yellow and orange and scarlet, a patch of delphiniums like a bit of blue sky in one corner. It was not a large garden, but it would be large enough.

She danced across the grass feeling rather like a pleased

child herself. Amy and Matt had tested the swing already and pronounced it serviceable, but Emily was glad she hadn't brought the children with her. Perhaps she should have, but for once she had not wanted their company, and she certainly did not want it now. The thought made her self-conscious again.

She turned back, wanting reassurance, to find that Richard stood in the doorway. He was watching her, frowning, perhaps because of the light. Sir Robert had said he suffered from headaches.

"Do you not like the garden?"

He walked slowly over to the bench and sat down on it. "Very much, Mrs. Foster."

"Emily," she corrected. She gave the swing a push and went to stand before him. The swing moved back and forth in shorter and shorter arcs.

In the afternoon light the marks of Richard's ordeal were plainer than they had been in the gentler light of the kitchen, and his eyes were troubled. He looked very tired. "Emily, then. I'm glad I found you here alone. The children are apt to be an impediment to rational speech."

Emily smiled. "True. What did you wish to say?"

"That I owe you an apology."

Emily stared, blank.

The headache, or frown, if that was what it was, still tugged at his brows. "You will have wondered why I didn't warn you long ago of my . . . inconvenient antecedents." He looked away.

Emily blinked. "Oh. Do you mean Lady Sarah and so on?"

"And so on," he repeated, grim. "I shan't pretend that I would have told you from the first, but I daresay I'd have got to it. I believed I'd seen the last of them, you see."

"I like Lady Sarah," Emily said feebly. "It's all over now. Isn't it?"

"I hope so."

"Sir Robert has been everything that is kind."

"Yes."

She sat gingerly at the other end of the bench and cocked her head, enquiring.

In the tree's shade his eyes were very dark. "Will you tell me something? If I'd made a clean breast of things from the first, from the time my solicitor answered your advertisement, would you have consented to take the children?"

She hesitated just too long.

He sighed and looked away. "Well, there you have my reason. Not very honourable, but I was desperate enough to be ruthless."

"I believe the Duke of Newsham did not know of their existence at the time," she offered by way of comfort.

"It didn't occur to me that he would discover them, either. My tactical blunder was Bevis. I'd forgot he's my mother's cousin, and would probably run into one or another of her children."

Emily turned that over in her mind. If Bevis were Richard's mother's cousin, then he was also Richard's cousin. She wondered if that fact had ever crossed either man's mind. "Then the encounter with Lady Sarah was almost inevitable?"

"I daresay."

Emily groped for the words to express her confused feelings. "Pray don't refine too much upon it. I've had a few anxious moments, but the children are happy and in the pink of health. That's what counts. Shall you come with me now to see them?"

He started to say something and stopped, rubbing at his forehead. "I thought . . . this evening." His hand dropped. "That is, what time do they go down for the night?"

"Tommy at half past eight and the other two at nine."

"Early."

Such hours were rather late for children. In winter they went to bed earlier. Emily suppressed a smile. Clearly Amy and Tommy would lead a strange life if, God forbid, their father took them off with him. Her amusement faded and she shivered a little. "Why don't you come to dinner? Papa and Aunt Fan are coming, and the vicar. They'd be very glad to welcome you. We dine at seven."

"I'd like to thank Sir Henry for the house." Richard hesitated, then smiled ruefully. "I confess I'd prefer not to display my famous one-handed fork trick just yet."

Emily flushed. That was the second time she'd forgot his disability. He would be thinking her remarkably insensitive. "If you'd rather not I won't press you, though I assure you no one would stare."

"I'm sure they're all far too well-bred. It's mostly vanity. I hate being so confounded clumsy." His smile faded. "If you dine at seven I can see that my coming at eight would be inconvenient to you. I'll walk up in the morning. I'd come now, but McGrath will appear at any moment bearing potions and salves and lint. If I don't cooperate he'll sit on my head."

Emily rose, reluctant to leave. "There's no need to wait till morning to see the children, Richard. Come at eight, before Tommy falls asleep. Phillida will show you up to the nursery for a nice private reunion and then, when you've seen the children, you can come down to the withdrawing room for a glass of Papa's sherry."

He demurred politely but Emily set herself to persuade him. She didn't intend to tell anyone but Phillida of his arrival. Let it be a surprise. A splendid surprise, as it had been to her.

He escorted her as far as the stile that led to the private footpath. McGrath had come with the inn porter, bearing the luggage, glowering. Peggy would have a reunion, too.

Emily walked slowly home, hugging her pleasure to herself. When she finally reached the house she hesitated to go in, for it seemed to her that her feelings must be written all over her face.

She looked in on the children's supper, mildly surprised to find them unchanged and unconscious of change. She settled a dispute between Matt and Amy, admired Tommy's expertise with the silver fork her father had given him, and catching Peggy's sharp eyes on her, escaped to make last minute arrangements for dinner.

That done, she dressed with great care in a new muslin trimmed in blue ribands. After critical inspection of her flushed cheeks, her bright blue eyes, her shining brown curls under the merest wisp of a lace cap, Emily decided that she didn't look in the least like a housemaid. What she looked was nervous.

— 26 —

The vicar, Mr. Wheeler, was coming for dinner. A fiftyish widower who instructed Matt and half a dozen other sprouts in the rudiments of Latin, Wheeler had already proposed to Emily three times, and she knew she would hear his heavy gallantries this night with special impatience. If the same florid phrases had fallen from Richard Falk's lips she would have drunk them in like a greedy shark. She wrinkled her nose at the hussy in the glass and stuck out her tongue. *Housemaid, indeed.* Laughing at herself, she went down to greet her aunt and father.

They had brought Mr. Wheeler with them, a circumstance which allowed Emily to put dinner forward a quarter hour. No one remarked the briskness of the preliminaries. Her father had spent the day making an extra crop of hay in his water meadow and declared himself sharp-set. Mr. Wheeler had no such excuse for appetite but dug in with relish anyway. Between masculine munching and Aunt Fan's detailed account of a visit with a widowed friend in Winchester, Emily had scarcely to say a word. The dining room lay at the back of the house overlooking the orchard. She had some hope that Richard's arrival might pass undetected—if Phillida had understood her instructions.

"Off your feed, Emma?"

Startled, Emily dropped her fork on the plate and met her father's disapproving gaze.

"Gel don't eat enough to keep a bird alive," Sir Henry grumbled.

"It's the heat, Henry." Aunt Fan cut a bit of sprout. "Debilitating."

How absurd they were. Emily swallowed a bubble of laughter. "Yes, indeed. If the good weather keeps on in this tiresome way I shall go into a decline. Do have one of those doves, Mr. Wheeler. Mrs. Harry is trying a new sauce and will be wanting your opinion. Wine, Papa?"

The moment passed. It was wonderful, however, what a tedious business a dinner could be. So many side dishes to be tasted and judged. So much fuss. Would Papa really insist on smelling the cork of that tolerable little hock Emily had purchased in Winchester? Would Richard's knock occur as Phillida was serving a course? Would the meal never end?

Eight o'clock whirred and bonged in the middle of the sweet, but nothing untoward happened. Perhaps Richard had suffered a relapse or just decided not to come. When Phillida brought in the savoury, however, it was obvious from the maid's air of portent—and from the way she dropped the cheese slicer and knocked over Mr. Wheeler's water glass—that Something had Occurred.

Emily mopped, apologised, and excused herself. She followed the flustered servant out into the hall.

"Has he come?"

"Oh, Mrs. Foster! Through the kitchen, and Mr. Mc-Grath with him. Didn't Mrs. Harry give a shriek." Phillida giggled. "I showed 'un up to nursery. Such a to-do as I never heard. Mrs. McGrath fair had the vapours."

"Hush, Phillida. Let us finish this meal in decent order. Try not to pour the coffee over Sir Henry." Emily returned to the dining room, suppressing her excitement as best she could.

"Clumsy wench, that Phillida," Sir Henry growled. "I wonder you put up with her, Emily."

Mr. Wheeler had leapt to hold Emily's chair. "But Mrs.

Foster's soft heart must prevent her turning off so faithful a servant, Sir Henry."

Emily bit back a snicker and slipped into her place. *Old softhearted Emily.*

"What's happening, Emily?" Aunt Fan, alive as usual upon all suits. "Out with it, gel."

Emily gave up. "Oh, it's just Colonel Falk."

Under their startled gaze her false insouciance deserted her. She gave Aunt Fan an apologetic glance, adding, "He came this afternoon. On the mail coach. Phillida has just taken him up to see the children."

Sir Henry exploded. "Upon my word! Have you no manners, Emma? Didn't you ask the poor devil to dine?"

Emily soothed and explained, and restrained her relations from trooping up to the schoolroom at once. Mr. Wheeler was struck dumb. He kept looking from one to another with the air of a bewildered horse. Sir Henry grumbled. Aunt Fan exclaimed. Emily began to enjoy the sensation of controlling events.

When she and her aunt retired to the withdrawing room, however, she found herself trembling a little. Aunt Fan gave her one piercing look and made her sit on the small sopha. "What's wrong?"

"Oh, aunt, nothing at all. He—Colonel Falk—surprised me, of course. He likes the house."

Aunt Fan snorted. "What's that to the point? How *is* he?"

Emily gathered her wits. "Tired from the journey, I think, but otherwise well enough. He told me I looked like a housemaid."

Aunt Fan gave her a queer look but for once did not pursue the subject.

Presently Sir Henry and Mr. Wheeler joined the ladies, and in the fullness of time Richard entered. He looked a trifle rumpled, as if he had been climbed over by small enthusiastic persons.

"How are the children?" Emily smiled at him.

"Beautiful."

Emily laughed. "I know that. Were they glad to see you?"

"I think so." He didn't look as if he had serious doubts. His eyes were bright. "They will be pestering you to bring them to me tomorrow. To carry off their Belgian loot, greedy little beasts. I wonder what they'd expect if I went to India?"

"You're not . . ." Horrible phantasies assailed Emily's mind. Sir Robert Wilson had promised that his brother-in-law would retire.

"Lord, no," Richard said hastily. "I'm out of it now, thank God. That's what kept me so long in London."

Emily meant to be absolutely sure. "You've retired?"

"Yes. As of the end of the month. Sir Henry." He turned to Emily's father who had stood listening to this little exchange with indulgent twitches of the eyebrows. "How do you, sir? I have to thank you for your good offices. The cottage is precisely what I want."

Sir Henry was heard to rumble a few doubts. He still thought a cottage a paltry dwelling for a gentleman and he made that clear, but Emily could tell that he was not displeased to see his tenant. Richard also said all the right things to Aunt Fan, whose delight in the meeting was betrayed largely by the gruffness of her exclamations and the way her back hair began to fall down. Aunt introduced Richard to Mr. Wheeler. Emily had half forgot the vicar's existence. *Rag-manners*, she told herself, vexed to have forgot so elementary a courtesy.

The company settled in with an air of spurious cosiness. Richard sat on Sir Henry's right hand, for Emily's father was going a little deaf in the left ear, Aunt Fan, aburst with questions, on Richard's right, and Mr. Wheeler, with the faint discomfortable look of one who finds himself intruding on a family reunion, on the sopha next to Emily. In good time every one was provided a glass of sherry, for Sir Henry did not believe in ladies drinking eyewash like ratafia.

Conversation rambled. The weather, everyone agreed, was the best in years, perfect for campaigning (Aunt Fan) and haymaking (Sir Henry). Hay led Sir Henry to horses and thence to Amy's equestrian prowess. Richard received Sir Henry's moving tribute to his daughter—"Good bottom, young Amy, steady hands, always throws her heart over a jump"—with the merest hint of a grin. He turned the conversation neatly from Amy to Matt with a question for Mr. Wheeler about Matt's Latin verbs (how had he found out about Matt's verbs, Emily wondered, bemused), and Mr. Wheeler spoke at length on the defects of modern education. A perfectly safe topic. Sir Henry's eyes glazed, Richard listened, Aunt tapped her foot. Mr. Wheeler worked his way gradually from Caesar to grouse shooting.

At the word *grouse* Sir Henry woke up and contributed a comment on Squire Talbert's coverts. That produced a little mild controversy to which Richard did not contribute. Sir Henry was in a tactful mood, however, and before Emily reached the screaming point he turned the question kindly to the state of Richard's health, and thence, after only a few cluckings about the inconvenience of one-handed existence, which Richard bore with resigned composure, to a chance recollection of Chelsea Hospital, Rane-lagh, and a set piece on the horrors of London in August.

That was too much for Aunt Fan's patience. She cut off Sir Henry's monologue with a single well-chosen phrase and plunged at once without transition into a series of questions about Water-loo, which somehow, as with most of Aunt's military conversations, turned into a lecture. Emily's heart sank.

In truth her aunt's expertise, which was genuine and based on passionately thorough reading and reflexion, embarrassed Emily, and she was ashamed of her shame. Why shouldn't Frances Mayne study military history if she found it interesting? It was not a very shocking eccentricity, surely. If only her aunt were not so intense. If only Aunt Fan's intensity did not render her vulnerable.

Emily listened to a masterful analysis of the charge of the Union Brigade with the pious but not very strong hope that Richard would restrain his satirical impulses. To her relief and surprise he listened politely enough and in one of Aunt's infrequent pauses for breath allowed that he wasn't a cavalryman.

"It's Bevis's opinion you should be seeking, ma'am. He was on General Picton's staff."

Aunt's eyes shone. "I had forgot that. Lord Bevis, eh? I've met him."

"Shall I give you his direction? I believe he is fixed in Paris with the occupation forces."

Aunt demurred. His lordship would be far too busy— she could not presume on so brief an acquaintance. And so on.

Richard's mouth gave a slight betraying twitch at the corners, but he said gravely, "I'm sure Bevis would be flattered to hear from you, Miss Mayne. He is not at all high in the instep, you know, and he remembers you very clearly. I think you ought to write him at once."

"Well then, I shall." There was a whiff of defiance in Aunt's voice, but Richard still did not smile.

He was, Emily concluded, far too pleased with the unsought opportunity to wreak vengeance on Bevis. She turned a laugh to a cough in the nick of time.

"This business of the Imperial Guard, now," Aunt went on, relentless. "What think you, sir?"

"Frances," said Sir Henry. "That is quite enough."

Emily gave her father a glance which she hoped expressed her heartfelt gratitude, but he was not looking at her. Indeed, he had been watching his sister and Richard from beneath twitching brows for some time. Now he rose.

"Time to be going home. Thank you, my dear." This to Emily. "An excellent dinner, as usual. Wheeler!"

Mr. Wheeler started and blinked. He had, all unnoticed, fallen asleep. *How he could*, Emily thought, indignant. Then justice compelled her to admit to herself that an outsider must have missed the tensions that had kept her on edge throughout Aunt Fan's military excursion.

"Time to go," Sir Henry repeated, authoritative. "Colonel Falk, I have my carriage and mean to drive Mr. Wheeler to the vicarage. Shall you ride with us?"

Richard had, perforce, risen when Sir Henry did. He accepted Sir Henry's offer. Emily thought he was relieved not to have to walk the half mile to Watkins's cottage. He looked very tired. She hoped Aunt Fan might not cross-examine him all the way home, but her hope was dim.

Richard thanked Emily quietly and said good night. Mr. Wheeler was rather more fulsome with less cause. Aunt Fan looked pleased with herself and only slightly guilty.

Emily stood at the door as her guests descended to the waiting carriage. Her father was the last to leave. As he bent to kiss her, Emily murmured, "Thank you, Papa."

"That young man should be on his sickbed. Estimable woman, m'sister. Sometimes wants good sense. Good night, my dear. You have a lively time ahead of you."

27

"DOWN, PAPA. WANT down."

Richard lifted his son from the paddock gate one-handed and set the little boy on the grass. Tommy was bored with pony watching. He wandered a few steps down the lane in search of dandelions.

In the paddock the redundant groom, who was soon to be absorbed into Sir Henry's stables, was giving Matt and Amy a last schooling on their ponies. Amy sat the sidesaddle with reluctance. Matt was showing off.

"He'll break his neck," Emily murmured.

"Not likely." Richard leaned on the gate.

They watched the young riders for a while in companionable silence. Emily had spent most of the day in Winchester with her aunt. The entire time they were in town she kept imagining she would return to find Richard gone, yet here he was, relaxed and sunburnt, leaning on the paddock gate as if his continued presence were in no way remarkable. He had been "home" nearly a week.

Nothing untoward happened in the paddock. Amy took three low jumps. Matt kept his heels in. Tommy ate a dandelion and decided he didn't care for the taste. It was all wonderfully routine. Presently Richard made his farewells and doubled back in the direction of Watkins's cottage.

Emily had resolved to keep her courtship at a low key. She told herself she didn't want to frighten Richard off, and indeed she did not wish to distract him from his pleasure in the children's company, which was unequivocal and warmly returned. Amy and Matt would cheerfully have camped in Watkins's cottage with him.

A pattern had already developed. Every day Emily brought Amy and Tommy in the gig as far as the cottage. They were met at the gate by Matt, who had morning lessons with Mr. Wheeler in the vicarage. Then they all took tea together in the cottage kitchen, the pewter mugs dripping sweet tea that was mostly milk on the oak table and the children chattering and gobbling bread and butter. Afterwards Emily would go on about her daily rounds alone. In an hour and a half or two hours she would return to find the children ashriek by the swing or sprawled on the Turkey carpet as Richard concocted a story for them, or seated at the round oak table in the kitchen in a marathon of spillikins.

Richard was very bad at left-handed spillikins. The children thought that hilarious. They were unselfconscious with him, even Matt, who was a little inclined to self-importance. Tommy took to his father without the coy shyness that sometimes afflicted him with strangers. Amy and Matt didn't spare Richard their squabbles, but they seemed to quarrel less at the cottage. The novelty had not yet worn off.

After their games Emily would load the reluctant children into the gig and take them home for a nuncheon and a nap. Later, when the weather permitted—and it was surprisingly pleasant most of the time—Amy and Matt would ride in the paddock and Richard would stroll over from the cottage to watch them. A natural routine. Almost they were turning into a family. Emily was afraid something would break the spell.

There was one fly in her ointment. Richard would not dine at Wellfield House. He declined her invitations with fair grace, but Emily was secretly hurt, especially when he did agree to dine with Sir Henry, Aunt Fan, and Emily at Mayne Hall. She complained to Aunt Fan when the ladies had withdrawn.

"He's probably heard the talk."

"What talk?"

Aunt Fan pursed her lips. "People gossip, Emma. So far no one is indulging phantasies, but you'll have to be circumspect. If Colonel Falk were to dine with you every night, or even several times a week, you could kiss farewell to your character."

Emily's cheeks burnt. "What a pleasure it is to live in a civilised society."

"My dear, that's the way of the world. I'd be cautious with your mother-in-law, if I were you. She has a malicious tongue, and she has never approved Amy and Tommy."

Emily bit her lip. Aunt Fan was right. The elder Mrs. Foster and Emily had maintained an armed truce for years, and the woman was a born gossip. "I mean to marry Richard, Aunt."

"Yes, I know," Aunt Fan said calmly.

Emily stared, resentment churning in her bosom. So much for concealment. So earthshaking an announcement ought to provoke at least a mild exclamation.

"You are going about it with a fair degree of finesse." Aunt pulled out her workbasket and took up a shift she was stitching for one of the cottagers' wives. "Don't rush your fences."

Emily fairly drowned in a wave of astonishment. "You approve?"

Aunt Fan threaded the needle. "From a worldly viewpoint it is not a good match."

Emily made an impatient noise.

Aunt smiled and bit off her thread. "I should not let worldly motives govern my judgement if I were you. He is an estimable man."

Emily sighed. "And Matt likes him."

Aunt's eyes twinkled. "That is certainly a consideration."

Emily felt her mouth twitch in an answering smile. "I won't rush my fences, Aunt Fan, but to tell you the truth

I'm impatient. Perhaps I *should* invite Richard to dinner every night."

Aunt Fan set a row of neat stitches. "Unwise, Emma. He might feel constrained to offer. Then you'd always be wondering—"

"Whether he made his offer freely. I was joking, Aunt." Emily heaved a sigh. "It astonishes me when I consider that Richard and I have spent a grand total of twelve days in one another's company—and we have known each other nearly three years. I do know him. I fell in love with his letters."

Aunt gave a sympathetic cluck.

"Do you know how he spends his time?"

"With the brats."

Emily shifted on the chair. "The rest of his time."

"How?"

"Practicing great *O*s with his left hand like a schoolboy. Amy and Matt find it mightily amusing." Emily sniffled.

Aunt Fan set her sewing aside and handed Emily a square of lawn embroidered in scallops. "Pull yourself together, my dear. Don't want to alarm Henry."

Emily blew her nose and pulled herself more or less together. It was one thing for Aunt Fan to guess her feelings, but quite another to betray her feelings to her father. He might accept Richard as a tenant and even grudgingly allow him some rights as Amy's father, but Emily knew very well that Sir Henry would kick up a dust at the prospect of his daughter wedding an unemployed army officer, even one with a pension. And though he had shown surprising complaisance about Richard's irregular connexion with the Duchess of Newsham, Emily did not for one moment suppose Mayne of Mayne Hall would embrace any bastard eagerly as a son-in-law.

Sir Henry and Richard left their port early, and Sir Henry appeared to have been well entertained. Emily gave Richard a ride home in her gig. He did not propose marriage, but he joked with her in his wry way, very much at his ease. Emily had perforce to be content with that, though she began to wonder if her tactics were right after all.

By and large, however, she was content with the routine of her courtship. The intrusion next day of Sir Robert and Lady Sarah into the children's morning tea ruffled her more than it ought. Sir Robert was expansive, even jocular, but Lady Sarah, though she made no criticism, was plainly appalled by Watkins's cottage. They did not stay very long. Richard saw them off and returned to the kitchen whistling perversely through his teeth.

Tommy had finished his milk and demanded a last push on the swing before he consented to go, so Richard took him into the garden.

"We didn't have our story," Matt grumbled through a mouthful of crumbs. He, too, disapproved the intrusion.

"Not with your mouth full," Emily corrected automatically.

"Why did Lady Sarah call on Papa?" Amy wiped away her milk moustache fastidiously. She still was not overfond of milk. "I thinked—*thought* she was *your* friend, Mama Em."

"She knew your father a long time ago, remember?" Emily felt her tongue tangle with hypocrisy and stopped and started over. "Sir Robert Wilson was very helpful to your papa when he was hurt in Belgium. I think they wished to assure themselves that Colonel Falk is well."

Amy was bored. "May I get down, please?"

Emily nodded.

"Me, too?" Matt swiped at his face and scrambled from his chair, but Amy dashed ahead of him out of the back door and into the sunlit garden.

"Me, too, Papa!" she shrieked.

"Me, too!" Matt crashed after her.

Emily remained. She stared at the crumb-bedecked table so long Peggy McGrath had to ask her twice if anything was wrong, but of course not. Everything was splendid.

Two days later McGrath walked up to Wellfield House

with a note from Richard, who had ridden over to Knowlton and would not be back in time for the afternoon riding exercise. Apologies. No explanation. He owed his sister a return call, but the break in their pleasant routine struck Emily as ominous.

28

"RICHARD! A PLEASANT surprise. Come in, come in." Sir Robert greeted him cheerfully.

His brother-in-law entered the bookroom dusty from his ride and unsmiling.

"Ought you to have ridden this far so soon?" Wilson's outstretched hand dropped. Something was wrong. "I could have sent the carriage for you, you know. Sarah will be glad to see you again, and the duchess has just come as well." He heard himself chattering and broke off.

"Timely." Richard took a paper from the breast pocket of his riding coat. "This came in the post, sir. I wish you to read it."

Sir? Bewildered, Wilson took the sheet of paper and read the clear, clerkly hand through twice. "I don't see . . . Whatley is Newsham's man of business."

"So I surmised."

"I don't understand," Wilson repeated.

"Don't understand what?"

Wilson was still blank with incomprehension. "The duke's reasons."

Richard gave a short, ugly laugh. "Does he need reasons? What do you suggest I do?"

Wilson gathered his wits. "I didn't foresee . . . that is—"

"He's offering me a bribe to leave the country."

"I daresay it can be construed that way." Wilson glanced at the letter once more.

"How else can I construe it?"

"As a settlement."

"I don't require a settlement of Newsham." Richard's voice was cold with fury. "I require to be left in peace. And I do not choose to take my children to North America."

Wilson drew a breath. "Now, don't be hasty."

"Thank you." Richard took the letter from him. "I can see the sort of advice I may expect from you. Good day, Wilson."

"Why must you leap to conclusions?" Wilson fairly shouted. "By God, you try me too far. Give me the blasted letter."

"There's no point."

"The letter, if you please." He held out his hand.

After a moment Richard shrugged and gave it back. He stalked over to the nearest window to glower down at the formal garden.

Wilson reread the letter. It was couched in language as formal as the garden. "It may be that Newsham has come to feel he *owes* you a settlement," he murmured, thinking aloud. "This could be taken as proof . . ."

Richard whirled, eyes blazing. The right sleeve of his coat flopped. "What would it take to convince the lot of you that I want nothing at all to do with the Ffouke family? Nothing means *nothing*."

Wilson felt his own temper rise again. "Do you include Sarah in your ban?"

"It was Lady Sarah who called my children to Newsham's attention—"

"That's not true—"

"And to the dowager's attention," Richard snapped. "Is there a difference? I don't question Sarah's motives, just her judgement."

"You're mad with suspicion, Richard. It poisons *your* judgement."

Richard stared at him for a long time. "Give me the letter, then, and I'll take my suspicions elsewhere." He held out his good hand. After a pause Wilson returned the letter.

223

He felt absurd, as if they had been passing schoolboy messages back and forth. Richard's mouth set in a hard line. He smoothed the letter and shoved it into his jacket.

"Richard, my dear!" Sarah, in the doorway.

Both men turned to her.

"Sally," Wilson began, warning.

Richard executed an exaggerated bow, sleeve flopping again. "Lady Sarah. I was just leaving."

Sarah flinched and cast Wilson a beseeching glance. He was suddenly very angry indeed. He contrived to keep his voice low, however. "Go back to the withdrawing room, Sally. I'll be with you directly."

"But *Maman* . . ." She looked from one to the other. Sarah was not slow-witted. "Very well. If it's Newsham again, Richard, I think you ought to acquaint *Maman* with the matter. In any case, you owe her some degree of civility. I'll tell her you're here." She left, her shoulders stiff with hurt dignity.

Wilson found he was trembling. All the pent-up resentment he had suppressed, all the exasperation of a bystander caught up in someone else's quarrel, possessed him. "I've had enough of your rag-manners and more than enough of your melodrama, Richard. By *God*, I have. Newsham has made you an offer. In a mean-minded, left-handed way, it might even be construed as generous, though I can see no reason why you should accept it. Decline, politely if possible, and put it out of your mind. That is my advice to you. Now, if you please, I'll accept your apology."

"I apologise for coming." Richard's tone was not conciliatory.

Wilson was not a quarrelsome man by nature. He was beginning to regret his own hot words. 'Left-handed' was not well chosen, nor 'melodrama.' He shook his head and went over to the table which bore the sherry tray. He poured a glass. "Sherry?"

"No."

"Then you'll have to pardon me. I need a soothing draught before we face the ladies." He took a careful sip.

'Ah. I beg your pardon if I used intemperate language, Richard. I think your apprehensions ill-founded, but I don't mean to dismiss them out of hand. Shall I ask Newsham to explain himself? I daresay he is still at Abbeymont, but I could write him."

"That won't be necessary. I'll follow your advice and write Whatley a fulsome letter declining the offer."

Stung, Wilson set his glass down. "I said nothing of fulsome letters."

"I beg your pardon. A civil letter."

Wilson mistrusted that. It was too carefully emotionless. But he did not wish to provoke further hostilities, and said, conscious that he sounded pompous, "I believe it to be the wisest course. If there are consequences, I trust you'll tell me so at once."

Richard did not reply.

"Well, well, we shall see." Wilson cleared his throat. "What do you hear from your publisher?"

"The galleys should be ready in a fortnight or so."

"Splendid. I'm looking forward to reading the book. By the by, I see from the *Times* that your friend, Major Conway, has succeeded to the earldom of Clanross. I had no idea he stood in the line of succession."

"What!" Richard was startled out of his impassive pose. He took a half step toward Wilson, frowning deeply.

"Did you not know?" Wilson indulged in another, soothing swallow of sherry. "It has set the Ton by the ears. Lord Clanross drowned on Lake Lucerne a fortnight ago, according to the *Times*. He had eight daughters. Your friend was the next male heir."

"My God."

Wilson set his glass down again. "You don't sound pleased."

Richard said flatly, "Tom is dying. He doesn't need to waste the time he has left haggling with lawyers."

Wilson was taken aback. "I'm sorry. A war injury, I collect."

Visibly distressed, Richard nodded without speaking.

"I'm sorry," Wilson repeated. "How easy it is to misread another man's fortune. I daresay Conway will be envied by the ignorant."

Richard rubbed his forehead. "I daresay."

Wilson rose. "Well, well, that is by the way. The ladies await us. Come and make your bow to the dowager, and, Richard . . ."

Richard looked at him, eyes dark.

"Try not to be too insulting. Your mother has already spiked Newsham's guns for you once. Best keep on her good side."

Richard's mouth was tight but he said nothing.

Wilson sighed, and led the way to the withdrawing room.

Wilson watched his mother-in-law. The dowager duchess had at all times a great deal of charm, and she now made a desultory attempt to exercise it on her son. On any other occasion, Wilson would have found her failure amusing, but Richard's blank indifference made Sir Robert extremely uncomfortable and distressed Sarah. The dowager did not reveal his feelings. She rarely did.

Neither mother nor son had seen one another in twenty years. To all appearances the reunion was as affecting as the presentation of a minor consul at a minor court. Sarah looked bewildered and unhappy, the duchess, after the first show of animation, cool. Richard addressed his mother as "your grace," and left after a mere quarter of an hour without mentioning Newsham's letter.

Wilson went out with him and waited whilst the groom retrieved Richard's horse. Both men stood silent.

"The dowager stops with us another fortnight," Wilson ventured when the silence began to pall.

"What? Ah, lucky for you. I say, Wilson, did the *Times* happen to mention where Tom was? Tom Conway," he added, impatient, when Wilson betrayed incomprehension. "The Earl of Clanross . . . Of all the stupid, unnecessary accidents. I daresay he can't refuse an earldom."

Wilson stared. He might have known better than to expect effusions of filial sentiment from his brother-in-law. The poor duchess. She did not perhaps deserve a great deal of this son, but she deserved something more than absolute indifference.

Wilson almost voiced his indignation, but at that point his groom led Richard's nag to the mounting block, and Wilson, taking a close look at the spavined beast, burst out, "Where in the devil did you find that?"

"Hired it. You cannot expect me to keep stables."

"But Mrs. Foster—"

"I'm not living with Mrs. Foster," Richard snarled.

"I didn't mean to imply . . ." Wilson took a breath. "You have a genius for forcing the worst possible construction on people's words. I meant, as you very well know, that you could hire a loose box from Mrs. Foster. You'll be requiring a horse. Indeed, I'd be glad to mount you. You can ride one of my hacks until you have time to buy your own."

"No." Richard swung into the saddle and adjusted the reins one-handed. "Thank you."

His sympathies thoroughly alienated, Wilson turned and stomped back into the house. Enough was enough.

But not quite.

Three weeks later Wilson, at Sarah's urging, drove over to Mellings Parva to make his peace. He found Richard gone. The cottage was locked and the grass overgrown. At Wellfield House he discovered that Mrs. Foster, her son, Richard's children, and their personal servants had also vanished. The housekeeper eyed him curiously. No, she couldn't say where they'd gone or how long they'd be away. Visiting Mrs. Foster's kin, likely. She couldn't say for sure. They'd left in an almighty hurry, certainly.

Wilson felt the stirrings of panic. Visions of forcible abduction, even murder, flashed before his mind's eye. He was not a prey to melodramatic suspicions, however, and he soon assured himself that Mrs. Foster and the children had departed in Sir Henry Mayne's carriage accompanied by Miss Mayne. Colonel Falk, it appeared, had left earlier, separately, for London. A perfectly ordinary set of circumstances. No need to worry.

Wilson told himself that half the way to Knowlton, and the rest of the way home, having granted the unlikelihood of the coincidence, worked himself into a fury with Richard. "Mark my words, your brother has inveigled that innocent lady into an unnecessary flight."

Sarah was white as curds. "Newsham."

"Newsham has nothing to do with it. They left in Mrs. Foster's father's carriage. No, my dear, they have not been abducted—unless your dear brother Richard has abducted them. He's mad as a March hare. Ought to be clapped into Bedlam."

"Where have they gone?"

"I don't know and I don't care. Richard," Wilson pronounced, "may go to the devil, with my blessing."

"I shall drive over to see Sir Henry Mayne."

"Oh no, my dear, you'll do no such thing. Nor will you go running to your mother with this fairy tale. We shall both stay out of your brother's affairs from now on."

At that Sarah flew into the boughs and they had a terrible quarrel, their first serious brangle in seven years of marriage. It left them frightened and spent. They clung to one another, appalled by the storm of fury, and repentant, both of them.

Part V
Tom Conway, Emily, Sir Robert Wilson
1815

=== 29 ===

My dear Tom,

I have just come from my brother-in-law Wilson, who tells me Lord Clanross is dead and you have succeeded. It sickens me that you should be dealt such a blow. Fate governs with a malign sense of humour, and nowhere more clearly than in this instance. I am sorry, Tom. If I can be of any use to you at all, pray command me.

Your servant, as always,
R.F.

P.S. This is probably my last right-handed scrawl. In future I shall be thoroughly and finally sinister.
Richard.

Tom Conway, tenth earl of Clanross, Viscount Brecon, Baron Breccan of Breccan, set the letter on his cluttered desk and walked slowly over to the narrow window of his makeshift study. The window overlooked the single pinched street of the Lancashire village in which he had now lived for more than a year. It was evening and the cottage windows flickered with friendly light. The village was not a beautiful place but Tom had begun to feel at home in it.

He had deciphered Richard's scrawl with difficulty. Now, staring into the dusk, Tom thought of the other letters he had received in the days since he had learned of his elevation to his cousin's lands and dignities.

Some of his friends had expressed conventional condolences. He didn't resent that, though it was mildly comic. Tom had disliked what he knew of Lord Clanross, had loathed being patronised by his wealthy kinsman, and had never met any of the Conway family. He felt no personal sense of loss at all.

Other friends had been gleeful—what a honeyfall! That was more realistic and as such more painful. Tom admitted to himself that in other circumstances he would have felt some pleasure in falling heir to one of the great estates. An unlimited income was any penniless subaltern's dream. But he was no longer a penniless subaltern, and he did not at all like the notion of being translated to the House of Lords.

As Tom watched, a black cat, tail erect, stalked into and out of the light from his window. *Seven years' bad luck, or is that mirrors?* He did not have seven years. That was what turned everything to ashes. Worse, he knew his engrained sense of duty would compel him to deal carefully with the legal difficulties attendant upon so unexpected an inheritance, and his conscience would compel him to see to the well-being of Lord Clanross's family and dependents. All that would take time, and he did not have time.

Two months before, he had suffered another surgery. The attacks were now more frequent, the pain barely manageable. What Tom chiefly felt was a vast dull resentment that he could not, in the brief time left to him, continue the absorbing work he had found. If his absorption was dogged, at least it was genuine, something more than mere distraction. Something productive. Richard had been right in that, as his letter was also right, a feat of pure imagination.

" 'Ere, Major—beg pardon, I'm sure. 'Ere, me lord. Wot about the lamp?" Sims brisked in, huge and blessedly unimaginative.

"Yes, light it." Tom smiled at his man. "I've had a letter from Richard Falk."

Sims was unimpressed. "Scribbling away again, is 'e?

Good luck to 'im." He trimmed the wick and lit the lamp with a spill from the fire.

"He's not doing very well, if his handwriting's a symptom. It's barely legible."

Sims snorted. " 'E should 'ire a sectary. Plump in the pocket now, ain't 'e. Colonel and all. *Chevalier* of France. Pah." The back of Sims's neck expressed his disdain of French orders.

"He's been pensioned."

"Chelsea ticket?"

"Yes."

"Humph. Was you 'ungry, me lord?"

"Confound you, no."

Sims looked injured. "I 'ave to get used to the ruddy title, 'aven't I then? Me lord."

"Don't be difficult. We're going to London."

Sims turned from the fire which he had been poking. "It's too bloody soon, Major. That last attack . . ."

Tom said wryly, "Or too bloody late. No time is a good time."

Sims scowled but forbore to protest further. When he left the room Tom returned to the desk and took up his friend's letter once more. "Sinister." Tom smiled. *Idiot*. He took out a sheet of paper and began to write.

Less than a week later he was lying more or less in state in his new *pied-à-terre*, a set of fusty rooms in St. James's Place that had once belonged to the late earl's deceased brother. It had only taken two days to reach London and two more to reach the high pitch of recuperation he now enjoyed. He regarded the ornamented ceiling and listened to Lord Bevis's account of their friends with the occupation forces in France and decided he wasn't dished yet. "I beg your pardon, Bevis."

"Expecting callers?" Bevis's head cocked.

Tom listened to the noise in the hallway. "Richard Falk, I think. I writ him I was coming to Town." He turned his head to look at Bevis, who was grimacing.

"Falk? I'm leaving."

Tom contented himself with a small grin. Richard had torn strips from Bevis's hide in their last encounter, or so Bevis insisted.

Richard's voice could now be heard. Bevis rose. "Shall I pop in tonight on my way to White's?"

"If you like."

Sims stuck his head in at the door. "Colonel Falk to see you, me lord."

"Tell him to come in, and don't lordship me to death." Tom craned his head gingerly.

When he entered, Richard noticed Bevis's presence first. *Richard always looks as if someone might jump him from behind*, Tom reflected, holding out his hand. "I'm under orders to be still, so I won't rise. It's good of you to come, Richard. I hope you didn't make a special journey."

"No. Had to see my publisher." Richard shook hands awkwardly, left-handed. His right reposed in a black silk sling. Tom had not seen his friend since Rye, two years before, and he looked Richard over narrowly.

The brown coat was better cut than the obnoxious French jacket that had offended Tom in their last encounter, and Richard wore his hair longer. The reason for that became apparent as he turned to greet Bevis. The scar of the head wound, jagged and new enough to show purple, scored the left side of his brow. A wing of thick brown hair covered it when you faced him straight on. Sidewise it was just visible. Richard looked about ten years older than Tom remembered, but he moved with the same contained energy, like a cat. That was reassuring. Tom let out a long breath.

Hesitating only briefly, Bevis offered Richard his hand. Left hand. Very tactful. After Water-loo Bevis's duties had taken him directly to Paris, whilst Richard sweated out his injuries in Brussels, so they had not met since. Bevis said something congratulatory about the Order of St. Lewis and Richard looked sardonic.

234

"Oughtn't to have refused a knighthood, Falk. Dash it, great honour."

"Certainly," Richard said politely. "I've been kicking myself ever since. It would sound impressive. Sir Richard F—"

"Restrain yourself, Dickon," Tom said, glancing at Bevis, who turned scarlet. Tom bit back a grin. In moments of exasperation Richard's subordinates had been used to refer to him by an inglorious cognomen very like his own adopted surname. Richard would have picked up on it. There was very little he did not pick up on.

Now he apparently decided he had tormented Bevis sufficiently, for he asked a question about the disposition of troops in the Parisian suburbs and allowed Bevis to master his confusion under cover of military technicalities. Very shortly thereafter Bevis left. He still looked ruffled.

Richard sat and stretched his legs out, admiring the sheen of his boots. "Sorry. I shouldn't do that."

"Bedevil Bevis? No, you should not. He's a good chap."

Richard leaned against the high-winged back of his chair, eyes closed. "The mail coach was delayed at Clapham last evening. The driver made up for lost time. Wonderful thing, his majesty's mail."

"Jostled?"

Richard opened one eye and grinned. "At least I had the wherewithal to ride inside this time. Squinched between a corn chandler and the Wife of Bath."

Tom smiled. "It's good to see you, and more or less in one piece, too."

Richard grimaced. "It marches. I seem to be obstinately right-handed, however. Did you know that a left-hander drags his sleeve across the wet ink as he writes? I must invest in a supply of paper cuffs."

"Sims says you ought to hire an amanuensis."

Richard's mouth quirked. "Your translation."

Tom nodded. "Why not hire a secretary?"

"My dear Tom, can you imagine me saying some of the

235

things I write aloud? I'd blush like a maiden. I'm much ruder on paper than I'd ever dare to be in speech."

Tom laughed. "That I cannot credit. Shall you write another novel?"

"I'll have to. As usual I've backed myself into a corner."

"And mean to write your way out of it. I wish I could write my way out of this mess I've fallen into." Tom forced a smile.

"Tell me," Richard said quietly.

So Tom did.

It was an act of trust, and not easy. He was not a man who was used to displaying his feelings. Richard listened, the slight habitual frown between his brows, without comment or interruption.

Tom told him of Clanross's death by drowning. Easy, because factual. Of the Conway solicitor's visit. Of other people's condolences and congratulations. It took a long time for him to put into words what really troubled him.

"Did you ever think of killing yourself?" He looked away from Richard and went on, groping, "I don't mean in a moment of emotion, but soberly, as a rational solution?"

Silence extended. "Yes."

Tom licked his dry lips. "But you didn't."

"No."

"Why not?" He made himself look at his friend.

Richard's mouth twisted in a smile. "Why not, you idiot?"

"You know I didn't mean—"

"Hush. It's a hard question to answer. Do you believe in Hell?"

"I . . . No."

"Neither do I. We make that here." Richard shivered. "I don't know why I didn't kill myself. I would think it through and be convinced, then somehow the time for it would pass and I'd be tangled up in living again. I never could think of a way of doing it without creating a mess someone else would have to clean up. I did try to step in the way of a French ball a couple of times, but you know the Frogs. Rotten marksmen."

An unwilling smile tugged at Tom's mouth. "They did well enough for both of us in the end."

"Half measures," Richard said lightly. "Very untidy." He looked Tom straight in the eye. "You're not asking for advice, are you?"

"No."

"Good. I'm fresh out of inspiration." He looked down at his hands, the right skeletal, the left clenched in a fist. He flexed the left, unclenching it deliberately finger by finger. "You'll do what you have to do."

"That's comforting."

"I know well it's not," Richard shot back, half angry. "There are loads of people who wouldn't know their plain duty if it sat up and bit 'em, but you're not that sort." The brief gust of anger blew itself out. "Just don't let the lawyers convince you to do more than you must. Sign their damned papers and let your man of business deal with the rest of it."

"Would you?"

"I'm unlikely to inherit an earldom or anything else," Richard said drily, "but yes, since you ask, I should. You owe Clanross's family nothing. Nor is there any reason why you should have to enact a charade in the Lords. What can they do to you if you don't take your seat? Cashier you? Unfrock you?"

Tom smiled. "De-belt me."

Richard hewed to his point. "When does Parliament sit?"

"After Michaelmas."

"Tell 'em you're ill. It's the truth. Put 'em off. The House of Lords will dodder along very well without you. It has done since the thirteenth century."

"True." This time Tom's smile was unforced. "I think you *have* advised me."

Richard flushed. "I beg your pardon, Tom. I was trying to imagine the difficulties."

"I've followed your advice before with good results. I may just take it again. I wish I could stay in Lancashire."

"Then stay there. Tell the lawyers you have an obligation to Dunarvon."

"I have," Tom said ruefully. "A large obligation. I must also find a replacement."

"Good. Take your time. And you can tell Dunarvon you have to train your replacement. Put 'em all off."

"You have a nefarious mind."

"So I've been told. How did Dunarvon respond to the news of your elevation?"

Tom chuckled. "Furious. He wasn't half as angry as I was, however." He sobered. "You know, Richard, Clanross never so much as warned me where I stood. I'd no idea—" He felt his old anger stir and broke off. No point in going into that. "I think my outrage deflated Dunarvon's. Or deflected it. He's taking it out on Bevis at the moment, for inducing him to hire me in the first place."

"Good. Let him."

"Poor Bevis."

Richard made a rude noise. "I daresay he thinks it's a splendid joke."

"Well, yes. And it is, in the abstract."

"We don't live in the abstract."

"No." Tom drew a long, ragged breath, and wriggled his shoulders experimentally against the supporting cushions. "It's been a hellish fortnight. You were the only one to see what a blow this business would serve me."

Richard, head bent, did not reply.

Time to change the subject. "Have you seen your publisher?"

Richard looked up, blinking. "What? Oh. No, not yet. He has some mad notion of reissuing the Don Alfonso books with my name on the title page. I'm not anxious to see him, but I daresay I must."

"Why is that a mad notion? It's time you took credit for Don Alfonso."

"Or blame?" Richard's smile went wry. "Just the thing to drive Newsham into a stew. No, I thank you. I've had enough notoriety for one year."

Tom's eyes narrowed. "Has the duke been at you?" When his friend did not reply at once Tom said, more sharply, "Has he, Richard?"

"No, of course not. I just don't want to give him an excuse to notice my ongoing existence. I met my mother the other day at Wilson's house, by the way."

Tom held his breath.

"I begin to understand why the French beheaded Marie Antoinette. I'm damned if the woman didn't try to charm me. *Me*, of all people."

"Did it work?"

"It must have done." Richard rose and regarded his friend with a dispassionate eye. "I was civil as an orange for fifteen minutes."

Tom laughed, his amusement sharpened by relief. "What happened after the fifteen minutes?"

"I left. Which is what I ought to do now. I'll stop by again in a day or so, if I may."

"I wish you will, Richard. Where do you stay?"

"Judy Cassidy's. She has a house in Chelsea."

"Good God, what kind of house?" Judy Cassidy was the widow of a Sergeant of Rifles, and there had been rumours, never confirmed, that she had pursued the oldest profession before Sergeant Cassidy swept her off to better things. Everyone liked Judy.

Richard smiled. "Not that kind of house. It's a grand house, thanks be to God, and everything tidy about it, including an enamelled clock from King Joseph's baggage train. Judy's a respectable householder and her son clerks at St. Katherine's Dock."

Bemused, Tom shook his head. "I can't take it in. Give her a kiss for me if she'll let you."

"If it came from you she might. Kissing privileges are reserved for the Rifles." Richard sketched a mock salute. "*À demain.*"

"Good-bye." Tom closed his eyes, tired suddenly. He was almost sure Richard had been lying to him—that the Duke of Newsham was causing trouble, and that Richard was worried.

=== 30 ===

IN THE NEXT three days Tom signed innumerable legal documents, approved routine expenditures whose sum made his hair stand on end, and rose from his couch long enough to receive a call from a son-in-law of the late earl who sat in Parliament for one of the Conway pocket boroughs. Not very restful. Certainly distracting. Richard did not come back.

When he still hadn't called by the next afternoon, Tom began to feel alarmed. "He said a day or so. It's been four."

Bevis, who was lounging in the wing-backed chair, yawned. "I can't think why you bother. I'd as soon converse with a cobra."

Tom rang for Sims. "Richard's a satirist. What do you expect of him, sugarplums? Sims, can you find your way to Judy Cassidy's house in Chelsea?"

"A course. Wot for, Major?"

"To bear a note to Colonel Falk. He's stopping there. Wait for a reply."

Bevis rose lazily. "I'll take you in my phaeton, Sims."

Sims beamed.

"That's unnecessary." Tom levered himself up with exquisite care and went to the dresser he'd been using as a desk. He stared at the paper for a moment, perplexed, then dashed off an innocuous message.

"It may be unnecessary," Bevis said with dignity, "but I haven't seen Judy Cassidy's house. I'm curious."

By the time the front door slammed Tom was beginning to feel foolish, but he didn't call Sims and Bevis back.

It was close on two hours before they returned. By that time Tom was lying down again, perforce. He held out a hand for Richard's reply. "Did you see him?"

"Yes." Bevis cleared his throat. "Look'ee, Tom, Falk's a bit under the weather. Er, met up with a pair of footpads three days ago on a back street. They roughed him up."

Tom's hand fell. He jerked his head round. "Damn you, Bevis, sit or stand, but do it where I can see you. What happened to Richard?"

Bevis sat in the wing-backed chair and made a heavy business of smoothing the skirts of his coat. Blue superfine, it was, cut by Weston in the first stare. "As I was saying, they roughed him up and he's feeling a trifle seedy. Better tomorrow, I daresay." He picked a bit of imaginary lint from one sleeve.

"You're lying to me."

Bevis's head came up. "Dash it, Tom, watch your language."

"Quit footling. Out with it."

"If anyone's lying, it's Falk," Bevis shot back, annoyed. "That was the Banbury tale he spun me."

"Sims."

Sims rattled the decanter. "Yes, me lord."

"God blast your impertinence. Did you talk to Judy?"

"I talked with Mrs. Cassidy," Bevis interjected, saving Sims's groats. "Thing is, they cut up his face somewhat with their fists and twisted his arm, but they didn't cut purse. He had a fiver and some odd coins on him, stickpin, watch fob, watch. None of 'em touched."

"Did Richard say—"

"That's what *she* said. Very shrewd woman, Mrs. Cassidy, and not best pleased with Falk at the moment. That sort of brouhaha lowers the tone of her establishment." Bevis shifted on the chair. "Falk sticks by his story."

"You say they hurt his arm. Badly? Which arm?"

"The right. The surgeon Mrs. Cassidy summoned bled him and strapped the arm so he can't move it. Nothing broken. No fever. Painful, of course."

Tom gritted his teeth. There were times when Bevis's gift for stating the obvious was hard to bear. "Newsham. I knew I should have made Richard tell me."

Bevis leaned forward, hands on his knees. "Jumping the gun, ain't you?"

"Perhaps," Tom said grimly. "We'll see tomorrow."

"Shall I fetch him for you?"

"If you will, Bevis. I don't fancy the idea of a hired hack."

"Glad to. He won't like it, though."

Tom swore. "He'll just have to put up with it."

Next day Tom waited for Bevis to return for a good hour, and the last half hour drove him to his feet. Pacing, in Tom's state, was an absorbing activity. When they finally came Richard followed Bevis into the room. Tom stalked over to him. Richard had a black eye and a cut lip and that was the least of it.

"You damned fool, did you fancy you could hide that shiner?"

"No. I meant to wait until it looked less dramatic before I paraded it in the streets, however."

"Sit."

Bevis pulled the wing-backed chair out for Richard. "Drove through the park. Should've thought twice about that. Old Peverel nearly fell from his phaeton staring."

Richard sat down gingerly. His arm was strapped tight, the wrist in an obtrusive white sling. No more discreet black silk.

Tom stood for a moment absorbing the lesser details of his friend's appearance and when he spoke his voice rang harsher than he intended. "Tell me what happened."

"I saw my publisher in Threadneedle Street. I took a hack as far as Chelsea Hospital and decided to walk from there." Richard shifted under Tom's gaze. "I needed to do some thinking, and I was careless. Two Mohawks jumped me from an alley. They beat on me for awhile. I blacked out. When I came to my senses they'd gone, so I walked to Judy Cassidy's. She called the sawbones."

Tom made an incredulous noise.

"That's *it*," Richard snapped. "Not an unheard-of event in that area. I should've waited to do my thinking indoors." Richard gave Tom stare for stare, quite a feat considering the black eye.

"Not unheard of, except you weren't robbed."

Richard's mouth hardened. "Someone has been dealing in backstairs gossip. Perhaps the gentlemen didn't like the cut of my coat."

"Is it Newsham?"

"I'm sure the duke has never set foot in that part of Chelsea."

"Cut line, Richard."

"I have told you what I know to be true," Richard said, more quietly. "Will you lie down, Tom?"

"I'm still capable of standing for ten minutes."

"Perhaps. I prefer not to be towered over, however. My neck's stiff."

Tom complied with bad grace. He resumed his semirecumbent pose on the daybed with some help from Bevis. Sims entered, took in the scene, cleared his throat ostentatiously.

"Yes, bring the decanter," Tom snapped.

Bevis pulled up a chair for himself and sat. "Dashed good idea. Now, Falk, no more foolery. Open your budget."

"It's possible I prefer to keep my own counsel." Richard regarded Bevis without enthusiasm.

Bevis bristled. "Bite your dashed tongue off, for all I care, but if you've a groat's worth of decency you'll think twice before you drive Tom wild with worry."

"Bevis . . ."

Bevis glowered at Tom. "I've no idea why you feel obliged to tie yourself in knots over a care-for-nobody like

Falk, but the bald fact is you do. Ain't the first time I've been tangled in his affairs, either. Open up, Falk."

"Does your lordship have any other little commands—either of your lordships?" Richard had gone white with fury.

Tom felt his own temper rise. "That's a foul thing to say, Richard."

Richard closed his eyes—eye, rather. The one was swollen shut. The muscle at the hinge of his jaw jumped. "All right, Tom, I'm sorry. But you ought to recall that it was Lord Bevis's damned easy habit of confiding my business to the world at large that brought Newsham down on me this spring. I think I have some reason to mistrust Bevis's discretion."

Tom was silent.

"I confided in Lady Sarah in good faith, Falk. Known her all my life. What's more, she's a good sort of woman. I'm dashed if I'll apologise again for something as natural as breathing." Bevis stood up. "I didn't intend to do you an injury. If I have, I want to know the consequences. Some sense of responsibility, dash it." He turned to Tom, his fair skin red with indignation. "Servant, Tom. I'll look in tomorrow."

"Oh, sit down," Richard said wearily. "It won't matter in the long run, and I daresay you have some right. To satisfy your curiosity, if nothing else."

"By God," Bevis spluttered.

Sims barged in with the replenished decanter. Sims had no tact. It was one of the things Tom liked about him.

"Pour, Bevis." Tom was exhausted past diplomacy.

Bevis obeyed. The indignant flush faded. He slammed Richard's glass down and brought Tom's to the occasional table that sat by the head of the couch. When Bevis had taken his own seat, Tom said, "Was it Newsham, Richard?"

"My publisher—" Richard drew a breath. "My *former* publisher told me that Josiah Whatley had bought the remaining copies of my old novels, and the plates and

245

galleys of the new one. Whatley is Newsham's man of business."

"Good God, he can't mean to destroy them!"

Richard's temper was now under strict control. "He told Hitchins that it would be unwise to print anything of mine in future. Politely, in indirect language." He toyed with his untasted brandy. "Hitchins took the hint. His is a small house and he can't afford to offend the Duke of Newsham. He was sorry, of course, but there it was. What else could he do?"

Bevis snorted. "Damned pigeon-livered piker."

"Hitchins is a prudent man. I don't think it's a coincidence that I was attacked on my way back from that interview. But of course there's no proof."

"He's mad!" Bevis exploded. "Loads of copies already out. The duke can't hope to suppress the books entirely. Dash it, everyone's read 'em. Read 'em myself."

Tom watched Richard start to say something rude and think better of it.

After a moment Richard went on, in the same controlled voice. "There is no question of suppressing the books that are already in print. Newsham means to encourage me to emigrate."

Tom's hand jerked and brandy slopped from his glass. He swore. "Explain, damn you."

"His man made me an offer some days ago which I incautiously refused."

"What kind of offer?" Bevis sounded bewildered, but Tom's stomach knotted.

"What was it, Dickon?"

"Passage to any North American port and an annuity to be settled on my children. Wilson," Richard added, dispassionate, "was of the opinion that the duke meant to acknowledge my claim against his family, and that I was starting at shadows. Wilson is a reasonable man. The duke is not."

Tom glowered at the ceiling. "A threat."

"I thought so at the time. It appears I was right."

Bevis jumped to his feet and began pacing. "That's Gothick. He can't do it."

"Newsham can do as he pleases," Richard said bleakly.

"But the law—"

"He is above the law, as your father would be. Or Tom, if he chose."

"That's a vile slander."

"If Tom and Dunarvon were men of Newsham's kidney it would be the truth. You're childish, my lord." Richard's eyes locked with Bevis's, and Bevis dropped his gaze first.

"What do you mean to do?" There was a bad taste in Tom's mouth. Like tin.

Richard swirled his untasted brandy slowly in the glass. "Call on Whatley tomorrow and tell him I've changed my mind, but that my health won't permit me to make the crossing until spring."

"You can't."

Richard looked at him. "No. I need to buy time. I'll tell him to book passage for three to Charleston in South Carolina. That's plausible. I've been there. Then, if he agrees to that, I'll instruct my solicitor to convert my assets to cash, pack up Amy and Tommy, and ship out on the first vessel bound for Spain."

Tom made a noise of protest.

Richard ignored him. "Isabel's brother can advise me as to which South American colony is least pestiferous. Montevideo, I think. The situation there is pleasant." He had clearly thought his escape route out. It was all terribly wrong.

"You're mad, Richard."

"No, I've finally come to my senses. I was mad to think I could raise my children in England. I took a gamble and lost. There will be no more gambles." He regarded Bevis impassively. "That is, if Lord Bevis can contrive to keep his tongue between his teeth."

"You have my word," Bevis said with stiff formality.

247

"Thank you." Richard rose. "Good-bye, Tom. You ought to go back to Lancashire as soon as may be."

"You can't do it," Tom exploded. "Think of Mrs. Foster."

"I have. I am."

"You'll break her heart."

Richard went over to the window which gave on Albemarle Street and stood staring down at the fashionable passersby.

"You can't do it," Tom repeated.

Richard turned. His face was pale, but quite composed. The bruises stood out like brushwork. "I'll have to. Neither Newsham nor his father ever showed any regard for bystanders. Emily Foster is a widow with a minor son."

It passed through Tom's mind how easily a house might be burnt or a carriage overturned. "There must be another solution."

"No," Richard said with weary finality. "If there were I'd have thought of it. I'm sorry you had to learn of this, Tom. Why the devil did you send for me? If I thought you'd oblige me I'd beg you to put this . . . this stupid melodrama out of your mind. I'll write you from Spain. Servant, Bevis." He went out of the room and presently Tom heard Sims hailing a hack from the front steps.

Bevis, who had listened to the later exchanges with an expression of bewildered horror on his features, came to life. "I'll fetch him back, Tom. Good God."

"No. Wait, Bevis. I have to think. Damn it, man, sit down."

=== 31 ===

AFTER FOUR YEARS of campaigning Bevis could no more sleep the morning out than Tom could. Tom took his friend's protests at being rousted out at an unfashionably early hour with a grain of salt and despatched him early next morning in the phaeton to find Richard. Tom and Bevis had spent the evening laying wild plots over a snug dinner and a noggin of brandy. With due respect to Richard's tragic dilemma, Tom had enjoyed the scheming. He was pleased with himself and feeling amazingly cheerful when Bevis and Richard returned.

Richard was not cheerful. He looked underslept and blue-devilled, too blue even for anger. He said without preamble, "I must call at Whatley's rooms before noon."

"Yes, of course. Richard, are you set on South America?" In spite of himself Tom could not entirely leash his elation and he knew that was the wrong note.

Richard said quietly, "Don't."

Tom paused. Heavy persuasion called for. "What if you and the children and Mrs. Foster were to give Newsham the slip in England?"

"He'd stumble on us sooner or later. Mrs. Foster's son is a landowner, after all. Matt can't disappear without arousing a hue and cry." Richard forced a smile. "I daresay you've constructed any number of plots worthy of the Light Bobs in winter quarters. D'you remember when Browning impersonated the *duque del Infantado*?"

"I remember," Tom said gently. Doña Isabel had been

induced to teach the counterfeit duque the fandango in a hilarious dress rehearsal. "Hear me out, Dickon."

Richard sat on the chair by the daybed. "Very well."

Tom decided that Richard being patient was worse than Richard snapping and snarling, and gave Bevis a cautionary glance. "I have a manor in Cornwall, or so I'm told. I've not seen it. It's remote, snug, furnished with discreet servants, and about as far as it can be from Newsham's principal seat. It's called Treglyn and it's not occupied." He outlined the skeleton of his plan quickly.

Richard listened without interrupting.

Tom awaited the inevitable refusal.

Richard just shook his head.

"Why?"

"It won't work."

"That's feeble."

Richard drew a ragged breath. "Feeble is what I feel. Look, Tom, it's kind in you to trouble yourself, but I've fought Newsham too long. I don't want to fight anymore."

"You want to run."

"In a nutshell. And pray don't bother to question my courage. I won't bite. Retreat is in order."

"There are retreats and retreats. I'm offering you a strategic withdrawal in place of a rout."

Richard frowned down at his clenched left hand. His black eye was turning a handsome shade of green.

Tom pressed on. "The first time I saw Emily Foster I proposed marriage to her."

Richard looked up, startled.

"She's an admirable lady, Richard. She deserves better than to be abandoned."

"Damn you, you know very well she'll be safer when we've gone. Cut the fanciful analogies."

"She may be safe, but she'll be wretchedly unhappy without your children."

Richard's mouth set. "I've admitted that."

"Then I wonder you won't at least try to work out an alternative. You owe her a debt."

Richard's good eye clenched shut. "For Christ's sake, I know it. Let be, Tom."

"Perhaps you're hesitating because you think I'll stick my spoon in the wall in the middle of this campaign. I don't think I shall. Even if I do, there are ways to—"

"You don't need to take on my problems. You've an estate to settle."

"Yes, and very boring I find it." With some effort Tom contrived to look wistful. "I think you might allow me to indulge myself one last time . . ." He allowed his voice to trail off in an affecting and dramatic way.

Richard stood up so abruptly Bevis started, spilling his coffee. "Here, I say!"

Richard ignored him and stalked over to Tom. "Don't ever do that to me."

Tom sighed. "Sorry. I thought I'd just give it a try. You're devilish hard to persuade, Richard."

Bevis was still swabbing at the coffee on his breeches. "Upon my word . . ."

"Hush," Tom murmured. "Richard objects to emotional blackmail. What a pity, Dickon. I was just thinking a spot of blackmail—the real thing—was the answer to your prayers. You've nothing to lose by my plan."

"If it works."

"We'll see that it does. You'll see to it. You've nothing to lose but a few months at worst, and a great deal to gain. Mrs. Foster's peace of mind, among other things. Go to Whatley and persuade him you're too ill to leave until March or April. From the look of you that shouldn't be difficult. Then come back here and we'll iron out the details."

"There is no way Mrs. Foster will agree to go into hiding."

"She will if you tell her the alternative."

Richard looked profoundly skeptical.

"When you've conveyed the children and Emily Foster safely to Treglyn, you will sit down in some quiet spot, your cottage perhaps, and write an exposé, a thinly disguised account of your situation."

"I can't write a *roman à clef*!" Richard exploded.

"Yes, you can. It need not have literary merit because it will probably never see the light of day."

"No, indeed," Richard said with awful sarcasm. "My dismembered corpse will be found floating in the Thames well before I finish it."

Bevis muffled a crack of laughter.

"I can't do it." Richard's jaw set obstinately.

"Nonsense. You're not a temperamental artist, you're a hack. How many times have you told me that?" Perilous ground. Tom hurried on, "Stop creating bogus obstacles."

"I can't write at all."

"Hire a secretary," Tom snapped. "I'm surprised at you, Richard. If I didn't know better I'd fancy you eager to drag your children off to some Latin American plague spot. Well?"

"It's a taradiddle and doomed to failure."

The protest was weaker and Tom knew it. He pressed his advantage. "When your manuscript is adequate to the purpose we'll have half a dozen copies printed privately— one for your solicitor, one for the duke, and one for yourself. You will then send an extra copy to Sir Robert Wilson with a full explanation of what has happened. If he's the man I take him to be, Wilson will bring Newsham to his knees."

"Your blasted plan is as full of holes as a *tirailleur's képi*." Richard was looking thoughtful.

"The sketch of a plan, merely." Tom experienced a twinge of doubt. He suppressed it. Not the time to be thinking of failure. "I'll leave you to work out the details."

"Two copies unaccounted for," Bevis interjected. "You said half a dozen, Tom."

"One for you and one for me."

Bevis grinned.

"It's still blackmail." Richard shifted in the chair.

Tom shook his head. "A bluff, Richard. It will work very handily."

At least Richard was thinking. He rubbed the scar on his forehead. After a long silence he said slowly, "I'll go to Whatley now. For the rest, I wish you may convince me. It's not a game to me."

"I know that, clunch. Bevis will drive you to the City."

"Happy to be of service." It was a tribute to Bevis's amiable nature that he didn't sound sarcastic.

"No, thank you." Richard looked at Bevis for a considering moment. "I'll take a hackney. I'll look far more abject without the cavalry at my back."

Bevis had stiffened at the refusal but Richard's oblique reference to his regiment mollified him.

Tom breathed a sigh of relief. "Off with you, then. Sims can find a hack for you."

By the time Richard finally returned Bevis had gone off to his club. Tom was lying in the high-ceilinged apartment, pretending to read a scientific journal and letting his thoughts drift.

Tom liked the flat better than the shrouded Conway town house, all marble and staircases and Chinese porcelain. The suite of rooms had been hired for the Hon. William Conway, a deceased brother of the late earl, on a ninety-year lease. Tom scandalised Mr. Brown, the Conway man of business, by bivouacking in it.

Tom liked the faintly shabby masculine furnishings and the aroma of ancient snuff. He would have loathed living alone in the vast town house and being waited on by phalanxes of disdainful servants. Here there were only a tweeny and an aged cook-housekeeper, and Sims dealt with them. And with everything else.

Now Sims ushered Richard in. "Colonel Falk, me lord."

Tom threw the journal at Sims's head. *Me lord, indeed.*

Sims fielded the journal imperturbably. " 'Ere you are, Colonel, sir. 'E's feeling a trifle testy."

Richard didn't enter into the badinage. He looked exhausted and rather green, and he sat in the wing-backed chair without invitation, as if his legs would hold him upright no longer.

"Leave us, Sims, if you please." Tom shifted on the cushions. "Bad, I take it?"

Richard said quietly, "If there's one thing I hate worse than a hypocrite, it's a sanctimonious hypocrite. That jumped-up hedge lawyer expected me to be *grateful*."

Tom waited.

"I was, too." Restless despite his evident weariness, Richard got up again and went to the window. "I abased myself."

Tom closed his eyes.

Richard gave a short laugh. "A convincing performance, if I say it. The place reeked of Newsham's money and Newsham's . . . purposes." His voice thickened. "I was afraid."

Tom said gently, "Why should you not be?"

Richard did not answer the question. After a moment he went on. "I shall certainly give Whatley a prominent role in my memoir." That sounded more like Richard.

"You mean to try my plan?" Tom held his breath.

Richard slowly crossed the room and sat down facing Tom. "I don't know. The devil—yes. I'm a damned fool. I don't think it will work. I'll probably wind up making a run for it in the dead of winter, but if there's an outside chance of embarrassing Newsham I'll take it. You're sure this manor of yours is secure?"

"You can make it secure," Tom said happily. "Hire a regiment, if necessary."

"A division at least will be required to move Emily Foster to Treglyn." A gleam of amusement lit Richard's eyes. "Not to mention Aunt Fan."

=== 32 ===

"I DARESAY YOU ran into a doorpost." Emily inspected the magnificent bruise which surrounded Richard's eye. Indignation and fright made her voice shrill.

Richard began to laugh. "No, I ran into an old friend." He was seated in Emily's bookroom, where they were safe from intrusive children.

Emily watched him succumb to the whoops without any impulse to join his mirth. Something was wrong—again. "Tom Conway," she uttered when she thought she would be heard.

"Who else?" He was still chuckling.

"I refuse to believe *he* has taken up pugilism."

Richard's amusement faded. "No, nor have I. Tom's health is not good, but he is otherwise very much himself. He asked to be remembered to you and your aunt. Emily—"

"You'd best just tell me the whole without roundaboutation." Emily folded her hands in her lap. "Begin with the black eye."

"I was jumped by a pair of footpads."

"Ah." She waited.

"It's going to sound Gothick."

"Thanks to you, I'm enured to the Gothick."

His mouth twitched in amused appreciation. When he had finished what she felt sure was an understated account of the fortnight's events, however, she felt no amusement at all, and wondered that he could.

Frozen between fear and fury, she could not speak. It was an index of her changed state of mind that the loss of Richard's publisher weighed with her almost as heavily as the implied threat to the children's safety, but for Emily the chief horror lay in the word *emigrate*.

When she could command her voice, she leaned toward him. "What do you mean to do? You cannot go off to America." Conscious that he was watching her, she forced herself to speak calmly. "You cannot. It is not to be thought of."

"But it must be thought of. It was the only solution I could come up with." He described for her in careful detail his appalling South American plan. "I still believe a complete disappearance the only course a prudent man would take."

"Oh God, no!"

"What other choice have I?"

Emily's mind skittered from one impossibility to another. She wanted to tell him that wherever he went she would follow, but she could not. Her first duty was to Matthew. Matt's place was in Hampshire. The Wellfield estate was Matt's birthright. She could not leave her son behind to follow Richard. For another woman that course might be possible. For Emily it was not. She also knew she could not drag Matt off into permanent exile. His grandparents on both sides would very properly object.

The thought presented her with an immediate vision of her father. She groaned. "You'd better tell me what is to be done, short of emigration. You said you had no other solution. Did Tom think of an alternative—" She interrupted herself. "What of Sir Robert and Lady Sarah? They have stood your friends."

"I'm sorry for it, but I must ask that you say nothing to either of them."

Emily stared. "I like Lady Sarah."

He met her eyes steadily. "Strange as it may seem, so do I, and I trust no harm will come to her. Indeed, she is far safer out of it entirely. You must see that."

Emily swallowed. She did see. "And the dowager?"

"She'll have to take her lumps. Tom does have a plan." Richard's eyes were grave.

Emily closed her own eyes briefly. "Then tell it me. It must be bizarre, or you'd have come out with it at once."

He rose. "Very well. Mind you, it may not succeed. I have strong reservations on principle. You'll have reason to resent the inconvenience, Emily, and I beg you will refuse entirely if you think the difficulties outweigh the prospects of success. It would be better—for you, and for Amy and Tommy—to make a clean break now than to drag out months of anxiety, only to fail in the end."

"You've forewarned me," Emily snapped. "Get on with it, sir."

Pacing the bookroom carpet, he told her of Tom's scheme. Emily heard him with growing incredulity.

"You've taken leave of your senses!"

"Very likely."

"I'd sooner cross the Channel in an oyster barrel than remove my son from his home."

"I thought you might feel that way."

Emily jumped up. "Who would oversee the apple harvest? The sale of fleeces? The rents? What of Matt's lessons? Oh no, indeed, Richard. You ask too much of me."

He said gently, "I have always done so."

Emily strode to the window. The orchard looked wonderfully tranquil in the noon sunlight. "What of my reputation? I daresay you don't care for trifles like that, but it is of some interest to *me*. My neighbours already regard me as an eccentric."

"I thought Miss Mayne might be persuaded to join you."

"Impossible." Panicked, Emily rounded on him. "The duke cannot be serving you such a turn! I think you must be mad, sir, mad with suspicion. There is no danger. You have created a dreadful phantasy and are acting it out."

He made a helpless gesture with his good hand. "Do you truly believe that?"

She licked her dry lips. "No—yes. I don't know!"

257

"I can show you Whatley's letter." He fumbled with the inside pocket of his coat, awkward, left-handed. The white sling impeded him.

"It's not necessary." Emily fought with her panick. "Oh God, I'm sorry, Richard. You did not smack yourself in the eye, twist your own arm, and buy up the plates of your novel. I believe you. I cannot do otherwise, but I don't want to believe. The reality frightens me."

His hand fell. His eyes were dark. "It frightens me, too."

"Will a threat of publick exposure succeed with the duke?"

He took a breath. "I can't guarantee it. His father wouldn't have been deterred, but I believe my half brother to be vulnerable to publick opinion. However, he is used to having his way." Richard frowned painfully. "Tom's backing could prove decisive. The earls of Clanross wield considerable political power. Tom's influence, by its very nature, poses a new threat. Keighley might be willing to shrug off a campaign of gossip such as Sarah could conduct, but he could not ignore questions in Parliament."

"Did Tom . . ."

Richard drifted to the desk and began to fiddle with the standish. "Tom has not yet come to terms with his new position. Even if he were in the habit of thinking politically, I don't believe he would consider using his power in so private a cause, but Keighley—Newsham, I mean— doesn't know Tom."

"I see." Emily resumed her seat, thinking hard. "Then perhaps my flight to Treglyn and your *roman à clef* are not even necessary. Couldn't Tom write Newsham a plain letter?"

"There's no proof yet." Richard rubbed his forehead. "None that would stand in a law court. Besides . . ."

"You want to try Tom's plan because it is Tom's plan."

"Yes."

Emily cocked her head. "Then let us make doubly sure it succeeds." She gave a single sharp nod of acquiescence. "Yes, very well. When?"

He turned from the desk and stood for a startled moment looking at her. "You're a remarkable woman, Emily."

Emily felt her cheeks burn. She did not wish to be called remarkable. Lovable, yes. "On the contrary, I'm a woman with her back to a stone wall. When, sir, and how?"

He hesitated. "Within the week."

Emily groaned.

He frowned, worried.

"Never mind, I'm just kicking against the prods. Friday, then. How?"

"I'll hire a carriage as far as Reading. Your eldest brother lives there, doesn't he? It wouldn't be thought odd if you were to seem to visit him."

"Only to anyone acquainted with Will and me. We fight like cat and dog."

"Oh."

Emily sat once more. Brooding, she tapped the arm of the chair with her forefinger. "We'd best take my father's travelling carriage. A hired coach would cause comment. I'll tell Papa we mean to visit my maternal Aunt Collingwood in Devon."

Richard sat too. "I ought to explain to Sir Henry."

Emily sighed. "We'll have to take Aunt Fan into our confidence. Papa, however . . ."

"He must be told."

"He'll kick up a dust."

"Yes."

Emily groaned again. "Well, let us persuade my father, then, and swear him to silence. Now, granted Papa's travelling carriage, why only as far as Reading? Why not all the way?"

"Tom suggested that you change discreetly to his carriage at some point to confuse the curious."

"Do you mean to say I'll be followed?"

"Not at once, but such an exchange, if it were made with care, would confuse questioners later. After all, we don't want anyone to pursue us."

"Us!"

"I mean to escort you."

"Wonderful. The duke's minions have only to ask if a carriage has passed bearing a load of females and squalling brats, escorted by a man with his arm in a sling. You are visible, Richard."

A gleam of rueful appreciation lit his eyes. "True, and you're a first-rate accomplice."

Emily said darkly, "Only since I met you. Before that I led a blameless, respectable life entirely without incident." She meant to make a joke, but she saw at once that he had taken her words at face value.

"I did you no favour bringing you my children, did I? I'm sorry, Emily."

He looked so beaten, suddenly, that Emily had to restrain herself from embracing him. After a moment she contrived to say lightly, "To tell you the truth, my blameless, respectable existence was also rather dull. Don't grudge me one small adventure. I've never seen Cornwall." *And never wanted to,* her prosaic self added.

After the first flurry of protests Aunt Fan proved persuadable, but Sir Henry Mayne was a tougher nut to crack, as Emily had thought he might be. She would have preferred to deceive him, she decided, as wave after wave of paternal fury crashed over her.

"Outrageous! I won't have it. You'll have to give the brats up." He prowled the carpet of his bookroom like a caged beast.

"No," Emily said, mildly but firmly.

"I'll put a stop to this harebrained plot. I'll write the Duke of Newsham."

Emily went cold. "If you betray Richard, Papa, I'll never see or speak to you again."

"Fustian!"

"Try me."

He stopped pacing and glowered. " 'Richard,' is it? Upon my word, have you no shame? You, a lady and respectably widowed, to be gallivanting all over England with a baseborn adventurer."

"That will do." Emily glared back, temper blazing to life.

"By God, I've had enough." Sir Henry's hand smashed onto the surface of his desk. A paper fluttered. "He is using you, madam."

"With my full consent. And Aunt Fan's."

"Your aunt is a dashed pander," Sir Henry said bitterly.

"If by that you mean to suggest there will be an irregular liaison, I assure you you are fair and far out. Colonel Falk does not come with us to Treglyn."

Sir Henry was not mollified. "It will *look* as if you've eloped with the man. To Edward's mother, for an instance. To your neighbours, who are already, I may add, impertinently curious about your relations with this . . . this . . ."

"Bastard?" Emily asked, her voice hard.

Sir Henry turned a deeper shade of purple. "Emma, you are my daughter. A *Mayne*. No scandal has ever attached to our name."

"Nonsense. I daresay there were any number of ramshackle Maynes. What of Matilda Mayne-Wilkins? She slept with Charles the Second, didn't she?" When she was a child Emily had heard the legend of Matilda's royal liaison from her father's lips. Embellished.

She almost made the mistake of pressing her point but she caught herself in time. Sir Henry did not relish having his inconsistencies thrown in his face.

She drew a careful breath. "Now, Papa, consider. If only you'll cooperate it will seem as if Aunt Fan and I have taken the children to visit Mama's sister. Nothing can be made of that. We'll spend the time quietly at Treglyn. When it's safe we'll return. No one will know the truth unless you peach."

"Mind your tongue." Sir Henry did not like Emily to use cant terms, but his protest was mechanical. There followed a baffled silence. "Why, Emma?" he asked finally. "Why? You ain't a fool in the general course of things."

"The children are in danger."

"So Falk says."

Emily leaned forward, earnest. "Richard was set upon in London by hired villains, Papa. You've seen his eye. They also damaged his injured arm."

"Pah, that's London. Could've happened to anyone. The children haven't been harmed, or even threatened."

Emily sighed. "Papa, Richard believes they are in danger. Perhaps he's wrong, but it's clear the duke means to exile him. I think Richard has earned a right that other Englishmen, my brothers, for example, consider as natural as breathing—the right to live and work and raise his children unmolested in his own country. He may be a bastard, but no one denies he is native-born." She blinked back unwelcome tears.

Sir Henry's eyes narrowed. "I'll tell you what, Emma, you're in love with the scoundrel."

Emily sat very still.

"Well? Eh? Eh?"

She raised her chin. "I'd marry him in a trice if he asked me."

"If he's trifled with you—"

"Oh, Papa, you know better. No one trifles with me." Try as she might she couldn't quite keep the regret from her voice.

Her father wasn't listening in any case. He sat heavily in his favourite armchair. "I only wish you happy, Emily."

Emily swallowed. "I know, Papa. But if I cannot be happy then I mean to be useful."

"He ain't worthy of you." Her father's voice was plaintive.

Emily smiled. "Dear Papa, so partial. Richard is a distinguished soldier, a writer of merit, and related, however indirectly, to half the peerage. He is a dear if sometimes exasperating man, and I love him very much."

"Nonsense. You love his brats."

"So do you." Emily had him at *point non plus* and they both knew it.

His shoulders slumped against the chair back. "But my God, to be leaving your home and traipsing all over the country on a wild-goose chase!"

"At least I shan't be following the drum."

Aghast, Sir Henry sat upright. "You'd never have done that!"

"Yes," Emily said slowly, surprising herself at this turnabout. "With backward glances and dragging feet, yes, I'd have followed the army if Richard had asked me to. Fortunately or unfortunately, all I intend now is to pay a little visit to Lord Clanross's Cornwall manor, fully countenanced by my aunt. Very respectable, Papa."

Sir Henry's eyebrows twitched wrathfully, but he was defeated and he knew it.

33

THE HOUSE LEANED drunkenly against its neighbour. Street vendors and urchins with shrill voices converged upon Sir Robert Wilson as he stepped down from his carriage. He held a scented handkerchief to his nose against the foul air.

In muffled tones Wilson directed his coachman to exercise the team, and picked his way through refuse to the peeling front door. His knock and question elicited a surly reply from a half clothed slattern. Third floor back.

He began to climb. The treads, upon which shreds of ancient carpet mouldered, creaked under his weight. He hoped he might not fall through a rotten floorboard. When he found what he assumed was the right door, he knocked again.

Richard, in shirt-sleeves, his arm in a sling, opened the door. "Ah, Wilson. Good of you to call."

Wilson lacked breath for a suitably scathing rejoinder. He took the proffered chair, one of two unmatched straight-backed chairs with which the room was furnished, and sat for a moment panting. Fortunately the air smelled rather better at that height.

He looked round him. A deal table bore the remains of a meal of bread and cheese at one end and writing implements and a neat stack of papers at the other. Against one wall—incongruously, it was freshly limed—a sprung couch leaned. A portmanteau had been shoved into one dark corner, and a washstand and shaving mirror by the lone window suggested that Richard lived in the room as well as writing in it.

Wilson took a last, puffing breath. "Where the devil have you been this past month? Where are the children? Sarah's frantic."

Richard watched him warily from the doorway. "The children are in a place of safety. I've been here most of the time."

"Why?"

"I'm writing a scurrilous memoir." A brief grin flickered across Richard's drawn features. "I like the neighbourhood."

Wilson was not amused. "Sarah has run half mad with worry."

"I'm sorry for it. I've felt a twinge or two of apprehension myself." Richard closed the door and went to the table. He propped himself against the edge. "Do you recall the letter I showed you from Newsham's man of business?"

"Very clearly." Wilson shifted in his chair. The wood creaked. "For God's sake, Richard, what have you done?"

"What have *I* done?" Richard drew a breath and said in a carefully reasonable voice, "Apart from conveying the children and Mrs. Foster out of harm's way, I've been sitting here writing."

Wilson leaned forward, hands on his knees. "Blast you, tell me what has happened!"

Richard complied, tersely, with a minimum of detail. There was no emotion in his voice, and Wilson had learned to mistrust that. As the tally of events unfolded Wilson's stomach churned, nor was Richard as cool as he sounded. His hand cramped on the edge of the scabrous table.

"Why did you not come to me at once?" Wilson burst out. "At *once*, when Newsham tampered with your publisher. Newsham broke his *word* to me. I'd have exposed him, I promise you." He stopped, choked with indignation.

Richard was examining the toes of his boots. He raised

his eyes. "There's been a small problem of doubt, has there not, Wilson? You acted for me this summer because it looked as if I'd be unable to act for myself. I was grateful to you. I still am."

"Richard—"

"But I could not risk doubts and hesitations. I had to act."

Silence lay between them.

"I've had help," Richard continued. "My friend—"

"Lord Clanross." It was a guess, but Wilson had had weeks to reflect on their last meeting.

Richard's brows drew together. "Tom had it in his power to provide a hiding place for the children. I'd not like his name to come into this, Wilson, if you please. He's not a well man."

Wilson nodded. He was hurt by Richard's failure of trust.

"My first impulse was to take my children abroad at once, without telling anyone, so that Newsham would lose the trace. Tom suggested another course. It was his plan that I compose a thinly disguised memoir which he would have privately printed in Dublin."

"Dublin!"

"Tom is convenient to the Irish packet—he's still fixed in Lancashire—and we thought it unlikely Newsham's surveillance of printers extended to Ireland. There was no thought of publishing the memoir." Richard brushed his hair from his forehead.

"Blackmail."

Richard's hand dropped. "If you like, though I believe blackmail involves making threats of exposure for gain."

The room had no hearth and was cold in the frosty October afternoon, but Wilson's face burned. "I beg your pardon."

Richard shrugged and went over to the window. "That was Tom's plan, to give me the freedom and the means to embarrass Newsham. However, it would have taken a great deal of time. I still write slowly. Even if I writ like lightning, making a book is a tedious business. I could not expect Mrs. Foster to absent herself from Wellfield House for months. She has had to give over the management of her son's estate to her father."

"What course *did* you take?"

Richard regarded the chimney pots and the dark bulk of the next house with grave attention. "Tom still supposes I'm holed up in some village writing my *roman à clef* in secret."

Wilson was not stupid. "Instead you've been sitting here like a dashed decoy, waiting for another assault."

"I thought I might come to Newsham's attention if I hid out in an obvious way." Smiling a little, Richard went to the table and straightened the papers on it. "You know, Wilson, I once earned my bread for a sixmonth by copying documents, and writing letters at tuppence a shot. It's not a lucrative profession. A fortnight ago I hired a copyist. I wasn't sure he was dishonest, but he looked hungry enough to be susceptible to Newsham's bribery." Richard's mouth twisted. "I'm a good judge of character."

"He betrayed you? Has there been another assault?"

Richard nodded. "Last evening."

"You might have been killed!" Wilson burst out. "For the love of God, Richard!"

"I was prepared for them." A defensive note crept into his voice. "This time I had my man, McGrath, by me. He's been following me home discreetly every evening from that inn down the street. When he saw my attackers McGrath rushed into the fray. He enjoys a brawl." A real smile lit his eyes. "They were the same two Mohawks who jumped me outside Judy Cassidy's lodging house." The smile faded. "Newsham ought to be more careful of his tools."

"Were you hurt?"

"A few bruises. Nothing to signify. We, er, detained one of the culprits. The other escaped, unfortunately. I'm less than adept at one-armed wrestling."

Wilson drank that in. "You're mad, Richard, utterly mad."

Richard took the other chair. "Do you think so? I had a long talk with my assailant last night. He is now reposing at Newgate and seems inclined to be frank."

Wilson studied his brother-in-law's thin, composed features. "Surely he cannot identify Newsham."

"Oh, no. I rather fancy his principal to be Lord George, though no names were uttered. My attacker has made a full confession, and claims he can point out the man who bought his services." Richard was rubbing the smooth silk of the sling with absent fingers. He looked up. "That surprises you."

"I'd not have expected Newsham to act in his own person, but I confess I thought better of George."

"He's been stupid, certainly."

Depressed, Wilson kept his silence. He could believe George's stupidity. It was the malice that surprised him.

Richard was watching him again from eyes that were shadowed with weariness. The sharp October light made the toll of his ordeal all too plain.

Wilson rose. "My carriage is below. Will you come with me to Newgate? I'd like to hear the man's story at first hand."

Not a tactful thing to say. Richard's jaw was set.

Hastily Wilson added, "I wish to be sure of details before I write Newsham of George's conduct. Shall you drop the charges?"

"If possible. I thought I might have to bring an action—"

"If I refused to persuade Newsham to deal with you. I see. You need not have doubted me in the face of such clear evidence of malice."

To his surprise his brother-in-law flushed and looked away. "I beg your pardon, Wilson. God knows, I have reason to trust you. This past month has been a little difficult."

It was an apology of sorts. Wilson had come prepared to

wrest an apology from Richard. He wondered why there was so little savour in it. "Well, come along, then. We can discuss our strategy in the carriage."

Richard took his coat from the chair back and shrugged into it. He did not try to put his right arm through the sleeve.

Watching the struggle, Wilson felt a stab of anger with Lord George that fairly shook him.

"I must speak with McGrath. Go down to your coachman. I'll meet you in the street directly. The devil, I nearly forgot."

"What?"

"My blackmailing screed." He bent over the stack of papers on the table. "This is a fair copy of the first fifty pages. I told you I was slow. You may need it."

Wilson reached for the sheaf. "I daresay Newsham has his own copy by now."

"Or Lord George." Richard handed Wilson the manuscript copy. For an unsmiling moment their eyes met.

"I shall have Newsham's head in a basket," Wilson said tightly. "He broke his word to me."

Richard's mouth relaxed. "Lead on."

Wilson returned to his town house before six with the stench of Newgate in his nostrils and wrath stiffening his backbone. It was one thing to contemplate criminality in the abstract and quite another to confront it in the flesh, whining for mercy and babbling betrayals.

Sarah met him in the foyer.

"I've seen your brother. He's well and his children are safe," Wilson said, answering the question in her eyes.

"Oh, thank God. Tell me."

"Will you await my explanations, my dear? I've been to Newgate Prison and I shan't be fit for decent company until I've had a hot bathe and fresh linen."

"Richard is not in gaol!"

"No, but it's a complicated business. Please, Sally."

269

"I'll tell *Maman* you've found them." Sarah's voice trembled. "But do not dally, Robin, I beg you." Sarah and Wilson had been ten days in Town, having failed to trace Richard and the children from Hampshire. The duchess, drawn by Sarah's apprehensive letters, had only arrived two days before.

Rather more than an hour later Wilson had completed his toilet and written Newsham a blunt note requesting the duke to call next morning. He thought he had revealed enough to ensure Newsham's response. That accomplished, Wilson descended to the withdrawing room in which, according to his man, his wife and mother-in-law awaited him.

Wilson made his bow to the dowager. Pulling the tails of his correct blue evening coat aside, he sat on the gold-striped sopha opposite her throne, a gilt chair with armrests which was reserved for her exclusive use.

As always the dowager sat very upright. Her small, slipper-shod feet rested on the striped satin cover of the footstool and her elegant hands were clasped decorously in front of her. She had dressed for dinner in some glowing fabric—shot silk perhaps—of a shade between brown and green. She wore a turban of the same hue. The fabric brought out the brilliance of her hazel eyes, which, bright and calm, were fixed upon Wilson.

Sarah was not calm. She had been seated at her mother's side when he entered. Now she jumped up from her perch and fairly flung herself onto the sopha by his side.

"Where are they, Robin?"

"The children? I don't know, my dear. Richard didn't tell me. I gather that Mrs. Foster and her son and aunt are with them."

"Thank God. If anything had happened to them—"

"Did my son account for his extraordinary conduct, Robert?" the dowager interrupted, her measured tones overriding Sarah's emotional outburst.

The sounds and stench of Newgate were still vivid in

Wilson's mind. He drew a long, purifying breath and explained what he knew. Sarah punctuated his tale with distressed exclamations. The dowager said nothing. She watched him, unwinking as a Buddha. She had gone rather white, however, and when he came to his interview with the imprisoned footpad she closed her eyes briefly. Wilson could have sworn her lips formed a name, but no sound reached him.

"I've asked Newsham and George to meet me here tomorrow at eleven," he concluded. "Richard will drop the charges when Newsham can be brought to agree to his terms."

"Then he means to prevent a scandal?"

Wilson met the dowager's brilliant gaze. "I believe so. If Newsham cooperates."

"He will cooperate," the dowager said with finality.

A brief silence ensued. Sarah broke it. "Is Richard coming early?"

"He's not coming here at all. He agreed to let me deal with Newsham."

"If I were Richard I'd want to *see* Newsham writhe," Sarah burst out.

"If you were Richard you'd probably wish to strangle Newsham." Wilson gave Sarah's hand a reassuring squeeze. It was ice cold. "At first Richard asked me to arrange a meeting. It was my idea to spare him the interview. He has been under considerable strain, and I doubt Newsham is capable of dealing with him civilly."

Wilson thought of the carriage ride from Newgate, Richard still and tense in the corner seat. It had occurred to Wilson that Newsham's arrogance might well prove the last straw. With that in mind he had volunteered to deal with Newsham alone, but he had half expected a sharp set-down.

Instead Richard stared at him with painful intensity. "Should you be more likely to succeed without me?"

After a moment Wilson said honestly, "I think you need

have no apprehensions either way. George's marplot has put Newsham in your hands. Name your terms. I'll convey them for you."

"When?"

"Tomorrow morning."

Richard drew a ragged breath. "Very well. If you will be so kind." And, after a pause, "I've been afraid I'd lose my temper and say something actionable."

"Or draw his grace's noble cork?"

"Or worse." Richard did not smile.

"I have my own bone to pick," Wilson said comfortably. "Let me at him."

"Fire-eater." Richard leaned back against the squabs, eyes closed. "I'll have to have a guarantee of some sort."

"Yes, in writing." The carriage swayed turning a corner and Wilson, who was leaning forward, grabbed the strap. "Tell me your terms, Richard."

"They haven't changed. No interference of any kind with me or my children or my friends." He opened his eyes and smiled at Wilson. "Or with any publisher unlucky enough to take me on. I nearly forgot that."

"Nothing else?"

"My God, isn't that enough?"

Wilson cleared his throat. "You're too easy by far."

"I'm out for peace, not revenge," Richard retorted. "Revenge is too damned exhausting. Boring, too. Have you ever read *The Revenger's Tragedy*?"

"Beaumont and Fletcher?"

"Tourneur, I think. Tedious stuff. Pure fustian."

At that very literary conclusion Wilson had to laugh.

As they came once more to the noisome street in which Richard's quarters lay, Wilson turned the conversation to practicalities. Remembering the footpads, he waited until Richard had disappeared into the house, then caused his coachman to drive home.

Now, safe on his own turf, Wilson met the dowager's enquiring gaze. "I expect a response from Newsham before dinner, if he has not gone out to his club."

"We need not spoil *our* dinner with waiting. Richard will be very much obliged to you, Robert, as I am." The duchess added, in measured tones, "You are a man of sound good sense."

Wilson flushed with pleasure even as a wry inner voice told him that the dowager—and Newsham—would indeed be obliged to him.

They made an excellent dinner. The saddle of mutton had travelled from Yorkshire with the dowager. Superb. The turbot was fresh as May.

When the ladies had withdrawn, Wilson's butler brought him a reply from Newsham on a silver salver. Tomorrow at eleven. Wilson savoured his port and rehearsed his strategy.

Next morning apprehension made his breakfast sit less easy than his dinner. Sarah picked at her buttered eggs and toast. Both of them drank too much coffee. The dowager was breaking her fast with tea and toast fingers in her own suite, so they were alone. Breakfast with Sarah was Wilson's favourite meal, but this morning they stared at one another and made nervous small talk.

The dowager rarely appeared belowstairs before one o'clock, so Wilson was startled, and not best pleased, to find her seated in the morning room when he and Sarah entered to await Newsham.

Sarah was also surprised. "*Maman!* You need not face Newsham. Ought you? Your heart . . ."

"Face Newsham, indeed. He will have to face me. Do stop dithering, Sally." The duchess set her elegant jaw and would not be budged.

Promptly at eleven Newsham was announced. Looking as much like an icicle as was possible in a man of his complexion, the duke entered the room with Lord George, who looked sheepish, trailing behind. Wilson was consoled to see that the dowager's presence flustered her sons. It had flustered him, too.

The formalities over, Newsham took the offensive. "George has something to say to you."

Lord George writhed. "Dash it, Keighley, not now!" He rolled a wild eye in the dowager's direction. She regarded him stonily.

"Now," Newsham said, grim.

"*I* hired the footpads." Lord George looked almost as miserable as he deserved to be.

Wilson gave him a cold stare. "I know you did."

"Without Newsham's knowledge," Lord George muttered.

"That I find hard to credit."

George scowled. "I can think for myself. Thing is, Keighley told me of his plan to send Falk abroad. Thought I'd help it along. Seemed to be working."

"Which of you corrupted Richard's publisher?" Scorn flushed Sarah's cheeks. Becomingly, Wilson thought. "Of all the low, despicable, mean-minded—"

"Sarah." Wilson shook his head. *No. Not yet.*

Sarah bit her lip. "Well, George?"

"Dash it, that was all Keighley's doing."

A silence fell.

"Thank you, George." Newsham took a pinch of snuff. "I am very much obliged to you in everything."

"By God, you are obliged to me," George shot back. "I found the scent again when you'd lost it. *I* found the copyist chap, didn't I? You was out of Town."

Newsham withered his brother with a stare, turning to Wilson. "At no time did George tell me of his private assassins."

"Assassins! No such thing." George was rosy with honest indignation. "Couple of bullyboys I met at a cockfight. Useful to me more than once. I told 'em to rough Falk up a bit. No intent to kill, either time."

"You relieve my mind, George." Wilson had taken his station by the fire, for the weather was chilly. "Richard had partial use of his right arm before your thugs set upon him. They contrived to finish what the French begun. His arm is now useless. I trust you're proud of your cowardly little private army." Out of patience, he turned on Newsham. "Do you understand that there's no point in pretending innocence?"

Newsham's tight mouth crimped with distaste. "I had nothing to do with the two assaults. So long as you understand that." The duke was seated in a gilt chair. One hand smoothed the velvet of the armrest.

"Oh, *I* understand it. A magistrate might find it incredible, in the light of your other intimidations. After all, it's a fairly drastic step to deprive a man of his livelihood. From there to direct assault is no great leap."

Newsham's eyes flashed. "If George hadn't interfered Falk would be long gone."

"Don't flatter yourself, duke. *Richard* is not a coward, whatever you and George may be. He now has you at *point non plus*. Admit it."

Newsham's hands clenched. Wilson thought the duke would rise and walk out, but he did not. "Very well. He has me at *point non plus*. Thanks to George." He shot his brother a venomous glance.

Wilson stuck to his guns. "What do you offer?"

"I'll double the annuity and settle five hundred pounds on both brats if Falk will leave the country at once."

Wilson stared, half admiring the man's effrontery. From her seat on the sopha Sarah began to splutter.

The dowager intervened. "You mistake the gravity of the situation, Newsham."

Wilson cast her a grateful look. "Between the threats in the letter you writ Richard on your father's death and this latest imbroglio, Richard has sufficient evidence for the courts."

"He'd never win an action at law." Newsham's eyes were hard with contempt.

"Do you wish to be brought to trial? You surprise me."

Newsham's eyes dropped.

"*I* think Richard ought to lay charges," Sarah burst out. "You should be flayed, both of you."

"Sally . . ."

She subsided, fuming.

The dowager kept calm. "I shall write *my* memoirs, Newsham. I have often been tempted to do so since your father's death."

Aghast, Newsham and George spoke together.

"By God, madam . . ."

"No, dash it, Mama, do you wish to destroy us all?"

Wilson, as startled as they, was hard put not to laugh. From being rather pale Newsham had turned a rich plum colour.

"Odd though it may seem, I do not, George." The dowager turned to regard the duke. "If I thought you meant to continue this ill-advised persecution of your brother, Newsham, I should take up my pen at once. I have interesting memories." She took a short, quick breath. It was the first sign that she was not as placid as she appeared to be. "Sarah!"

Sarah went to her mother's chair.

"Your arm, my dear." The dowager rose slowly and stood leaning on her taller daughter. Her sons must, perforce, stand, too. She stared Newsham down. "I am weary of you all. Newsham, you will submit to whatever terms Colonel Falk requires, and you will go abroad for a calendar year, bag and baggage. Those are *my* terms. Take George with you. He needs a keeper." She walked to the door, still leaning on Sarah. "Come, Sally. Robert will deal with your brothers freer in our absence." Sarah looked too stunned to rebel.

Wilson was enjoying himself for the first time in a month. The door closed on the ladies. For a frozen moment none of the three men moved. Then Newsham began to pace.

George collapsed into his chair. "She can't mean it."

"Shall you put her to the test?"

"Be still, George, if you can say nothing intelligent." Newsham came to a halt at Wilson's side. "Tell me what I must do." He was so close Wilson could see tiny beads of sweat on his immaculately shaven upper lip.

Wilson walked to the empty sopha and seated himself with deliberation, crossing one pantaloon-clad leg over the other and admiring the gleam of his Hessians. "Richard wants what he always wanted—to be left in peace. I tried to persuade him to ask for reparations, but the fact is he wants nothing whatever to do with either of you. Quixotic, but there it is."

Lord George took a step forward. "What of the succession?"

"Content you. There is the dowager's sworn statement. Besides, Richard has already given Newsham his word that he will make no claim on the estate. *Richard's* word is not in question."

"I say!" Lord George flushed at the insult.

Newsham was too dispirited to resent the implications of Wilson's remark. "What else?"

"I require a stronger guarantee than your word this time, Newsham." Turning the screws.

The duke's mouth thinned.

Bland, Wilson went on, "I want a written statement of culpability from you and from George. I mean to call in witnesses to your signatures."

Newsham made a strangling noise in his throat.

Wilson gave him a straight look. "If ever I hear of the least interference, if Richard or his children or Mrs. Foster or Matthew Foster should suffer an accident of any sort, I shall see to it that you are prosecuted to the full extent of the law. In the House of Lords, if need be. Is that clear?"

"No, dash it," George protested. "Might be overturned in a carriage."

"Then you'd both best pray for their safety." Wilson now felt no amusement at all. "I warn you, I'm in earnest. And no more tampering with publishers and copyists. If Richard's livelihood is interrupted again, I'll see to it myself that copies of his memoir are sent to every leader of the Ton and the entire peerage, with a gloss for the slow-witted. And you can send Richard the galleys of the book you purloined from his printer, Newsham. I trust you haven't destroyed them as well as the plates."

"The galleys are with my solicitor."

"I want the book in Richard's hands by two o'clock. That gives you little time to write your sordid confessions, so you'll have to be brisk about it. From the beginning of your persecution, Newsham, if you please. Eighteen eight, I believe. There is paper. Write."

To Wilson's surprise there were no more protests. He knew that Newsham was now his enemy, and discovered, with the same relief he had felt as a child when he discovered a guy was only a turnip dressed to frighten children, that he didn't mind at all.

=== 34 ===

WHEN WILSON CALLED for his carriage at half past two, having tucked into a cold nuncheon with restored appetite, he found that he was not to carry the good news *solus*. Bonneted and buttoned into their best pelisses, Sarah and the dowager awaited him in the foyer. Her grace was leaning on a silver-headed cane.

"No, Duchess. Absolutely not."

The duchess gave him a cool stare. "Do you deny me your escort?"

"Yes, ma'am, and you'd not go far in that neighbourhood without it, I assure you."

"I'm not afraid of a few vulgar loungers."

"Then you ought to be afraid of three flights of very steep, badly lit stairs."

She blinked at that. "You could carry me up."

"I can scarce carry myself up." He softened. "Indeed, ma'am, you need not exert yourself. I'll bear any message you like."

"Sarah?"

"Perhaps he's right, *Maman*. Pray allow James to help you to your rooms. I'll go with Robert and report to you afterwards."

"Oh, very well," the dowager grumbled. She was an elderly lady, after all, and she sounded elderly. "I consider you vastly disobliging, Robert. Is he well?"

"Richard?" The abrupt question startled Wilson. The

dowager had shown no great interest in Richard's health after Water-loo, when she had had more cause for concern.

"He seemed well enough," Wilson admitted when he had mastered his surprise. "Tired, and not in an easy frame of mind. I daresay he'll cheer up when Sarah and I have given him the good word. Now we must go or he'll be imagining I've failed him."

Sarah's concept of London extended as far as St. James's Palace. She was a creature of Westminster, and indeed, of the safer precincts of that borough. There were worse kennels in London, but in all conscience Richard's chosen territory was bad enough.

As it had on the previous day, the carriage attracted a swarm of beggars and urchins, some hopeful, some merely curious, but all vocal. By the time she and Wilson had passed the slatternly landlady, Sarah had heard more direct insults than in her life to that point. Fortunately most of the comments were couched in terms so obscure Wilson doubted she understood them. Sarah was not pigeon-livered, however. In the dim, skylit hallway he could see spots of colour burning on her cheekbones, but her chin was up. Her husband regarded her with a sympathy he was too out of breath to express.

"Go in to him, Robin," she said quietly. "Warn him I've come. He does not expect me."

"Very well." Wilson tried the door and found it un-latched.

Richard was leaning on the table reading from a stack of galley proofs. He looked over his shoulder as Wilson entered. "Hullo. In good time. Is this your doing?" He tapped the papers.

"Yes. I induced Newsham to disgorge his spoils."

"I'm obliged to you."

"Richard, I've brought Sarah."

Richard straightened and turned. "Well, good God, don't leave her out in that hallway!"

Amused by this display of brotherly protectiveness,

Wilson pulled the door wide. "Come in, my dear. Richard is not disposed to eat you."

After one incredulous look round the cold, half furnished room, Sarah forced a smile. "I'm glad to see you well, Richard."

"Thank you." Richard turned back to Wilson. "Did something go amiss?"

"No."

Richard let out a long breath and shoved his hair from his forehead. "I thought it must be so when Newsham's servant brought the galleys. Newsham gave you a written assurance?"

"The duke and George. Assurances and confessions. I have them here." Wilson patted his breast pocket. "You'll want to read them and decide what to do with them." He drew the carefully folded sheets out.

Richard went to the window. The room was poorly lit. He fumbled the papers open one-handed. "If Sarah wants to risk it, the cane chair should bear her," he said absently.

Sarah was watching her brother. When Wilson pulled the chair for her she came out of her trance and made a *moue* of distaste. She sat, keeping her skirts raised above the grimy floorboards. Wilson lifted Richard's wet cloak from the other chair and sat as well. The chair creaked but held him.

Either Richard had been out or the damp cloak lied. He was dressed for it. This time he had slipped his right arm through his coat sleeve. The right shoulder was already noticeably lower than the left. Wilson felt another stab of anger. Damn George and his hirelings to perdition. That morning George had been embarrassed, resentful, indignant, but he had shown no remorse at all. Wilson thought him incapable of it.

Having read the confessions with frowning attention, Richard rattled the papers and swore under his breath. "Here. I can't fold them properly. Will you keep them for me, Wilson?"

Surprised and moved by the trust implicit in the request, Wilson nodded his agreement.

"Thank you." Richard's mouth quirked. "Did no one ever teach Lord George to spell?"

Wilson laughed. Sarah smiled, too. "Tallie always swore George read backwards. Do you remember Tallie, Richard?"

"Miss Talcott? Yes." Richard leaned against the table. "I daresay you mean to cross-examine me about my offspring, Sarah. You might as well begin."

"Where are they?"

He glanced briefly at Wilson. "Treglyn."

Sarah looked blank.

"Lord Clanross's Cornwall estate, I fancy," Wilson murmured.

"Oh, thank God!" Sarah's relief was disproportionate, Wilson thought, puzzled.

Comprehension dawned upon her brother. "Did you imagine I had bestowed them here in the top floor back?"

Sarah flushed. "I didn't know."

Richard was not entirely amused. "What a good idea. Pity I didn't think of it."

Sarah made a swift recover. "I'm persuaded that Emily Foster would have objected."

That did amuse him. "When I consider the objections she raised to a journey to Cornwall, I shudder to think what she'd say to this rookery. I have a letter of her. Do you care to read it?"

"Of all things—if you don't mind, Richard."

He raised his brows. "Why should I mind?"

"Manner of speaking," Sarah mumbled.

Richard surveyed the strewn table. "Where the devil did I put it? Oh, my coat." He withdrew a sheet with a broken seal from his pocket. The paper was crossed in Mrs. Foster's neat hand. "She says Amy and Matt have taken to running footraces in the gallery. I hope Tom's ancestors have stopped whirling in their graves."

Sarah smiled. "I wish I might see the children."

"So do I," Richard rejoined, his voice dry. He turned to Wilson. "I mean to go down to Cornwall tonight on the mail unless you think there's some urgent reason for me to stay in Town."

Wilson considered. Beside him Sarah, absorbed in the letter, gave a subdued snort of mirth. Wilson shifted on the stiff chair. "Everything is well in hand. I foresee no difficulties."

"Good. I bought our places on the coach this morning. McGrath goes with me." Richard walked to the window again and stood looking down. "I can return when I've restored Mrs. Foster to Wellfield House. A week, say, or ten days."

Wilson rose with a creaking of chair joints and joined him. Two curs were snarling over a bone in the alley. "That won't be necessary. Newsham and George should be safely in exile by then. You may make whatever arrangements you wish at your leisure."

"Exile?" Richard's brows drew together.

Wilson explained the dowager's *coup*. "I confess I did not expect that of your mother. She is the most redoubtable lady."

"I should think it very much in her style," Richard said quietly. "Out of sight, out of mind."

Wilson could think of no comfortable reply. He glanced back at Sarah. She was finishing the letter and appeared unconscious of the exchange.

Smiling, she looked up at the two men. "What a delightful letter Emily writes. I can almost see Tommy confronting the housekeeper." She sprang up. "You ought to marry her."

Wilson went cold.

"A splendid notion." Richard took the letter from his sister and restored it to his coat. "I've already embarrassed Mrs. Foster sufficiently without flinging my liabilities at her feet as well. Why don't you take up rescuing chimney

283

sweeps or fallen women, Sarah," he added, well and truly losing his temper, "and stay out of my life? It's chaotic enough at the moment without your help."

Sarah looked as if she had been struck.

For once Wilson felt no impulse to rescue her, but he was by nature a tactful man, so he interposed a question about the still imprisoned footpad, leaving Sarah to stare out the window in her turn. He thought she was crying.

Richard, still ruffled, snapped an answer at random, drew a breath, and put his mind to the problem of the footpad. He meant to see the man released and on his way out of the country that afternoon, and had made tentative arrangements. Efficient.

"That's an expence you oughtn't to bear," Wilson said bluntly.

"I collect you ought to," Richard jeered, still angry.

"No. Lord George is the appropriate party, I fancy." Wilson held Richard's gaze. After an explosive moment, he had the satisfaction of seeing his brother-in-law's mouth relax in a grin.

"He'll balk."

"I think not. At the moment George is thoroughly subdued."

"*Rompré?*"

"If I understand the meaning of the term. How much, Richard?"

"Fifty guineas."

Wilson nodded. "I'll direct George to send your banker a draught at once."

"He'd be better advised to send it to Tom Conway's banker. I had to draw on Tom's letter of credit. He banks with Coutts."

"Very well."

An indignant sniff recalled Sarah's presence to their minds. Wilson met Richard's eyes. Richard grimaced, but he went to the window and touched his sister's stiff shoulder.

"*Pax*, Sarah. I'm sorry I snarled at you, but you really must give up your meddling ways."

"Meddling!"

"I daresay you always act from the best motives, but from my viewpoint it feels remarkably like being overrun by heavy cavalry."

"Oh, Richard," Sarah wailed. "I'm sorry. It's all been my fault." She burst into tears.

Richard patted her and rolled his eyes at Wilson. "Help."

In a moment, Wilson mouthed. He extracted a large lawn handkerchief from his pocket. When the first throes of the storm had subsided he retrieved his wife from her brother's damp bosom and seated her once more on the cane-bottomed chair.

Sarah blew her nose violently.

"Come, that's better, my dear. Cheer up." Wilson tidied her bonnet, which was askew. "All's well that ends well, after all, and you'll be giving Richard a very odd notion of your understanding if you insist on blaming yourself for Newsham's deeds."

One bloodshot hazel eye peered at him from behind the handkerchief. She hiccoughed on a sob.

"I rather think Newsham has done me a favour," Richard ventured, eyeing his sister warily.

Sarah gave an incredulous sniff.

Wilson squeezed her shoulder. "How so?"

"I've been rereading my novel, and it's a good thing it never reached the bookstalls. It sounds as if I were unconscious when I writ it. I probably was."

Wilson chuckled. "Shall you look for a new publisher at once?"

"When I've revised it."

Sarah drew a shuddering breath. "I collect we're to be grateful to Newsham for saving you from the reviewers' shafts."

"Just so."

"Ha."

Wilson, his hand still on her shoulder, felt her shiver, more from reaction, he thought than from cold, though the room was cold enough in all conscience.

"I can't think why you chose such a miserable kennel to hide out in," Sarah muttered. "Surely you could have found a snugger lair."

"No doubt, but few so convenient for entrapping foot-pads. Let be, Sally."

"Oh, very well. Shall we go, Robin?"

"Yes, if I wish to keep John Coachman's goodwill." Wilson gave Sarah his hand.

She rose, straightening her skirts and gathering up her gloves and reticule from the table. "Shall you call on us when the dust settles, Richard?"

He hesitated, but acquiesced with fair grace, and Sarah gave him a sisterly peck on the cheek. Wilson and Sarah made their way down to the besieged carriage. Richard followed them out.

When they were seated, Richard stuck his head in the door. "Good-bye, Sarah, Wilson."

Sir Robert remembered to hold out his left hand. "Good-bye."

"Thank you." Richard's handclasp was brief but warm, his eyes grave.

The door slammed to and Richard's voice rang out on the chill air. "Hi, you lot!"

The gabble of voices from the tattered crowd devilling Wilson's coachman stilled.

"Here. A drink to the lady's eyes." Richard tossed a handful of coppers. There was a burst of good-natured laughter and a scrabble for the coins. The horses' path cleared miraculously and the carriage swayed into motion.

Wilson pulled down the glass. "Thanks!"

Richard gave a casual wave from the steps and disappeared into the house.

Wilson and Sarah rode in silence through the squalid

streets. When the carriage turned into the wider stretch of the new Regent Street, which was still in construction, Sarah heaved a relieved sigh. "I'm glad you didn't allow *Maman* to come. What a dreadful place."

"I ought to have forbade you to come, too, Sal."

"Well, you couldn't."

"I know." He smiled at her. Sarah was still ruffled, red-nosed from crying, and pretty as new paint. "Neither to hold nor to bind, are you?"

She looked remorseful. "I had to see Richard."

"I know it."

"Forgive me?"

"There's nothing to forgive, my dear. You're my wife."

She leaned against his shoulder. "Yes, and glad of it. Can we go home to Knowlton soon, Robin?"

"In a few days."

"Richard will have reached Cornwall by then."

Thank God, said Wilson to himself. He was yearning for a little peace and quiet.

"That slumming kennel . . ."

"Such language!"

"It *was* a back slum. I daresay Richard was clever to find the place, but he could just as well have chosen an inn in some decayed area that would have served his purposes."

"But not at so low a rent."

She had been leaning against his arm and now sat upright, stiff as a poker. "He said—"

"I know what he said."

Sarah's mouth compressed. "Men!"

"We're all vainglorious creatures." Wilson smiled at her. "I daresay Richard was afraid you'd dash out and pop your pearls for him. Sarah to the rescue again."

Sarah flushed.

"No more meddling, Sally." He patted her hand. "I must admit I was relieved to hear he has Clanross's letter of credit to draw on, for I must otherwise have had to offer

him a loan of money. I'm not turning miser," he added a
she bridled, "but I was sure he'd plant me a facer if
offered."

"Such language," Sarah mimicked.

Wilson grinned.

Her face clouded. "What's to be done?"

"Nothing, my dear. Richard will come about. He has the
pension, after all. In the circumstances, though, it was
doubly tactless in you to prescribe matrimony."

She shot him a defiant look out of the corner of her eye.
"It would be an excellent match."

"For Richard."

"For them both. Emily Foster loves him."

It was Wilson's turn to be startled. "She confided in
you?"

"Not in so many words."

Wilson laughed. "Wishful thinking, Sally."

Her neatly gloved hands clenched into fists. "Stop dealing with me as if I were a ninnyhammer. I have eyes. When
I brought her your letters from Brussels this summer I
watched Emily narrowly. I could tell what she felt."

"What, then?" he asked, skeptical.

"Exactly what I'd have felt had you been lying ill in a
foreign place."

That took a moment to register. Wilson's cheeks burned
with astonished pleasure. He felt as if he had been given the
Garter.

Unaware that she had made a gratifying revelation,
Sarah went on. "If Richard asked her, Emily would marry
him like a shot."

"An impecunious, illegitimate, unemployed, one-armed
scribbler of satires? Why should she consider him? Mrs.
Foster is a woman of the first respectability and may look
higher for a husband than your half brother."

"Robin!"

"My dear, that's not what I think, and, whatever her
sentiments, not what Emily Foster thinks either." He

leaned toward her, earnest. "It's a fair approximation of what Richard feels, however, and with some reason. Besides," he added as her eyes darkened with distress, "we do not know Richard's tastes. Perhaps he favours opera dancers."

Her eyes narrowed to slits. "Black-eyed señoritas, more likely. It's not fair."

"Certainly not. There are few señoritas in rural Hampshire."

Sarah fetched him a blow to the midsection that left him gasping and laughing. He had to placate her.

Presently revolted passersby in the vicinity of Cavendish Square could observe a plump, middle-aged gentleman and a woman old enough to know better embracing in a carriage in broad daylight, a clear instance of the decay of modern manners.

Epilogue
Emily
Cornwall
1815

= 35 =

It was Amy's birthday. She had been unnaturally virtuous all day. Richard had posted the obligatory doll well in advance, and Emily was set to produce it at the little girl's birthday dinner, but the magic had begun to fade from Amy's dolls in the past year. Emily thought the child would have preferred her father's presence to any number of gifts.

Amy and Matt missed Richard almost as much as they missed their ponies. They were always asking Emily impossible questions, the worst being "When he is coming to take us home?" Only Tommy, unmoved by nostalgia, existed at Treglyn in a state of perfect bliss. Peg had weaned him that summer, and today, as the culmination of a week of heroick continence, he was to be breeched.

"Like Matt!"

"Certainly, darling."

Tommy was beside himself with joy, but fortunately not to the point of neglecting to use the requisite domestic offices. Before they left Wellfield, Emily had caused her seamstress to stitch up half a dozen tiny pairs of nankeen trousers. Now she brought out a pair and she and Tommy stood together by the pier glass in Emily's dressing room, admiring them.

"Brishes?"

"Nankeens," Emily said. "Nankeen breeches. Or trousers, more correctly."

"Trows." Tommy indicated vigourously that the time had come for his transformation.

"It's early . . . Oh, very well, Tommy."

They had a struggle with the buttons. Presently, however, Tommy preened before the mirror in the compleat dress of a little English gentleman—black pumps, white stockings, nankeens, frilled shirt, blue jacket with brass buttons. An English gentleman *manqué*. *He looks incorrigibly Spanish*, Emily thought, her eyes filling with sentimental tears. *My baby. And Amy is just five years old.*

"Nankies," Tommy shouted and roared out into the hall, breeched legs twinkling.

Emily caught up with him outside the schoolroom. He was still too short to open the door. When the other children had applauded him and Peggy had shed her own quota of sentimental tears, there was a lull in the action, for it was still half an hour to the birthday dinner. In a spirit of generosity Matt decided to teach Tommy naughts and crosses. Amy took up her station at the window.

The Treglyn schoolroom overlooked the front entrance and the long carriageway. In the past week Amy had spent every unoccupied waking moment staring down the carriageway. She meant to be the first to announce her father's coming.

Emily grieved for her. "I really don't think he can be coming so soon, darling. Next month, perhaps."

"He'll come." Amy pressed her nose to the glass.

It was blowing a modest gale and the child could surely not see far through the rain and dusk. When Amy breathed out she made patches of fog on the panes. Presently she was drawing interesting faces in the mist. Relieved to see her distracted, Emily didn't try to stop her.

Aunt Fan came in and was properly awed by Tommy's trousers. Emily had just decided to smooth her own hair a last time in the schoolroom mirror before leading the party downstairs to dinner when Amy gave a shriek.

"Good heavens, child, what is it?" Aunt Fan peered out the window.

"Papa!" Amy gave another whoop and added, complaisant, "I thaid he'd come." She had lately lost her front teeth. The result was a fine Castillian lisp.

Unwilling to credit the announcement and unwilling not to, Emily stood frozen.

Aunt Fan squinted. After a judicious moment she said, "I believe the child is right, Emma. There are two men walking up the drive. The taller appears to be Colonel Falk."

Emily leapt over the boys, who were stretched out on the carpet drawing *X*s and *O*s on a slate, and dashed to the window. "Where?"

Aunt Fan pointed.

"Papapapapapa!" Amy was chanting happily.

"Do stop bouncing, Amy." Emily peered. Her heart tripped along like one of the steam hammers Tom Conway raved about in his letters. "I can't see—oh." She swallowed hard. "Yes, so it is."

She exchanged glances with her aunt. Had something gone wrong?

"Wonder what brings him so soon?" Aunt Fan murmured.

"My birthday," Amy crowed. "Whoop!" And she was off, streaking for the door.

"Catch her, Peggy!" Emily picked up her skirts and pursued, alas, too late. Amy had made good her escape.

By now the boys had caught fire, too, and were hopping about like fleas. Emily, almost as giddy as they were, began to laugh. "Yes, dears, we'll go down, too. Only please, a little slower."

"Nankies!" Tommy shouted, bouncing.

"Come on, Mama." Matt dragged her hand.

Emily cast a last rueful look at Aunt Fan and Peggy, and allowed the boys to sweep her out into the hall. Aunt and Peggy followed at a more sedate pace.

"Oh, saints preserve us all, they'll be breaking their

necks, all three of 'em," Peggy could be heard wailing as Emily and her two headlong escorts clattered down the first flight of steep polished stairs.

"No, Matt, not the bannister!" Emily gasped, laughing, as they reached the first floor landing.

"Oh, Mama."

"*No!*" Tommy was clutching her hand for balance but he seemed bent on jumping his way down. She grabbed the tail of his new blue coat.

Matt grasped the bannister with both hands and compromised by leaping and slithering sidewise the rest of the way. He made a terrific clatter.

By this time the commotion had stirred the servants to life, and the aged Treglyn butler creaked into the foyer bearing a branch of lit candles. He was followed by the gaping footman and the housekeeper.

Dancing with impatience, Amy struggled with the latch of the huge oak door.

"Now, Miss Amy . . ." The butler set his candles on the hall table.

"It'th my papa! Open it, pleathe, Turvey." She gave him her famous gap-toothed smile. "Pleathe."

"Amy, wait!" Emily called from the stairs. She'd got halfway down the last flight with Tommy jumping and shrieking beside her.

Amy was far too agile for the ancient Turvey. He made the mistake of unlatching the door. Casting an impudent grin over her shoulder, she slipped out under his elbow into the night. Turvey peered after her, clucking.

"Lord, she'll take her death. No, Matt. Oh, Turvey, I beg your pardon." Emily finally achieved the foyer, panting. "Thank you, Charles." This to the footman who had collared a red-faced Matt. "It's Amy's father, you see, come from London. She saw him from the schoolroom and there was no holding her. The rest of us"—she gave Matt a Meaningful Look and tightened her grip on Tommy's hand—"will await him here in a civilised manner."

296

The servants looked sympathetic, if bewildered. They knew of Richard, but hadn't met him. Matt squirmed.

"It's Amy's birthday, Matt," Emily said gently.

Matt made a face but subsided.

"Will you be requiring another place for dinner, then, m'dear?" Mrs. Denning, the housekeeper, was a Cornishwoman with a strong sense of order. It had taken Emily a week to realise the woman enjoyed the challenge their visit represented.

"Yes—ah, no. Colonel Falk may take Mrs. McGrath's place. She will want to greet her husband properly. If a chamber could be prepared for Colonel Falk, hot water, of course. And I daresay dinner ought to be put back half an hour. Yes."

"Very good, missus." Mrs. Denning gave an approving nod. She liked a decisive manner, or so Aunt Fan said. Emily had been cultivating a decisive manner for a month. Smiling, Mrs. Denning vanished into the domestic netherland.

In the next minutes Emily's eagerness was undermined by the horrible conviction that something must have gone wrong with Tom Conway's scheme. Probably Richard was going to gather the children up and fly to the Antipodes. Emily wondered if her father would visit her in Van Dieman's Land, and banished the thought as unworthy. Probably Richard would spurn her, if she offered to come. Probably he would sail to Montevideo and marry a wealthy Spanish lady at once, and Emily would never see him or the children again.

"Charles, do you assist Colonel Falk and his man." Turvey, quavering but authoritative. "I believe they have . . . yes, a portmanteau and saddlebags. At once, if you please."

The footman leapt to obey. Voices could be heard but Turvey's bent back blocked the view.

"If you will just step inside, sir. I am Turvey. Welcome to Treglyn." Turvey threw the door wide.

Richard entered, dripping. "Thank you, Turvey. I seem to have acquired a very damp child." He was carrying Amy under his cloak. She stuck her head out and grinned.

Turvey removed Richard's hat and cloak, shaking the water from them onto the black and white tiles of the entryway, and Richard set his daughter down. Wet and beaming, she clung to his side.

"How do you do, Richard?" Emily croaked. She took a step forward.

Blinking against the light, he looked over at her and smiled. "Very well and very wet. I'm glad to see you."

Emily's knees quivered and her heart lurched, but she contrived to utter her most urgent thought. "Has anything gone wrong?"

"No, no. Everything's splendid. Amy, *querida*, dislodge yourself from my leg so I can move." Amy bounced a few feet away.

Richard took Emily's hand. His was cold but his smile was warm. "It's all right. I didn't mean to alarm you. I thought McGrath and I should arrive as soon as a letter, so here we are."

Emily heaved a sigh of pure relief and smiled at him shakily. "I'm so glad to see you. But you must be frozen, and McGrath, too. Did you walk from the village?"

"From the coaching inn."

"Good heavens, that's three miles!"

"It felt like ten," he said ruefully. "Poor McGrath is half dead from dragging that portmanteau. We didn't realize Treglyn was so far."

Peggy had spotted her wet spouse. She gave a screech and flung herself down the last stairs, uttering a barrage of greetings and predictions of imminent pneumonia. The baffled Turvey, who was not accustomed to admitting anyone's servants by the front door, freed McGrath from his greatcoat. The batman scowled round him and grunted.

"Er, perhaps Charles could show McGrath down to the kitchen to dry off," Emily ventured. "It's warm there."

Charles, the footman, damp and laden with portmanteau and saddlebags, had slipped in the door, too. Turvey shut it. Turvey regarded McGrath with a stern eye. "An excellent idea, madam."

McGrath dripped and shivered.

Turvey softened. "A small glass of brandy might be in order, if I may be so bold."

"Faith, lead me to it," McGrath growled.

Emily stared. She had not thought him capable of articulate speech.

Richard laughed. "A *large* glass of brandy, I think, Turvey. Jerry, I'm obliged to you, as usual. Give over wailing, Pegeen, and see to your man's comfort." He gave Peg an affectionate squeeze of the shoulders and shoved his servants off in Charles's wake.

All this time Aunt Fan had been descending the stairs with unimpaired dignity. Stately as a galleon, she gained the foyer and advanced, hand outstretched. "Colonel Falk, a welcome sight. Trust your mission was successful."

Richard's eyes gleamed. He bowed over her hand. "It was, Miss Mayne. We rolled 'em up, foot, horse, and guns. And in short order, too."

"Excellent. We shall await your account with great interest. And now, sir, I believe you should retire to your room to dry off. Wet to the bone."

"In a minute." Richard looked round. "I think I see Matt over there by the hatrack. And who's that with him?"

"Nankies!" Tommy shrieked and flew at his father like a whirlwind.

Richard knelt in time to catch the little boy and hug him tightly. "So I see. All grown up, Tomkin? Like Matt." He smiled over Tommy's head at Matthew who, unaccountably shy, had hung back. "Hiding, Matt?"

Matt grinned, shamefaced, and advanced to be hugged in his turn. Watching Richard disentangle himself gently from the two boys, Emily decided to propose marriage at the first opportune moment.

The moment did not present itself that evening.

Amy's dinner could not help turning out a smashing success, for all that the food was a trifle overdone. The guest of honour, having drenched her best gown, had been hastily towelled and stuffed into an ordinary blue wool, but nothing could quench her high spirits. Amy's doll—beside whom her other gifts faded into temporary insignificance— was seen to be a tiny, splendidly haughty English lady in the first stare of the mode.

"What'th her name?" Amy demanded.

Richard looked startled. "Er, I've forgot. Just a moment. It'll come to me."

Emily smiled at him. So he didn't think of everything.

"Whopstraw," he said firmly, avoiding Emily's eyes. "Lady Whopstraw. Yes, I'm sure that was it, but you'll have to christen her yourself, Amy. My acquaintance with her was so brief we never reached first-name intimacy."

Amy's brow furrowed. "I know! Lady Tharah." She tested it on her tongue. "Lady Tharah Whopthtraw."

Richard fell into the whoops.

Everyone regarded him with sympathetic tolerance, even Amy. Emily was hard put not to laugh, too. So he had had further commerce with Sir Robert and Lady Sarah.

"It's a good name, Amy." Emily bestowed an approving nod on the puzzled child. "Doña Barbara and Doña Inez will be happy to receive Lady Sarah."

Sheepish and still chuckling, Richard wiped his eyes. "Sorry."

"That'th all right, Papa." Amy had already examined the fabric of the doll's gown. She gave a small satisfied nod and began to remove Lady Sarah's bonnet. She was very critical of her dolls' hair.

Richard said out of the corner of his mouth, "Tell me her teeth will grow back thoon."

"I trust they may. Matt's did." Emily choked on a laugh. Richard was certainly in tearing high spirits.

"Show us your fangs, Matt."

Matt grinned cheekily around a mouthful of cake.

"My God, aren't they rather large?"

"Matt's face will grow to accommodate his teeth in due time,"Aunt Fan offered.

"How old are you now, Matt?"

"Seven and a quarter. On my birthday," Matt pronounced, "I want a few de joy, like the king."

Richard winced. "Can you possibly mean a *feu de joie*?"

Matt looked at Emily.

"It is a French phrase," Emily said blandly. "We must defer to Colonel Falk's pronunciation, Matt. After all, he has the Order of Saint Lewis."

Richard flushed and grinned. "I knew there had to be a use for it. I'll set myself up as a tutor. French and deportment at a shilling a week."

Matt stared at him wide-eyed. Aunt Fan looked rather shocked. The sight of her aunt's disapproving face sent *Emily* into the whoops. It was plain that the gathering had begun to disintegrate. Tommy, worn out with glory, was half asleep in his plate.

The children safely abed, Emily and Aunt Fan carried Richard bodily off to the withdrawing room for explanations. Aunt Fan deserved that courtesy, though Emily had begun to wish herself and Richard marooned on a desert isle.

Would they never be alone together? Not that Richard seemed conscious of any such desire. Having spent two nights on the mail coach, he was by then nearly unconscious in the absolute sense of the word. A pot of strong tea and the intricacies of his narrative woke him up sufficiently for coherent speech, though he continued to suppress yawns at the most hair-raising points in the story.

When it sank in at last that he had been using himself as bait to entrap Newsham's agents, Emily's temper flew out the window. Her denunciation was vivid and comprehensive. Richard bore it meekly. In the end Aunt Fan interrupted the tirade and sent him off to bed.

As the door closed behind him, Emily came down out of the boughs with a thud. "What have I done?"

Aunt Fan regarded her enigmatically.

Emily held out her hands. "Look at me, Aunt. I'm shaking like a blancmange. I can't stand this much longer."

Aunt Fan shook her head. "When I was a gel I fancied myself in love with one of your father's Oxford friends. Showed all the symptoms—fits of crying, poor appetite, daydreams, short temper. Threw a brush at my abigail. Gave me pause."

"Oh, Aunt."

"Fortunately I recovered. Take a dose of salts, Emma, and go to bed."

Emily bored herself very much by bursting into tears.

Resigned, Aunt Fan mopped the excess and administered halfhearted pats.

"Why is it," Emily gasped between sobs, "that I'm only eloquent"—gasp—"when I'm furious with Richard?"

Aunt Fan considered the problem. "Love," she pronounced after a moment. "Form of madness."

"He's sent for Tom's carriage."

"Yes."

"And writ Papa we're coming home."

"So he said."

"Oh, Aunt, there's no time! We'll go back to Hampshire and everything will be just as it was." Emily gulped. "I don't want that anymore. It's not enough."

Aunt Fan made a soothing noise but Emily was not comforted.

The gale blew itself out before morning. Emily woke very early after a restless night. From the slant of light she decided it could not be eight o'clock. Scarcely dawn. Thanks to the wind, no morning mist hovered. The leaded casement of her bedchamber window framed the theatrical green-and-rust-streaked cliffs that bounded the manor. Beyond, the sea glimmered. The air was so clear she thought she could make out the French coast, but that was unlikely. It did not feel like the last week of October. The wind-whipped air fizzed like champagne.

Pulling her thick winter robe about her shoulders and scuffing into her slippers, Emily took up her hairbrush and returned to the window. She stood there, brushing and gazing dreamily across the park and avoiding conscious thought, for perhaps five minutes. Then it dawned on her that Richard was walking along the meandering path that led to the cliffs. Alone. She froze, brush half raised. Her heart did its lurching and thumping trick. *Now or never.*

She flung the brush at the dressing table and threw off her robe and night rail. A button popped. In a twinkling she was dressed in a serge walking dress and stout shoes. Clattering down the stairs, she startled one of the chamber-maids.

Emily slowed her pace, gritting her teeth with impatience. "Beautiful morning. Going for a walk." The girl gaped at her.

Emily contrived to leave by the garden doors with the semblance of dignity. Then she ran. Richard was no longer in sight. Puffing, she gained the path—and came to her senses. She stopped dead. What business had she, Emily Foster—thirty, widow, mother, so to speak, of three—to be chasing a man in blatant, hoyden style across half a mile of Cornish cliff? He had given no sign of wishing to be chased.

Gloom settled like a fog about Emily's shoulders and she drifted aimlessly along the path, still gasping a bit from her run. As her breathing steadied, she began to think less erratically. She would find Richard and they could talk about the children and the weather, and she could apologise for ripping up at him the night before. *What harm in that? Alas, what good in that?*

The steady wind, warm for October, blew against her right cheek as she walked, whipping the strings of her bonnet. She stopped and retied the ribbons and started off again. There was a viewpoint beyond a small clump of wind-sculpted gorse.

As she gained the bush she crashed into Richard. He had been walking in the opposite direction. They both jumped, startled.

Richard made a swifter recover. "You're up early." He took her arm briefly to steady her.

"It's a beautiful morning." A dim thing to say. Emily felt his hand on her elbow even after he dropped it.

"Perfect for tripping along the edges of cliffs. That's quite a drop."

"I know." She paced to the rim of the turf and looked down at the sea, boiling around the rocks so far below that the sound of crashing surf came to them as no more than a murmur. "When we first arrived I was terrified that one of the children would tumble over." *Possibly I should tumble over and end it all*, she reflected. The extravagance of her thought jolted her back to sanity and she laughed at herself.

"What is it?" Richard smiled at her.

Emily's pulse thumped. "Nothing. Richard?"

"Yes?"

"I didn't bump into you by accident. I saw you from my window and came to find you."

"That's flattering," he said amiably. "If you're spoiling for another fight, however, I warn you I'm feeling peaceful."

Emily blushed to the roots of her hair. "I ought to apologise for last evening."

"Good God, what is this? I thought you were in earnest." He mimed astonishment, hazel eyes sparkling.

"I was. Am. Oh, do stop teasing." Confusion tangled Emily's tongue. "When does Tom's carriage come?"

"You may count on arriving in Hampshire in time for Guy Fawkes day."

"It *is* a major family festival." They were drifting back

the way he had come. The sea stretched before them, green and glittering in the morning sun. Two gulls hung almost motionless at the cliff edge.

Emily stiffened her resolve. "May I ask you a question?"

He cocked his head. "To be sure." His eyes were friendly but puzzled, and perfectly clear from a blissful night's sleep. He wore no hat and the wind had stung colour into his cheeks. The scar on his brow was fading. In another year or so it would scarcely be noticeable. Emily thought he looked splendid.

Her courage deserted her. "What do you mean to do? That is, now this business of your—the duke— is settled."

He shrugged. "I thought of London. I like London. It would be convenient to publishers, but of course the distance to Hampshire is too great. My lease of the cottage runs through November, doesn't it? I might take rooms in Winchester. That's close enough so I could come to see the children every week, and it would be a good place to write. I've friends in the barracks." He bent to pick up a handful of loose pebbles and began tossing them sidearm over the edge of the cliff. Practicing left-handed pitching.

Winchester sounded dreadful to Emily. "Why?" she wailed, despairing. "What's wrong with the cottage? Papa would give you a longer lease. I thought you liked it."

"I do." He threw the last pebble in a long flat arc and admired the trajectory. "I daresay there would be talk."

"So?"

He turned, sober. "I've no wish to compromise you, Emily. I'm too much in your debt."

Emily could have screamed. "You are the *most* exasperating man."

He frowned.

"I wish you *may* compromise me," she exploded.

Richard stared.

In for a lamb, in for a sheep. "I w-want to m-marry you." There. It was said. Emily gulped and turned away from him, her cowardice rushing back. "That is, not if you dislike it . . ." Her voice trailed off. She knew her cheeks were scarlet.

"Why?" He sounded as if he had been whacked on the head.

A great lump constricted Emily's throat. She shook her head, helpless to speak. She could not look at him. She had never done anything half so brass-faced in her life.

"Why, Emily?" His obtuseness broke the spell.

"Oh, good God, because I love you!" she cried, turning and facing him at last.

He looked rather white.

"I have loved you any time these two years." Really, this was remarkably difficult. Emily began to feel sick. She raised her chin, which was quivering. "However, if you do not return my regard—"

"Hush. You must know I do, for all that I've never told you." His eyes were dark, his voice rough. "You cannot have thought it through, however—"

"In two years," Emily interrupted, "I have thought every thought, and doubted every doubt, and none of them matters a whit. I mean to marry you."

He still said nothing, frowning. She held his gaze. "Last year I spent a sixmonth terrified for you, dreading every post and listening for every post. This summer, when you were wounded, I wanted to fly to you at once. I was green with envy of Sir Robert Wilson. I am tired of caution and tired of propriety. For God's sake, Richard, you cannot go off to Winchester!" That was something of an anticlimax. Emily blushed.

Richard's eyes were bright with laughter and something warmer. His mouth quirked. "Well, perhaps another month in Watkins's cottage."

"Fiend!" Emily was lost to shame. She threw her arms about him. He returned her embrace with sufficient enthusiasm to quiet any lingering doubts she might have felt as to his sentiments. In fact their first kiss left both of them speechless.

Emily recovered first. "I shall write Papa to procure a special licence." She licked her lips, tasting the kiss.

Richard groaned.

"What is it, dear heart?"

"Sir Henry."

Emily laughed. She felt giddy, light as air, as if she could fly out over the cliffs like a gull. "How do you fancy I persuaded him to allow me to come to Treglyn in the first place?"

Richard stared. "Good God. But your aunt—"

"Oh, Aunt Fan is awake upon all suits. She has always been your partisan." Emily gave him a mischievous glance. "I took a great deal for granted, didn't I?"

"By God, you did, madam. I've half a mind to catch the first coach back to London." He kissed her on the mouth and neither of them spoke for some time thereafter. There was no need.

If you have enjoyed this book and would like to receive details of other Walker Regency romances, please write to:

Regency Editor
Walker and Company
720 Fifth Avenue
New York, N.Y., 10019